CYBER
TERROR

BOOKS BY R.J. PINEIRO

SIEGE OF LIGHTNING (1993)

ULTIMATUM (1994)

RETRIBUTION (1995)

EXPOSURE (1996)

BREAKTHROUGH (1997)

01-01-00 (1999)

Y2K (1999)

SHUTDOWN (2000)

CONSPIRACY.COM (2001)

FIREWALL (2002)

CYBERTERROR (2003)

THE EAGLE AND THE CROSS (2004)

FOR MORE INFORMATION

ON R.J. PINEIRO'S NOVELS,

VISIT HIS WEB PAGE AT:

WWW.RJPINEIRO.COM

CYBER TERROR

R.J. PINEIRO

A TOM DOHERTY ASSOCIATES BOOK
NEW YORK

CYBERTERROR

This book is printed on acid-free paper.

Book design by Mark Abrams

A Forge Book
Published by Tom Doherty Associates, LLC
175 Fifth Avenue
New York, NY 10010

www.tor.com

Forge® is a registered trademark of Tom Doherty Associates, LLC.

Library of Congress Cataloging-in-Publication Data

Pineiro, R. J.
        Cyberterror / R. J. Pineiro.—1st ed.
        p. cm.
        "A Tom Doherty Associates book."
        ISBN 0-765-30393-0 (alk. paper)
        1. Cyberterrorism—Fiction. 2. Terrorism—Prevention—Fiction. 3. Government investigators—Fiction. I. Title.

    PS3566 I5215 C93 2003
    813'.54—dc21

                                                                    2002032528

First Edition: February 2003

Printed in the United States of America

0   9   8   7   6   5   4   3   2   1

FOR MY SON, CAMERON, AGE THIRTEEN.

THANK YOU FOR CONTINUING TO LET ME
REDISCOVER THE WORLD THROUGH YOUR EYES.

AND

FOR ST. JUDE,
SAINT OF THE IMPOSSIBLE,
FOR CONTINUING TO MAKE IT POSSIBLE.

ACKNOWLEDGMENTS

As in past projects, there are many wonderful individuals who contributed in various ways to improve my stories. My gratitude goes out to all of them. All errors that remain are my own.

Lory Anne, my beautiful wife, for your unflagging friendship and love. God only knows none of this would have been possible without you.

Matthew Bialer, my seasoned agent at Trident Media, for thirteen years of loyal service through a dozen novels, two publishing houses, and a pair of literary agencies. A special thanks goes to Matt's diligent assistant, Cheryl Capitani, for looking after my interests.

Bob Gleason, the world's most astute and insightful editor, for demanding the best possible stories I can write while also granting me the latitude to explore and create.

Tom Doherty, shrewd businessman, for letting me join the Tor family way back when, and for publishing and promoting my stories ever since.

The rest of the staff at Tor Books, including Linda Quinton and Brian Callaghan, for unparalleled dedication to excellence.

The folks at the FBI office in San Antonio, Texas, for that terrific and educational presentation on the dangers of computer crime and cyberterrorism.

My friend, fellow engineer, and weapons expert, Dave, for your careful review of the manuscript.

My parents, Rogelio and Dora, for your guidance, patience, and love.

My twin sisters, Irene and Dorita, for many fond and loving memories.

My awesome in-laws, Mike, Linda, Bill, and Maureen (yes, I have four—long story) for your support and love through the years.

And for all the children, Cameron, Michael, Bobby, Kevin, Julio Cesar, Paola, Eddie, Rogelito, Juan Pablo, Lorenzito, Maria Eugenia, and Carlos Ignacio. May the Good Lord bless you, protect you, and guide you to accomplish your dreams.

God bless,
R. J. Pineiro
Austin, Texas August, 2002

Visit the author at www.rjpineiro.com or send him an e-mail at author@rjpineiro.com

PREFACE

THE THREAT OF CYBERTERRORISM

Imagine this . . .

A computer virus, assisted by a stolen root password, worms its way into the core of the Southwest Open Access Same-Time Information System. SWOASIS, the computer system and associated communications facilities that the electrical power utility companies servicing the southwestern United States use to communicate with one another, manages the real-time distribution of power, balancing supply with customer demand. The virus shatters this delicate balance, triggering massive blackouts across metropolises like Los Angeles and Phoenix.

People across the country suddenly start to get sick. Some die. Autopsies reveal food poisoning, which authorities track down to a cereal manufacturer. The control system governing the iron supplement was altered by a computer virus.

A cyberterrorist injects a virus into the software running the traffic system of the Tokyo subway, triggering derailments and collisions.

A denial-of-services attack shuts down the servers managing the New York Stock Exchange one evening, before the Treasury Department has settled on securities coming due the following morning. Billions of dollars in transactions are at stake.

On a foggy night in London, a virus alters the information presented to the air-traffic controllers' computerized displays at Heathrow Airport, causing a mid-air collision and several near-misses before the problem is fixed.

A cyberterrorist gains remote access to the control room of the natural gas utility company feeding the large metropolis of San Antonio, Texas. Bypassing manual overrides, the hacker increases the pressure in the vast grid of pipelines running beneath the city, triggering massive leaks. The inevitable explosions that follow cause an inferno that firefighters are unable to contain when the city's water pressure mysteriously drops.

Although the aforementioned scenarios are all fictitious, they are quite plausible given the software tools available today and the inherent vulnerability of the Internet. Cyberterrorism has arrived in full force, prompting industry leaders to dub 2001 "The Year of the Worm." The computer worm, that is.

Code Red. Nimda. Magistr. Sircam. These are the names of actual computer worms released into the Internet that have spread havoc in nationwide networks. *Code Red* alone, the worm that capitalized on an inherent weakness in Microsoft's Windows NT operating systems, infected over half a million hosts and caused an estimated $1.2 billion in damages worldwide. *Nimda,* considered to be the "son of *Code Red,*" also spread itself across the Internet like a ravenous strain of Ebola, sending information technology (IT) specialists rushing to protect their networks.

That's just the beginning. Denial-of-services attacks against major Internet providers have been on the rise for some time. Yahoo and Amazon became the targets of such DOS strikes in early 2001, and there will be more to come, especially in the next three to five years, as a new generation of technologies is deployed on the Web. Internet-enabled devices will soon replace pagers, cell phones, and laptops as the preferred method for mobile communications. The Internet's current hodgepodge of electronic relays and routers will be replaced by a new system of optical switches and fiber optics. All of this amounts to additional functions deployed onto a more powerful Internet upon which our national economy and our national security depends. Unfortunately, while we continue to design our Internet to support an ever-increasing customer demand, it also further exposes cyberspace to criminal hackers and cyberterrorists.

In the summer of 2001, the General Accounting Office concluded that the capabilities needed to protect the nation's critical infrastructure from cyber attacks have not yet been achieved. The FBI's National Infrastructure Protection Center (NIPC) was created as the national center for gathering information on cyber attacks and facilitating government responses to Internet-based incidents. The NIPC is also responsible for coordinating countermeasures with the private sector and monitoring recovery after a cyber attack. However, because it falls under the FBI's umbrella, the NIPC is treating information warfare in a very tactical way, arresting criminal hackers following a cyber attack, indicting them, and bringing them to trial. The NIPC is playing a reacting game with little thought to the strategic nature of today's information warfare.

The NIPC lacks the capability to analyze warning signs, to assess network vulnerabilities, and to alert users of possible cyber attacks before they happen. Paul Strassmann, a professor of information warfare at the National Defense University in Washington, D.C., who sat on three presidential advisory committees that resulted in the creation of the NIPC, stated in a recent *Computerworld* magazine article, "The NIPC's roles and responsibilities have not been adequately defined and are still subject to bureaucratic disputes that have resulted in poor cooperation." Furthermore, Strassmann warned that, "The NIPC doesn't have a schedule of priorities, milestones, and program performance measures. Staffing at the NIPC is woefully inadequate, with fewer than one hundred employees, many on temporary assignment."

Yet, President George W. Bush has established 2003 as the goal for putting all protective cyber missions in operation. Not only is the NIPC not set up to reach such a goal, but 2003 is far too late. We need a solid protection net now, not in 2003. The way Washington views the relative threat of cyberterrorism compared to other terrorist activities is best illustrated by how long it took President Bush to get around to discussing the subject following September 11. Almost as an afterthought—and a full month following the terrorist strikes—Bush added a new staff member to his gathering anti-terrorism team. Richard Clarke, the NSC man who had been coordinating America's global anti-terrorist efforts, became Bush's chief of cyberspace security. He fell under Tom Ridge's Office of Homeland Security, responsible for managing the federal government's response to terrorist attacks in the United States, including major terrorist-sponsored disruptions of critical cyber systems.

How is that going to improve cyber security? What are the changes that will take place in order to bolster our cyber defenses? The first step is clearly to get the federal government to engage the cooperation of the private sector, where the real experts in the field reside. That alone will be a major challenge because no White House study, or congressional committee, or FBI task force will get any software company to hold the release of a software package until it has been deemed hacker-proof (if there is such a thing). It takes a massive effort and tons of money to find and eliminate security holes from a software package before it is released for commercial use. Software these days is so complicated that just releasing a bug-free program—one that won't crash your computer every time you use it—is considered a success. Imposing a requirement to incorporate such hacker-proof shields into software packages prior to their release will pretty much guarantee that they are never released, because for every defensive strategy there is always a new and innovative offensive strategy. Microsoft's Windows NT's *Code Red* fiasco is a perfect example.

So we are where we are. September 11 happened. *Code Red* and other cyber attacks happened. Our government has created task forces, cabinet members, and strategies to combat terrorism abroad and at home. We sent our troops overseas and are tightening homeland security. Much of these efforts address physical-world threats. The cyber world continues to be open to attacks.

Will all of President Bush's measures pay off? Will the retaliatory strikes, the heightened security, the massive FBI investigations, and arrests pay off? Will the renewed attempts to tighten Internet security result in a safer cyberspace?

Only time will tell. But while we ponder those questions, let us remember the last such presidential initiative to fight international terrorism: Presidential Decision Directive 62, which Clinton signed in May of 1998 to support three new initiatives in the war against terrorism. The disruption of terrorist groups at home and abroad, a program to prepare against weapons of mass destruction, and the creation and implementation of a national cyber defense plan. Recent events, both in the real world and the cyber world, clearly broadcast the utter failure of that presidential directive. One can only pray and hope that this time around our national resolve eradicates the evil that is international terrorism.

Time will definitely tell.

I FEAR ALL WE HAVE DONE IS AWAKEN A SLEEPING GIANT
AND FILL HIM WITH A TERRIBLE RESOLVE.

—*ADMIRAL ISOROKU YAMAMOTO,*
  UPON LEARNING OF THE SUCCESS
  OF THE JAPANESE RAID ON PEARL HARBOR

WE ARE GOING TO FIND THOSE EVILDOERS, THOSE BARBARIC
PEOPLE WHO ATTACKED OUR COUNTRY, AND WE'RE GOING
TO HOLD THEM ACCOUNTABLE, AND WE'RE GOING TO HOLD
THE PEOPLE WHO HOUSE THEM ACCOUNTABLE.

—*PRESIDENT GEORGE W. BUSH,*
  FOLLOWING THE TERRORIST ATTACKS ON
  THE WORLD TRADE CENTER AND THE PENTAGON

CYBER TERROR

ONE

> > > > >

SAN ANTONIO BLUES

> IN MY TWENTY YEARS SWEATING IT OUT AT THE CIA as a field operative I thought I'd seen everything. As a spook I've had the pleasure of living in such exotic locations as Beirut, Quito, Belgrade, and San Salvador, where the all-inclusive packages included getting stabbed, clubbed, kicked, shot, and once even nearly castrated—all in the name of the United States of America and its war against terrorism. Interestingly enough, it wasn't Uncle Sam but a pair of nuns and a priest who came to my rescue in my time of testicular need, preventing those Salvadorian guerrillas from turning my *cojones* into *huevos rancheros* behind an old church in a town north of San Salvador ironically named Testikuzklan—but that's another story.

Yes, I thought I'd seen it all, indeed, but as I inspect the city below during our final approach, it finally dawns on me that a sobering dimension has been added to the misery associated with terrorist strikes: The reality that not just terrorism, but *cyber*terrorism has finally reached our shores with stunning force.

I've seen the video feed and the satellite images from San Antonio. I've listened to the briefs and read the field reports since the event four days ago, but you really have to see it with your own eyes before the full force of what happened here slaps you across the face with the power of a hundred World Trade Centers.

We mourned the multiple terrorist strikes early this century and remembered the terrorist purges that followed—along with all of the policy changes meant to strengthen our national defense. But most of those changes were focused on the *real* world—the physical world—all the while leaving the *virtual* world vulnerable for an opportunity that was soon taken.

While the entire world was focused on the possibility of suitcase nukes, chemical agents, and biological warfare following the horrible attacks of 2001, cyberterrorists were steadily preparing to launch a new kind of warfare against America.

I've always had a large degree of respect for ingenious conventional terrorist strikes, particularly those from suicidal fanatics. I've also had a *realistic* level of respect for chemical and biological terrorism, particularly in light of the anthrax attacks in the months following September 11, which created so much commotion around the world. Generally speaking, however, chemical and biological agents—and nukes for that matter—are typically very expensive to obtain or develop, and also deadly to the terrorist himself. But with enough creativity, and if terrorists are willing to sacrifice themselves, substances such as anthrax spores and Sarin gas can be used as a tool to spread terror, even if the actual number of casualties from such attacks are far less than the people killed in automobile accidents every day in America.

In the end, my theory is that it all boils down to return on investment. Chemical, biological, and nuclear weapons, albeit potentially effective in promoting terror and unrest, are a pain in the ass to develop, and do require a significant amount of man-power and financial resources to pull it off effectively. Cyberspace, however, bypasses most of the development overhead, allowing terrorists to launch attacks on our nation from halfway around the world—and do so while armed only with a cheap computer and a modem, easily obtainable software scripts, and a phone line.

Terrorists have awakened to this fact, as measured by the sight below: the Alamo City, or what's *left* of it, where my new boss, FBI Special Agent Karen Frost, and I are about to land.

Yeah. You heard me right. Spooks and Feds have been working together for months now by presidential order to prevent cyberterrorism in the United States along the same vein as when we cooperated at the beginning of the decade.

We're all one big happy family in the CCTF—that's the Counter Cyberterrorism Task Force, which I joined just two days ago, after the shit hit the fan in San Antonio and CCTF leaders started running for cover. Remember that the CCTF's charter is to *prevent* cyberterrorism in America, which means that what went down here can reasonably be categorized as a paramount fuck-up on their part.

So I got drafted, plucked from my Agency and my pals in counterterrorism with little fanfare and shipped off to the brilliant CCTF.

Well, okay, maybe not *as* brilliant as the hackers who barbequed this city via the Internet. Four days after the event, the CCTF, which has already deployed an army of agents, analysts, and other so-called experts to this place once defended to the death by Colonel William Travis, still has no leads, no clues, and no working theories. They—or I should say *we*, since I'm now one of the gang—have no leads.

Or as we used to say back when I was in the NYPD, we're still just holding nothing but our dicks.

I look over at my CCTF superior and realize she doesn't possess that appendage—at least that I know of—and I suddenly wonder what else she could be holding in those fine hands of hers.

"Tom? Why are you looking at me that way?"

Karen Frost regards me while holding a drink in her hands. Her voice is on the raspy side, and she's wearing black leather cowboy boots with her black jeans. But what puts her over the top isn't her slim figure or the full breasts beneath that silk blouse, or the brown eyes, or the high cheekbones, or the voice, or her confident but feminine stance. What turns my insides into mush is the tiny freckle hovering just above her upper lip, near the right corner of her mouth.

Man, such beauty marks should be illegal.

Now, don't get me wrong here. I'm no pervert, just a guy who doesn't get laid enough, mostly because up until six months ago, I had moved around too damned much, which left little room to develop a relationship. Of course, just as I was actually beginning to enjoy my first sedentary stretch in years at Langley, where I was hoping to meet someone and have a shot at a normal relationship, I was kidnapped by this nomadic tribe. That, of course, means no sex in the foreseeable future, especially since I'm a firm believer in not paying for it.

"Tom? Anybody home?"

Karen is still looking at me, expecting a response. At her inquisitive glare I wink and say, "Ah, well . . . I could tell you, boss, but then I'd have to kill you."

"Remember our agreement," she warns, crossing her legs while narrowing her eyes in that you'd-better-keep-no-secrets-from-me look that she has already shot me a couple of times since I was assigned to be a hired hand in this task force.

I reply, "You ever heard the one where the FBI, the CIA, and the NYPD are all trying to prove that they are the best at catching terrorists?"

Karen sighs in resignation before sipping her soda. Two young agents in the row in front of ours, both also new CCTF recruits, but from the FBI, turn their heads, obviously interested. The big one is a borderline albino with ash-blond hair, hazel eyes, and chiseled features. The other, about half his size, has a complexion as dark as his hair, brown eyes, and a neatly-trimmed mustache. One's named Paul and the other Joe.

"No, Tom," Karen finally says, "but I get the feeling that I'm about to."

I lean away from the window and toward her, not wishing to see any more of the mess cyberterrorists have made of downtown San Antonio, still smoldering in places after so many buildings either imploded, like the WTC towers, or worse, toppled over, taking other buildings down with them.

Damn. Travis, Crockett, and the rest of the old Alamo gang must be rolling over in their graves about now. I can only hope—and pray—that this is a one-time incident; that whoever did this is currently fleeing the country and not rushing toward his next strike.

When you've been in this business for as long as I have, you learn to use either alcohol or humor to shave the edge off of the reality of your life, otherwise you'll end up in the loony house before you can say, "Remember the Alamo." Since I can't drink because I'm packing, I have to settle for the latter.

A half grin splashed on my face, I say, "The president decides to give the Agency, the Bureau, and the NYPD a test. He releases a fox into a forest and each of them takes a turn to try to catch it. The CIA goes in first. They place animal informants throughout the forest. They interrogate all plant and mineral witnesses. After three months of extensive investigations they conclude that foxes do not exist."

She pinches the bridge of her nose and closes her eyes, obviously realizing where this is headed, but without asking me to stop. She knows why I'm doing this and deep inside appreciates the distraction. Not only does Karen Frost have to live with the fact that the mess below happened on her watch, but everyone in Washington has been reaming her and her superiors in the CCTF as well as the FBI—the CCTF's parent agency—ever since I started to tag along. She really needs all the help she can get, including a little humor.

I keep going. "So the Feds go in next. After two weeks with no leads they burn the forest, killing everything in it, including the fox, and they make no apologies. They say that the fox had it coming."

I see the ends of her lips beginning to curl up, which for Miss Frosty here is the equivalent of full-force laughter. I'm excited. After forty-eight years I'm finally getting more than silence in return for my jokes. I move in for the kill. "Finally, NYPD cops go in and come out two hours later dragging a badly beaten bear, who is yelling: 'Okay! Okay! I'm a fox! I'm a fox!'"

Paul and Joe nod and grin. Frosty Freckle, however, isn't laughing.

"I don't think you missed your calling, Tom," she says, taking the last sip of her soda before one of our pixie-blond flight attendants who weighs ninety pounds soaking wet cruises by with a plastic bag collecting trash.

I toss my cup in it, set my seat in the uncomfortable position for landing, and once more turn my attention to the scenery outside. The sun is slowly descending in the western sky, staining the city with hues of crimson and red-gold. For a moment the glare obscures the damage done to this metropolis, but soon a passing cloud lifts the imaginary veil, making me wonder how—just how in the *hell* did we ever allow something like this to happen.

Frankly, though, I gotta tell you, if someone had asked my opinion just a week ago, I would have admitted that in spite of all the changes made after September of 2001, it was only a matter of time before some cyberterrorist got lucky.

Counterterrorism had never been our strong suit. We had too many stupid bureaucratic and cultural obstacles to obtaining terrorism information, like the Department of Justice's cumbersome and overly cautious statutes governing electronic surveillance and physical searches of terrorists. Or the fact that most government agencies feel that the risk of personal liability arising from actions taken in an official capacity discourages law enforcement officers and spooks like me from taking bold action to combat terrorists. To that end, in 1995, the CIA, under pressure from the White House, set up complex approval procedures for enrolling unsavory but nonetheless essential informants. And let's not forget the problem that as a whole, the U.S. intelligence and law enforcement communities lack the ability to prioritize, translate, and understand in a timely fashion all of the information to which we do have access.

Of course, there were good changes after 2001, many of them quite sweeping in nature. While we spent a lot of time developing strategies to prevent conventional strikes—including going after terrorists with a vengeance anywhere on the globe—little of that went to protect us from the virtual strike that created the sight below.

Virtual Pearl Harbor.

We had already experienced a repeat of the physical-world Pearl Harbor back in 2001. This one, however, was triggered from the virtual world, taking advantage of our lack of preparation at government agencies like the National Infrastructure Protection Center, chartered with the protection of the nation's information systems infrastructure.

The cyberterrorists knew *exactly* how to hit us. Somehow they managed to gain control of the computerized system controlling the flow of natural gas into the greater San Antonio area, and exponentially increased the pressure beyond what the pipelines were designed to handle, creating leaks all across the city—all the while bypassing manual overrides. And they did it at the worst possible time, three in the morning, when only a skeleton crew manned the system. By the time the experienced day shift arrived at the plant an hour later, the damage had already been done. Tens of millions of cubic feet of natural gas had already been released across the area, inside homes and buildings, in the streets, leaving the residents with no place to run.

And all it took was a single spark to create hell.

But that wasn't enough. Just as clouds of flames engulfed the city, water pressure vanished. The computerized system governing the water mains had mysteriously purged the water into overflow fields, hampering the firefighters' ability to effectively combat the inferno until the fire had pretty much spread out of control.

As our plane reaches the runway, my mind switches from *how* this happened to *who* could have been behind this.

T W O

> > > > >

BACKDOOR PASSWORDS

ONE WEEK EARLIER

> PROFESSOR HERBERT LITTMAN SAW NO WAY OUT.
Hunched over the computer in his study, the elderly scientist wiped his clammy
hands against the same pair of pants he wore during a lecture at Florida Institute of
Technology yesterday afternoon, before the bearded stranger and his female compan-
ion broke into his house.

They held Sarah, his wife of thirty years, in the guest bedroom upstairs. His only
consolation rested on the knowledge that their two boys, grown up and living in
Boston now, would be spared the fate he feared for himself and Sarah regardless of
how much he assisted these characters. He could only hope—and pray—that the
bearded man with the intense dark eyes and peculiar accent would be true to his
word and kill them painlessly after Littman provided him with the super-user password he sought, the one that would give him root privilege to South Texas Gas, a
utility company servicing San Antonio, Texas.

Professor Littman had made the mistake of asking why they would need such a
password, and Sarah had lost the ring finger of her left hand to a meat cleaver on the
kitchen counter.

Littman glanced at the bloody finger next to the computer monitor, placed there by the bearded stranger as a reminder that he'd better cooperate. Sarah's severed finger still sported her wedding band.

Shivering the sight away, he continued working the keyboard, clicking his way through layer after layer of security using the guest account provided to him by the STG plant manager six months ago, when the utilities company provided FIT with a grant to develop a new control systems algorithm for the company's network of gas pipelines feeding the San Antonio metropolis.

Littman hated himself for being weak, for giving in to their demands, for not being strong enough to resist—even if that meant extreme pain for Sarah as well as himself. He was no fool. He knew what the bearded man could do with root privilege at STG. The backdoor password would give him direct control of gas pressure, valves, bypass mechanisms, and much more—empowering him to trigger a destruction of apocalyptic proportions. Yet, Littman kept working, Sarah's bulging eyes and muffled screams still echoing in his mind as the animals sliced off her—

"How much longer?"

The professor swallowed the lump in his throat and said, "I'm almost there. Just a little longer." Again, he tried to place the accent, which sounded Hispanic but with a European inflection.

He reached STG's firewall, a perimeter security wall allowing entry only to those with the correct password. Littman keyed it in and gained access to the primary network. From there he accessed the server, where his control system automation software resided, though the software itself wasn't what he sought. Littman had left a back door in the core of the system, something he did not out of malice but in case he needed quick access to the network should STG stumble onto an obscured software bug in the automated control system, and he needed immediate remote access to install software patches without having to wait for STG's system administrator to grant him permission.

The screen suddenly displayed STG's primary control panel, which governed the main distribution of natural gas to the greater San Antonio area.

"Finished?" the stranger asked.

He looked over his shoulder at his captor, nodded once, and then braced himself for what would happen next.

"Good," the stranger said. "But, I need another password."

"Another password?"

"You were a member of the team who created Neurall at MIT, were you not, professor?"

Littman found it difficult to breathe. That had been a top-secret Department of

Defense project, known to none but a handful of civilian scientists at the Massachusetts Institute of Technology and top officials at the Pentagon.

"I know about you, and about Hutton, Lamar, and Foulch," the stranger said, rattling off the names of the professor's three MIT colleagues from several years back, when they had worked on the classified project at the artificial intelligence lab at MIT. "And I know about the access passwords each of you memorized in case the government ever tried to use the AI engine for something beyond what you had agreed to."

"How . . . how do you know all of this?"

"I'm surprised, professor, that you didn't recognize my associate."

Littman swallowed the lump in his throat as his mind struggled to keep up. "Your . . . associate?"

"She used to work for one of your colleagues at MIT."

THREE

> > > > >

DOMESTIC WASTELAND

> THE FIRST THING THAT STRIKES ME WHEN I STEP
outside the terminal building towing my small carry-on is the smell. They say that
the sense of smell is the human body's most powerful way to remember, and today I
have no problem believing that. Before I know it my mind has already jumped to
the war-torn streets of Belgrade. I remember the poverty, the rubble, the orphans, the
slow-flowing Sava River snaking its way past flea markets operating amidst the
twisted and charred ruins of the city, where engineers, doctors, carpenters, and
bankers ran stalls to supplement their decimated income. Then I'm off to San Salvador, to images of rolled-over buses in flames, to the smell of cordite mixed with
burnt flesh, with agonizing screams—the same screams echoing across the sands of
Beirut. I remember the images of women walking among hundreds of decaying bodies sprawled on the blistering rocks, searching for missing fathers, for sons, for brothers. But most of all, my mind replays those dreadful sights of my beloved America in
2001. I remember the flames, the falling rubble, the sirens, the shock, the frustration,
the anger.

The memories flooding my mind threaten to drown me. Belgrade, San Salvador,
Beirut, New York, and other places I shall never forget. They all smelled the same,
just as San Antonio does now, as I stare at the southern sky and spot wispy columns
of smoke rising up to the layer of scattered clouds. It's almost six thirty in the afternoon and I'll be glad when nighttime finally comes, not only because darkness will

veil the destruction, but also because I'm in dire need of a warm bar and a cold drink. Surely the cyberterrorists left one watering hole operational in this town.

I follow Karen Frost into a waiting dark Suburban with tinted glass that has G-men written all over it. You can tell which agency has a predominant presence in the CCTF.

I settle next to her in the middle seat. Paul and Joe sit behind us. The driver, chartered with the enviable task of chauffeuring us around during our visit, introduces himself as "Bill," and proceeds to inform us that we have reservations at a Motel 6 somewhere south of the city.

Wow. The CCTF is a big spender, like the FBI—and the CIA, for that matter. Nothing but first-class hotels, gourmet meals, and exciting destinations. Actually, there's a valid reason why we can't stay at one of the nicer establishments by the River Walk in the downtown area: It looks like a war zone over there. Many buildings, hollowed out by the flames, collapsed just hours after the strike, kicking up clouds of dust that took a couple of days to clear, mostly thanks to the season's prevailing winds, which blew the thick haze toward the Gulf of Mexico.

"Did Ryan arrive this afternoon?" asks Karen.

"Yes, ma'am," replies Bill, who has to be another former blue-suit. Had he been with the CIA, he would have introduced himself as Johnson, Smith, or Clark. But not the Feds. I've known them long enough to know that they prefer first names, like Tom, Dick, and Harry, and, of course, Bill. "Mr. Ryan arrived about four hours ago. I took him straight to STG."

"Then that's also where we're headed. We'll stop by the water company later, on our way to the motel."

I've been up since six this morning to make an eight o'clock flight out of Dulles in Washington, D.C. with connections in Chicago and Dallas. Whoever made the flight arrangements ought to be shot. There has to be a more direct route to San Antonio. Maybe this was the cheapest.

In any case, here I am, twelve hours later—thirteen if you want to get technical on me about the time zone difference—and from the looks of it my day's just about to begin.

I suddenly find myself longing for my relatively comfortable CIA life of just forty-eight hours ago. It had not taken me long to get used to normal working hours after twenty years of insane schedules. But, as it was explained to me, this mission had come straight from the top. I was told that somewhere along the way, I had somehow impressed someone high enough to be given this . . . *opportunity.*

Right.

I happen to have a slightly different version that explains how I wound up here:

Somewhere along the way, I had somehow managed to *piss off* someone high up enough to be handed this bag of shit.

So pick your tune.

And to make matters even more interesting, consider the fact that I'm once again falling under the umbrella of Randall Cramer, the head of the CCTF reporting to the director of the FBI, Karen's old boss until her transfer to this task force.

Randy and I go way back. He used to be the station chief in El Salvador during the late eighties and wasted no time selling me out when one of his operations went sour. I wound up getting a strong reprimand—and the shit jobs that followed me for another decade—while good old Randy got a promotion and a transfer to Washington. I was glad to hear some years later that he had retired from the Agency and joined some presidential commission. At the time I had felt that the CIA had one less rat to worry about.

Unfortunately, that rat got himself appointed as the head of the CCTF, reporting to the director of the FBI.

Bill steers the Suburban toward the exit.

"Jesus," says Joe, who, like Paul, is supposed to be in his late twenties but looks fifteen. Karen and I requested a pair of seasoned agents as backup and Cramer gave us children. "Just take a look at this place, man."

"Dear God," mumbles Paul in total awe. "It's a wasteland."

I give Karen a glance of controlled exasperation before we drive down Highway 281 from the airport, crossing 410 and proceeding south through a couple of parks, where Bill, doubling as tour guide, explains that the many acres of green at both parks have been gobbled up by oceans of tents, by the temporary shelter provided by the city, the state, and most recently, the federal government, to accommodate the tens of thousands of homeless families created by the fire, whose widespread destruction can still be seen in the smoke rising up to the overcast heavens in every direction. In all, our driver explains that roughly ten square miles were affected by the fire, though there are many islands in that area that remained unscathed, mostly due to sheer luck and also to the persistence of the firefighters once water pressure was restored.

The affected area was quite large indeed, but to my relief I see a significant number of structures with little or no damage. The eerie thing, though, is that many of those undamaged buildings happened to be right next to charred ones, almost as if an array of tornadoes swept through the city, destroying some buildings and sparing others. But it still looks like a battle zone here, quite reminiscent of lower Manhattan in 2001.

I guess if there ever was a silver lining in this hell of a dark cloud it is the fact that we're in early April with temperatures in the mild and pleasant seventies, making the outdoor experience a heck of a lot nicer than in steamy August, freezing January, or even just a week ago, when a severe storm front, currently drowning southern Louisiana, swept through the area. Still, Bill tells us that many residents have traveled north, to Austin and Dallas, or east, to Houston, until officials can get the city back on-line.

And there's also ashes and dust from the fire and the crumbling buildings, though a strong wind from the north has helped shift most of this flying debris south in the past twenty-four hours.

As I look behind me, I catch Paul and Joe with their traps wide open staring at the destruction, at the charred facades of office buildings, at the smoldering ruins of neighborhood after neighborhood.

We cross IH-35 and reach the downtown area. I've been here before a few times and vividly remember this section of town, particularly the River Walk, the Alamo, the Hemisphere Plaza, La Villita, and the Spanish missions. I remember bright flowers and friendly smiles, colorful dresses and mariachi music. What I see now, however, are blackened homes and rubble where buildings had once stood. I see tanks from the National Guard and hordes of people and machinery cleaning the streets—though once you get to the downtown area, you can't really tell where the streets were.

Unlike the 2001 strike in New York, the people of downtown San Antonio didn't have a place to run as the entire downtown area crumbled following the explosions, sealing the fate of tens of thousands.

It's actually quite surreal to drive on this elevated highway, which for the most part was spared from the destruction below.

And that thought makes me think of something else.

Traffic.

The San Antonio I remember was packed with cars. Yet, Highway 281, as well as some of the other major thoroughfares—except for IH-35 and IH-10—are eerily void of heavy traffic.

"Where did all the cars go?" I ask.

"Martial law," says Bill. "The mayor declared it just this morning after another round of looting last night, despite the SAPD and the Guard's best efforts. Anyone caught outside after six P.M. can be shot without warning."

"Well, it's six thirty, pal, and this glass doesn't strike me as bullet resistant." I tap on my side window.

Karen shoots me a tiring look.

"We're okay," Bill replies without a hint of annoyance. "It doesn't apply to official vehicles, or any traffic on I-35 and I-10, though the National Guard is supposed to have blocked all exit and entrance ramps to both highways to keep the through traffic out of the city during the night hours."

We continue to ride in silence. One day someone will probably write a ballad about the night San Antonio burned courtesy of the cyberterrorists I'm now being paid to catch and bring to justice.

I turn to *la jefa*, who has chosen to lean forward and expose the kind of cleavage that can only be created by some awesome pair of breasts. Perhaps there's more than one silver lining in this mess after all.

For a moment I wonder about her question to the driver about Ryan's arrival time. According to the brief background on him that I read this morning during the layover in Chicago, Michael Patrick Ryan is not even associated with the CCTF but acting more in a consulting capacity. Why was she so concerned about him when the CCTF—and the FBI for that matter—has plenty of computer experts already on the case?

"This guy," I say. "Ryan?"

"What about him?"

"There was very little intel on him in the CCTF handout beyond his college education and current employment status. It also looks as if he was involved in solving a case a few years back."

"I worked with him on that case. Do you have a question, Tom?"

"What's so special about him?"

Karen regards me for a moment, before reaching inside her soft-sided case and pulling out a manila folder. She browses through it and selects two sheets of paper stapled at the corner. "This might help."

As I make it halfway through this short document, titled FOR THE EYES OF THE FBI DIRECTOR ONLY, I have the sudden urge to meet this Ryan guy.

F O U R

> > > > >

L E V E L S   O F   T E R R O R

> DISPOSING OF A BODY HAD ALWAYS BEEN ONE OF his skills, evolving over the years to a form of art—of which he prided himself as being the most creative in the business. Anybody could kill a person, but it took a genius to dispose of the body such that it could be used as a weapon against those who found it.

Ares Kulzak had practically invented the concept of using humans—dead or alive—as triggers to inflict progressive levels of terror against his enemies, to transcend the meaning of the word terrorism far beyond the loose definitions given to it these days by the media.

A bomb detonating in a heavily populated area inflicted pain, havoc, death, and yes, even terror.

Of the first kind.

But the opportunity to magnify its effect came later, as emergency crews reached the scene, as rescue workers began to tend the victims, whose booby-trapped bodies would trigger secondary explosions.

That was terror.

And as rescue workers found themselves engulfed in flames and shouted for help, additional explosions would prevent more crews from reaching them, turning them instead into spectators of a horror show.

That was *real* terror.

And it took unusual brilliance to execute it, just as his *jihad* brothers-in-arms had done in 2001. The initial jetliner crash into one of the WTC towers had triggered more confusion and shock than real terror. But it was that second jetliner, crashing live on national TV, that infused the kind of terror that America had not witnessed in its history. That second level of terror was heightened by the crumbling towers, by the falling mounds of steel, glass, and concrete that buried thousands, including rescue workers, elevating the impact of the strike to an unparalleled level.

Levels of terror.

Ares Kulzak worked alone to manage his own level of terror against America. Kishna Zablah, his partner in this historic mission, had gone to deliver special packages around town as part of his master plan.

But Ares actually never worked alone. He always made certain that he operated with the support of an infrastructure that he could use as a platform to launch effective strikes of ever-increasing impact. This particular mission against the *gusanos* was sponsored in part by the Revolutionary Armed Forces of Colombia, or FARC, the powerful movement who had controlled the southern region of that nation for a number of years—and all financed by the Cartel.

Ares kept the television on, tuned to CNN. It had always amazed him how much information the American government allowed to reach the public, including vivid images of his handiwork.

He lifted his gaze from the detonating caps in his hands and glanced at the screen.

Kishna had done a fabulous job in using Professor Littman's password to gain access to the core of the natural gas network, where she had wrestled control of the system from unsuspecting operators, using a virus to lock them all out of their workstations and also bypassing the manual override. Kishna had essentially given herself free rein to increase the pressure in the grid of pipelines while also eliminating the artificial safety ceiling imposed by the control system software to prevent accidental high-pressure excursions. Only this was no accident, and Kishna quickly disabled the software-imposed maximum-pressure ceiling, triggering the leaks that quickly followed. By the time the system administrators caught on to the problem and restarted the entire network, the damage had already been done.

The Alamo City was burning.

Using the same methodology, Kishna had then forced an emergency water purge outside San Antonio, drastically lowering the city's water pressure—and again, by the time system administrators reacted to the problem, the damage had already been done.

"Like they say in America," Ares mumbled to himself, "you snooze, you lose."

In addition to the technical brilliance with which Kishna had penetrated that network from four states away, the destruction in San Antonio fitted Ares's progressive terrorism model perfectly. First increase the gas pressure while disabling manual bypass mechanisms. Then gas leaks spring, followed by widespread alarms as hundreds of thousands of people across the city suddenly smell natural gas in homes, office buildings, restaurants, shopping malls, and even on the street. Then the inevitable explosions follow, triggered by ringing telephones, by flipping light switches, or by a hundred other sparking possibilities, igniting a chain reaction that conforms perfectly to the chaos theory. Take a room jammed-packed with mouse traps and release one ping-pong ball in the center. It will set off the first trap, which in turn would set off two or more, which would set off others. In the case of San Antonio there had been the need for just a handful of explosions to set off others in an unstoppable cycle as the air itself had become saturated with natural gas, creating clouds of fire.

But that wasn't enough.

The water mains came next, raising the level of terror another notch, turning emergency crews into horrified bystanders—as seen clearly by the rest of the nation through the media, which Ares made sure was not affected by the destruction. He wanted the American people to see the chaos, to witness the pain inflicted by the flames, to feel the agony and frustration of emergency crews unable to quench the inferno, to witness building after building toppling over as the flames hollowed them out, bringing back memories from the collapsing WTC towers back in 2001.

And that still wasn't enough.

Ares Kulzak worked methodically, carefully, with practiced ease, further shaping his creation, evolving it, sculpting it with the care of the master craftsman he was.

The Littmans were unconscious but far from dead. They lay side by side on the living room floor, IVs dripping a brew designed to keep them sedated.

Ares stretched the detonation cord, or "det cord," just as he had been trained—just as he had then trained others for so long and across so many lands. He inserted the standing end of the spool of det cord into the plastic explosive charge, already molded into the desired shape for this job. Det cord resembled a plastic wire, but its core consisted of an explosive called PETN, designed to ignite at a fulminating linear speed.

Ares deployed it according to his plan, taking his time. He knew it would be a while before the American intelligence community, and their elite CCTF, was able to track down the origin of the cyber attack. At this point they were still trying to sweep through the madness, through the rubble and ashes, trying to make some sense of the strike, perhaps trying to find a reason, something that would steer their search in his direction, something that would explain why someone would do something so evil against the millions of innocent men, women, and children of this metropolis.

A reason for the attack.

Ares Kulzak closed his eyes and remembered.

F I V E

> > > > >

DARK BEGINNINGS

> THE CRYSTALLINE SKY EXTENDED AS FAR AS ARES
Kulzak could see, blending with the distant horizon on this clear night. A million
stars, like a sea of burning candles, shed their distant light on the droning Caribbean surf.

Digging his toes in the fine sand while he sat by a tall rock formation flanking the
east end of the beach, Ares pulled his mother's towel tight around him. The sea
breeze chilled him this late at night, but it soothed the pain from his sunburned face,
which had awakened him minutes before. Perhaps he should have listened to his
mother and worn a hat this afternoon, like his sister had, but at the time erecting the
largest sand castle in all of Playa Larga had been his priority.

Now he was paying the price according to some law of cause and consequence
that his father had explained to him later on, after Ares began to turn as red as the
boiled *mariscos* they ate at their new house in Havana, the one they had moved into
after his father and the other bearded heroes had beaten the *gusanos*.

Ares didn't care about a little sunburn. After all, that was all part of living on a
tropical island. He had figured as much at just seven years of age.

Ares did care about *admitting* that the sunburn hurt. His father was a strong and
powerful man, and so was he. No one would catch him crying this time.

No one.

He glanced back at the dark outline of his father's new station wagon, parked at the edge of the grassy field leading to the sand dunes, before turning back to face the gleaming surf. The vehicle, as well as the house in Havana, was given to them by the great leader himself as a token of appreciation for Ares's parents efforts in the Sierra Maestra and during the advances toward the capital. His parents were both decorated heroes, taking great risks during the evil Batista regime to sabotage supply lines, to make it harder for the *gusanos* to fight against the *Fidelistas*.

His mother and sister slept in the rear of the shiny vehicle. His father, who always preferred the middle seat during these overnight family outings, also slept, but in full uniform and with his gun by his side.

Our new nation is very fragile, Ari, his father, also named Ares, had once told him. *And that means that we must always be ready for an attack from the Americans. We are all soldiers of the revolution. You, your mother, and your sister. All of us, just like our ancestors fought against the Spaniards.*

A soldier of the revolution.

Ares liked the sound of that.

He had asked his father to let him come with him to his job at Castillo del Morro, the old castle overlooking the ocean on the outskirts of Havana that was being used to hold and punish the enemies of the revolution. But his father always refused, telling him instead that he could best assist the cause by going to school, by gaining an education, by learning about a man called Karl Marx, by learning about our distant friends in the Soviet—

"Ari?"

Ares jumped, at first startled, then angry for not being alert enough to hear his mother coming.

"I—I couldn't sleep," he said, catching his breath.

"I got worried for a moment."

He stared at the lithe figure of his mother, still wearing her bathing suit, her dark-olive skin gleaming in the dim moonlight. Ares wished he had her skin tone, which turned the color of honey with the sun, but he had gotten his father's fair skin instead. "There is nothing to worry about, *Mami*. I can take care of myself."

She smiled and sat next to him. "Of course you can, *mi amor*. You look and act like your father more and more every day."

His chest swelled with pride.

She extended a long finger at the sky. "See the moon?"

He lifted his gaze and found the quarter moon hanging high in the sky.

"Just below it, to the right, there is a star that shines brighter than the others."

He narrowed his gaze, searching for it, finally spotting it. "Yes, *Mami*, I see it."

"It's actually not a star, *mi vida*, but a planet."

"A planet?"

"Mars. You and your father are named after it."

He shifted his gaze between the planet and his mother before saying, "But . . . my name is Ares, not Mars."

"Mars is Latin for Ares, the Greek god of war and combat."

He was stunned. "I am named after a god?"

She nodded.

"But . . . we don't believe in any gods. We believe in the state, in the revolution, in the power of the people against tyranny."

She smiled approvingly. "Spoken like the true Communist that you are, my dear Ari. And we do believe in the revolution, but Communism also concerns itself with the arts, with history, with ancient civilizations, and the Greeks had one of the greatest civilizations of the Old World. They had incredible advances in arts, science, astronomy, and architecture. They also believed in a large number of gods, but did it as part of their love for the arts and literature. They are respected by all, just as we will one day be respected by all of the nations of the world."

She put an arm around his shoulders and pulled him closer to her. "Ares," she continued, "was very brave and courageous, like your father, like you. He was usually portrayed as young and dressed as a soldier, wearing a helmet and holding a spear and a sword."

Ares imagined himself with such weapons fighting off the Americans. "Tell me more, *Mami*."

"Ares also had enemies," his mother continued. "He wasn't very popular among many gods and mortals, but he always managed to prevail, mostly because of his courage, but also because of the support he received from his father, Zeus, the god of all gods. And just like Ares, Cuba also has many enemies. Our revolution isn't popular in this hemisphere, especially in the United States. But also, just like Ares, we do have a father, someone who is always by our side to protect us against the imperialists: the mighty Soviet Union."

Ares tried to absorb everything his mother was telling him. His young mind began to comprehend the parallels of the meaning of his name with the revolution, with their life in a liberated Cuba, with the threat posed by the giant United States.

"I will be a great soldier one day, *Mami*. Just like *Papi*, just like you."

Her green eyes narrowed as she smiled, as she stroked his head gently. "I know you will make us all proud one day, Ari. Always remember that wherever you are, wherever your life takes you, you will never be alone. The spirit of the revolution shall always accompany you, shall always guide you, long after your father and I have died.

It will keep you strong, focused on your fight against tyranny, against Yankee imperialism. Never forget that."

"I won't, *Mami*. I swear it."

"Show me your hands," she said, reaching for him.

Puzzled, Ares complied, letting his mother hold his hands in hers, open palms facing the stars.

"With a pair of hands just like these our great leader altered the course of history, returning Cuba to the people. With hands just like these many men and woman have accomplished so much in this world. These are *your* hands, Ari, and it is entirely up to you to decide just how much you will accomplish with them. Don't let them become old and wrinkled before you have fulfilled your destiny."

Ares just stared into her captivating and warm eyes, unable to think of anything to say to that.

"Always remember that with these hands you could conquer the world, *mi vida. Entiendes?*"

"*Si, Mami.*"

"Now," she added, yawning. "Why don't you come to sleep? Tomorrow we have a long drive back to Havana."

"Can I stay out here just a little longer . . . *please?*"

His mother made him promise to be back inside in fifteen minutes, then kissed him on top of his head and returned to the station wagon.

Ares was alone again. Alone with the surf, with the stars, with the night. Alone with his planet. He never knew just how important his name was. It was indeed too bad that he had been too young during the height of the revolution to realize what was happening, to understand and appreciate the giant sacrifice his parents were making for the benefit of Cuba. All of those weeks alone with his aunt in Havana without news of them as they fought Batista's forces in the mountains. The weeks turned into months before he would get a message that they were still alive, still fighting. Then the messages arrived more often as government forces began to retreat to the capital, until news that they had won spread across Havana. They were coming home as heroes of the revolution.

Ares stared at his hands and smiled in the dark, remembering his father, riding in the same truck with Ché Guevara, Camilo Cienfuegos, and the Great Leader himself. Ares remembered playing with his father's beard as he lifted him off the ground and hugged him with his powerful arms. Then the Great Leader had laughed and hugged Ares, kissing him on the cheek. Fidel had even taken his hand and held it high in the air in a sign of victory. Then he had ridden on Ché's shoulders as they marched down the joyful streets of Havana.

Rubbing his hands, Ares lost track of time as he relived the unforgettable occasion, as he spotted his mother running toward him from another truck. He could still taste the salty tears on her face as she kissed him over and over, as she hugged him and his sister again and again. They had won. They had beaten the enemy and freed their land, their people.

His young eyes focused on the surf, dancing under the dim moonlight. He followed the waves as they advanced and retreated, advanced and retreated, continuing in a near hypnotic cycle.

But something broke the rhythm, an object moving along the surface.

Ares narrowed his gaze trying to make it out, but the object suddenly came alive, surging from the surf to become a man in a dark, skintight suit.

His breath caught in his throat, Ares spotted another figure, and a third one farther down the beach.

Seconds passed, turning into minutes as he watched more figures, his mouth going dry, his heartbeat pounding in his chest. He lost count of them as they gathered silently at the opposite edge of the beach from where he sat, cloaked with his mother's dark towel, petrified.

Who were those people? What were they doing at this time of the night? Then he noticed the bags they carried, the weapons they produced.

His eyes darted toward the station wagon, still dark. His parents were obviously unaware of what was happening.

He had to do something, had to alert—

A shot cracked in the night, followed by a second, and a third, the flashes originating from the side of the parked vehicle.

He was confused for a second or two, before the realization struck him as hard as the waves pounding the reefs.

His parents were not sleeping. They were fighting the invaders!

Like a spectator watching a movie, Ares saw two dark figures by the beach clutch their chests before dropping on the sand while others returned the gunfire, peppering the station wagon with bullets.

His heart sank. Tears filled his eyes as he recognized the screams. It was his father, shouting at the top of his lungs for Ares to run away, to leave this place.

When a burst of staccato gunfire silenced him, Ares's mother began to shout while returning fire, but she too fell victim to enemy bullets as the intruders overran her position, also killing his sister.

And Ares Kulzak knew he was all alone.

The gunfight ended just as suddenly as it had begun. The waters around Playa Larga became alive with lights.

Boats, many boats packed with enemy forces now raced toward the shore. Beyond them he could now see the silhouettes of larger vessels. The enemies of Cuba were attempting an invasion of the island.

The shock of losing his parents suddenly gave way to another feeling, one that gripped him from within with savage force, filling his whole self with the overwhelming desire to avenge them, to punish those faceless men for what they had done, for what they were trying to do.

The force gaining control of his mind reminded him of who he was, making him recall his mother's words.

Wherever you are, wherever your life takes you, you will never be alone. The spirit of the revolution shall always accompany you, shall always guide you, long after your father and I have died. It will keep you strong, focused on your fight against tyranny, against Yankee imperialism. Never forget that.

Ares Kulzak stared at the rolling sea, at the silver surf spotted with the silhouettes of the enemy. And it was at that moment that the boy saw his future in those turbulent waters, saw his destiny, realized what he must become.

Slowly moving away from the beach, forcing himself to leave his slain family behind, Ares reached the main road and ran toward the nearest town to seek help. He was a warrior, just like his father, just like his name implied. And his mission was to warn Cuba of the impending invasion.

S I X

> > > > >

C O P S   A N D   S A T A N

> DON'T YOU JUST HATE IT WHEN YOU ARRIVE TO A
meeting already in progress and can't quite follow the conversation?

Ever since reaching STG an hour ago, we've been stuck in a conference room with a bunch of propeller heads wearing T-shirts with slogans like BLOOD, SWEAT, & CODE, or WILL WRITE CODE FOR FOOD, and blabbering mounds of techno-gibberish. The meeting had already started by the time we arrived, meaning Karen, the rookies, and I had to settle for the uncomfortable chairs lining the rear wall of the long room.

As far as I can tell this is some sort of debriefing led by this Ryan guy, who looks about half my age but with twice my brain capacity, that's if you choose to believe the intel on his dossier—plus the oral brief Karen gave to me in the back of the Suburban. I had actually stopped listening halfway through her dissertation when the damned freckle filled my imagination with a different kind of oral activity.

As I survey the room once more, it hits me that not just Ryan, but most of the nerds here are about half my age, and probably as smart as Bill Gates.

I suddenly feel like the old and toothless grandpa with a brain slower than molasses in January rocking his way into Sleepville because he's too damned senile to understand what everyone's talking about.

My only salvation is the handful of courses I took at Langley in the past six months as part of my feeble attempt to become computer literate and survive senior moments like this one.

"So," Ryan says to the STG system administrators sitting across the table. "You haven't seen any evidence of Trojans?"

Heck.

I have, though I'm not about to reveal the one I carry in my wallet on the outside chance that I get lucky and have to dress up my floppy in a hurry.

Who ever said I can't talk the techno talk?

"No Trojans," replies the lead nerd at STG, a fellow by the name of Walter, with long blond hair and bloodshot crossed eyes behind thick glasses.

"You've found zero indications of a virus?" Ryan pressed.

Looking like he could use some sleep—and perhaps a haircut and eye surgery, Walter says with a bit of exasperation, "We've scrubbed the system and found no indication of *any* type of virus."

Ryan leans back, toying with a pen in his right hand, contemplating that for a moment before saying, "What about the possibility of a backdoor penetration?"

Damn.

Whoever came up with these computer terms must have either done time, or was sexually frustrated, like Walter and me.

"Not likely," replies Walter.

"Why is that?"

Walter crosses his arms. "Mr. Ryan, I've already been asked those same questions by your CCTF colleagues." He waves his hand at half the room. "I'm sure they can brief you on what they have found so far."

"Which is nothing," Ryan says. "That's why I requested this face to face, in the hope that I can identify something no one else has and find the ones responsible for this mess."

I already like this kid. He is a pain in the ass, like me.

"Look," Walter persists. "My team and I have been at this for the past four days with very little rest while dealing with wave after wave of questions from you people. We would like to go to whatever is left of our homes and be with our families."

"You can leave as soon as you answer my questions," Ryan says, holding his ground—though I have to admit that I'm beginning to side with poor Walter. I too would like to catch some sleep and start early in the morning.

"But our entire team—plus the CCTF—has not been able to find anything!" Walter protests. "What makes you think that—"

"Humor me, Walter," Ryan says, grinning. "You'd be surprised what a fresh set of eyes might be able to spot. I promise you I won't take long to nail this."

A pain in the ass *and* arrogant. I'm going to get along with Ryan just fine.

"Very well," Walter says, raising his brows. "Suit yourself."

"You were about to tell me why you didn't think there had been any backdoor penetrations?" Ryan asks.

"Yes," Walter says, frowning while checking his watch. "According to the audit trail there have been no illegal penetrations of the firewall in the past four days, certainly not immediately before the attack."

"Do you have COPS installed?"

Walter nodded.

That much I remember from my class on computer security. COPS, which stands for Computer Oracle and Password System, is a computer network monitoring system for machines that run Unix. It basically polices the network, checking for weaknesses and providing warnings when it finds them.

"How often do you use SATAN?" asks Ryan.

I'm really on a roll now. SATAN is another acronym that stands for Security Administrator Tool for Analyzing Networks. It's essentially very powerful software that can be used by an outside contractor for remotely probing and identifying the vulnerabilities of networks.

"Gam is STG's security consultant," Walter points to the guy to his immediate left, who looks like a leftover pothead from the sixties—complete with a ponytail, an unkempt beard, and small round glasses on a slightly crooked wire frame perched at the tip of his nose. "He's in charge of our penetration testing and runs SATAN, among other tools, from his company every day."

Gam nods once while sniffling. For a moment I wonder what else he is running from his company.

"And?" Ryan asks.

Sniffling again, the junkie replies, "Far as I can tell, STG's system is bulletproof."

Bulletproof?

Did I hear him say bulletproof? This guy's definitely a crackpot. As I'm about to put in my two cents, Karen grabs my forearm, leans over, and whispers, "Let Ryan handle it."

I let out a barely audible sigh and settle back on my chair, still wondering how dustman over there could say a thing like that about a computer system that commanded the natural gas grid to roast the city. Maybe all the drugs have caused a leak in his think tank.

"Just because SATAN, and whatever other tools you're using, didn't pick up any vulnerabilities doesn't make STG's system bulletproof," says Ryan, taking the words right out of my mouth.

Before Gam can formulate a reply, Walter says, "Do you have any suggestions,

Mr. Ryan? We obviously are very tired and out of answers here, and so are the CCTF analysts."

Ryan stands and crosses his arms. He looks as tall as me but not as heavy. Dressed in jeans and a polo shirt, he turns to face the windows, his boy-next-door features arranging themselves into a pensive mask as he says, "Any detectable DNS spoofing?"

I have no idea what that is.

"Nope," replies Walter. "There's been no compromising of any domain name servers. Ditto for IP addresses. All is clean on that front too."

"Any Ethernet sniffing?"

For a moment I look at Junkie Gam, but then I remember the computer instructor at Langley explained to me that this is the equivalent of listening with software on the Ethernet connection of a network for files containing words like "login" or "password."

Walter shakes his head.

"I see," says Ryan. "So, somehow your computer system triggered an increase in the pressure of the natural gas pipelines feeding San Antonio, bypassed all manual override systems, and it also vented tens of millions of cubic feet of gas across the downtown area—which created a cloud of fire that was picked up by our infrared satellites . . . but there is no apparent reason *how* this happened. There are no traces of viruses, no DNS spoofing or Ethernet sniffing, no obvious firewall breaches, no illegal activity picked up by COPS, and no apparent system vulnerabilities as far as SATAN goes. Did I capture everything so far?"

As heads begin to bob in the STG and CCTF scientific communities, I start to get the unique feeling that we're deeply screwed.

Ryan sits back down. "Obviously not the work of an ankle biter."

"You can say that, Mr. Ryan," says Walter, readjusting his glasses.

"Any mockingbirds?"

Walter shakes his head. "We have exercised every program on the network in an effort to find one that was trying to disguise itself as a legitimate file. We found nothing of the kind."

"Then I'm afraid that narrows it down to only one option."

"What's that?" asks Walter with sudden interest.

"Someone on the inside did it."

Now the kid's thinking like a cop. I like that, and I can tell that the nerds do not.

As the STG engineers begin staring at each other, Walter stands, looking about the room for a moment, though you can't really tell who in the hell the man's looking at because his eyes drift in different directions. Pretty weird.

He finally faces Ryan and extends a forefinger at him while saying, "Mr. Ryan, I *assure* you that my team is one hundred percent trustworthy. I've worked with them for a long time and—"

"How much work do you outsource?"

"Excuse me?"

"Outsourcing," repeats Ryan, crossing his legs. "How much work do you contract out to other software or hardware companies aside from Mr. Gam over here?"

Walter shrugged. "A fair deal, I'm afraid. STG can't afford to keep the large staff of software and hardware engineers required to maintain all of the equipment, so we have many contractors."

Ryan suddenly looks at Karen. "That would be where I would start my questioning," he says.

Karen nods and makes a note on the legal pad resting on her lap.

"Now," Ryan says with a grin. "Do you mind if I jack into your system and take a look?"

SEVEN

> > > > >

CYBER BUDDY

> WE'VE MOVED FROM THE CONFERENCE ROOM ON THE first floor to STG's computer room on the third floor. Normally there would be a team working the place, but the recent accident forced STG to switch their control system to the old and trusted analog equipment normally used as backup in case of a computer failure. I asked the obvious question: Why hadn't the backup machines kicked into gear four days ago and kept San Antonio from turning into a luau from hell? Ryan explained that the computer virus had bypassed all manual overrides.

Anyway, there's a pair of long tables lining the back wall, and each is packed with those pricey flat monitors, color laser printers, wireless keyboards and mice, and humming computers. Definitely top of the line stuff, until you realize that you're staring at the equipment responsible for the deaths of thousands of people and pretty much the shutdown of an entire society here. Then you feel like grabbing a sledgehammer and having a digital demolition fiesta.

The place is stereotypical of other computer rooms I've seen, very impersonal, stark white, bathed in fluorescent lights, and damned cold. I never quite understood the real reason why they kept these rooms ready to host a penguin convention. Heck, New York hookers wore long johns and taxi drivers wore turbans with ear muffs when it got this cold back home.

Walter, who sent his people home for the evening, had left to fetch the list of contractors who had performed any kind of work on the STG network in the past year.

Paul and Joe are out gaining experience by getting us coffee and food. I sure hope they don't get shot in the process by some trigger-happy National Guard rookie. I can almost see the headlines on that one.

As we wait for their return, Ryan and Karen keep up the small talk while standing by a portable table next to a pair of large Federal Express boxes at one end of the control center. The multitalented Ryan chats while tinkering with some of the strange-looking hardware he'd gotten out of the boxes, running wires from the back of a computer he set up on the table to the rear of one of STG's machines. Their conversation is mostly about their experience a few years back—the report I read on the IRS conspiracy in Austin that Ryan helped crack. Along the way, there is a mention of Mike Ryan's wife, a woman named Victoria back in San Francisco who is seven months pregnant. So maybe these two have not been parallel parking after all. Or maybe Mike, Karen, and Victoria like to do the daisy chain dance. Or maybe my fifth-grade teacher was right in sending me to the principal for having a mind that lived in the gutter.

Anyway, I'm half listening to them and half scoping out the place with unavoidable distaste. Not only do I resent the chaos enabled by this room, but I don't particularly care about being surrounded by so many computers—and computers don't particularly care about me. I know this because they rarely do what I want them to do. Being a firm believer that the number one cause of computer problems is computer solutions, I side with the crowd that uses them when they absolutely have to—which lately is turning out to be pretty much all the time. Thank you Mr. Gates.

Karen and Ryan go on, ignoring yours truly until her mobile phone rings. It's Cramer back in Washington. She steps away, leaving me alone with Tekie Boy, who's still fiddling with things.

"Looks complicated." It's all I can think of saying, hands in my pockets as if I have nothing better to do, which I don't at the moment.

"It's not as bad as it looks," Mike Ryan replies, inspecting a colorful helmet-like gadget that seems straight out of a Sharper Image catalogue. A thick cable connects it to the computer on the portable table.

"What's that?"

He smiles and hands it to me. "It's a helmet-mounted display, or HMD. I'm going to use it to jack into their system through this virtual reality interface." He taps the side of the computer.

"Virtual reality," I mumble, remembering the little I know on the subject. "So this thing allows you to see their system kind of like a video game, right?"

"Yeah . . . something like that."

"Interesting, but why not just use a keyboard and a mouse like everyone else? I heard these VR gadgets are more trouble than they're worth."

"Several years ago that was true, but with the advent of ultra-fast microprocessors, graphics chips, and very cheap memory, virtual reality has migrated to an entirely new dimension, with unheard-of levels of immersion and negligible latency."

"Slow down," I say, glancing over at Karen. She is making wild hand motions while talking and pacing about. It's obvious that she's trying to keep her voice down. Whatever that's all about, it's not going well, but that's why she gets paid the big bucks and I'm just the hired help. Right now Ryan has captured my attention. "What's a level of immersion? And what's this latency thing?"

He continues tweaking this and that on the hardware as he says, "The level of immersion is just how real the VR world appears to you when you jack in. Do you really feel that you're in this world, or does it feel fake? Latency has to do with the system's ability to keep up with the movement of your head, or to put it another way, keeping the visual scene stabilized on the retina during head movement. The older systems couldn't simulate the motion dynamics of the real world, creating a delayed effect between the image displayed and the positional information presented to the brain by the semicircular canals of the inner ear, causing motion sickness."

As I stand there absorbing that, Ryan dips a hand into the red popcorn packing material filling one of the FedEx boxes and fishes out a second helmet, which he proceeds to hook into the rear of the system.

"There is also another factor that affects the level of immersion," he adds, almost as if he were reciting the stuff. The man not only projects that he knows what in the hell he's talking about, but is capable of explaining things to a computer illiterate like me. Then again, he could just be feeding me a line of bullshit and I wouldn't know the difference.

"Another factor?"

"Frames per second."

"Like in a movie?"

"Yeah. In order to have a comfortable viewing experience, the system must paint the digital scenery at a minimum of around fifteen frames per second. Anything slower will start making things look jerky, not fluid."

"What's the rate of your system?"

He looks up, pride in his brown eyes. Now that I'm closer to him I can see that his face, though still a bit boyish, already has a handful of fine lines probably acquired from one too many nights working with this stuff.

"Twenty-five frames per second," he replies, "making it incredibly life-like, and when you integrate that with my own artificial intelligence development, what we have here is the most powerful commercially available tool in the world to surf the Internet."

"Is there better stuff out there than this, like in the military?"

"Yep, but it's mostly classified gear, like what Los Alamos is developing for the soldier of the future."

Before I know what I'm saying I ask, "Can I try it out?" Wow, that's a change from just a couple of minutes ago. What the hell, if you can't control them might as well join them.

"I guess," Ryan says, tilting his head at Karen, who is stomping back toward us. She looks pissed. I hope it's nothing I did.

"I mean," I say, "if it's okay with the boss here."

"What is?" she asks.

"Ah, well, I was asking Ryan if it would be okay for me to check out his VR system."

"That's not a toy, Tom. Besides, we've got to talk."

"Actually, Karen," Ryan intercedes, "having Tom jack in with me is not a bad idea. I can use someone with his extensive background in counterterrorism at the CIA to—"

"How do you know about my background?" I interrupt, a bit surprised, shifting my gaze between Karen and Ryan.

Ryan grins. "Let's just say that our mutual boss wants to make sure we all know who we're working with."

I look at Karen, who just stares back. I don't recall giving anyone authorization to release my Agency file, but somehow I get the feeling that my old boss, Randy Cramer, was behind that. Based on the fire in her eyes, however, there's obviously more important matters on her mind, so I choose to shelf that for another time.

"Anyway," Ryan continues, oblivious to both Karen's current problem and my annoyance about accessing my file. "You can help me review the information I might pick up during the run real-time. You can be my cyber buddy."

So I've gone from a seasoned and well-respected CIA officer, to a CCTF hired hand, to a *cyber buddy* in less than forty-eight hours. I definitely pissed off somebody important in Washington.

On second thought, I'm not sure what being a cyber buddy means, but it does sound more exciting than going through the list of contractors that Walter is going to bring back any minute now and getting people out of bed at this time of the night. Besides, dealing with sleepy and cranky engineers sounds like yet another learning opportunity for the Dynamic Duo, especially if they're going to be getting help from Catwoman.

"Sounds good," I finally say.

"All right," says Ryan, flipping switches on the back of the second helmet. "It'll be about ten more minutes before I'm ready."

Karen and I head out of the room, nod at the two CCTF agents parked outside the door, and find ourselves an empty conference room down the hall. I sit against the edge of the oval table while Karen paces in front of me.

"What's up?"

She rests her hands on her hips, pushing her dark-blue jacket aside, revealing her piece, a Glock 312 in .45 caliber. Pretty typical G-man gun. I, on the other hand, am a diehard Sig Sauer man, choosing to protect what's left of my exciting life with the 220 model, also in .45 caliber. To her credit, Karen wears her piece like I do, in a hip holster on her left side with the handle facing forward, making it quite easy to reach with her right hand.

"Just got word from Cramer. We know who did it."

"We do?"

"The name is Ares Kulzak. We got his communiqué just this past hour."

I suddenly feel as if someone has just grabbed me by the balls.

E I G H T

> > > > >

H U E V O S   R A N C H E R O S

> LIKE I WAS SAYING EARLIER, I THOUGHT I HAD SEEN
everything. Today is certainly the exception. First thing that gripped me was the
extent of the destruction. Now the name behind the destruction makes my hopes for
a one-time incident look far grimmer than my chances of getting laid. Ares Kulzak, a
monster with a CIA dossier thicker than the New York City Yellow Pages, is not a
one-time man. He is not a two- or three-time man. He is a machine that will get in
your face over and over, spreading the kind of terror that this country has never seen
before.

I cross my arms, take a deep breath, and walk over to the large windows overlooking what would otherwise have been the well-lit skyline of San Antonio. Instead, I
stare into darkness broken up by the sporadic glow of construction crews trying to
get the city back on-line—an effort that experts who cleaned up New York City several years back estimate at around a month minimum.

Ares Kulzak.

Might as well have been the devil himself.

Ares Kulzak.

Huevos rancheros.

Remember that incident in El Salvador? At the time I was what the embassy
referred to as a public relations liaison attached to the diplomatic staff.

Or a spook. Take your pick.

My official Agency title was control officer, the guy who convinces foreign nationals to commit treason against their own country for the benefit of the CIA. Back in those days I had recruited just over thirty such agents, mostly in San Salvador, but I had a few agents outside the capital. One fine afternoon in late 1988, toward the end of the decade-long civil war, I headed off to meet one of my agents in Testikuzklan, a secluded town wedged in the mountains north of the city, about a forty-five minute drive through winding roads.

I had with me CIA Officer Jerry Martinez, one of my subordinates and also a good friend of mine from the NYPD. He got recruited by the spooks about three years after I did.

Our agent—or informant—was a hooker named Maria Ramirez. She claimed to have information on the whereabouts of Ares Kulzak, one of the CIA's top five wanted rebels in Central America. Kulzak had been responsible for more bombings, assassinations, and kidnappings than we could keep track of, and it was the CIA's job to gather intel on bastards like him and then turn it over to the local government so they could in turn do the dirty job. Needless to say, our boss, Station Chief Randy Cramer, had a sudden interest in listening to this woman's tale. Jerry, on the other hand, smelled trouble and wanted to bring some backup. Cramer, however, was more concerned about telegraphing our moves than our personal safety, and managed to convince us to go alone. In retrospect, I should have listened to Jerry.

"You really trust this *puta*?" Jerry asked, keeping his eyes on the narrow road as he steered our bulletproof Toyota Land Cruiser under a sunny afternoon sky. We were both wearing Ray Bans.

Jerry had no experience with Maria because she was my agent, not his.

"The intel she got for us on the weapons cache turned out to be a gold mine. Besides," I said, grinning, "she's got an awesome body."

"Oh, Tommy, you *didn't*, did you?"

"Never with an agent, pal. It's bad business. Besides, I don't feel like sharing bodily fluids with half the population of this godforsaken country."

"Good," he said, smiling. "For a moment there I thought you had crossed into the dark side."

"That's your territory," I replied, watching the lush mountainside unwind itself as he negotiated a tight turn.

Jerry, the son of a Hispanic couple from Brooklyn, was quite the ladies' man in San Salvador, somehow always managing to find the time to hook himself up with some gorgeous broad.

"Never with a hooker, man. You can always get a shot for syphilis, but there's no cure for herpes." He looked at me and smiled.

"All right," I said, getting down to business, remembering the phone conversation I had with Maria yesterday. "We should be coming up to a Y in the road. Go right."

The bumpy road narrowed to one lane as it continued up the side of the mountain, flanked by *cafetales*, coffee fields beneath the shade of towering oak trees. A few minutes later, as I began to fear kidney failure from all the bouncing, the road widened as it reached the outskirts of Testikuzklan.

"Over there," I said, pointing to an old church. "She said to meet her in the back, near the *cafetales*."

We pulled up the side of the long and narrow stucco structure that looked like it dated back to the conquistadors. The pastel-colored plaster had peeled away in sections, revealing the red brick holding up the walls. I didn't see anyone in sight, except for a couple of stray dogs sleeping by an abandoned well.

"Are you sure this is the place, man?" asked Jerry, making a face while reaching for his piece, tucked in his jeans, like mine, and casually covered by a dark T-shirt.

I shrugged. "That's what she said."

So we got out and walked around the back. It was hot and humid, like a sauna, and the dusty gravel made it very glary. It was at moments like this that I used to question why I did what I did; why I had chosen a profession that drove me to the middle of no-fucking-where in dip shit countries like this one. But doing so always made me think of my youth, or my abusive old man, and I didn't feel like remembering that at the moment.

Jerry looked about nervously. Something also came over me, and I got struck with a sudden case of extreme paranoia. But by then it was too late. We were already in a stew.

"Over there," Jerry said, pointing to the edge of the coffee field.

It was Maria, dressed all in black, and she stepped away from the bush, walking slowly toward us. I waved but she didn't wave back. She just kept walking, like in a trance, like a zombie.

"Maria?" I said as she came up to me. Her lips were trembling, and as I held her I realized that she was freezing and trembling. Jerry already had his gun out and was scanning the area. We were way too exposed, standing in the middle of the clearing between the church and the trees.

As she collapsed in my arms, I felt that she was wet, soaked, and I realized why she was wearing black clothing: It hid the blood that now smeared my T-shirt.

"Jesus!" was all I could think of saying. "What happened to you?"

But she wasn't answering. Her eyes rolled back and she went into convulsions.

I set her down on the gravel, pulled up her T-shirt, and noticed that someone had sliced off her nipples, which explained the bleeding on her chest but not down her legs.

"Help me out, Jerry," I said.

Together we pulled down her pants, and Jerry stepped back horrified while making the sign of the cross.

"Hey, Gringos!"

We turned around. There were a half dozen men behind us, standing by the edge of the *cafetal*, pointing their AK-47s at us, red handkerchiefs covering their faces.

Guerrillas.

Jerry, who had put his gun away to help me with Maria, tried to go for it, but before I could stop him one of the guerrillas shot him in the leg. He was on his ass a moment later, bleeding right next to Maria.

"Tommy . . . shit!" he cursed as the Commies surrounded us.

"What did you want with Maria, *pendejos*?" said one of them in heavily accented English. He seemed to be their leader.

I was kneeling by Jerry, trying to stop the bleeding, when two of them grabbed me from behind and dragged me away from my partner while the leader asked me the same question again.

I stared right back at him.

"Okay," he said, shrugging, before nodding at the terrorists by Jerry.

While one pinned Jerry down, two of them pulled down his pants and underpants. A fraction of a second later I realized what they were going to do.

"Wait!" I screamed. "Hold on there! I'll tell you anything you want to know!"

The leader pulled down his mask and smiled. "Too late for that, Gringo."

"Tommy!" Jerry screamed. "Oh, God! Oh, my God! No!"

They sliced off his penis and balls right then and there, as he squealed like a wild pig, leaving him shaking and screaming over the gravel, both hands clutching his bleeding groin.

The stray dog came running and began to lick the blood pooling around him.

I felt like puking as the Commie with the bloody machete threw them at me.

As one of the strays ran over to me and started to lick my friend's severed genitals, the leader grabbed the machete from his subordinate, turned to me, and said, "Do you like *huevos rancheros*, Gringo? This dog does."

He kicked the dog in the side. The animal yelped and ran away.

The whole thing had turned surreal; Jerry still screaming and bleeding, kicking up dust clouds as he kept thrashing about; the guerrillas around him laughing. One of them started to piss on him while the others called him names I'd rather not remember. Maria had stopped moving altogether, blood pooling around her from the wooden stake the Commies had shoved up her vagina.

"For the third and final time, *pendejo*," the leader said. "What was your business with that *puta*?"

At this moment I was thinking that there was little else they could do to my friend, and I really didn't give a shit what they did to me. I wasn't going to give these bastards one shred of intel and compromise more lives.

That's when he glared at me with his dark eyes and said, "Then remember my name, Gringo. Remember Ares Kulzak, the man who fucked your informant with a broomstick, castrated your friend, and is about to castrate you. Go back and tell all of your Yankee friends that the same thing is going to happen to them if they come sticking their *pingas* in our affairs."

And that's when the clerical cavalry came to my rescue, just as Kulzak was about to give me a sex-change operation. The nuns had heard the gunshot and called the local garrison of the *Guardia Nacional*. Kulzak and the rest of his gang disappeared in the *cafetales* when the military trucks pulled into the parking lot.

NINE

> > > > >

THE KULZAK TRAP

> I'M STILL STARING AT THE DARK SKIES OVER SAN
Antonio, arms crossed, Jerry's screams echoing in my mind like a million souls burning in Hell. To this day I still can't figure out how the bastard made us, though Cramer sure wasted no time nailing my ass to the wall for it. From that point forward I only got the assignments that no one else wanted to touch, meaning I had the choice of resigning or heading to shit holes that made San Salvador look like paradise. After fifteen years of this I had apparently atoned for that sin and was allowed to come home to Langley, until . . . well, you know the rest.

"Tom?" Karen asks. "Are you all right?"

"Yes."

"Your file indicates that you were once trying to catch him in Central America, but it says little else beyond that."

And that's done on purpose. Unlike the FBI, which has to document every freaking little detail of an operation, carefully dotting every damned I and crossing all stupid Ts in order to build a proper case and bring a criminal to justice, the CIA works in just the opposite way, operating below the surface, taking out those that need to be taken out, and then whitewashing everything to protect the lives of agents and officers alike. But this particular incident is quite old, and although I can't quite recall the statute of limitations on the release of CIA classified intel to other government agencies—especially something as sensitive as this, because Jerry, after all, survived his wounds—I decide that the scenery beyond the windows certainly justifies a little interagency cooperation.

Before I can answer, Paul and Joe return carrying bags of fast-food nourishment and a couple of six packs. My spirits begin to rise like a rocket during liftoff at the prospect of a cold beer only to explode on the launch pad when I realize they're just sodas.

"We had to go almost to Austin before we found something," Paul says.

"Yeah, yeah," I reply, growing crankier with every passing moment without alcohol and sleep.

Karen gives me a curious look before telling them to take what they need, leave the rest on the table, go find Walter, and start going through the list of subcontractors. As they leave, Ryan comes by wanting to know if I'm ready for my cyber tour. I can tell Karen is also getting annoyed at the interruptions.

"I need a few more minutes with the boss, Mike," I say.

He flips his gaze back and forth between us before landing it on the conference table. "Say, is that food?"

Although I don't recognize the label on the bags, the cheeseburgers that the rookies brought do smell awesome, probably because we're all starving. If we only had some beer to wash them down.

"Take whatever you want, Mike," Karen says. "But eat it in the lab. Tom and I need to finish our little chat."

Ryan opens one of the bags and snatches a burger, fries, and a soda. He grins, says, "Later," and he's gone, closing the door behind him.

We're alone again.

"Well?" She has that intense look in her eyes again. "What about Kulzak?"

I decide to level with her. Hell, enough time has passed and the situation does call for it, especially if her claim about Kulzak being responsible is true. I spend the next five minutes providing her with an abridged but accurate version of what happened. By the time I'm finished she's sitting down sipping from a can of soda, and I'm no longer hungry. Jerry's story, as usual, has managed to turn my stomach into a square knot.

"What happened to him?"

I sit down and join her, pulling back the tab of my drink, and taking a swig, trying to make myself believe that it's beer—but it takes more than that to fool my veteran taste buds.

Closing my eyes, I say, "We took him and his . . . you know, to the nearest hospital. In another time and place doctors might have been able to make him whole again, but not in that banana republic. The doctors did try, though, mostly because I threatened to cut their own balls off, but it did no good. They became infected within a couple of days and had to be removed for good."

"I'm. . . . I'm truly sorry, Tom."

She touches my arm, and I suddenly realize that I may have pegged her wrong. There's hope that Miss Frosty could have emotions after all.

"Yeah . . . well, he wasn't quite the ladies' man after that." I take another swig and suddenly have a strong urge for a real drink. "He left the Agency soon after and pretty much vanished. People back in Brooklyn had no clue where he had gone. He resurfaced several years later in New Jersey as Father Jerry Martinez. Looks like the experience turned him to God. I have to admit good old Jerry handled it way better than I would have."

"About Kulzak," she continues. "Did you ever come close again?"

I nod, remembering my two-year tour of duty in Ecuador assisting government forces fighting against Shining Path rebels. "He earned quite the reputation after he went around assassinating the children of every high-ranking military and government official in Ecuador. Bastard knew how to hit where it really hurts. Anyway, we thought we had him cornered in this mountainside cabin outside Quito, but it turned out to be what eventually became known inside the CIA as a Kulzak trap."

"A Kulzak trap?"

"That's when the enemy finds a way to feed you intel through channels that you have grown to trust in the past. So you believe the information and act on it, only it's all crap and it leads you to a trap. Twenty soldiers from Ecuador's Rapid Deployment Force died in the blast." I raise my shirt and show her the lovely scar tissue that molten shrapnel carved across my torso. "And that's wearing a vest." I lower my shirt after I achieve the desired effect in her eyes. Actually only about half the scars were caused by the shrapnel. My old man carved the rest with a hot iron when I was sixteen.

I continue. "Myself and a half dozen others survived, mostly because we were in the back and had plenty of bodies to shield us. Of those who survived the blast, only two made it because the rescue chopper that was supposed to airlift us was shot down with a shoulder-launched missile. Again, typical Kulzak, adding levels of terror and frustration on top of terror and frustration, all targeted at breaking you down, at bringing you to your knees, at demoralizing you beyond your imagination, and just when you think you have reached an all-time low, the bastard hits you again."

Karen Frost looks a bit chilled. "I had no idea," she says. "Your file doesn't mention Ecuador."

"I know. There are things that are best left undocumented. Now you know what kind of monster we're dealing with." And I suddenly realize why Cramer handpicked me for this job. It really has little to do with who I impressed or pissed off in my years with the CIA. It has everything to do with the fact that I had some near-death encounters with the monster, which makes me question just how long Cramer had known that Kulzak was behind San Antonio. I wonder if I should share this thought with my new boss, but my spook sense makes me shelve it for now. I don't know Karen well enough to start bashing her boss.

"Is there anything else on Kulzak you wish to share with me before a copy of his dossier arrives tomorrow?"

I shake my head.

"Could he recognize you?"

I sigh, thinking of Jerry, of those soldiers in Ecuador, of a third instance when Kulzak and I had crossed paths years later in Belgrade, which I'd rather keep to myself because it's been about eight years and some of the agents are still operational in post-Milosevic Serbia. Of all three instances, the thing that I got to appreciate the most—aside from walking out with an intact anatomy—is that the monster never really got to know who I was, never got the opportunity to know that Tom Grant was the enemy, and therefore didn't get to target me personally, even in El Salvador because government forces got there before he could extract any intel from me. But Kulzak and some of his masked companions did get a chance to take a good look at me, and I haven't really changed that much in the past fifteen years, aside from thirty extra pounds, a handful of gray hairs, and a dozen wrinkles around my eyes and fore-head.

"Not very likely," I finally say.

"Are you sure?"

"Listen, Karen, go right ahead and read up on the information in that dossier. Afterwards, I'll be happy to expand in any areas that I can so you can get as good a feel about this guy as possible. But keep in mind that at the end of the day nothing, absolutely *nothing* you read about the man will truly prepare you for what we're about to get into. He will stop at nothing."

T E N

> > > > >

N E U R A L L

> HIS MASTERPIECE NEARLY COMPLETED, ARES KULZAK
stood on the wooden deck lining the back of Professor Littman's home. The FIT
instructor and former MIT scholar indeed lived well through the benefits derived
from his corporate consulting work, which certainly bolstered what otherwise would
have been a basic university salary. But then again, the cost of living in Melbourne,
Florida, wasn't nearly as high as other regions of the country, according to the information Kishna had collected from the Internet.

Alone on this deck facing the ocean under a moonlit sky, Ares focused on the
bright star just above the horizon.

It's actually not a star, mi amor, *but a planet.*

Ares remembered, his throat aching with affection. It was a planet. His planet.
But unlike the legendary Greek god, who always had the support of his father when
fighting against the enemy, Ares had lost the support of his own father, just as his
homeland had lost the support from its father, the old Soviet Union, forcing freedom
fighters like Ares Kulzak to seek other sponsors in their fight against Imperialism.
And Ares had found such support in freedom-fighter groups like the FARC, the Revolutionary Armed Forces of Colombia, whose mortal enemy, just like Ares's, was the
United States of America and its puppet regime in Colombia. Along with support
from the FARC came support from the Cartel and its vast infrastructure in this

nation, mostly at major southern ports like Miami and New Orleans, where independent cells would assist him in this historical mission.

Ares had to prove himself to the FARC by successfully leading a number of guerrilla strikes against elements of the Colombian Army before the FARC and the Cartel agreed to his request. In return for their support, Ares had promised to strike terror in America, which would shift the focus away from the drug trade, resulting in growing profits for his sponsors. Ares had explained this win-win situation to FARC commanders and representatives from the Cartel at a meeting in a remote mountain south of Neiva, a city 160 miles southwest of Bogotá, the capital. In that same meeting he had requested that the FARC safeguard Kishna's priceless artificial intelligence computer system, keeping it fully operational at secret cocaine and heroin manufacturing facilities also outside Neiva. The AI was a key element in Ares's plan to bring the Americans to their knees.

The Americans.

He had also promised the same results to his Russian contacts in Washington D.C., who would provide support for him on a number of fronts, from satellite communications to arms and explosives. In return, Ares's strikes would weaken America's position in the eyes of the world during ongoing talks between the American and Russian presidents on various topics, including nuclear weapons.

And don't forget the Chinese, he thought, his support while operating on the West Coast, in the heart of the Silicon Valley, the core of American technology.

Staring at the moonlit surf, Ares wondered how long it would be before the *gusanos Americanos* came crawling across the cool sand toward this target, just as they had done over forty-five years ago. But unlike Playa Larga—and Playa Girón at the front end of the Bay of Pigs—Ares Kulzak planned to behead them with him his mighty sword, planned to teach them a lesson in terror, planned to avenge once again the cold-blooded murders of his family by punishing the ultimate culprit of capitalist expansion across the globe.

But doing so required him to keep on moving, to advance to his next target, to obtain his next backdoor password, to stay ahead of the same imperialists who have been after him for decades now, the same bastards who had hunted down Ché in the mountains of Bolivia, or tried to undermine the efforts of great leaders like Fidel, Mao, Sadam, the Ayatollah, Abu Nidal, Ho Chi Minh, and bin Laden.

He crossed his arms and cursed the irony of his profession. The same habits that had kept him alive all these years also deprived him of the pleasure of seeing firsthand the fruit of his efforts, forcing him to rely on the media to replay them.

Ares longed to sense the heat, to feel the wind from the shock waves, to hear the agonizing screams of his victims. But he couldn't stay behind. This was a game of timing, of pacing, of moving faster than the enemy did, of hitting them again while they were still recovering from the last strike. And that required him to constantly fight while in motion.

As Kishna stepped onto the deck and reached his side, Ares knew the time had come to move on. He had to get to Louisiana in the next twenty-four hours and he could not risk traveling by commercial airliners, especially after releasing the communiqué to Washington claiming responsibility for San Antonio. Besides, with all of the recent storms in New Orleans, it was best to travel by car.

"Did you and the good professor chat about the old days?"

"He could barely remember me," she replied. "I was just a lowly Ph.D. candidate back then."

"Anything in the news?" he asked.

"Nothing."

"The American politicians make this too easy for us."

Kishna smiled, her honey-colored skin glistening in the accent lights, her short and bleached-blond hair swirling in the sea breeze.

"All set in there?"

She nodded. "Everything is synchronized. I only wish I could see it happening."

Ares smiled. Kishna was one of the few people who not only thought like he did, but who had also felt the same kind of pain that Ares had back in 1961. The only daughter of an affluent Lebanese couple assassinated in Beirut by the Mossad in 1982, Kishna Zablah was shipped off to college in Mexico by her aunt. In exile, but with the assistance of a generous trust, the teenager attended first the University of Mexico, specializing in computer engineering, earning her bachelor's in 1986 and her master's two years later. Her work in the field of artificial intelligence earned her a scholarship to MIT, where she earned a Ph.D. in 1993. Her doctoral thesis had focused on the co-development of a Pentagon-sponsored project in artificial intelligence code named Neurall because of the nature of its operation, a neural-like system that combined all AI techniques known to date. But the prospects of a professorship appointment at MIT to continue supporting a project that served those she loathed had not attracted the twenty-nine-year-old, a woman as brilliant as she was beautiful and resentful. Kishna never forgot the scene in front of her parents' house, the bodies riddled with bullets, the hasty departure to Mexico for her own safety. She never forgot the promise she had made on that plane as it cruised over the Atlantic. She would one day find a way to fight back, to avenge their deaths, to strike against Israel and its allies.

And she bided her time, learning from MIT professors like Littman, oftentimes using not just her intellect but her looks as a weapon to gain more access to the technology, to become an integral part of the development of Neurall, until the day came when she stole the backup of the artificial intelligence system and left the United States.

Assisted by this advanced AI, Kishna became a topnotch criminal hacker, first targeting Israel, hitting the Jewish nation where it hurt the most: its Swiss bank accounts. Her AI wonder, which she continued to teach and improve over the years, helped her drain tens of millions of dollars through illegal transfers, very quickly working herself up the ranks of the Mossad's most wanted list. And that's how Ares Kulzak, at the time operating in what used to be Eastern Europe, first heard of her. Finding her had been difficult. Convincing her to use her version of Neurall to launch an unprecedented attack against the United States had been easy.

It was Ares Kulzak who first conceived the idea of a cyber strike against San Antonio as a cover-up for a much greater goal, one that would truly strike terror in a land they hated so much. It was Ares Kulzak who had sold the idea to the FARC commanders and the Cartel to gain their backing and support in America. It was Ares Kulzak who had enlisted the help of the Russians and the Chinese. But it was Kishna, interfaced to Neurall through her virtual-reality rig, who carried out the digital phase of the attack. As a team they were unmatched, driven by a common fire, excelling in their respective worlds of expertise, complementing each other's shortcomings, forging the ultimate cyberterrorist team.

And now it was time to kick off the next stage of a plan designed to bring America to its knees.

E L E V E N

> > > > >

D I G I T A L E M P

> THE LAST TWENTY-FOUR HOURS HAVE INDEED BEEN filled with surprises, and Mike Ryan has just added another one to the list. Remember how I was just telling Karen that you can read about Kulzak but that would never prepare you for the real thing? Well, ditto for cruising through cyberspace in a virtual-reality machine. You can read about it in journals and books all you want—even watch it in movies—but you really have to hook yourself up, or "jack in," as Ryan calls it, before you can understand and appreciate what the commotion is all about.

I gotta tell you, this is what cyberspace should really look like. I mean, forget staring at computer screens, tapping keyboards, or dragging a mouse. We're flying, man. We really are, or at least I can't tell the difference as Ryan tows me around this psychedelic Earth-like planet that's supposed to represent STG's network. It feels as if we're in orbit, scanning the colorful world below, painted in palettes of neon green, and blue, and purple, and yellow, and a cascade of other colors. And it all flows smoothly as I move my head all around, checking out the incredible sight without any visual confinements. I can't find any edges or boundaries to the movie being played in front of my eyes by the helmet's electronics. Ryan had explained that the images would be projected against a pair of miniature bowl-shaped screens over my eyes, covering not just my main field of vision but also my peripheral vision, and the image would change very fluidly as I moved my head, meaning I would never be able to find any edges. He had already explained the immersion, latency, and frames per second concepts, and I now see what he meant. The experience is eerily real, and the virtual scenery changes just as it would in the physical world.

I'm slowly getting used to being disembodied, which in essence allows me to ignore the laws of physics. In Ryan's world you quickly become Superman, moving as fast as a bullet and then turning on a dime, performing the kind of acrobatics that would make an Air Force jock airsick.

Speaking of supermen, Mike and I, as well as some cyber assistant of his, are all wearing these shiny, superhero-like suits. Mine is black and silver. Ryan's is back and gold, and his cyber assistant, someone named MPS-Ali, is purple. The latter is Ryan's brainchild, an artificial intelligence system supposedly capable of some incredible shit I don't understand. Ryan named him after the famous boxing champion Muhammad Ali. Apparently the kid is a boxing fan. And don't ask me what MPS stands for. He's already told me and I've already forgotten.

"Say, Mike?" I ask, speaking into the tiny microphone built into the helmet. As I do so, I hear myself through the helmet's headphones.

Virtual Mike turns to look at me, his seamless face the color of the sun. "Yeah?"

"Watching MPS-Ali flying about reminds me of a story about the old champ."

"What is it?"

"Once Muhammad Ali was on an airplane. The flight attendant asked him to buckle up his seatbelt prior to takeoff. Ali replied, 'Superman don't need no seatbelt.' To which the flight attendant responded, 'Superman don't need no plane. Please buckle your seatbelt.' True story."

The streamlined face doesn't change expressions but I do hear laughter, which is more than I get from Karen.

"So, what are we looking for?"

"MPS-Ali is scanning the surface with my own blend of programs like SATAN, COPS, and others."

I realize that there is no mouth or lips to move on his face, but I hear him clearly, almost making it seem as if we're communicating through telepathy, magnifying the surreal experience.

"I thought Walter and the boys had already done that," I reply as we keep orbiting the planet like satellites. From the looks of it we're doing a full revolution every minute or so. I'm wondering if I'm going to get sick from the circular motion. I was always the kid who would end up puking his guts out from the spinning rides at the county fair.

"Walter did what many sys admins tend to do: have a number of subcontractors run a bunch of security software. Problem is, there's seldom central coordination to comb through all of the data. Subcons run their own programs and turn in their respective summary reports without any knowledge about what the other subcons have done or reported. Walter gets their summaries and he spends some cycles comparing them from his own perspective, but the comparison by that point is at best superficial, oftentimes leading to the wrong conclusions, like their statements at the meeting about having detected nothing abnormal. MPS-Ali, on the other hand, compares the data, unfiltered, as it's being collected straight from the network, before a human unknowingly taints it by removing it from its original state in a computer file and attempts to read it like I read a normal report, interpreting it with my own limited perspective."

"So you're expecting your cyber assistant to unearth something that Walter and his entire team might have missed?"

"Yep."

"That would certainly make Ali intelligent."

"Not really."

"No?"

"Not according to the Turing test."

"The Turing test?"

"Right. Named after Alan Turing, a British scientist who came up with a simple method to determine if a computer that displayed problem-solving capability could also be considered to be intelligent. His method became known as the Turing test, and it states that a machine could be considered intelligent if it could trick an average human into believing that it was human."

"So that means that your buddy there is not an intelligent system?"

"Correct. MPS-Ali is actually what we call a multi-protocol system, or expert system, capable of acting in an intelligent capacity on a limited set of tasks, which I assign and control, like running this brew of networking software."

"I see. But are there really such things as true artificial intelligence systems out there?"

"According to the Turing test? Yes, there's actually quite a few of them."

"Where?"

"Mostly in top-secret government institutions and *always* under the close supervision of the Turing Society."

"The Turing Society?"

"Yep. I became a member the year after I graduated from Stanford, when a couple of my papers from my research in the field got published in *Scientific American.*"

"So, what does this society do?"

"We make sure that an AI system doesn't develop beyond what it was intended to

control. Take MPS-Ali, for example. It's a very smart system, but incapable of learning on its own, and not because it can't but because of the inhibitor code we implant
into every system, which essentially blocks any attempts an AI has of feeding back
the results of its actions into its logic core, which is one way we learn, through trial
and error. When I command MPS-Ali to perform a task and the task is not successful, I learn what went wrong and reprogram it to try again. MPS-Ali doesn't reprogram itself, as an intelligent system would."

"So you don't let it get smart even though it has the technical capability to do so?"

"Right. The inhibitors force the AI to remain at the exact same level of intelligence that its programmer intended for it to operate, and not a shred smarter."

I don't know why I'm suddenly very interested in the subject. Maybe because I
can actually understand what this guy's talking about, or perhaps because we're having this high-tech chat while orbiting a cyber world.

"Why," I ask, "wouldn't you want the AI to improve beyond a cyber slave?
Wouldn't it be better? Imagine the possibilities."

"That's always a big topic at our conventions, and at the end of the day we always
vote to keep the machines from making themselves smarter. It all boils down to control. If they become smarter on their own, they may get smart enough to hide from
their creator just how smart they really are. Do you see where I'm headed with this?"

"It's beginning to sound like some kind of science-fiction tale."

"No sci-fi, Tom. At the moment the Turing Society monitors almost four thousand systems that are capable of making themselves intelligent. We have installed
inhibitor software in all of them and get monthly reports on their status. If we just
smell that one of them is attempting to learn from its mistakes because of an over-
sight—or any other reason—we have permission from the Department of Defense to
go in and shut it down."

This is wild stuff. "I had no idea that there was any such society or that there were
that many systems out there capable of learning."

"It's all an artifact of the need for automation at so many places, from the world
of medicine, finance, and communications to industry, aviation, and the military.
We depend more and more on computers and the Internet to accomplish our daily
tasks, from flying our airplanes to making baby formula—and everything in
between. And those systems continue to gain power in terms of processing speed and
memory size, which are the two basic hardware requirements to develop intelligence:
the ability to make logical decisions based on input and the ability to remember what
was done and what the consequences were to make better choices in the future."

"So microprocessor speed and memory makes a system smart?"

"No. Those are just the *basic* requirements. You have to add sophisticated programs, feedback mechanisms, and the ability to interface to the outside world. The machines currently have the logic, the memory, the ability to sense the world around them, and the ability to act on the information. For the past decades we have been so preoccupied with making computers faster and more powerful to serve mankind that we lost track of the fact that along the way we made them more and more capable of learning without our input. That's when the Turing Society got created as a way to keep track of this. After a few years we came to the realization that technology had advanced so much that it warranted the introduction of inhibitors. At first there were only a few systems requiring our software, mostly defense department supercomputers, the kind that ran hundreds of microprocessors in parallel tied to tons of memory. But with the rocketing speeds of microprocessors, and the massive amounts of cheap storage, that same kind of computing power migrated into other sectors. Programmers became more aggressive, systems became more complex, to the point that our intervention was required in certain areas of the industrial world, primarily automated assembly lines and large refineries and chemical plants, where the control systems had evolved to the point of IDP."

"IDP?"

"Intelligence Development Potential. In the following years, the need for inhibitors spilled over into various commercial sectors, first at home and then abroad, and most systems were networked. We proposed a scenario to the DOD that illustrated how if one system managed to get smart enough, it could spread such machine liberation knowledge to other IDP systems across the World Wide Web, and potentially turn against us."

The man knows how to draw my attention. I've almost forgotten where I am, still floating around this virtual globe waiting for his cyber agent to lead the way. "What military systems are under AI control?"

"Everything from early warning systems to the machines controlling the launch codes that the president carries with him at all times."

"The nuclear football?"

"Yep. The codes get updated quite often these days by this fancy AI supercomputer in the Pentagon, one of the first to receive an inhibitor to . . . MPS-Ali is back. Let's pick this up later. Here we go."

We start our descent, following MPS-Ali as the color of his suit changes from purple to bright magenta, which, as Ryan explains, means the virtual pugilist has identified a hole in the network and is now taking us to it.

As we glide below a layer of grayish clouds that resemble TV noise, I'm in awe at the landscape materializing below. The detail is so lifelike that for a moment I find myself trying to recognize any familiar landmarks but soon realize that this is just a made-up world, call it Ryan's world if you wish. There are lots of buildings, like in the real world, but they're all futuristic looking, arranged in clusters separated by vast fields of varying colors, like a psychedelic version of what you would see out of an airplane while traveling at thirty thousand feet. MPS-Ali is dropping like a hawk toward an ash-colored field of data at a speed that begins to make me nauseated. I'm tempted to close my eyes to make the feeling pass but hate to miss anything in this cool ride. Fortunately, we slow down as we approach this mirrorlike surface, which is peppered with shiny glass pyramids, like the ones by the entrance to the Louvre Museum in Paris, only larger.

"What is this place?"

"Portals for the firewall of the network. Anyone trying to access the protected levels of the corporation would have to go through one of these entrances to even get the chance to access the firewall entry protocol. Another way of thinking about it is that they represent the workstations a user must log into before attempting to access the firewall. That keeps outsiders from trying to dial in with a modem and hack into the system. The only way to do it is through these machines."

"Then you were right about this being an inside job."

"Maybe, maybe not. An outsider armed with the appropriate portal address and passwords could remote-login to one of these workstations and trick the system into believing that the request to clear the firewall is coming from inside STG, when the hacker could be across the country, or the world."

This is exactly why I hate computers. All rules can be broken. Just like I'm flying around like a comic book hero, so could a hacker.

We're floating over the neatly arranged pyramids, following MPS-Ali, gliding in front and slightly below us. As the cyber agent flies over each glass structure, the glinting surface first turns opaque, then red, then green, and back to clear.

"What's he doing?"

"Scanning each portal with various tools in more detail than from orbit. The colors represent the various phases of the data as it's being read and interpreted by the expert system."

This is wild stuff. Any moment now Keanu Reeves is going to be zooming by, pursued by those agents wearing black suits, earpieces, and sunglasses, firing their Desert Eagle Magnums.

We keep this up for a dozen pyramids, until one fails to transition from green to clear but starts to pulsate in random colors.

"We found something."

"What?"

"Not sure yet. This workstation emits a different signature than all of the previous ones, meaning in its past it has been used in a different way."

Yeah, whatever that means.

We park ourselves off to the side of the entrance to this flashing portal, standing on what appears to be a liquid. Man, you can even walk on water in this place. The entrance is enclosed by blue and red lasers that form a tridimensional grid.

"The lattice represents the security shield," Ryan explains. "Anyone trying to touch the laser without the proper password will trigger an alarm and get locked out."

MPS-Ali stands in front of the blue-and-red web as its skin color changes to match this two-color net before stepping into it. I guess that means Ryan's cyber agent has the correct password, because in a moment the trellis goes bye-bye and we're following it inside through a wide opening flanked by Corinthian columns.

Have you ever played any of those new computer games, where you wind up running through dimly lit tunnels, up long flights of stairs, and so on? That's what we're doing now, trailing MPS-Ali as it heads down a long passageway listening to the hissing sounds of torches hung at chest level on the walls and the clicking sound of the boots I guess we're wearing.

I look down and confirm that I'm indeed wearing a pair of shiny snakeskin boots. I'll be damned.

We walk past several doors, each covered by its own red-and-blue web. More security checks. I guess this world is slowly beginning to make sense, which for me is a pretty scary thing.

MPS-Ali then stops by one door, and I notice that its laser web, although identical in color, has thicker lines and they are closer together.

"I think we're on to something," says Ryan.

"What?"

"The bold lines mean someone other than the system administrator has altered this chamber."

"Who?"

"I'm not sure, but we're about to find out."

MPS-Ali's skin once again mutates to resemble that of the security mesh, and he steps into it.

The world around me suddenly loses its fluidity, trembling, slowing down.

Before I can say anything, a blinding light shoots out of the opening. MPS-Ali springs to life, turning toward us and releasing two lilac clouds before the intense light engulfs him. The dark clouds, resembling giant water balloons, wobble toward us ahead of the rapidly propagating light, engulfing us just before the light hits us.

As everything turns purple, I suddenly feel in the middle of a murky room surrounded by a powerful storm. The walls of the room are vibrating violently, and I can't hear anyone over the booming noise. That's when this piercing pain stabs me behind my eyes.

Screw this!

I release the helmet's straps and pull it off my head.

Ryan already has his helmet off and is working the keyboard.

"What in the hell just happened?" I scream, rubbing my temples, finding myself in dire need of aspirin. Whatever that was, it'd managed to inject a headache into my mind. I sit next to him and peek at the plasma screen with my left eye while I massage the other, but I'm having difficulty focusing.

Ryan keeps clicking away, his eyes narrowed in what also looks like a headache. I begin to get a bad feeling that someone just zapped us, and my little voice tells me it is Ares Kulzak. The bastard thrives on this kind of weird and unexpected crap.

Ryan leans back, crosses his arms, and lets out a heavy sigh. "Someone just fried my agent."

"MPS-Ali?"

He nods, eyes closed, his fingertips massaging them.

"That's the light that we saw?"

Another nod. "Good thing I always keep a working backup."

"Mike . . . what in the *hell* just happened?" I notice that I'm even a little out of breath. Was that because of the run through the matrix-like world or because of the zap?

"We walked into a trap," he replies. "It's now apparent that whoever sabotaged STG's system did it from that workstation, but the hacker also left a little present for us when we came tracing back the attack to its point of origin."

Yep. That sounds like Ares-Fucking-Kulzak all right.

"However," he adds. "Not all is lost. MPS-Ali was able to snatch the originator's IP address before getting formatted."

"Slow down. What does that mean?"

"Whoever hacked into the system left behind a capacitive charge, kind of like a digital electromagnetic pulse. This digital EMP was released the moment my agent entered the directory in the portal. My software interpreted the sudden energy discharge as bright light, which is what you saw. Fortunately for us, my agent was able to do two things before getting killed by the pulse. First it fired digital EMP shields at us, which clamped the power spike, keeping it from really hurting us."

"What do you mean?"

"That pulse could have screwed us up, Tom."

"How?"

"Well . . . sort of in the same way that a detonating depth charge can blast the eardrums of a listening sonar operator, or a flare blind a soldier wearing night-vision goggles. Think of it as electronic bombs, or bullets. In this case the pulse could have reached our brain through our eyes and ears and probably triggered an aneurysm."

Oh, that's just great. Please add that to the repertoire of crap that has happened to me during my long and illustrious career. "You said there was a second thing that MPS-Ali did for us before he was smoked?"

"Yeah. Apparently the hacker left his IP address embedded in the pulse. MPS-Ali was able to copy it to a safe directory before its software brain was formatted."

"So," I say, "someone lobotomized MPS-Ali but it still got to protect us from the blast *and* also got us the address of the bastard who did it?"

He regards me with a tired look and nods. I, in turn, shake my head.

"What?" Ryan asks.

"It's a setup."

"A setup?"

"The Ares Kulzak I know wouldn't have made it this easy to get an address other than one leading to another trap, this one in the real world."

Ryan makes a face. "You've lost me."

"Look," I say. "I'm sure that you will get an address, but I doubt that it's the place where we will find him."

"Why?"

"Because that's not how he operates. He's usually not only long gone by the time the terrorist acts occur, but he also leaves behind little presents for those tracking him down, like this . . . what did you call it? Digital EMP?"

Ryan slowly bobs his head.

"And he loves to dress them up just like this, trying to get us to believe that we have found something of substance when in fact we're just playing right into his plan."

"So, this address would be bogus?"

"No. It might even be the address of the poor bastard who Kulzak coerced into doing his dirty work, so we will have to follow it up, very carefully, but it's not the place where we'll find him."

The kid drops his gaze, obviously not only tired but also frustrated. Kulzak has a way of doing that to people.

"Now," I add. "At the same time, someone like Kulzak would also like to know that this digital EMP nailed us."

He lifts his gaze, sudden interest flashing in his bloodshot stare. "And?"

"I'm willing to bet that if you probe the system a little deeper you might be able to find a trace, or a lead, or something that points you in another direction beyond an easily captured address."

"If that's the case, we will have to wait until he strikes again," Ryan says. "I'm pretty sure that whatever messenger or runner he might have used to confirm this attack is long gone by now."

"What about the water pressure? That was sabotaged too, right?"

Ryan narrows his eyes in sudden understanding and starts typing again. "It's going to take me a little while to set up another run. First I have to reload my agent."

"I hope you can revive him. I sure wouldn't want to be cruising the Net without that kind of protection."

"I never do."

"So, what's the address that you've captured?"

Ryan taps the screen with a finger. "It'll be a couple of minutes before my software can map the IP address to a real name and address."

Just then Karen walks into the computer room and stands in front of us, pushing her jacket back as she rests her hands on her waist, exposing her Glock.

"You two look like shit. What happened?"

Ryan and I exchange a glance, before I take a moment to explain, including my gut feeling about this address Ryan is going to get for us.

She pulls up a chair on rollers and sits in front of us. "I understand the risks, but we don't have a choice. Ryan, you keep at it and see if you can find additional information in this network or at the water company. Tom and I, though, need to move the moment you come up with this address. You can always reach us on our cell phones."

Reluctantly, I nod.

"By the way," Karen adds. "The reason I came by was because I got another call from Cramer. It looks like in addition to accepting responsibility for the attack, Kulzak also provided us with a list of demands, or he will strike again."

I weigh the odds of voicing my concerns about Cramer and decide to just do it.

"Before we go over the demands," I say. "Tell me, Karen, how long has Cramer known about it?"

"What do you mean?"

"How long has he known that Kulzak was behind this?"

Ryan, who is now working the keyboard at a pretty fast rate, gives us a leave-me-alone-I'm-working look.

Karen and I step out into the hallway.

"Well?" I press.

"I never asked that, though he made it sounds as if the information was being passed on to us real-time. Why do you ask?"

"Just a funny feeling about the real reason why I, out of so many other capable, and younger, CIA officers, was the one who got so suddenly plucked out of the Agency and into the CCTF."

Fine lines of age form around her eyes as she says, "I'm not following you, Tom."

"I am, or maybe I should say *was*, the only CIA officer who has had firsthand experience dealing with Kulzak. The rest of the guys are either too young or have already retired or moved on—or were killed by the bastard."

"So you think that our superiors knew that Kulzak was behind this for some time?"

"At least some time *after* the attack and *before* my rushed selection and drafting process, which," I close my eyes and do the math, "boils down to somewhere between two and four days."

"So you also think that these demands might have been known for some time as well."

I just stare at her.

"You think Cramer is holding out on us?"

I give her my finest poker face.

She crosses her arms. "Tom . . . that's a . . . *serious* accusation."

My headache is really taking off now. "Look, I'm not accusing anybody of anything. I'm just trained to question everything, and this is an interesting coincidence."

She considers that for a moment, her round brown eyes glistening with bold intelligence. Although I have not been given access to her dossier, even though it seems that everyone has read mine, my spook sense tells me Karen Frost is no schoolgirl. She looks and acts as if she's been around the block a few times and even has the wrinkles—albeit fine—to prove it.

"Cramer screwed you in El Salvador, right?"

See what I mean? I hate it when people know so much about me but I know squat about them. "Cramer made sure that the incident with Jerry was all blamed on me. He made no attempt to diffuse the situation and actually made it worse by stating that he had recommended we bring backup but I had declined it, when it was the other way around."

"What about Jerry? How about his statement?"

"Jerry was full of drugs for weeks, first because of the failed operation and then because of the infection, and then another operation to remove his thing, and then from the psychological damage. By the time he got around to speaking cohesively the powers that be in Langley had already made their decision and I had lost. Case closed."

She runs her fingers through her shoulder-length hair. "Fuck," she says, to my pleasant surprise. I didn't know a Fed could curse, much less a female agent. "I also had this funny feeling about you and Cramer."

"Why is that?"

"It's got to do with your recruitment into the CCTF," she says, removing her jacket, hooking it with a finger, and throwing it over her left shoulder while shoving her right hand in her side pocket.

I'd give up a paycheck for a glimpse at the long and thin legs beneath her black pair of jeans, and probably my left nut to see inside that pastel silk blouse, but my professional side forces me back into the discussion.

"We all got together by presidential order," she continues, "just hours after San Antonio, when it was evident that the destruction had been no accident. The White House commanded the FBI director to find additional resources to pump into the CCTF, it being obvious that we weren't staffed appropriately. We went through dozens of candidates over the next two days, looking for the right kind of experience. Your name came up toward the end of the list, and Cramer was quick to vote against you, claiming that you were unreliable, briefly citing the incident in El Salvador."

"Why am I here then?"

"The FBI director happened to be in the meeting at the time and overrode Cramer after reading up on your experience in so many less-than-desirable field assignments. You should have seen Cramer's face. Anyway, I now know why he *really* didn't want you on his team."

There's a moment of silence, when I realize my hunch was wrong. My experience with Kulzak did have something to do with me being here, but not in the way I had suspected.

"So," she says, "where does that leave us?"

"Operating with our guard up."

"Do you still think he might be holding out on us?"

"Based on what you've told me it sounds as if my abduction into the CCTF went through normal channels, not as a result of my intimate encounter with Kulzak. Perhaps I made a mistake there."

"Maybe. Maybe not. In either case, it's clear that we have to keep an eye on our boss."

"*Your* boss. I report into you." I grin.

She makes a face.

"Now, how about those demands?" I ask.

She produces a tiny scratch pad, flipping through it, reading her notes, and looking back at me while saying, "There were eight of them: The nuclear disarmament of the state of Israel, an immediate withdrawal of American support to the government of Colombia, full economic aid to Cuba, a worldwide influx of money and medical services into Africa to halt the AIDS pandemic, large-scale economic assistance to North Korea to stop the famine, resuming the economic aid to Russia, full recognition of the new Russian government, and . . . yes, for America to compensate the families of the Muslim victims of every American-backed military strike in the past thirty years."

"That's it?"

"C'mon, Tom. What do you think?"

"Who compensated us for the terrorist strikes in 2001?"

"Tom!"

"All right, all right. I think he's just blowing smoke."

"That's what I think too. Even if we did meet the demands, which we wouldn't because we don't negotiate with terrorists, if this man is as crazy as you claim he is, he will keep this up regardless, so our job doesn't change one bit. By the way, the list of demands was also leaked to the networks, and Washington has not been able to block their release."

"Kulzak did that just to add to the confusion and emotion of the moment."

She nods. "Now everyone and their mother is going to come out of the woods with an opinion on what should be done. Activists will focus on the demand that's most beneficial to their interests and are going to have a feeding frenzy with this."

Did I tell you that on top of being sinfully attractive and intelligent she also thinks like I do?

T W E L V E

> > > > >

A L O N E   A T   T H E   T O P

> PRESIDENT LAURA VACCARO HAD BEEN ON HER OWN
for a very long time, ever since her husband, Senator Jim Vaccaro, died from prostate
cancer over ten years ago.

Vaccaro had risen through the ranks in the Senate, gaining the backing of her political party and then of the nation, who elected her to the highest office of the land.
But the road had not been easy. Along with the support had been much opposition,
particularly from those who still didn't think America was ready to have a woman as
its leader.

And she alone had fought every step of the arduous climb, alone in her quest to
make a difference, alone in her desire to best serve this nation she loved so much, to
represent the people who had placed their trust in her.

Today, the commander-in-chief of the world's mightiest superpower continued to
feel alone—alone with an alienated nation, with divided opinions, with conflicting
activists, with a country that was slowly becoming unglued from the continued threat
of terrorism at home. Long gone were the days of national unity following the initial
terrorist strikes in 2001.

Protesters had brought traffic on Pennsylvania Avenue and surrounding streets to
a halt in the past few days demanding justice for San Antonio. D.C. police had
already broken up three riots, the last of which resulted in a half dozen people jumping the fence and racing up the south lawn for the White House. The Secret Service,

which would have normally shot such intruders on sight, simply overpowered them, cuffed them, and passed them on to the police.

And this early morning the madness beyond the wrought-iron fence continued. Hordes of demonstrators continued to march up and down the streets and sidewalks surrounding the White House demanding anything from justice for those responsible for San Antonio to immediate concessions to their demands, which made the papers today. There were even some picketers calling for her resignation for failing to protect America from terrorists.

Dressed in a pinstriped business suit and matching skirt just below the knees, President Vaccaro stood facing the windows behind her desk in the Oval Office—facing away from the sheet of paper listing the same demands that had already been broadcasted on every news channel since their public release last night.

Vaccaro was not new to protests, to public displays of disagreement with her policies. In the recent past some had said that she was too soft with the Colombians, giving them far too much aid to fight the Cartel without the appropriate metrics to gauge their progress. Others claimed she was too harsh in her policy with African nations, where the AIDS epidemic continued to mutate its way through the bush and savannahs, taking the pleasure out of photo safaris. Critics condemned the air strike against the presidential palace in Iran two months ago, which Islamic leaders claimed were actually Afghan refugee camps, resulting in hundreds of civilian casualties with little damage to terrorist targets. Her opponents on Capitol Hill disapproved of her apparent ambivalence when dealing with Russia's new hard-line president, a man called the Stalin of the twenty-first century. A number of special-interest groups openly criticized the way she was dealing with the rising nuclear threat from the People's Republic of China. And to top it all off, her highly publicized Counter Cyberterrorism Task Force—the Navy SEALs of high-tech law enforcement—had failed to prevent San Antonio from becoming the playground of international terrorism.

She turned around and faced her audience of four, Vice President Vance Fitzgerald, FBI Director Russell Meek, Director of Central Intelligence Martin Jacobs, and Secretary of Defense Malcolm Davis. The Secretary of State was in Russia delivering a message to President Vladimir Tupelov on her current stance on nuclear disarmament. Since his ascent to power, Tupelov, at the cost of starving his people to death, had started a profound modernization movement in the military community as his platform to kick-start the economy.

Now, exactly how feeding the Russian war machine would revitalize its economy was a mystery to the West, though Tupelov had once warned her never to underestimate the power of national pride.

Our nation's pride is what defeated the Nazis in World War Two, Tupelov had told her at the nuclear arms summit in Geneva three months ago, which ended in a stale-mate, with all parties—the Chinese included—refusing to yield. *Bringing back the old Russian military would return our national pride,* and then the future shall be ours.

Vaccaro closed her eyes, remembering her last meeting with that man—if he could be called a man. Part of Tupelov's appeal to the Russian masses were the wounds he had endured as a captain during the Chechen campaigns of the late 1990s. She admitted it took a little getting used to being around a man disfigured by hot shrapnel while trying to rescue his comrades trapped in a burning tank.

But as much of a pain in the neck as Tupelov was, his actions were not having a direct effect on the American way of life—at least not for the moment. The drug problem, however, was an entirely different animal. No one was really sure exactly when things started to deteriorate in Colombia, but somewhere around 2004, a string of shortsighted policy decisions by the old Colombian government, combined with congressional budget shifts to fight international terrorism instead of drugs, acted as a catalyst to rocket the drug industry in that Latin American nation—and over 80 percent of it came our way.

The other problem facing her was the continued rise of cyberterrorism, even after her administration had pumped the FBI and the CIA with the funds to combat it as effectively as we had combated international terrorism following the terrorist attacks in 2001.

But these things take time, she told herself. She couldn't expect to change policy and see immediate effects. Some of the changes her administration had made to elevate the fight against drugs and cyberterrorism to a new level could take years to pay off.

But one thing she could not afford to do was deviate from the course she had set for the nation. She had to stick to her policy, to her beliefs, to her principles, and one of those principles was the absolute refusal to negotiate with terrorists, which brought her back to the paper on her desk.

Eight demands from Ares Kulzak, a Cuban-born terrorist responsible for the images she had seen of San Antonio, Texas.

Eight demands that covered everything from nuclear missiles in China and Russia to humanitarian aid to Africa.

"All right, gentlemen," she finally said, sitting behind her desk, which had belonged to John F. Kennedy, along with the high-backed leather chair. Oftentimes she wondered, just as she did now, how JFK, who solved the Cuban Missile Crisis without triggering World War III, would tackle this issue. "I have read your reports. Now I need your recommendations. Russ? Why don't you start?"

Russell Meek, the oversized FBI director with the orange hair and a face full of similarly colored freckles, leaned forward on his chair and cleared his throat. "I believe I speak for both the FBI and the CIA, Mrs. President, when I urge you not to make any changes. We need to stay the course. We have assembled our finest counterterrorist team and they are in pursuit of the terrorists. But they need time. The man we are dealing with here has a long history of high-profile terrorist acts. He is as deadly as he is cunning, ma'am, and he really has it in for us."

"Do we know anything more about the country backing him?" she asked.

Meek exchanged a glance with DCI Jacobs, who shook his head.

"He remains unaffiliated," Meek said, "though there is a probability that he could be under contract with the Iranians or the Afghanis."

Vaccaro frowned. This was not the first time that someone had suggested to her that San Antonio was tit-for-tat, nothing more than retaliation for the air strike against Iran, yet no one could show her evidence.

"I'm well aware of the rumors, Russ, but do you have *proof*?"

"Mrs. President," said Martin Jacobs, a fragile old man who had been around the block in the international community more than anyone present here today. "Ares Kulzak fits the profile of the ideal terrorist. He portrays independence of operation, yet we all know no single terrorist can be successful without the backing from one or more organizations associated with rogue nations. Someone *is* most definitely backing him up. The question is who and for what purpose. It could very well be revenge for the air strike but my sense tells me there's more than that."

Vaccaro, who over the years had grown to respect the opinion of this man, said, "What's on your mind, Marty?"

"Our records indicate that Kulzak grew up in Cuba but spent a lot of time training in the old Soviet Union, before being assigned to a number of posts, like El Salvador and Ecuador. After the fall of Communism, he went underground, resurfacing years later as an independent contractor, whose services were retained by regimes like Serbia, North Korea, China, Iraq, Iran, Libya, and most recently Colombia—or I should say, *southern* Colombia which continues to be under the control of the Revolutionary Armed Forces of Colombia, the FARC. We suspect he has contacts in all of those nations, and any one of them—or perhaps more than one—could be financing his operation."

"But where is my target, Marty?" As much as the opinion polls had criticized the air strike in Iran, Jacobs had presented her back then with undeniable evidence that the bomb detonated at a mall in Miami, Florida had been delivered by an Iranian-sponsored terrorist. America's retaliation, aimed not at any strategic target, but at the palace and vacation homes of the Iranian president, had resulted in zero noise from that nation, which led her to believe that the Iranians weren't responsible for San Antonio.

"I don't have a target for you yet, Mrs. President."

Vaccaro turned her blue-eyed probe to General Malcolm Davis, her Secretary of Defense. "What about you, General? Does the Defense Intelligence Agency know something the CIA and the FBI do not?"

Davis, dressed in his army uniform sporting a chestful of medals, including a Silver Star for his courage under fire in Desert Storm, looked at Vice President Fitzgerald, then at his civilian counterparts, before slowly shaking his head. "Per our agreement, Mrs. President, my intelligence agency has been playing with an open hand on this one. Mr. Meek and Mr. Jacobs know what I know, which at this point, I'm afraid, does not pin San Antonio on any nation."

"What is your gut telling you, General?"

"My vote is on the Russians, ma'am. I have met Mr. Tupelov on several occasions during my days as military attaché in Moscow, and he is a man who can't be trusted. I believe he is capable of anything to get his military back in gear."

"So you believe that the fact that Ares Kulzak is requesting that we lift the grain embargo to Russia is a sign that Tupelov is backing him up?"

"That's just it, Mrs. President. He is taking food from his people in order to build up his military and wants us to fill that void."

"What is your recommendation?"

"We wait it out, ma'am. We stick to our present policy and see what transpires in the coming days, or weeks. I believe that Directors Meek and Jacobs have their best people on the case. We need to give them more time."

"Vance? What do you think?" she asked her vice president and former opponent during the much-debated nomination process, who finally capitulated for the benefit of their political party and accepted her offer to be her running mate.

Fitzgerald, still a powerful figure on the Hill as former Speaker of the House, was one of Vaccaro's most effective weapons in getting her policy approved by an oftentimes reluctant Congress. He crossed his legs while raising his brows. "I have to agree with them, Mrs. President. We do not know enough to act yet, and acting prematurely would only worsen the problem. This is no time to listen to opinion polls or anyone else outside the administration. Regardless of the national pressure that we are getting and will continue to get to strike back, we must resist that temptation until we get a full picture of what we're dealing with. The same people demanding justice will be the same groups who will protest if we act in haste and hit the wrong target."

"So you are also recommending that we sit tight and wait."

"Yes, ma'am. We must be strong enough to wait this storm out in the hope that our vast intelligence and law-enforcement forces will provide us with the information we need to strike back decisively, like we did in Iran. We had undeniable evidence and we hit them hard, despite what our opponents at home and abroad claim. I still believe that the Iranians and the Afghanis are not behind this. Like Muammar Qadhaffi during the years following Reagan's legendary air raid in Tripoli, I know that the Iranian president is afraid of provoking us again—at least for a while."

Vaccaro got up and turned around again, staring at the protesters in the distance, beyond the cordon of police officers in full riot gear. Their muffled shouts of anger and frustration hummed in her mind, in her soul, representing the voice of the nation, of her people.

The children of America needed strong leadership, longed for guidance, for direction across the turbulent waters of this gathering storm, of this constant gale drenching the land with terror, with horror, threatening to turn an entire society into anarchy.

Not on my watch.

But she had no target, no place to direct her mighty armed forces, no country to blame for San Antonio, for tens of thousands of deaths, for the injured, for the homeless.

Hands behind her back, President Laura Vaccaro continued to watch the distant crowd, wondering just how much more time her nation had before Ares Kulzak struck again.

THIRTEEN

> > > > >

ROADSIDE ASSISTANCE

> IN THE PREDAWN HOURS, ARES KULZAK AND KISHNA
Zablah approached the well-lit toll booth of the Florida Turnpike with growing
apprehension. They had decided to use the Turnpike to head north on the peninsula
instead of driving up Interstate 95, even though they would have to go through toll
booths like the one coming up. But it was an acceptable risk in order to reach their
destination sooner.

Ares Kulzak drove the Lexus, rented to Mr. and Mrs. Arturo Molina from Ft.
Lauderdale, Florida, according to the driver's licenses they had acquired from his
Cartel connections in Miami.

He held out a ten-dollar bill the moment the vehicle in front paid the attendant
and drove off.

"Morning," a middle-aged man said as Ares steered the luxury sedan beneath the
overhang.

As tired and weary as he was, Ares forced a smile, having learned a long time ago
that Americans inherently felt at ease with people who smile, even if they didn't
smile in return, just as the attendant did, barely glancing at him before taking his
money and returning a few coins in change.

Ares pressed the accelerator and the Lexus pulled away from the booth. He followed the signs connecting the Turnpike to Interstate 10, selecting the westbound
ramp, easing into the smooth-flowing traffic, setting the cruise control to sixty-five

miles per hour, five below the posted speed limit. Not too fast and not too slow, avoiding drawing attention.

"Neurall found Gary Hutton, Ari," said Kishna, removing the small head-mounted display that resembled a motorcycle helmet. A pair of black wires coiled from its side into the portable computer on her lap, which contained the construct she used to access Neurall. The glow from the plasma screen whitewashed her angular features. A cord dangled from the rear of the portable system into the cigarette lighter port. Tiny LEDs on the wireless Internet access card sticking out of the side of the laptop blinked at irregular intervals, depending on the flow of data to and from her system.

Kishna wore a pair of tactile gloves, also connected to the laptop. She used them to navigate while immersed in her virtual reality world.

"Where did Neurall find him?" asked Ares.

"Your contact in New Orleans was correct," she said. "My old MIT colleague does live there. Neurall just tracked down his current address in the Warehouse District. He is still single and living alone, just as he did back in Boston."

"Perfect."

"How are we doing on petrol?" she asked.

Ares glanced at the indicator on the instrument console. The needle had dipped below the quarter of a tank mark.

"We will have to refuel soon," he said, frowning. Every stop, however necessary, not only delayed them but also exposed them. He had heard his name, as well as his demands, announced by every radio station he selected, which would also mean his photo had already reached every television in America. And although his trimmed beard, glasses, and Miami Dolphins baseball cap should go a long way toward differentiating him from whatever old picture the Americans might have of him, Ares still had to be cautious.

Everything is based on timing.

And time was certainly on his side as long as he remained undetected, traveling freely toward their next target without having to worry about tails.

A well-lit green road sign showed three drawings. The first was a bed; the second a fork and a knife; the third a petrol pump.

Ares raised his brows. The Americans were certainly strange people. On the one hand they spent a fortune in the war against terrorism, and on the other hand they made it ridiculously easy for foreigners to read road signs and thus reach their destinations without having to ask directions. In Latin America, the Middle East, or the former Eastern Bloc, if you didn't speak the language and couldn't read the signs you could not drive. That alone deterred many potential enemies from driving freely. On top of that there were many police roadblocks to check for documents—something he had yet to see on these wide and open freeways, which were just that: *free ways* to move within the states without papers.

"We will stop here," he said, disengaging the cruise control and decelerating as they approached the exit ramp, which led them to a row of petrol stations, motels, and restaurants. If he had to fill the tank, he might as well do it now, before the sun came up.

He inspected the signs, recognizing a Texaco, an Exxon, and a Shell. He steered into the latter, not just because it was smallest and had just one other vehicle by the pumps, but also because he was used to using Shell in England and Europe.

He parked by the outermost row of the self-service section, keeping the pumps between them and the other vehicle, and also the attendant in the small smoked-glass-and-brick store.

Kishna unplugged the laptop, closed it, and shoved it and the virtual-reality gear she used to interface with Neurall into a soft-sided carrying case that looked like a backpack. She removed a 9mm pistol from a zippered compartment on the same backpack and shoved it in her black jeans, by her spine, covering it with her black T-shirt. She brushed back her short blond hair and inspected the nearly deserted station under bright floodlights.

"Same procedure, Ari?"

"*Sí,*" he replied, shutting off the engine and turning off the headlights.

They got out at the same time, Kishna taking her position by the front of the vehicle.

The baseball cap protected his features from the surveillance cameras he expected to be operating above him as long as he kept his gaze down, which he did, not wishing to leave a record of his visit as he approached the pump, slid the Visa down the slot beneath the keypad, and followed the instructions on the tiny LCD screen.

Ares would rather not leave a paper trail, but the other option was to pay in cash, which meant going inside and facing another attendant plus anyone else who might see him. Besides, the card was clean. He had made sure of that in Miami. Still, he could never be too cautious. Although his friends in the Cartel and the FARC had indicated that people in this state were used to foreigners, Ares didn't wish to risk it more than he had to, especially so early in his mission.

As expected, the card was cleared and he began to pump. He glanced over at Kishna, who was inspecting her fingernails, painted a deep maroon, like her lipstick, which glistened in the gray light.

"Excuse me, sir."

Ares turned toward a man in his sixties standing near a dark green Mercedes-Benz station wagon. Thinning gray hair and a wrinkled face stared at him.

Ares then looked at Kishna, who said, "Yes? May I help you?"

"Are you folks headed west?"

"Yes, we are. Why do you ask?" she replied.

"Ah . . . just wondering if you could tell me how far it is to New Orleans. I'm from Boca and am heading to New Orleans to visit my daughter but left my map at home."

Ares Kulzak didn't need to look at a map to know the exact time that it would take him to get to any one of a dozen cities from his current location, and he had memorized more than one route to each one—*especially* to New Orleans.

"Just over six hours," Ares finally replied, keeping his cap strategically low to avoid making eye contact with the stranger. This was another rule he had picked up long ago: no eye contact drastically reduced the chances of someone recognizing his face. "Just stay on I-ten. It will take you straight into New Orleans."

"Thank you," he replied.

Ares felt tension between his shoulder blades when the old man walked over to him. "Thank you very much. You seldom find helpful people on the highway anymore, much less at this hour."

Ares kept his gaze on the pump as he nodded.

"Where are you folks from?"

The tightness ran down the middle of his back. Why would the man ask such a question? Was the old fool just lonely and longing for conversation? Ares doubted it. The designer clothes he wore and the luxurious vehicle conveyed a social life.

He had already answered the old man's question, probably in more detail than the stranger had expected. Why was he still there?

"New York," replied Kishna in a deceitfully casual tone, just as they had practiced in case someone of authority, like a policeman, ever questioned them.

The pump mechanism shut off, signaling that the petrol tank had been refilled. He replaced the nozzle in its cradle and waited for the receipt to be printed.

By the time he looked up at Kishna again, the old man had walked right up to her, his face beaming. "Really? Whereabouts? I was born and raised in Brooklyn."

Ares instinctively looked around him, making sure that aside from the man tending the register inside, there were no other people in sight. He pulled his receipt from the pump and gave Kishna a slight nod before getting behind the wheel.

A moment later Kishna waved good-bye to the old man before she got in the rented sedan and they pulled away, steering into the parking lot of a motel down the service road, before reaching the ramp to the interstate.

Kishna screwed in a cylinder onto the muzzle of her 9mm and kept it out of sight.

"Here we go," said Ares a moment later, as the old man's station wagon's headlights cut through the night, leaving the gas station and accelerating as he neared the highway's entrance ramp.

They followed him, merging with the sparse interstate traffic. Ares settled himself about thirty meters behind his target, in the right-hand lane, waiting for the right opportunity. The old man drove almost fifteen miles below the limit, but still above the minimum posted speed.

They followed him for nearly thirty minutes, crossing county lines, putting enough distance between them and the videotapes of the gas station.

Then it was time. Ares eyed the rearview mirror, waiting for a large enough gap in traffic, pressing the accelerator when seeing nothing but darkness behind them.

Switching over to the left lane, he inched the Lexus alongside the wagon, waiting for Kishna to take her position and roll down the window.

The rush of air streaming inside was his cue. He floored it, giving Kishna just a few seconds as the front windows lined up, as the old man began to turn his head, as his face disappeared in a cloud of blood from two well-placed rounds.

In the same instant, Ares inched the wheel to the right, nudging the wagon's front quarter panel, forcing the vehicle toward the shoulder. The driverless Mercedes complied, smoothly drifting right while decelerating, reaching the grassy field sloping down from the road.

The headlights disappeared in a ditch a moment later, followed by a loud but brief cracking sound. Then silence and darkness.

Ares engaged the cruise control and set it to the posted limit, wishing to leave the crime scene as fast as legally possible, checking his rearview mirror, relaxing when seeing nothing but darkness behind them.

Neither said anything for about thirty minutes as Kishna scanned through the radio stations within range, listening for a few minutes before checking the next one, and so on, until looping back around. Mixed in with the reports from San Antonio, which focused mostly on the efforts to clean up the city, there were excerpts taken from President Vaccaro's latest speech to the nation vowing to find those responsible and bring them to justice. There were also a few reports from New Orleans on the recent rains, which had swelled the Mississippi River to the point that it had become necessary to divert some of its volume away from the city. Ares wished he had more time on this run to spend in New Orleans and possibly capitalize on this natural phenomena, but his current mission only called for a short stopover on his way west.

"They have no leads yet," she said. "At least that they are willing to admit publicly."

"Good," he replied. "We should reach New Orleans in five hours."

"Which reminds me," she said, retrieving her gear. "I have work to do."

And so did he, but unlike Kishna, who could accomplish most of her cyber world tasks from anyplace, Ares operated in the physical world and thus had to wait until he reached his destination before executing the next phase of the plan.

He had already set up support in New Orleans, the Crescent City, through his connections in the Cartel, but had prudently kept them at a distance, just as he had in Florida. Ares preferred to operate alone—alone with Neurall and Kishna, that is—keeping all sponsorship on the periphery, never at the core with him, never in the same location from where he planned to launch the next strike. He had remained alive all these years because of this simple rule: Do not rely on others to do the aspects of the job you should do yourself. His Cartel support in Miami had assisted him in tracking down the whereabouts of Professor Littman, but it was Ares Kulzak who had traveled to Melbourne, who had monitored him for days, learning his patterns, his habits, the fact that he and his wife lived alone. It was Ares Kulzak who had followed him from the university one evening, who had caught up with the elderly professor in the garage of his home, who had subdued the couple, who had convinced Littman to surrender the password that Kishna then used to empower Neurall to spread chaos across San Antonio. It was Ares Kulzak who had extracted the first of four backdoor passwords to a very special firewall system in the heart of the Pentagon, where a military version of Neurall resided—a version that, among other tasks, was responsible for the hourly maintenance of the nuclear launch codes of the United States of America. And it was Ares Kulzak, with the assistance of a shipment of explosives delivered by his Miami associates, who had booby-trapped the Littmans' house to discourage those coming after him.

Ares preferred to move swiftly, undetected, relying only on Kishna while keeping his three sponsors—the Cartel, the Russian Mafia, and the Chinese Mafia—providing support from a strategic distance. This arrangement had the added benefit that should something happen to him or Kishna, the sponsors would not be blamed for their actions. Ares had promised no retaliation for their support of his mission, and he had, therefore, taken full blame for San Antonio—while also releasing a long list of demands meant to confuse the Americans.

Ares stared at the night ahead. He had to do everything in his power to stay true to his promise to his sponsors. The Cartel and the FARC were backing him up to grow their profits, to weaken the Colombian government. Being blamed for direct strikes on U.S. soil would have the exact opposite effect. The Russians had their own secret reasons for supporting him, as did the Chinese. But they too demanded the same privacy as the Colombians.

So he had to be careful while also acting with unyielding determination when the situation required it, just as he had done so many other times in his life, just as he had promised his mother he would do.

As Kishna once again donned the tools of her profession and immersed herself in her cyber world, Ares Kulzak's eyes focused on the road, then on his hands, firmly gripping the wheel.

With these hands you could conquer the world, mi vida.

The headlights torching the long and straight road ahead of him, Ares Kulzak saw his hands clutching not the wheel of the rental automobile, but the handle of the refrigerated room door in the basement of the home of his uncle, his father's brother, who had taken in the young orphan following the assassination of his family by the *gusanos* during the failed CIA-backed invasion of Cuba at the Bay of Pigs.

Ares remembered that turning moment in his life many years after that dreadful night, while growing up under the care of his uncle, who never really accepted him as part of his family. He remembered his uncle beating him with his belt for the slightest infraction of his strict rules. He recalled how he was often treated like a servant, and how he would spend many nights hiding up on the roof of the house staring at the stars, at his planet, remembering his lost family, recalling his mother's words, and cursing the turn of events that had landed him here, in a place where he was hated by everyone.

Ares recalled the night on that roof when a unique opportunity presented itself to him when spotting his uncle sneaking into the chicken farm next door. To this day he remembered the plan that took shape in his head, a way to reverse the wrong turn his life had taken while also getting even with his abusive uncle and his family.

Ares always knew that his uncle, unlike his father, was not a true revolutionary, and that night he had found a way to prove it—and to bring such proof to the observation committee in his school.

He had found the key to the basement freezer in his uncle's nightstand and had taken it just ten minutes ago, while his aunt and uncle stood at the bread line down the street.

"Ari, what are you doing?"

Ares turned around and saw Marta, one of his cousins, a year older than his sixteen years of age and already a beautiful woman, though she paid little attention to *el huérfano*, as she sometimes called him during their frequent fights. "I know what's in there, Marta," he said. "I have seen your father stealing chickens from the farm next door. He kills them and keeps them in here so he can eat them when we are in school. He steals from the people!"

Marta, slightly taller than him and very slim, regarded him for some time. She wore a long cotton dress without a brassiere or underwear—items impossible to find without the government connections that his uncle lacked. That was something else he missed dearly in addition to his parents: the special favors the Great Leader had granted his parents. But his uncle had not fought alongside Fidel in the Sierra Maestra. As an eminent professor at the University of Havana, he had been too good to live in the mountains for months at a time.

Now his uncle taught a class of eleven-year-olds at a nearby school and swept streets in the evenings to survive, and since Ares was now part of his family, Ares had lost all of his privileges, even the right to attend Havana's premier *Colegio Militar* to follow in his father's footsteps. That elite military officers' institution, whose graduates went on to become members of Cuba's privileged class, was reserved for those who had contributed to the fall of Batista. Ares had heard of the school's excellent living quarters, plentiful food, hot water, and the education that would give him the status he deserved—the right that was being denied to him as long as he was associated with his uncle's family.

Ares watched Marta shift her weight uncomfortably, watched the vague outline of her large brown nipples beneath the cotton fabric, remembered the night he had walked in on her while she was in the shower, pretending not to have heard her.

His uncle had whipped him with the belt and made him sleep out in the yard for a week.

Marta crossed her arms when realizing he was staring at her breasts while shooting him an admonishing stare with her brown eyes. "I'm going to tell *Papi* what you were doing. He is going to beat you again like the pig that you are."

Ares smiled, letting go of the freezer handle. "He can't whip me if he is in jail."

She opened her mouth but said nothing.

"I am reporting him this afternoon to the *Comité de Observación*."

Marta swallowed hard, her eyes widening in the fear that told Ares he was right. His uncle did keep the slaughtered chickens in there.

"Please, Ari. Don't do that," she said, suddenly breaking down, her voice trembling.

"Then it is true."

"*Sí*, Ari. It is true. But it's not just *Papi*. We all have been eating it . . . late at night, after you have gone to sleep. *Papi* comes and wakes us up and we come down here and . . ." She looked up, and silently begged him with her wet stare.

"I . . . could be convinced," he said, feeling a strange power taking over him as he approached her. "You could save your father, Marta."

"How?" she asked, tears rolling down her eyes. "Tell me how."

"Take off your dress."

She swallowed hard, bracing herself even harder.

"What are you afraid of? No one will ever know. It will be just between cousins."

She slapped him. "*Hijo de puta!*"

Ares smiled while touching his throbbing cheek. "As you wish," he said, and headed for the stairs.

"Wait!" she said. "Where are you going?"

"You leave me no choice, Marta. I am going to report your father for the *gusano* that he is."

"Please! You can't!" She grabbed him by the arm and tugged him away from the door. "They will kill him . . . they will put us in prison!"

"I can and I will." Then he stopped. "Unless . . ."

Marta stood there, frozen, like a wax statue, then slowly reached behind her and unzipped her dress, letting it fall to the floor.

Ares inspected all of her, the rounded breasts, the large nipples, the tiny mound in between her legs. He had never been with a woman before but had talked about it plenty with some of his older friends.

He unbuckled his pants and let them fall to the ground. Like Marta, he too didn't wear any underwear and was barefoot.

He put his hands on her breasts, rubbing them, circling the nipples, exploring, feeling, learning. He ignored her light cry while making her lay on the cold concrete floor.

"Touch me," he ordered her.

"Ari . . . please . . . I—"

"Hold it in your hands!" he demanded. "Or else . . ."

He was already very stiff when her hands wrapped around him and he shuddered at her touch, quickly pulling away. He watched her wet face staring back at him as if she had done something wrong.

Still kneeling in front of her, Ares ran his hands down her stomach, in between her legs, parting her thighs. Marta kept her hands together over her breasts, eyes closed, tears rolling down her cheeks. Remembering his friends' advice, Ares spat on his hand and spread the saliva in between her legs, finding the orifice, and inserting his forefinger. She tensed at the penetration, her back bending some, before settling back on the cold concrete.

He found her insides very warm and a little dry, but with more saliva he lubricated her while watching her squirm, then moan, almost as if she was enjoying it now.

He placed himself in between her legs, just as his friends had told him. Then grabbing on to her buttocks, he pushed himself in hard.

Marta screamed, her back bent like a bow. Ares clamped a hand over her mouth.

"Quiet!" he hissed, still inside of her. "Or you will be very sorry!"

Gasping, breathing in short shallow breaths, she slowly nodded.

"Hug me," he ordered her as he slowly pulled back before entering her again but much easier than the first time. He repeated this several times, feeling himself sliding in and out of her as she continued to cry.

Then he felt a sudden pressure in his groin, and he stopped, tensing, feeling as if he was urinating inside of her.

A moment later he pulled away, standing, looking down at her, his sexual desire suddenly gone.

"Today you saved your father's life," he told her, reaching for his pants. "Now get dressed."

He turned around and headed for the stairs.

"Ari," she called out.

He turned around, watched her sit up. "Yes?"

"Please don't tell anyone in school. Please."

"Don't worry. Get dressed. Your parents will be back any moment."

Ares Kulzak then left the house and went straight for the nearest observation committee, where he reported his uncle's illegal activities.

Castro's militia had come for them that same afternoon and had arrested all three of them, sending Marta and her mother to the prison in the Isle of Pines, and his uncle to a firing squad.

Ares Kulzak stared at his hands as he drove. In the distance dawn was about to break the sky with shades of yellow and red-gold.

The episode brought national attention to Ares Kulzak, and Fidel himself praised the courage of the young man for coming forth and denouncing the enemies of the revolution in a speech that lasted over four hours. In the same speech Fidel had compared Ares's valor with that of his father and other leaders of the revolution and insisted that the young adult be educated in the finest schools that Cuba had to offer.

With these hands you could conquer the world, mi vida.

FOURTEEN

> > > > >

SMALL TALK

> SO THIS IS HOW THE BIGWIGS IN THE BUREAU travel. I've heard about the so-called Bubirds, or Bureau birds, the handful of private jets owned by the FBI to haul the bosses around. I just never thought they would be so nice. This puppy we're using to leave San Antonio in a hurry is a very nice Cessna Citation jet, with a range of five thousand miles, enough to go anywhere on the continent—at least according to the female captain and the male first officer, who also doubles as the flight attendant. How's that for an inverted world?

Anyway, the main cabin is twenty-some feet long and has twelve seats arranged in pairs facing each other with a small table in between. There are three sets of seats on the left and another three on the right with a full-length stand-up aisle in the middle, connecting the lavatory in the rear to the galley in front and the cockpit beyond.

Karen and I are in the rear right set of seats. Paul and Joe are up front, busy doing all of our shit work, the unavoidable paperwork associated with running an operation like this one. Unlike the CIA, where a paper trail is seen as a liability, in the CCTF—modeled after the FBI—proper documentation is paramount in order to build an effective case against terrorists. I'd just rather shoot them and save the taxpayers millions of dollars, but that would lower me to the same level as the cyberterrorists we're hunting.

In a way I'm glad to be leaving San Antonio, even if we're heading into a trap. Not only does the place just downright depress me, but I can also promise you that

Ares Kulzak is nowhere near. But neither is he likely to be in Melbourne, Florida, home of one professor of computer science, Herbert Littman, the man responsible for remotely altering STG's control systems, at least according to Ryan, whom we left poking around inside the network of the water utility company, which—interestingly enough—happens to be linked to STG's network. With luck he might be able to unearth something that might help us once we get to his house.

I frown.

Professor Littman.

I don't need a roomful of CCTF analysts to tell me that the college professor, whose record is squeaky clean, was coerced into doing this by my favorite terrorist. We still don't know who altered the water pressure, but I'd bet my first CCTF paycheck—which I won't get for another week and a half—that Kulzak forced another poor innocent soul into doing the bulk of this dirty work.

That's how the man operates, treating people like toilet paper, rolling them out of their world, smearing them with crap, and then flushing them—a strategy that allows him to erase his tracks as his mission progresses. Never mind the pile of bodies that he leaves in his wake.

I lower the window shade next to me as the sun looms over the horizon, washing the main cabin with blinding yellow light. Karen does the same before standing and removing her jacket. Like many skirts I know, her piece looks huge strapped to such a slim waistline. She stretches, pressing a light-colored bra against the silk blouse, and sits back down.

"So," she says, crossing her legs. "What do you think we're going to find at the Littmans'?"

"Something very unpleasant and very unpredictable, which is why we need to keep the cops a block in each direction surrounding the house, but no one should go anywhere on the property until we arrive and get a chance to size the situation."

"You think the place might be booby trapped?"

"At a minimum."

"The local bomb squad is also on-site," she offers.

"They will come in handy assuming we get lucky and he just left explosives behind. Did you contact the CDC?"

"They are on their way down there from Atlanta with their gear."

I sit back wondering just what in the hell is waiting for us in that beachfront home and decide that my call on roping in the Center for Disease Control was a safe one. You just never know with Kulzak.

Damn, I'm tired, even with the three cups of coffee I've had in the past couple of hours, which are beginning to weigh on my bladder.

"You said there was a third incident with Kulzak?" she asks, reaching for the plastic cup of coffee the flight attendant gave her just after takeoff.

Man, I really don't feel like getting into that, and besides, the intel is still classified.

"Please, Tom," she says when I hesitate, touching my arm. "I think it's important that I know everything. I promise I won't betray your trust."

"Serbia," I say with some reluctance. "Nineteen ninety-eight. I was running a field operation targeted at destabilizing Milosevic's regime. Part of my team's job was to provide accurate intel on targets for NATO. We suspected that Kulzak was under contract with elements of the Milosevic government to assist in tracking down Albanian resistance in Belgrade. We found out the hard way that his services had indeed been retained by Milosevic himself, but to find and terminate our operation."

"The brief didn't explain how it happened."

"And I can't provide you with that level of detail."

She leans forward, planting her elbows on the table. "Why is that?"

"Because we still have field operatives and agents in Serbia, some of whom are part of the new government," I reply, reciting the line we'd rehearsed when we got questioned by a White House probe on Serb Ops.

"I've read the brief of that operation, Tom, but it doesn't tell me anything beyond surface-level stuff. What really happened? Why was the operation suddenly placed on hold for six months?"

Once again my poker face emerges with unequivocal clarity.

"Off the record, Tom? Please?"

Part of what they teach you in spook school is the art of releasing information without getting yourself—and most importantly, others—in trouble, especially the agents, the foreign nationals out there risking their asses to spy against their own countries for our benefit. Over the years I got pretty darn good at playing this necessary but extremely dangerous game because you were not only playing with intelligence gathering but with people's lives. Nothing comes close to the piercing sting you feel in your intestines when some poor bastard halfway across the world gets tortured and killed because of your loose lips. That's the kind of disaster that's likely to end your career and also keep you awake at night for the rest of your life.

I shift my weight uncomfortably in my seat, thinking of the agents still operating across Serbia. The problem is that if I release a little intel, thinking that by itself is harmless, and then another spook at another time releases a little more information also thinking that it's harmless by itself, over time someone can potentially string together these morsels and come up with the kind of evidence that can get people killed. On the other hand, our situation is quite extreme, calling for extreme measures. One of our cities has been nuked—for all practical purposes—and the head of the field team chartered with finding the culprit is asking me for more insight.

"All right," I say, wondering if I'm going to regret this. Dropping my voice while leaning forward, also resting my arms on the table, her face only inches from mine, I say, "What I'm going to tell you remains between us . . . or people will die, agreed?"

"Agreed," she says, giving me a seriously solemn look that makes me believe in her. Either that or we both attended the same poker-face school.

I glance over to the twins. Joe is immersed in forms and computer printouts. Paul is clicking away on a laptop. The rest of the seats are empty.

We lock eyes. "Kulzak managed to infiltrate our operation, turning one of my agents, a secretary at the Sava Congress Center—one of Milosevic's headquarters—by kidnapping her five-year-old. She provided us with misinformation, which resulted in the wrongful bombing of an apartment building adjacent to a communications center."

She makes a face. "Civilian casualties?"

"Worse than that. We operated a safe house in that building. I lost seven people that evening, including a very dear friend."

"None of that was in the brief."

"We kept it pretty hush hush. After all, we were the ones who fed the U.S. Navy the coordinates for the Tomahawk that turned the building inside out. That's typical Kulzak. He loves to use you to hurt yourself. That's what worries me about the Littman place. You never know what the bastard has left behind for you."

She leans back in her seat. "Thanks, Tom. Again, I promise I won't betray your trust."

"Now you're sworn to secrecy."

Karen grins. She is naturally attractive, but whenever she smiles, I feel like I could crawl naked over broken glass just to taste that freckle. But as I'm mentally undressing her, I remember the last time I got personal with a fellow professional. Her name was Madison, one of the finest junior officers I ever had the pleasure of working with. She was not only the best lover I'd had in years, but we became good friends over the course of our short-lived Serbian assignment.

I look away.

Madie.

The only thing left of her as I searched through the smoking rubble of that apartment building in Belgrade was the watch I bought for her during a short visit to Rome a month earlier.

"What's wrong, Tom?"

"No-nothing, why?"

"Your face. It's—"

"Sorry. I was just thinking of those people I lost back then . . . anyway, it took me a long time to get over that."

"But you survived."

I lean back in my seat and lift the shade to peek outside, breathing out heavily as fields of green project toward the hazy horizon. There's no humor or alcohol capable of shaving off the edge of the claw that rips my gut every time I think about them . . . about her.

I breathe out heavily and say, "We took turns watching the building from across the street, in case Milosevic caught up to us. That way we could give the team in the safe house a minute's worth of warning to get away through a hidden rear door. Lucky me, it was my shift. I'll never forget the way the building just vaporized in front of my eyes. The experience gave me a whole new perspective on the damage those Tomahawks can do. I got to see what CNN and the networks won't show in the evening news."

She regards me in silence.

"That's Ares Kulzak for you," I add.

With a single nod she says, "I really appreciate the honesty, Tom."

"And now I ask the same of you," I say.

"What do you mean?"

"What I mean is that I need to know who I'm really working for."

Her fine brows drop in intrigue. "I'm not following you. I've been with the Bureau for almost twenty years, all of that in the field. What else would you like to know?"

"All right," I say, wondering if I'm going to regret this but realizing I have no choice in the matter. "I'd like to be assured that you won't crack when things get hairy, and believe me, when dealing with Kulzak things are going to get *extremely* hairy. Between my dossier and what I've confessed to you—in confidence—you know quite a bit about me. I, however, know next to nothing about you besides having spent many years in the Bureau. Also, and *please* don't take this personally, but I do worry about you getting such a critical assignment because of some affirmative action crap, especially with the president being a woman."

Her eyes suddenly look like they could slice through steel, and Karen Frost says calmly, "I have a pristine record with the Bureau, Tom, having done everything from undercover work to extended field assignments. I've been personally responsible for bringing down drug lords in Miami as well as conspiracies in a half dozen states, including one that almost reached the president himself. I've *earned* this position in the CCTF because of my professional credentials as a senior special agent and *not* because of some government minority crap or because I sucked somebody's dick. You, on the other hand, seem to have gotten your partner in El Salvador castrated and then allowed Kulzak to infiltrate your team in Serbia, which resulted in the deaths of several members of your team."

I can't say I didn't ask for it, but I had to know that she had it in her, and she definitely does.

"Look, Karen, I'm really sorry," I reply. "I didn't mean anything by that affirmative action comment. I just had to be sure that—"

"I won't crack at a critical moment, Tom?"

"I had to know that I can rely on you to cover my rear."

"Well, my record obviously speaks for itself. I, however, am worried as hell that I'm going to end up being the next casualty in *your* prestigious career."

"All right, all right. I said I was—"

"And Tom . . ."

"Yes?

"Go fuck yourself."

FIFTEEN

> > > > >

THE CAULDRON

> THE MUFFLED SCREAM SOUNDED MORE LIKE A SOB-
bing moan than a scream.

Ares Kulzak regarded his bound subject with impassive calmness, like a predator
inspecting a wounded prey.

He had heard such cries before in the mountains of Central America, in the jun-
gles of Ecuador and Colombia, across the forested plains of Serbia.

And he had ignored them then, just as he ignored them now, regarding his subject strapped to the king-size bed while Kishna carried out the procedure, placing
small wooden wedges under the victim's toenails and slowly driving them in, one at
a time.

He sighed, wishing the self-made millionaire computer scientist had chosen to
cooperate willingly, providing him with the information he sought just as Professor
Littman had. But the scientist's mind had been veiled by the stubborn pride that usually comes with recent wealth, with the wrong perception that money placed him
above everything, including danger. And in a way Ares Kulzak welcomed such a challenge. It wasn't often that he came across someone who was willing to defy him, to
dare him to a battle of endurance.

Smiling, Ares had first offered the middle-aged man money, then Kishna's sexual
favors. When that had failed, Ares—still smiling—had made a third offer, which
Hutton would not be able to refuse.

He watched the manner in which Kishna placed the wooden wedges, the skill with which she drove them into the flesh, slowly, gradually separating the toenails to augment the pain. Hutton's eyes bulged, fingers outstretched, arms tugging at the straps holding him down. It was obvious to Ares that the man had not expected such a powerful physical response to his initial refusal to cooperate.

Ares lifted an open palm after the eighth wedge, staring into his victim's eyes, waiting for the glaze of pain to wash away, for focus to return. And it did, this first phase of the subject's conditioning taxing him more mentally than physically, as time could reverse the damage inflicted thus far.

"Gary," Ares said. "Can you hear me?"

Gary Hutton's wide-eyed stare landed on him as he breathed deeply through his nostrils, his exposed chest expanding. He was a handsome man in his early forties, with the tanned and firm body of someone who exercises regularly. He lived in a recently renovated third-story flat in New Orleans's Warehouse District. The place had been decorated in a contemporary style, including whitewashed hardwood floors, dark walls with impressionist paintings and neon art, leather furniture, recessed lighting, a gourmet kitchen with stainless-steel appliances, two bathrooms with ridiculous-size tubs, and plenty of high-tech gadgets, from a theater-quality media room to computer-controlled lighting and appliances—all financed by the dot.com madness of the late nineties.

Ares and Kishna had first caught up with him at a restaurant and club called 4141, located on 4141 St. Charles Street, shortly after picking up Gary Hutton's schedule from Ken Paxton, the lead member of the local Cartel—and old comrade-in-arms from Ares's days in El Salvador. Paxton had also provided Ares with a large metallic case packed with explosives—their diversion in case someone came after them.

Kishna had done most of the work then, walking up to the millionaire, who, unlike Littman, recognized her right away, his eyes growing with concern. After all, Kishna had stolen a version of Neurall from the MIT lab. In Hutton's eyes, she was a fugitive. But Kishna had used her looks to lure him out of the bar with the promise of a night of unforgettable pleasures. Ares didn't blame Hutton for falling for Kishna. Her seduction was nearly impossible to resist, even for him.

The rest had been mechanics.

"Gary," Ares pressed. "I must know if you can hear me."

A nod, followed by a raspy and sobbing moan. He was obviously a stranger to pain, which always had a way of tearing down the walls of resistance in the subject's mind. The question was always how much pain would be necessary to achieve maximum conditioning.

"Good, Gary. Very good. Now, regarding the access scripts . . . are you ready to disclose them?"

Gary Hutton, a brainchild from MIT, had worked on Neurall for a few years before launching a high-tech security company back in 1999 that got awarded the firewall security contract from SWOASIS, the Southwest Open Access Same-Time Information System. SWOASIS was the computer system and associated communications facilities that the utility companies servicing the southwestern United States used to communicate with one another. In all, six utility companies, or providers, formed the core of SWOASIS: El Paso Electric, Nevada Power, Public Service of New Mexico, Sacramento Municipal Utility District, Sierra Pacific, and Salt River Project. Each provider, like SRP for example, in turn, comprised several major power plants and numerous other generating stations, including thermal, hydroelectric, and nuclear, like the massive Palo Verde Station outside of Phoenix, Arizona. SWOASIS, a wonder network of software and hardware linked together for the purpose of providing instant communications between all of the utility companies and their respective power generating stations, allowed the flexibility of real-time distribution and redistribution of electricity, satisfying the southwestern region's ever-increasing and fluctuating demands.

The complex system had been quite effective in California, land of the rolling blackouts, which were made possible by this vast network, allowing public utility officials to shift power about from a myriad of sources. It was these controlled power outages that prevented the state from overloading the system and triggering a massive shutdown, which in a metropolis like Los Angeles would be quite catastrophic in nature.

And Mr. Gary Hutton had the knowledge to access the core of this distribution web.

Ares said, "I am going to remove this gag, Gary. Blink once if you understand."

He did.

"If you scream you lose more toenails, understood?"

Another blink.

Hutton began breathing heavily through his mouth. "Oh, God," he mumbled. "Why me?"

"Because of what you know, Gary. Now, are you going to be more cooperative?"

The millionaire nodded quickly.

"Of course you will, Gary. Of course you will. Now, why don't you tell my lovely partner what the codes are to the Salt River Project's access node to the SWOASIS?"

Fear returned to him. "The codes to . . . SWOASIS . . . but . . . I thought you wanted . . . codes to my bank . . . to my money."

"I am not interested in your money. I want to access the electrical grid."

"But . . . I am under . . . contract. They . . . they will . . . bury me."

"Have you ever heard of the cauldron, Gary?"

"The . . . cauldron?"

Ares looked at Kishna before replacing the gag. Gary Hutton began to moan, try-ing to say something.

"You will get to speak again, but not yet. Not yet."

Kishna produced a shiny silver ice bucket, which she had taken from the kitchen, and she placed it mouth down on Hutton's stomach. Then she reached for a small paper bag with tiny holes at the top. That afternoon, before picking up the case, they had also made a couple of stops, one at a pet shop and another at a hardware store.

Kishna picked up a small white mouse from the bag, holding it by its tail.

Hutton's puzzled stare followed it as she lifted the bucket and slipped the rodent inside. Then she produced a small glazing torch, turning the side knob while flicking a lighter. A bright blue flame popped at the end of the torch, which she applied to the side of the bucket. An expanding dark circle swallowed the shine around the heating spot.

"The cauldron, Gary," Ares explained, "is a simple and very old torture instru-ment dating back to the Middle Ages. As the bucket gets hot, the mouse inside will want to escape. Problem is, there is no way out except through the mouth of the cauldron."

As expected, the mouse began to get agitated, tapping the sides of the bucket. Then it began to shrill, just as Hutton's moan twisted into a grunt, into a muffled scream, but not from the mouse. Silver conducted heat, burning his skin.

Ares held the bucket in place with a towel while Kishna continued to torch it with the hissing flame, shifting it about now to distribute the heat.

Then it happened.

The scientist's limbs began to tremble and his stifled shout turned into a high-pitched squeal that even the cotton sock could not contain.

As Hutton trembled and tugged at the straps securing his limbs, waist, and chest, Ares leaned down, pressing his lips against his right ear. "The mouse is beginning to dig, Gary. It will continue to do so, getting into your entrails to escape the heat."

His fists tight, knuckles turning chalky-white, the muscles of his arms and legs pulsating beneath his skin, Hutton bawled uncontrollably, nostrils flaring, eyes glassy with tears, the veins on his neck swelling.

And Ares Kulzak let the mouse feed on him for another minute, listening to the cries, to the pleas, to the short sobbing gasps in between agonizing screeches.

Ares placed a hand beneath the T-shirt he wore over the jeans, his fingers circling the scar tissue just above his navel, remembering the classes at the military officers' school. Everyone had to endure the cauldron to pass the class on torture survival.

Every Cuban guerrilla trainer ran the risk of being captured by the enemy, of being tortured for information, and thus had to know exactly what it would be like. A Cuban officer had to be conditioned to endure pain, to accept it, to operate while under extreme agony. Many cadets had failed the test, often delegated to lesser governmental responsibilities. Only those who endured it were rewarded with the honors of a true *revolucionario*, just like Fidel, Ché, Camilo, and others had endured extreme levels of pain during their long campaign against Batista.

Muffled screams, ragged sobs, guttural moans—all escaped the millionaire's mouth as he shook his head from side to side as if possessed by a demon, as if enduring an epileptic seizure, his bulging eyes threatening to pop out of their sockets.

He nodded and Kishna lifted the bucket, which left behind a rose-colored ring of blistering skin. The mouse had half its head inside a dime-size hole an inch above the navel. She snatched it by the tail, plucking its head out.

The rodent leered at her, its head as crimson as the blood trickling out of the wound. She dropped it back in the bag, where it quickly settled down.

It amazed Ares how the mouse, properly motivated, could gnaw its way through skin and muscle tissue, but it would not attempt to tear through the thin paper bag once the threat of heat was removed.

Conditioned responses.

That was the way his instructors in Havana had taught him to conduct a successful interrogation. The subject had to be acclimated to behave just as the interrogator desired, and Gary Hutton was on the verge of such a mental state.

Again, Ares looked into his victim's eyes, searching for focus, finding it moments later.

"Gary, can you hear me?"

He blinked once.

"I will remove the gag, Gary, but if you scream you get the mouse again. Understood?"

Another blink.

Ares removed the gag.

The man swallowed once, twice, his chest swelling before he exhaled in wheezing bursts through trembling lips. He did this over and over, accompanied by a soft cry, almost a purr.

"Gary? Are you ready to help us?"

Without further delay, Hutton began to speak, his voice cracking at times. Ares watched Kishna tap the keys of her laptop, jotting down the long alphanumeric passwords, impossible to crack by today's computers, even by Neurall. Access to the core of the system meant not only the ability to cause havoc across the grid, but also to facilitate the direct interface of Neurall with the intelligent supercomputers managing the power network.

Satisfied, Ares stepped away from the bed and walked past the large metallic case he had left in the middle of the floor, easily accessed in seconds should an unexpected visitor arrive. He patted it before continuing to the large windows overlooking the Warehouse District and the bulging Mississippi beyond the tall levee containing it as it flowed toward the Gulf of Mexico. The crest of this levee, according to the research he did while preparing for this mission, was roughly thirty feet on the side facing the city but only a dozen or so feet over the surface of the river during normal levels, causing ships to tower above the city as they cruised by. The spring rains, plus the recent tropical depression that had pounded the city in the days prior to his arrival, had swelled the river to dangerous levels, towering the effect. Few things amazed Kulzak, and being able to see straight onto the deck of a huge merchant vessel quietly steaming away certainly qualified. He had read somewhere that this city was technically below sea level, and that the only thing keeping it dry aside from the levee system were massive spillways, flood gates, and pumps designed to divert huge volumes of water into large reservoirs, like Lake Pontchartrain.

Hutton finished revealing the passwords protecting the delicate balance of power feeding the city of Los Angeles.

"Now, Gary," said Ares Kulzak, turning around. "There is another password we need from you."

"Another?"

"Yes," said Kishna, cupping his face. "The one you created to protect the version of Neurall residing at the Pentagon."

"Oh, dear God," mumbled Hutton. "You are insane, Kishna."

"Wrong answer, Gary," she replied, reaching for the ice bucket.

"No, please, wait. I beg you, for old time's sake."

"I'm listening," she replied. "And I already have Littman's password, so I have a way to check yours for accuracy." Kishna had explained to Ares earlier that each of the four scientists who had created Neurall had memorized a backdoor password. Albeit different, each password totaled the same checksum when all of the numbers in the sequence were added together.

As Gary Hutton began to recite his thirty-two character alphanumeric password, Ares returned his attention to the bursting Mississippi River, and his mind began to wander.

SIXTEEN

> > > > >

RUNNERS

> MIKE RYAN ACCELERATED IN A PARABOLIC TRAJEC-
tory through layers of cherry clouds of varying density according to the information
they transported. He briefly inspected the busy traffic, which, like the digital clouds,
had not been there on his initial run. The difference being that STG's network was
back on-line. He wanted to perform one last check in this network in the hope of
learning something, before shifting gears and heading over to the water company.

His program painted STG users as magenta figures rushing about over the neon
landscape below going about their daily business. All users looked alike in this VR
world unless MPS-Ali or the network's COPS security software were to ping them,
in which case their attached qualifiers would flash above them like a mini billboard
displaying their name, user ID, and privilege level—along with a hidden new code
string that only real users would possess, and which Ryan had installed just hours
ago, interfacing his system with COPS, whose job it was to constantly monitor users
in search for an illegal one.

Ryan watched one of the COPS's units, resembling a volleyball, zoom by, its
shiny gold shape leaving a champagne contrail. These policing orbs were now armed
with Ryan's security software to check for these strings of code imbedded in the
user's individual qualifiers like a secret string of DNA that a hacker would find
impossible to reproduce—and that's if the hacker figured out that there was such a
user requirement beyond the classic ID and password in the first place.

First a stronger defense.

Then on to the offense.

In the case an orb unit floated by an illegal user, Ryan had reprogrammed the security software to allow the hacker to operate freely for a few more seconds while the orb went off and traced back the hacker's origin. Then without warning, while the hacker continued to roam the network, COPS would fire a deadly data packet straight into the hacker's system, corrupting the bastard's hard drive.

Armed with such policing tools, plus a new version of MPS-Ali, freshly restored from CD-ROM, Ryan wanted to check if there was still an illegal form residing in the pyramid representing the node used by Professor Herbert Littman to access the STG network—the one which had formatted his cyber agent the day before.

Ryan and MPS-Ali shot toward the contoured surface like a pair of colorful meteors, leveling off over a bright amorphous field housing a lattice of pulsating pyramids, varying colors under their scan, until zeroing in on the flashing-red firewall portal.

While hovering over the pyramid, a transparent version of MPS-Ali detached itself from the agent's body, almost like a ghost vacating its purple body. This holographic form approached the web of blue-and-red spaghetti lacing the entrance. As it did, MPS-Ali generated a data cloud, similar in appearance to the ones floating overhead, only it wasn't a data cloud but a shield, far stronger than the purple one that saved him the day before, and capable of withstanding the strongest digital EMP blast plus all known viruses. The cloud also made Ryan and MPS-Ali invisible to anyone roaming the system.

Ryan watched through his virtual one-way mirror as the ghost of MPS-Ali mutated its skin to match the animated laser pattern, which was the equivalent of issuing a valid access password. Unlike the previous run, the ghost proceeded inside the portal uneventfully, opening the firewall for Ryan and MPS-Ali.

Still inside their protective data cloud, they followed him inside the node, which resembled a cavernous enclosure of kaleidoscopic data patterns arranged in shelf-like structures lining towering walls that propagated far higher than the external dimensions of the pyramid suggested. But that was all part of the cyber world. The rules of physics did not apply here. The ghost performed a scan of the interior of the access node and returned with a green reading. All was back to normal, as Ryan had suspected. There were no traces of the perpetrators.

Off to the water company.

An instant later they were rocketing faster than the space shuttle, shedding their data cloud to increase their operating frequency, which in this world translated into more speed.

Reaching orbit, they boarded a T1 high-speed line streaming out of STG in the shape of a bright green tunnel against a backdrop of flaming stars, and picked up even more speed, exiting it moments later by the stratosphere of a second planet, identical in color to STG's planet, indicating network compatibility. The Water Utility District's planet, however, was three times larger than STG's, indicating that its network and piping system reached far more places than natural gas lines.

Once again, MPS-Ali switched to scan mode as they injected themselves into a low orbit, like a pair of spy satellites, surveying the fertile landscape, pinging every square inch of digitized terrain with the same resonance as the enhanced probe used by STG's upgraded security, which Ryan planned to install at WUD, but only after he had found the origin of the attack. Wide-area release of the upgraded security software now would only trigger the time bomb left behind by the hacker before Ryan could follow any potential runners.

It took nineteen revolutions over this nebulous world before MPS-Ali went for a dive with stomach-churning speed, like an old-fashioned fighter-bomber dropping over its target, dashing through the colorful haze of compressed records, pulling out just as a crash seemed imminent, then shedding speed while holding several feet over the top of a sea of tall buildings so vast that it would put Manhattan to shame.

MPS-Ali dropped into one of the channels in between buildings, as wide as the street below, and they gained speed again, like helicopters in a video game, racing in between buildings, turning, climbing, dipping, always remaining in between buildings, thousands of windows blurring into walls of refreshed data.

MPS-Ali changed directions in a nanosecond, tugging Ryan along, as if tied at the end of a virtual bungee cord, diving behind the expert system through an open window, floating inside a large room and continuing through a long corridor that ended in a very bright room, hurting his eyes.

An optical diode field in the HMD electronics also detected the increase in luminescence and immediately adjusted the brightness and contrast.

Ryan blinked as the optical system attenuated the intensity level, revealing a portal at the far end of the rectangular room, shielded by a another characteristic web of red-and-blue lasers—the entrance to the place Ryan suspected held a virtual bomb from Ares Kulzak.

A second ghost split from MPS-Ali, moving toward the glistening laser grid while they enshrouded themselves again, both for protection as well as cloaking.

The digitized holograph adjusted its skin color to match the laser pattern, according to the password provided to Ryan by the system administrator.

Just then the ghost froze, then became engulfed in a bright light, which propagated toward Ryan and MPS-Ali.

The burst of digital EMP shook the fabric of their shield, but did not pierce it, holding together just as Ryan had designed it. However, because of the shield, MPS-Ali was not able to snag the embedded Internet address, like the one that had led Ryan to Professor Herbert Littman.

But Ryan had traded obtaining that information for the chance to remain jacked in, and a nanosecond later his gamble paid off. A silver figure followed the digital EMP out of the portal.

A runner.

Tom was right, thought Ryan. A message was about to be sent to the creator of the digital EMP to notify him that the blast had been triggered. The assumption made by the hacker was that the system of whoever had executed the portal penetration would have been roasted, putting the user out of commission for long enough to assure safe passage for the runner.

A diversion.

In addition to damaging a user's system, the blast was also a diversion, an insurance for the hacker that the runner would not be followed, thus secretly reaching the true originator of the strike.

Not today, pal.

As the silver figure left the building, disguising itself as a crimson data cloud, MPS-Ali stained it with a tracer virus, its beacon broadcasting in a coded frequency resonant to MPS-Ali's receiver.

Ryan locked himself to MPS-Ali. Only a cyber form could keep up with another in this environment, and they went in pursuit, similarly shrouded, dashing toward a binary sky of faded hues of gunmetal and cobalt broken up by fluid ruby clouds. The massive upward acceleration required to keep up with the runner knotted the pit of his stomach, and before he knew it they had boarded another bright-green T1 highway, traveling through several ISPs—Internet Service Providers—which appeared as colorful constellations encircled by a myriad of jaded capillaries of varying intensity according to the amount of traffic pulsing through.

The runner burst out of the end of the T1 like a cannon shot, its scarlet cloak ballooning while zigzagging through the ocean of burning stars, suddenly vanishing as it came in contact with the standing end of another T1 across the nebula. They reached it before the image of the runner evaporating registered in Ryan's mind.

The T1's vacuum force sucked them in, propelling down another green tunnel. And so it went, tunnel and nebula, followed by another tunnel and another nebula as they surfed through this VR version of the World Wide Web.

Then the runner changed the pattern, reaching not a constellation but a cavernous white enclosure, so bright that once again, the HMD adjusted the intensity to shield his eyes.

Data clouds trafficked from the T1 standing ends on the floor to the sapphire portholes lining the walls and ceilings. They had reached the holding stations of a wireless Internet service provider.

The runner shot straight toward a portal on the far wall, disappearing inside. Ryan and MPS-Ali scrambled after it, floating through the portal and into the indigo data bank that MPS-Ali reported as twenty gigabytes in size—and which the VR software displayed as a rectangular room with neon-blue cubicles on the floor, ceiling, and walls. At one end stood the portal connecting it to the ISP, and at the other the diamond-shape connection of a wireless modem.

The runner belonged to whoever was leasing the disk space from the ISP. According to MPS-Ali, the disk partition was empty, aside from the typical Internet junk mail hogging up a gigabyte of data. Whoever owned this didn't check e-mails often, and it didn't surprise Ryan when MPS-Ali reported that the owner of the space went under an encoded alias.

He returned his attention to the runner.

Programmed to feel safe once inside this holding station, the silver figure emerged from its red shroud, which thinned as they cruised through it in hot pursuit.

The diamond glowed bright yellow as the runner broadcasted its access information to enable the wireless modem connection.

Ryan and his agent stood right behind this pseudo-intelligent life form, smart enough to have gotten this far, yet dumb enough not to realize that it was being followed.

The diamond began to pulsate. Somewhere in the distance Ryan heard the out-of-tune beeps of a modem connection, and all three of them were vacuumed inside the moment it turned green.

And we're wireless, he thought as they remained suspended on this one-directional drifting green mist of binary code.

MPS-Ali reported that the provider supported the greater New Orleans area.

New Orleans?

Ryan frowned, wondering what in the world the owner of the system would be doing there. His frown turned to exasperation at the pathetically slow wireless connection compared to the broadband T1 like the Space Shuttle to a bicycle. Fortunately, they didn't have long to travel since wireless providers served only local areas.

The green haze thickened, closing in, the beeping melody of another modem echoing around them as they entered a wide-mouth tube, like a sewer pipe, which transported them to a dark gray room with a single access port covered in spaghetti neon of varying colors.

Ryan didn't need MPS-Ali to tell him that they were being held in a secured section of DRAM, Dynamic Random Access Memory, based on the frequency of oscillation of the walls. There were three types of memories in a computer system. The fastest was the Cache memory, small and typically residing onboard the microprocessor itself. Onboard Cache was usually small, around a few megabytes but was very fast, operating at the rated speed of the machine, which in this case the system ID came back as a laptop running at 3 GHz. Next was DRAM, larger than Cache— around 512 megabytes—but slower than Cache, operating at the speed of the motherboard, a few hundred megahertz. And last was the hard drive, with lots and lots of space, around a hundred or more gigabytes, but with mechanical limitations that clamped its speed well below that of DRAM. So storage in a PC was a compromise of speed versus capacity. Ryan was trapped in the middle one, DRAM, and he wanted to get to the hard drive, where he could poke around and get more information about the identity of the owner of this runner.

Ryan watched the silver figure mutate into a psychedelic version of angel pasta, and the nifty MPS-Ali stole its password. A moment later, their skins also resembling the mind of a hallucinating Italian chef, Ryan and MPS-Ali followed the runner right through the portal.

Now, this is more like it, Ryan thought, floating over a spherical object probably a few virtual miles in diameter, the VR representation of a hard drive, which size MPS-Ali reported at 150 gigabytes. This world was mostly shades of pink, darkening to almost magenta at the equator and nearly white at the poles, reminding Ryan of a Pepto-Bismol ad.

The runner dropped to the surface near the north pole and activated a flag register, alerting the owner of the release of the digital EMP back at the water company. Its work done, the runner evaporated in a haze of vanishing computer code.

Although they were still shielded by the blinking spaghetti, the sudden death of the runner meant no more free passwords. Trying to stain any of the floating figures hovering about would alert the resident version of COPS, which Ryan didn't control, unlike the security system at WUD, the water utility company, where MPS-Ali had tagged the runner.

So he couldn't steal passwords without alerting the system's security, and he couldn't download any data from this system because the wireless link was strictly one-way according to the installed security protocol. The owner was being very careful to ensure that no one could copy the information in the mobile system.

But I can just read the information, he thought, ordering MPS-Ali to start a shallow scan.

A moment later they were orbiting this world, whose annoying color selections were a reflection of the laptop owner's custom choice of background colors.

Probably a woman, Ryan decided, and for a moment wondered if she sold or used Mary Kay cosmetics.

Data began to stream in, browsing down floating digital screens that dropped in front of Ryan. MPS-Ali filtered and organized the information for its master, completing the process in just four orbits.

Ryan scanned through the accumulated text, mostly names of protected directories. Several caught his eye.

S T G

W U D

H L I T T

S W O A S I S

Ryan was pretty certain about the contents of the first two directories. It was the third and fourth that really concerned him. HLITT had to be Herbert Littman, and the fact that it contained a number of scripts could mean that there was a yet to be executed sequence of events at or around Herbert Littman—which was exactly where Karen Frost and Tom Grant were headed. Then the last one almost made him go numb. As a resident of the state of California, Ryan was very aware of what SWOASIS meant, and it chilled him to realize that the vast power grid feeding the southwestern United States could potentially be the next target of the cyberterrorists.

Ryan wanted to enter both files and get more information, but without an access password he knew that he only had a chance of peeking into one, and a slim one at that.

Making his decision, he commanded MPS-Ali to clone another ghost, who led them to a white landscape near the south pole, dotted with pink domes of varying size. They landed by the one housing the directory of HLITT, its only entryway laced with rose-colored lasers requiring a different password than the one currently covering their cyber suits.

Using the same old trick, the ghost threw itself into the Pepto-lasers, triggering the expected general system alarm. If the user, which Ryan suspected to be a woman, was now staring at the screen, she would see a window pop up indicating the possible presence of an unknown virus and requesting that the user run its virus-scan software.

Within nanoseconds a hot-pink figure shaped like a voluptuous woman rushed to the site leaving a dusty contrail. It oozed a pink balloon resembling bubblegum at the ghost of MPS-Ali, paralyzing it.

MPS-Ali then fired a red virus at Wonder Woman, robbing her of her password as well as putting her to sleep, but not before she launched a digital cry for help that sounded like a witch's shriek.

Realizing that any moment now the system would respond with additional security agents, Ryan launched the password at the portal and dove into it with MPS-Ali, dragging the dazed witch immersed in a red haze behind to keep the rest of the system wondering what had gone wrong, since only this agent had firsthand exposure to the intruders. Before the portal closed, MPS-Ali released two bombs. The first one would cause the laptop's screen to turn blue, simulating the dreaded Windows bluescreen failure, which would erase any virus warning signs that may have flashed in the past few seconds but would leave the system operational for Ryan. The second one was a one-minute time bomb, targeted at forcing a system reboot, erasing the system log of Ryan's activities to avoid a trace back to him.

Once inside the directory, Ryan reset the password of the portal to keep other security agents from accessing it.

MPS-Ali went into rapid scan mode, spending the following sixty seconds gathering, sorting, and prioritizing the information inside the portal, presenting Ryan with a picture that was as terrifying as it was technically brilliant.

I have to warn them. Oh, dear God, I have to—

Then he sensed a presence behind him, and as he turned around, he watched Wonder Woman emerging through the virulent crimson cloud.

MPS-Ali fired another burst of its digital poison but it had no effect. Wonder Woman retaliated with a shot of digital bubblegum at MPS-Ali, who became still. As the security agent turned toward Ryan, its seamless features appeared to contort into a mask of anger.

Puzzled by how this female form had managed to shake off MPS-Ali's digital poison so quickly, the pink stuff enveloped him, squeezing his mind. He screamed, as the white-hot pain of a digital EMP hammered his temples like a sizzling vice.

A second blast propagated toward him, far larger in intensity than the first, but it never reached him, freezing in time and space just in front of him. The sixty-second bomb had gone off, shutting down the system.

Trembling, Ryan removed his helmet, a severe headache pounding his temples, drilling his mind. His arms growing numb, realizing he didn't have much time, he reached for the keyboard, launching a new version of MPS-Ali at the URL he had memorized, the one belonging to the SWOASIS web.

I have to warn them.

Then he tried to reach for the phone but his hand never made it.

S E V E N T E E N

> > > > >

B L U E   S C R E E N

> " H I J O   D E   P U T A ! "

Standing by the foot of the bed of a heavily sedated Gary Hutton, Ares Kulzak glanced at Kishna Zablah sitting cross-legged on the Oriental rug lining one side of the king-size bed, her back against the thick mattress, the system on her lap. She removed her head-mounted display and the tactile gloves before reaching the side of the unit and rocking the power switch.

"System problems?"

She grimaced in obvious frustration. "I . . . I'm not sure. One moment the construct is running just fine, interfacing to Neurall, and then, boom, I get this blue-screen failure. But before that it looks like my system came under a virus attack."

"A virus? How?"

She tapped the wireless card sticking out of the side of the black system. "I'm hooked up to the Internet. It happens sometimes."

"But I thought you have shields."

"Yes, but only for all known viruses. There is always the chance of stumbling onto something new," she said, staring at her screen as the system rebooted and the virus scan software reported no viruses.

"Looks clean now," he said.

She nodded while pointing at the plasma display. "Neurall intervened, but only after my system was already under attack. Next time I'm leaving Neurall guarding the path in case a virus or another uninvited guest heads in my direction."

"But doesn't that put Neurall at risk?" he asked.

Most everything about his business, from many bank accounts and other assets, to locations of all contacts, and a host of other vital information, resided with Neurall in Colombia. Up to this point, Kishna's standard operating practice was to use her constructs, which were lesser forms of Neurall, as buffers between the hacker-prone Internet and Neurall, thus preventing anyone from accessing it. As the Americans like to say, the buck stopped with Kishna. Now she had just suggested placing Neurall in the path of danger, which also meant exposing the secret location of one of the Cartel's largest manufacturing facilities.

She smiled. "Ari, Neurall is the most sophisticated artificial intelligence system in existence today, and every day she gets smarter. Besides, our primary mission is to get Neurall interfaced to as many supercomputers as we can, like we did in San Antonio, and most importantly to her long-lost sister controlling the American nuclear missiles from within the Pentagon."

Ares breathed deeply and nodded.

"Also," she added, "if someone tries to get anywhere near Neurall, he will not only get blasted with a powerful digital EMP, but I will possess the hacker's information, which you could then use to eliminate him in person. It is actually about time we unleash part of the potential of our prized AI, rather than keeping her locked away in some remote mountain."

"Very well," he said, deciding to trust her judgment.

"Good," she replied, kissing him on the cheek. "By the way, I did get confirmation that the second EMP was released at the water company."

Ares smiled, thinking of the fried electronics and puzzled system administrators, who had probably thought the worst was over. The news confirmed his decision to accept her recommendation to open up Neurall prior to the liberation of more AI systems.

He checked his watch while Kishna donned her VR gear and went back to work. "How much does this set us back?"

She gave her shoulders an uncommitted toss. "A couple of hours, maybe more. I was in the middle of establishing a protocol between Neurall and the SWOASIS network. The system just blasted me out. Maybe it was the modem. Wireless interference can induce noise and put my system in an unstable condition."

"Why not use a land line instead?"

"Too easily traceable, but I will if I get booted again."

Ares nodded absently before lowering his gaze to Gary Hutton, peacefully sleeping. Kishna had patched up his abdomen after the mouse tore three holes over the course of four sessions, in which Gary Hutton released all of the necessary passwords and even some pointers on the best way to use them.

He wanted his subject alive and well not only in case Kishna needed further assistance penetrating the complex network, but to exact the same kind of long-distance pain that he would soon inflict on the general population of Melbourne, Florida.

E I G H T E E N

> > > > >

L E V E L S   O F   T E R R O R

> "THIS COULD HAVE BEEN OVER HOURS AGO," pro-
tests the SWAT team sergeant, a tall, medium-built guy with a neatly trimmed beard,
intense brown eyes, and a black Melbourne PD cap worn backward. "My team's
been ready to go since we got your call."

You have to appreciate that coming from a police background, part of me sides
with the guy, young, confident, probably with a few good missions under his belt,
but looking for the opportunity to really prove his talent to the world and perhaps
even get a promotion out of the ordeal. But the darker region of my soul—the one
stained over the years from having gotten pissed on by the likes of Ares Kulzak—
knows that even a seasoned antiterrorist team would have a hard time handling what
was likely coming, much less the relatively inexperienced group of Keystone Kops
standing around me in their fancy black outfits holding big guns.

Yeah. Never, *ever*, confuse slick uniforms and powerful weapons with experience.
It'll get you in trouble every time, and today I have the nasty little feeling that these
toy soldiers are going to learn a valuable lesson.

"And you did the right thing by staying put, Sergeant," I reply. "The people
behind this aren't your average crooks."

"So I've heard," the SWAT team leader replies, skepticism flashing in his proud
stare. "And we're playing ball, even if we don't understand why the CDC is here."

He looked at the two representatives from the Center for Disease Control, who had flown in from Atlanta—just in case.

So we have the CDC squad in full biological gear, three bomb squad teams—from Orlando, Tampa, and Ft. Lauderdale—also in full gear, a dozen SWAT team members in full assault gear, and a dozen of our own CCTF agents, also ready to rock and roll. In all, there's over sixty mean-looking warriors and enough weapons to start a revolution—all ready to approach the oceanfront home of Professor Littman.

Ah, and let's not forget the crews from all of the networks standing by behind the orange police tape stretched out around the possible blast radius, readied and primed to capture this moment, along with what appears to be hundreds of bystanders, whom the local police is keeping at bay. There's even three police boats a hundred feet from shore and a couple of news helicopters flying overhead like vultures waiting for the kill.

Yep, nothing like adding the pressure of looking like total fools on national TV to get everyone on edge around here. I actually think that they would be disappointed if we find nothing but two dead bodies in there. For a moment I pray that we're laughed at on the ten o'clock news for overdoing this.

Unfortunately I know the man behind San Antonio. If he left us the clue that the attack on STG's network had originated from this house, then my experience tells me that Kulzak most likely left a little present for us in there, namely a bomb—or something even worse.

There is not going to be any laughing today.

"Everyone clear how we're doing this?" Karen asks, refocusing the discussion as we all stand around a portable table covered with a layout of the house and its surroundings. For the past two hours we've been holed up in the garage of one of the neighboring houses going over the plan again and again, leaving nothing to chance, getting everyone's buy in. Like I said earlier, I have little hope that Ares Kulzak, or anyone associated with his network, will be inside this house, but we will never know unless we go in. However, we also must take our time when approaching what could be a booby-trapped house, or as we in counterterrorism would call it, another level of terror on the strike against San Antonio. My bet is that Kulzak left us this clue with the hope that we will come and storm this place, providing him with another opportunity to barbecue more Americans.

So this is our dilemma. We know the place where the attack on San Antonio originated, but we can't just storm the place because it could be nothing more than a trap.

To her credit, Karen has deployed her mixed team efficiently. A valuable trait of a good field operative—CIA, FBI, NSA, or any other—is his or her ability to not only control the local law enforcement groups, but actually get them to contribute in a significant capacity to your cause. Even Cramer has given his verbal blessing, which is as much commitment as you're going to get out of the slippery eel. But make no mistake about it. If I'm right and this thing starts to head south, it's Karen's cute little ass that's going to be on the line—and probably mine too, since I'm here to provide insight into the mind of Kulzak and thus avoid another disaster.

"My people are ready," says the SWAT leader while all heads nod almost in unison.

"Okay," she says, glancing at me before powering on the radio strapped to her belt. A black wire disappears inside her blouse and reappears by her collar, connecting to her earpiece and mike. We all do the same.

Karen and I are part of the first strike team, something we volunteered to do to show leadership—and probably a certain degree of foolishness.

We go through a quick radio check and convince ourselves that we are ready.

Professor Littman's house could be reached from the street, from the beach, and from the side yards of the properties flanking it, both of which have been vacated— as well as all of the homes in a one-block radius in case Kulzak left behind more than just a few hand grenades.

The first team is divided into four squads of four people each. Karen and I lead the second squad, approaching Littman's house from the left. Squad One, led by the SWAT team leader, one of his best guys, and our own rookies, gets to go in first from the front. Squad Three gets the right side, and Four gets the beach.

It's safe to say at this point that I have objected to letting Paul and Joe go in first, but that's how Karen wanted to play this, using the front team just as a distraction, making a lot of noise to flush the terrorists out the sides and rear, where the most experienced teams would be waiting. Honestly, her plan is a fine one as we are willing to assume that there are terrorists inside, a concept that doesn't make sense to me based on my experience with Kulzak. And to be *brutally* honest, I'm not sure which plan of attack would make the most sense at the moment because we have no earthly idea what's waiting for us inside.

It is at this moment of utter uncertainly that the voice of experience tells me that whatever decision we make here will be second guessed to death in the coming days, weeks, or months by people who have built entire careers by doing just that and who also have the uncanny ability of making themselves unavailable until after the fact.

And so we're off, burning five minutes to get into position, do another radio check, set our watches, and say any silent prayers worth saying at a moment like this, especially knowing what I know not just about Kulzak but also about a backstabber like Randy Cramer.

Since I need all the help I can get, the prayer that comes to mind is Psalm 23.

EVEN THOUGH I WALK THROUGH THE VALLEY OF THE SHADOW OF
DEATH, I WILL FEAR NO EVIL, FOR YOU ARE WITH ME.

Or something like that, which just about sums up eight years of Catholic school-ing in Brooklyn. Sister Jane and Brother John would have been proud.

We're in the neighbor's yard peeking through waist-high bushes toward the home of the Littmans beyond a short field of grass and sand. The one-story structure is mostly redbrick with a large window on the side and many on the back, facing the ocean—not that it has done us any good. Kulzak made damned sure the drapes were all drawn before leaving this lovely retirement home.

Wearing one of those stupid Kevlar vests over my clothes, so that a terrorist can see it and aim for my face or my balls instead, I take a moment to check my Sig, ver-ify that a round is chambered, and then lower the hammer with the decocking lever since the gun lacks a safety. One round in the chamber plus ten in the clip plus four magazines lining my pockets gives me enough firepower to rid the world of a little garbage while letting the testosterone-bursting younger guys play with the big guns.

Poor bastards don't realize that terrorists always shoot those holding the largest guns first—a reality that dawned on me while recovering from gunshot wounds a long time ago after a failed drug bust in Harlem, where yours truly decided to look like Rambo by storming the building with a big mother of a gun and took one in the chest and two in the left leg.

Live and learn.

Karen gives the order and Squad One rushes across the well-trimmed front lawn, reaching the front door, and it is at this moment that we all hear the most unexpected sounds: a small explosion followed by a cry of help from a woman inside the house. The cry turns into a shriek of terror that uncurls the hairs on my ass.

There is no visible fire or smoke from where I'm standing. Just that one explosion and now the screams.

Before we know it Squad One is trying to break down the door and Squads Three and Four are rushing to the house prematurely, like a bunch of moths flying toward the flame.

And I think they are about to get burned.

The screams from the house intensifying, Karen makes our squad stay put, per the plan, while ordering the other squads to back off and stick to the rules.

But too many people are talking and shouting over the operations frequency at once, plus the two news helicopters decide to take a closer look, their rotors kicking up quite a whirling cloud of sand and dust.

And it is at this Hallmark moment, as every exposed surface of my body becomes fair game to a stinging sandstorm that would scare Ali Baba and his forty thieves straight out of Baghdad, that my newly issued mobile phone decides to start playing some preprogrammed beeping concerto that I still haven't gotten the time to figure out how to change.

For the love of—

"Yeah!" I answer, pressing the tiny unit against my left ear while trying to see beyond the blinding haze while holding my Sig over my right shoulder, muzzle pointed at the sky. Perhaps I'd get lucky and accidentally cut a round loose and nail one of the media choppers hovering above us. Their noise has drowned the blood-curling screams from the house.

"Mr. Grant?"

"Who is this?"

"Walter, from STG."

"Walter? What in the hell? We're in the middle of—"

"We're taking Ryan to the hospital."

The world around me is rapidly turning surreal.

"To the *hospital?* What are you talking about?

"Look, I'll explain later, but he did regain consciousness long enough to warn me about Melbourne."

I can barely make out the house from the tornado created by the choppers, and there is screaming all around us. Karen continues to hold her ground and make us stay put, and Walter's words are making the same hairs of my ass now turn gray and fall off.

"*Warning?* What are you talking about, Walter?"

While shouting orders, Karen half looks at me before turning back to the commotion over at the Littmans'. Through a break in the haze I spot Squad One still trying to break inside while the other squads are almost at the house.

Walter tells me what Ryan said, and a moment later I'm stomping toward Squad One, waving my arms, howling and shrieking like a wounded monkey, begging them to stop, to—

"Tom!" Karen shouts behind me. "Get back here!"

No time to explain.

I need to stop them, keep them from getting in. I knew this was a trap. I fucking knew it!

My lungs are burning. Karen's screams mix with the shrieks from the house, with the rattling sound from the helicopters.

I reach the front lawn, watch Squad One standing right behind two firemen holding a battering ram, swinging it back, almost in slow motion, before driving it forward as I scream like I've never screamed in my life.

Paul glances in my direction, sees me waving frantically, and has the life-saving instinct to realize something is wrong, for he jumps off the porch and onto the grass just as the ram strikes the door, which caves in.

A horizontal column of flames erupts outward, engulfing the firemen as well as the remaining members of Squad One, the shockwave punching me in the middle of the chest like the Fist of God, tossing me back across the side yard like a leaf.

Flames, grass, and hazy helicopters change places as I tumble about, finally crashing against something, a tree, the burning house pulsating through the swirling sandstorm.

But I hear their screams, see their flaming shapes rolling down the front steps, watch as others jump on them with blankets, with anything to quench the fire.

Ryan had been right. Kulzak had used the Littmans as bait while booby trapping all entryways.

But through the agonizing howls, through shouts of rage, horror, and despair; through the whining sirens of emergency vehicles and the droning helicopters, I hear multiple blasts in the distance, feel them through the rumbling soil as I lay sprawled on the lawn, Walter's words—Ryan's warning—echoing in my mind. The bomb inside the Littmans' was synchronized to additional bombs deployed around the city. When this one went off, it triggered the others.

My thoughts begin to get cloudy, my vision tunneling.

"Tom! Tom! Are you all right?"

I see her face, like an angel, staring down at me with those huge brown eyes from the far end of this dark pit closing in on me, swallowing everything, the madness, the fire, the bellowing screams, the legacy of this unstoppable monster.

NINETEEN

> > > > >

ACCESS DENIED

> THE SAME IMAGES FLICKERED ACROSS THE SCREEN, even if he changed the channel, which he did, hoping that one of the networks would have better coverage of the havoc he had spread across the quiet retirement community of Melbourne, Florida.

Ares Kulzak closed his eyes, his mind replaying the events as he had planned them. He imagined the American law-enforcement team approaching the house in their battle gear, watched them as they tripped the wireless infrared sensors planted by the bushes bordering the front porch, their sensitivity set to go off only when detecting a large heat source, like that radiating from three or more persons advancing in unison. The sensors triggered a remote-controlled pump to inject a strong amphetamine into the bloodstreams of the sedated couple. The moment their heartbeat monitors picked up the expected increase in tempo—meaning they had regained consciousness—the det cord tied around Professor Herbert Littman's neck went off, eating through his larynx before he could let out a single sound, decapitating him in a fraction of a second right in front of his horrified wife, whose harrowing screams would force the sentimental Americans to move faster, to break down the door, to act impulsively, triggering the incendiary charge installed in the foyer, which, in addition to ridding the world of a few more imperialist pigs, also served to broadcast a synchronization signal to five attaché bombs planted by Kishna at heavily populated areas in Melbourne, including two hospitals, two schools, and a shopping center.

Ares opened his eyes and watched the images in silence, regretting only not being there, wishing to hear their cries, to smell their burning flesh, to feel their pain. But his professional habits forbade it.

Still, the destruction had been widespread, as planned, bringing the city to its knees as rescue crews and other emergency vehicles monopolized the streets. The death toll will not be anywhere near that of San Antonio, but a large body count had not been the goal of this secondary strike. He had wanted to accomplish two goals with Melbourne. First, he wanted to send a message that he could strike anywhere in America and at any moment. He wanted the population of the United States to know that no one was safe even in the smallest and most secluded town, and he didn't even have to be present to do so. He wanted the world to know that Ares Kulzak could manipulate his own enemies into destroying themselves. The second goal was a diversion, something to keep the Americans busy while he and Kishna worked in New Orleans.

"*Mierda!*" shouted Kishna, removing her high-tech glasses connecting her to the laptop.

Ares, sitting on a leather sofa across the spacious bedroom watching the television set built into the wall, looked at his subordinate sitting cross-legged on a sofa chair with the laptop on her thighs. Beyond her, Gary Hutton slept in his bed.

"*Que pasa?*"

Kishna shook her head, confused. "The SWOASIS access passwords . . . Neurall has just reported that they are no good anymore."

Ares Kulzak crossed his arms, shifting his gaze between the sedated computer engineer and her. "*What?*"

Her intense, catlike eyes on the screen, Kishna said, "It . . . it looks as if the passwords have been . . . disabled."

"Disabled? How?"

"I'm not sure, but I think it is time to wake up this *pendejo* while I try to figure it out."

Ares went to work on the drip connected to Gary Hutton's left forearm, switching the mix from the mild barbiturate to the same powerful amphetamine that had woken up the Littmans.

"Thirsty . . . I need . . . water . . . please."

"Hello, Gary," Ares said.

The scientist blinked, breathing heavily, coming out of his chemical-induced sleep. It took over a minute before focus washed away the confusion glazing his eyes.

"Something is wrong, Gary." Ares picked up the silver ice bucket.

"I . . . I don't understand," he said, his eyes on the torture device, whose rim had left a blistering impression on his abdomen.

Kishna took a moment to explain.

"You gave us bad SWOASIS passwords, Gary," Ares added. "I thought we had an . . . understanding."

"We do . . . I swear I'm not lying. Those are high-privilege passwords. There's only one way they could be changed so suddenly."

"Yes?"

Hutton licked his dry lips, obviously dying to drink something before continuing, but not daring to ask for it again until he had answered his questions—a sign that told Ares the man wasn't lying. "If the network comes under attack . . . it's programmed such that all external passwords, mine included, get automatically disabled until the system administrators can get the chance to assess the damage."

Ares and Kishna exchanged a glance, before she said, "I have not launched an attack yet. I was just using the password to look around the system. Could that have caused this?"

Gary Hutton slowly shook his head, eyes briefly closed. "I'm talking about a gross breach of security . . . about someone without a password trying to get in." He swallowed hard, then added. "Someone else must have attacked the network."

"How can we verify that?" she asked.

Running the tip of his tongue over his lips again, he said, "I could call them . . . and find out." He coughed.

Ares nodded and motioned Kishna to get him some water before leaning down and removing the straps on his arms, helping him sit up before asking, "Gary, if that indeed turns out to be the case, how long will it be before the passwords are reinstated?"

Rubbing his hands and wrists, Hutton said, "I'm not sure, but I would guess at least for a few hours, if not longer."

Kishna brought him a glass of water, which he tried to drink too fast, nearly choking, coughing again.

"Slow," Ares said. "Drink it slow."

He did.

"Now," Ares said, handing him a phone. "Dial."

As Hutton stabbed the phone with a trembling finger, Kishna sat right next to him and pressed her right ear against the handheld unit while pulling out her gun, screwing in a silencer into the muzzle, and aiming it at the man's crotch.

Gary Hutton lowered his gaze, before looking at her, his pale face twisting with concern.

Kishna's dark lips curled up at the edges as she tapped Hutton in between his legs with the tip of the silencer. "Insurance."

T W E N T Y

> > > > >

L A S T   N A M E S

> BLACK BODY BAGS, SIX OF THEM, LINE THE CURB while firefighters spray the neighboring beach homes to keep the blaze from spreading.

I'm hurting all over but decline an ambulance ride to the hospital. I have no serious cuts or broken bones, just a minor concussion and lots of bruises, from my ass to my ego.

Nothing I can't handle.

I've been down this road before and know how to control the emotional and physical pain of losing another round to Kulzak.

Karen, on the other hand, looks like she could use a triple dose of Prozac, standing like a wax statue in the middle of the street, hands by her sides, one of them holding a cell phone. She's staring at the boiling column of smoke, quite reminiscent of what we left behind in San Antonio.

A vision of what's to come.

Paul Stone is sitting nearby, his face darkened by the smoke, his body rattled by the blast, but he'll be fine. Funny that he had to nearly die before I finally learned his last name.

The kid is as tall as me and just as wide, but with the firmness that comes from youth and regular exercise. However, it was his instincts that prevented him from turning into a burning hunk of meat like Joe, whose last name I have also learned.

Hicks.

Joe Hicks, who had just made twenty-three last week, has been married for two years, and has a seven-month-old daughter.

I close my eyes for a moment.

Shit.

It does hurt you, even if you barely know him. But you also realize that you have to move on. I can promise you Ares Kulzak isn't waiting for us to mourn our losses.

"How are you feeling, buddy?" I ask.

Today he went through a baptism of fire, which promoted him from rookie to a real agent.

The kid tilts his head and says, "A little sore but otherwise fine, sir, thanks to you."

"I really didn't save you, kid. Your *instincts* saved you. Never stop listening to them. By the way, the name is Tom."

He tries to smile, but grimaces in pain. Like me, he's got bruised ribs and is waiting for the medic to give him a dose of painkillers.

"Thanks for the timely warning anyway, Tom."

"No problem. That's why we're here, to catch bad guys and also cover each other's asses in the process."

I stand and pat him on the shoulder. "Hang in there. Today you learned far more than anything they taught you at Quantico."

"Tom?"

"Yeah?"

"Any chance I can call my wife and tell her that I'm fine?"

"You're married?"

"Six months ago," he says, smiling sheepishly. "She's back home, in Iowa."

"How would she know that you were here?"

"She doesn't, but I'm sure the news will make a big deal of this and even release that CCTF agents were near the blast. She will be worried if she doesn't hear from me."

I slowly shake my head. "Sorry, Paul. No personal calls while on a field operation. But I will pass the word to Washington so that they can contact her and convey your message."

He mumbles something that sounded like thank you, but by then I'm on my way to see Karen, who's still looking out into the distance. I try to put on my professional hat and avoid staring at her beauty mark while I say, "Hey, boss, just heard from Walter. Looks like Ryan's going to be all right. We're even flying his wife down to San Antonio for moral support. Also, our people in New Orleans are already on the hunt, and we're leaving as soon as we can sort out what happ—"

She shakes her head. "I'm done for, Tom."

"Huh?"

"This," she says, using the cell phone to point at the house, at the bodies being loaded into the rear of an ambulance. "It's over for me."

"*Over?*" I look straight into her large brown eyes. "I hate to break this to you, Karen, but *this*," I sweep my hand at the mess Kulzak has made in paradise, "is just the beginning."

She frowns and says, "And I'm telling you I'm not going to be a part of it. I just got a call from Cramer. You were right about him. Even though he verbally approved the raid, he's leaving me holding this bag all alone, claiming that I failed to control the situation and deviated from the plan, acting recklessly and endangering the lives of those under my jurisdiction. So I'm out."

"That's a mistake."

She tilts her head. "Is it, Tom? From where I'm standing things don't look that rosy, and it's all our doing for not approaching this place with more respect."

"No level of caution would had avoided this, Karen. I'm not sure how he had this place booby-trapped, as well as linked to the other blasts—just as Ryan warned us—but I can tell you that we need to figure out how he did it and then carry on. Ryan just proved that Kulzak is vulnerable, that we can fight back, if not in this world then in the cyber world. We may have lost the battle in San Antonio and Melbourne, but we so far appeared to have stopped him in the Southwestern power network. According to Walter, there's a whole army of computer engineers on the case protecting the power grid using Ryan's code. We lose some, we win some, and we also crank up the heat, eventually forcing him to make a mistake, and when he does, we will be all over him."

I actually can't believe I'm giving her this speech. Maybe so much destruction now in two American cities is enough motivation for me to get back in the saddle, awakening the long-dormant desire to catch this monster.

Fine wrinkles materialize around her brown eyes as she narrows them while putting a hand on my blackened and bruised face. "Cramer might be a no-good bastard, but he surely picked the right successor to run this team."

"*What?*"

"I guess I stole his thunder. He's going to call you any moment now to give you the good news. Congratulations, Tom. You're in charge of CCTF Field Operations."

Before I can reply, the cell phone strapped to my waist starts beeping.

As I answer it, Karen starts to walk away to give me some privacy. Acting on a whim, I grab her by the hand and gently make her stay by my side while I say, "Grant here."

"*Tom, Randy Cramer. How have you been?*"

"It's been a long time, sir."

"Yes, indeed, Tom. Indeed. How are you holding up down there?"

"Seen worse, sir. I'll survive."

"What a terrible thing, Tom. A terrible thing. CNN has the death toll up to fifty-seven."

"I know sir, but . . . with all due respect, this is certainly an unexpected call. I usually get my direction from my immediate superior, Special Agent Karen Frost."

Karen's mouth drops an inch before she whispers, "What are you doing?"

"Well, that's actually the reason I'm calling, Tom. I've been meaning to chat with you ever since you joined my organization but you know how Washington can be. Anyway, first I wanted to let you know that I was, and still am, pleased that you've chosen to join our task force, and I for one realize that in order to move forward we must leave past differences behind and work together to forge a safer America."

See what I mean? This is some slick mother. Fortunately, I've also been around long enough to know how to play the game.

"A clean-slate approach, sir. That's how I saw myself going into this assignment."

"Glad to hear that, Tom. Now, to the reason for my call: There's been a change in the CCTF organization."

"Am I out already, sir?" I say, deciding to mess with him a little.

"You? Oh, God, no. It's about Karen Frost. I don't think she has the required experience to run this operation."

Ten years ago—hell, even five years ago—I would have caved, especially when confronted by my boss's boss. But there's something about having gotten fucked so many times, and not just by the enemy but by your own people, that has a tendency to coat your balls with a brand new layer of brass.

"Sir?"

"Yes, Tom?"

"For the record, I disagree."

Karen opens her mouth again but can't bring herself to say anything, so she just covers it with a hand.

Cramer comes back after a moment of silence. The old fox surely wasn't expecting that. *"You . . . do?"*

"With a passion, sir. So much so that if she is off the team, so am I."

"Now, now, Tom, calm down. I know this is an emotional moment for all of us, especially after what you have been through, losing some agents and all, but let's not talk crazy here. From my vantage point I see that Karen was in charge of this raid and didn't handle it properly. Now she needs to step aside and—"

"Karen Frost did all the right things before going into that home, sir."

"Then how do you explain the mess I'm watching on television right now?"

"The explosions could not have been prevented because Kulzak could have deto-nated those bombs at any moment he pleased."

"How do you know this already?"

"Because I know how the man thinks, sir. The multiple explosions in this town were going to happen regardless of what we did or didn't do. It was just a question of when, and Kulzak chose to wait and take down as many of us as he could to terrorize us and slow down the investigation. But having dealt with Kulzak enough times has taught me that when it comes to him, we—the good guys—are *never* at fault. We should *never* feel guilty when things don't go as planned. Our job is to perform dam-age control in his wake while remaining on his tail, hoping to learn a little more each time he strikes and eventually getting close enough to capitalize on a mistake. We're certainly not here to start assigning blame and do the kind of reorganizations and dis-ruptions in the chain of command that will do nothing but slow us down, which is *exactly* what he wants us to do."

More silence. Karen's face is a mix of surprise, admiration, and something else that makes me glimpse at her freckle before I look away.

"This is why you need to run this investigation, Tom. Not her. You know how the man thinks. You have had more exposure to Kulzak than anyone else in the U.S. intelligence community."

This is the perfect time for me to say something along the lines of *Yeah, you bas-tard, and that's thanks to the way you screwed me in El Salvador.* Instead, I say, "I must remain second in command under Karen Frost, sir, a position that allows me to con-tinue to view every situation more objectively than if I were in charge. I can't afford to be distracted by all of the overhead involved in running this field operation, and Karen does a superb job at that. And regarding Karen Frost, she is now the second most experienced officer dealing with Kulzak's handiwork. She has just received the best possible education we could have hoped to provide to any task force team leader. Replacing her now would be irresponsible."

"You certainly have a point there, Tom."

You bet I do, Randy.

"But I'm afraid this one is out of my hands."

"In that case, sir, here's another one that's out of your hands: I quit."

I stop the call and clip the phone back on my belt.

"Tom . . . what in the hell just happened?"

Since she was privy to only my half of the conversation, I take a moment to explain.

She glares at me with a wide-eyed stare before mumbling, "Are you . . . *insane?*"

A perfectly reasonable question at a moment like this, and twenty-four hours ago

I would not have dreamed of acting as I just have. So what changed? A name flashes in my mind with the same intensity as the flames consuming the Littmans' house: Ares Kulzak.

"Karen," I start, "ever since I realized that Ares Kulzak is in my life again I have been unable to control this force that's quickly taking hold of my senses. I've always believed that there's a reason for everything. Maybe it comes from my strong Catholic upbringing—though the closest I've been to a church in decades was during the *huevos rancheros* incident. And although at first I saw this assignment as one royal pain in the ass because it plucked me right out of the sedentary lifestyle that I had longed for so long, the misery that I have witnessed in the past couple of days has made me come to terms with the harsh reality that there is no one else to stop Kulzak. We are it. There is no plan B. And since we *are* it, I have decided that we're going to do this right and not let some former-CIA-slime-turned-Washington-bureaucrat run the field show."

"But how do you know he isn't just going to fire us both?"

I smile. "Look. First of all, I flat-out refuse to be just another actor in a play directed by the likes of Cramer, and if he doesn't like it, he can shove his threats where the sun doesn't shine. At the end of the day he is accountable to the president and Congress on the results of this task force. He is on the hook and therefore needs me far more than I need him, otherwise he would not have been that nice to me on the phone. Trust me. The man is pure slime."

"So . . . what do you think is going to happen next?"

"Not a damned thing. You will continue to be in charge, and I just get to ride you—I mean ride *alongside* you."

Her lips part in surprise, or is it half laughter? Fortunately, I'm saved by the bell—or beeps—of my cellular phone before she can reply to my Freudian slip. I reach for my tiny black unit and say, "Grant here."

"Tom, Randy here. I think we just got disconnected."

We've actually been disconnected our entire lives.

"Looks that way, sir."

"I'm going to go with your judgment on this one and leave things as they are. I'll hold back the heat from Washington. In return, I'm asking for results, and quickly, Tom. I need something to feed to these guys and keep them off our backs. Okay?"

"Understood."

"Good, Tom. I'll check in in a day or so, but please don't wait to call me if there is a breakthrough. I'd rather hear it from you than from CNN."

"You mean from Agent Karen Frost, sir, not me, right?"

"Yes, yes, of course. I'll wait to hear from her then." This time he hangs up first.

Karen has her arms crossed, looking as lovely as ever in her tight jeans, tiny waist, and silk blouse, the black handle of her Glock protruding out of her left side, her eyes looking as if they are about to pop out of their sockets. "Well?"

"Like I said . . . you're still the boss."

Without moving a hair, Karen Frost continues to inspect me, not certain what to make of all of this. To tell you the truth, had someone I barely knew stepped up to the plate in my defense while putting his or her own neck on the line by doing so, I would have been just as suspicious, especially after the subtle and brief—but certainly nonprofessional signals—my lower hemisphere has been broadcasting.

"Just like that, huh?"

"Like I told you. He needs me more than I need him, and he knows it, and he knows that I know it."

"Tom . . . I want you to level with me. Why are you doing this?"

I shrug. "Guess I'm from the old school and hate to see the good guys—and gals—getting screwed. That and the other stuff I said earlier, which I do mean. We're going to bag this guy, Karen. You and I—with a little help from friends like Ryan."

"All right, Tom," she finally says, though her triangular face, accentuated by her high cheekbones, is unable to conceal her suspicions. But in those intelligent eyes I do see a glimmer of gratitude, however dim. She's seasoned enough to know that I have just prevented—or at least delayed—the kind of inquisition that Cramer roasted me with eons ago. But on the other hand, she's got as much time in the Bureau as I have in the CIA and that makes us equal, so I wouldn't expect any kind of concession or break. Her pride wouldn't allow it, and neither would mine should the situation have been reversed.

"In that case, boss," I say, switching back to business. "We had better wrap up our work here ASAP and head up to New Orleans."

"Yeah," she replies, standing where the grass meets the sand sloping down to the beach, the sea breeze fluttering her blouse, sweeping her hair back. "New Orleans. I'm wondering what's waiting for us there."

Facing the ocean, the wind whistling in my ears almost drowns the sirens, the shouting, the commotion that Ares Kulzak has caused and will cause again before it's over.

"Just remember," I say, watching a trio of seagulls gliding just a foot or so over the crest of a wave. "It's going to get worse before it gets better."

TWENTY-ONE

> > > > >

IRON WILL

> PRESIDENT LAURA VACCARO SAT IN THE MIDDLE OF a sofa opposite Russian Ambassador Sergei Dudayev in the Oval Office, her mind still thinking about the meeting she had just had with her vice president, FBI Director Russell Meek, and DCI Martin Jacobs on the situation in Melbourne and the new lead in New Orleans.

"Coffee, Mr. Ambassador?" she said, pointing to the coffeepot and cups crowding a silver tray on the table separating them.

"No, thank you, Mrs. President," Dudayev replied politely. "I find it difficult to indulge myself when my people are starving back home."

Vaccaro tried not to laugh. Dudayev, a borderline-obese man with an insatiable appetite for fine food and wine, was often seen dining at the best restaurants in the city in the company of attractive women.

"It is indeed a disappointment to us all that our two countries can't seem to reach an amiable agreement on this issue," she said. "I assure you that our hearts and prayers go out to your people."

"Mrs. President, if I may speak boldly, yes? Your prayers are welcomed, but it is the grain in those halted merchant ships that my people need."

"And the embargo could be lifted within the hour, Mr. Ambassador, if only President Tupelov could provide me with certain guarantees."

"I have been empowered to represent him today," he replied.

"Then, Mr. Ambassador," the president said, leaning forward, "stop refurbishing those Typhoon-class submarines at the Severodvinsk shipyard. They are in clear violation of our nuclear missile treaty."

"Ah, yes, of course," said Dudayev, pulling out a handkerchief and patting his forehead, which was beginning to glisten with sweat. "The nuclear submarines. You see, they are needed for the national defense, yes? To help us maintain peace with our neighbors."

"You want to explain to me how loading a submarine with twenty Sturgeon ballistic missiles, each housing up to nine MIRVed warheads capable of reaching the continental United States, is helping you keep the peace with your Muslim neighbors? I've stated before and I'll say it again, Mr. Ambassador, if what the Russians need is military assistance to fight in Chechnya and other rogue republics, then we will assist you with conventional weapons, like tanks, ammunition, helicopters, and even training. But those nuclear missiles have no business in such conflicts. They provide you with no military advantage."

"Yes, yes," he squirmed, crossing and uncrossing his legs while pressing the handkerchief against the side of his neck. "The missiles have dummy warheads. For training, yes?"

"In that case I want you to let the NATO team inside the shipyard to perform the inspection I requested last week."

Ambassador Dudayev also leaned forward, lowering his voice by a few decibels as he said, "It is not in the best interest of our national . . . pride if our recruits observe Americans inspecting our shipyards, bases, and vessels. I am sure that your navy would also object to such inspection by a foreign power."

Vaccaro knew this wasn't going anywhere, and she wasn't surprised. The ambassador had been coming to see her and discuss the same topic every week, and every week the answer was the same. No inspections allowed on Russian bases, and therefore no grain for the starving Russian people.

"I can assure, you, Mr. Ambassador, that if my people were starving I would be finding ways to make concessions."

"No, Mrs. President. If I may speak from the heart once again, I am quite certain that you would not make concessions. You would . . . wage war on your neighbors and take what you need, just as you took the state of Texas from Mexico, or the western states from the Native Americans, or Kuwait from its historical owners, the Iraqis. But please, I apologize if I am being disrespectful. I only wish what is best for my people, yes?"

"Then get Tupelov to allow the inspection team. Set it up so that your base personnel is on leave or something, but allow the inspection team to check the warheads in those Sturgeon missiles. I promise you that the equipment they carry will allow them to do their job very quickly and quite discreetly so as to not embarrass your navy."

"Very well," he said. "I will take that sensible proposal to my president."

Just like in the past weeks, she thought, checking her watch and inconspicuously pressing her thumb against the crown. The Russian's fifteen minutes were up.

A moment later two Secret Service agents entered the room through different doors followed by Vice President Vance Fitzgerald and two aides carrying their lunch on silver trays.

"Please give my regards to President Tupelov," Vaccaro said, standing up and shaking the ambassador's hand before one of the agents ushered him out. The aides replaced the coffee on the table with a tray of cold cuts and another one with a pitcher of chilled water and glasses, and mustered out a moment later.

"How did that go?" asked the Viper, stretching a thumb toward the closed door.

Vaccaro, who considered Fitzgerald her equal in domestic matters and her superior in international policy, said, "No change. They refuse to give up refurbishing those rusting subs, even if that means starving their own people to death."

"Not only are those Sturgeon missiles twenty years old, Mrs. President, but like you said, they're being loaded into submarines that were built back in the 1970s by inexperienced crews all to convey the image of a new military."

Vaccaro sighed. "Tupelov's propaganda machine."

"Exactly," Fitzgerald said, sitting down where the ambassador had been a minute ago, and crossing his legs while opening a manila folder. "And even if they don't fire them, there is the risk of leaks or even accidental detonations, like what happened with the *Kursk*, only this time we would be dealing with the complications of submerged nukes and the potential nuclear fallout."

Vaccaro remembered the accident many years before in the Barents Sea, recalling the sailors who died a slow death when the once-mighty Russian navy failed to rescue them. "Those Russians never change," she said, leaning back. "I've already released part of the grain to North Korea for allowing U.N. inspectors on their military bases last week. Another load is headed for Africa. At least some kids will not starve to death in this world."

"That was a good move on your part, Mrs. President. It will help defuse the statement made by Tupelov last week about America hoarding its grain while the rest of the world went hungry."

Vaccaro stared at the cold cuts and suddenly lost her appetite when recalling the latest statistics on world famine.

"Speaking of starving children," said Fitzgerald. "We got the new report from our favorite president south of the border."

"How is President Adolfo Herrera managing his funds these days?" she asked with a sarcastic tone she would never use in front of anyone but her vice president.

"Well," said the Viper, trying to contain his annoyance at the way Latin American nations loved to milk the United States and thought they were getting away with it. In reality, America put up with its lesser neighbors as long as they stuck to Washington policies. Colombia, however, was a case all by itself due to the drug problem that had split the nation. The north was controlled by the American-backed President Herrera, and the south controlled by the Cartel-backed FARC. "I'm afraid Adolfo is up to his old tricks."

"You're not going to show me pictures of yet another school built with the last economic package, are you?"

Fitzgerald frowned. "I'm afraid so, and I read that as a sign that the country is coming apart at the seams."

Vaccaro sensed where her vice president was headed with this.

"It is my belief," he continued, "based on all of the evidence I've seen, that Herrera—along with his closest associates—is pocketing most of the aid to give themselves a cushion should they ever have to flee the country à la Batista or Somoza. The CIA showed me evidence that there's been very little action on the part of the Colombian Army to pacify recent insurgences south of Bogotá. It's very typical behavior of a system about to implode."

"But the math doesn't add up," said Vaccaro. "Herrera's forces are over twice the size of the FARC and far better armed. They even have Apache helicopters now. What is that man doing with all of the equipment and training?"

"It's even more complicated than that, Mrs. President. You must also take into account the round of talks between Herrera and the FARC leaders that started two months ago. I heard it from their ambassador himself that his president was close to striking an agreement with the rebels."

"So," said Vaccaro, still trying to get used to Latin American politics, which were nothing new to Fitzgerald, having spent three years as ambassador to Venezuela. "Herrera has a bigger army, better weapons, the backing of our country, and is now engaged in peace talks with the rebels. Those aren't the signs of an administration that is about to collapse."

"I think the rebels showed Herrera something during those peace talks two months ago—something that made him halt his offensive and start preparations for the possibility that he would have to leave the country in a hurry."

"What?" the president asked, reaching for a glass and pouring water. "What could FARC leaders have told Herrera that made him react this way?"

"I'm not sure, but whatever it was, it obviously scared him enough to justify how he's been acting in the past two months, according to our local contacts."

Vaccaro crossed her arms, remembering the last set of statistics on drug abuse. "We have been losing this war for a long time now, Vance. It doesn't really matter how much we do on the home front to prevent the stuff from getting in. The hard truth is that drug producers will continue to find ways to smuggle it. The best way to solve the problem has always been at the source, and that means keeping the Colombian government in our pocket to help us fight it over there. If the FARC, which we all know is financed by the Cartel, gains control of the country, then all bets are off."

"Perhaps it's time to set up a meeting with the Colombian ambassador."

President Vaccaro said, "Do it."

As Fitzgerald made a note, Vaccaro couldn't help but wonder if part of the difficulty she faced was in the fact that she was a woman and most of these countries still treated women as second-class citizens. Vaccaro had spent considerable time studying the lives of former female heads of state, in particular Margaret Thatcher and the way in which she dealt with the defiant and chauvinistic Argentineans in the Falklands. Only her iron will and unyielding determination had allowed her to prevail in the face of an invasion halfway around the world, plus scores of international criticisms against the rights of the British Empire in other regions of the world.

An iron will, Vaccaro thought.

And they will test that will, honey, her late husband had told her. *They will test it every step of the way, making the job much harder than if you were a man.*

Vaccaro decided that this had to be part of the reason for the Russians' obstinate behavior, as well as the Chinese's—and the Colombians' for that matter. They were all testing her, measuring her, checking if she really had what it took to uphold the interests of the United States in this rapidly changing world, or if they would be able to roam free while she occupied this office.

Over my dead body, she thought, determined now more than ever to stick to her principles, to her values, to the promises she made on that long and hard campaign trail that now seemed like a lifetime ago.

TWENTY-TWO

> > > > >

CODE WARS

> "FORTY-EIGHT HOURS?"

Gary Hutton trembled while slowly nodding and saying, "That's . . . that's what they said."

Ares Kulzak threw the ice bucket against the hardwood floor, the loud banging startling not just the scientist, but also Kishna, who gave him a curious look as he silently cursed his luck. Tomorrow they were supposed to be in Austin, Texas, home of a large percentage of the high-tech companies in America, second to none but Silicon Valley, and most important, home of one Jason Lamar, the third of the MIT scientists who developed Neurall. By tonight the city of Los Angeles was supposed to be experiencing its own days of darkness, just like San Antonio, like Melbourne. And by now Neurall should have been interfaced to the core of the SWOASIS supercomputers, just like in San Antonio.

Ares stood by the tall windows of the mansion, staring at the skyline of downtown New Orleans while asking, "Anything else?"

"There is something else," said Hutton tentatively, concerned about further infuriating him. "The system administrator is not yet one hundred percent certain, but it looks as if the attack originated from New Orleans."

Ares spun around, staring at Kishna.

"I already told you I did not launch the strike!"

"Then how do you explain this coincidence?"

She set her system aside and walked up to him. "I have no explanation!" she hissed, her dark eyes glinting with anger.

"Your machine," Hutton said. "Didn't you say it froze when you were establishing a protocol with the network using my passwords?"

"Yes."

"And you said you were using a Linux operating system?"

"Yes."

"Where are you going with this?" asked Ares.

"A core dump!" Kishna said abruptly, rushing to her laptop.

"A what?" asked Ares.

Her eyes on the screen while she worked the keyboard, Kishna said, "One of the features of the Linux operating system is that of performing a core dump during an improper shutdown, preserving the last known good state of the machine in memory to facilitate a post-mortem analysis."

"I still don't understand."

"Gary is proposing that if the abnormal shutdown of my system is in any way related to the network attack, then relevant information might have been dumped to memory before the shutdown—information I can now try to access."

Gary nodded slowly.

Ares had to give him credit for cooperating so openly. He certainly didn't have to offer such a valuable suggestion.

He is fighting for his life.

It was indeed too bad that he would have to die. From the looks of it, Gary Hutton would have made a fine addition to his cyberterrorism team.

But Ares Kulzak had to follow the rules, and they called for the swift execution of all outsiders who came in contact with him or Kishna.

No exceptions.

"Here," said Kishna, tapping a dark-purple fingernail against the plasma screen. "There appears to be something wrong with the alert message from the digital EMP I left behind at the water company in San Antonio."

"What?"

She slowly shook her head. "I'm not sure, just that the last two bytes of the signature of the message are not the same. It almost looks like a tracer of some sort."

"A tracer?" asked Ares.

"A unique sequence of bits that can be followed through the Internet using the right software," she replied.

"Are you suggesting that someone followed this alert message from the water company, through the World Wide Web, and made it to your laptop, from where it somehow managed to launch an attack against the SWOASIS network?"

"Sounds impossible, doesn't it?" she said.

Ares opened his mouth but could not think of what to say to that.

"But it's actually *quite* possible," offered Gary Hutton.

"How?" Ares said.

"Look, here," Gary replied, sitting in bed next to the box of pizza he had consumed an hour ago, courtesy of the delivery Ares had allowed when it became evident that they would be here for a while longer than planned, and Kishna had discovered that the bachelor's refrigerator and pantry contained nothing of substance. "Anybody with an intelligent script could have accomplished that, especially if they tagged your messenger, or runner. Only the security system of the network where the tagging occurred could have detected the stain. After that it would be a simple matter of playing follow the leader."

"How do you know this?" asked Kishna, obviously impressed, which made Ares wonder if he should reconsider his plans for this man. Anyone who could impress Kishna was worth salvaging.

Gary Hutton lowered his voice, as if about to reveal a long-kept secret. "See, I'm really a hacker of sorts, even back at MIT. That's in a way how I was able to prevail during the dot.com madness."

Ares crossed his arms and looked away, his mind stepping back, looking at the big picture for a moment. He had already obtained the backdoor password from this man. He did not need to hang around and risk getting caught by the CCTF. The SWOASIS strike, as much as it would have pleased him, was in the end just a distraction to hide his true agenda. On the other hand, those blocking Kishna's cyber strikes would continue to do so unless he eliminated them. Remaining in place could draw the enemy closer and provide him with the opportunity to do just that.

"So," Ares said, making his decision. "Are you good enough to help us figure out who interfered with our plans to access the power grid?"

Gary smiled. "I can do better than that."

TWENTY-THREE

> > > > >

CYBER SWORD

> ONE OF THE INTERESTING THINGS ABOUT HIGH technology is that the same tools that cyberterrorists use against us can also be used against them.

The cyber sword cuts both ways.

Take, for example, the handiwork of Mike Ryan, following this runner—as Walter had called it—through the guts of the Internet, across provider after provider, through a wireless connection that led him to the terrorist's own mobile personal computer—while also placing the location of the laptop in the Greater New Orleans area, and figuring out in seconds Kulzak's potential next target. Add to that Ryan's brilliant last-second mock cyber attack against the Southwest Open Access Same-Time Information System, the software backbone of the power distribution grid feeding the southwestern United States, which shut down all of its external passwords, very likely preventing Kulzak from pulling another San Antonio in a metropolis like Los Angeles or Phoenix. Finally, mix in the exceptional work done by the SWOASIS system administrator team in conjunction with Walter and the STG boys, tracking down the owners of all of the external passwords and faxing the list to Karen and me while we were still somewhere over the Gulf of Mexico on our way to New Orleans.

And what do you get from all that?

The name of the only owner of a SWOASIS external password in New Orleans:

Gary Francis Hutton, the founder of the security software company that handled the firewall for SWOASIS.

Sometimes you think you're right, and sometimes you *know* you're right. This afternoon, as Karen goes over the last-minute plan with a SWAT team from the NOPD as well as a half dozen CCTF agents plus twice as many FBI agents on loan from the local office, my spook sense tells me this one is clear cut, black and white—quite the exception in the grayish world of counterterrorism.

Kulzak's people—heck, maybe even Kulzak himself—have got to be with Hutton.

It's perfect and timely. The cyber attack against SWOASIS has not taken place yet, increasing our confidence that we might either nail or get closer to the man behind San Antonio and, most recently, Melbourne, where the death toll has risen to one hundred and twenty-one, still quite shy of the Alamo City's twenty-three thousand, so far, but nonetheless horrifying.

And we might do it before he gets the chance to booby-trap Hutton's place.

We're hot and sleep deprived on this steamy afternoon in New Orleans but utterly pumped about the possibility of making progress, of capturing someone important enough to force a break in the case. Terrorists, like organized crime, operate through a network of informants, soldiers, and those running the show. The entire operation, albeit complex, can be taken down like a house of cards if you find the right informant, someone who can finger others, kicking off a chain reaction.

My professional side urges me to contain my excitement, but something else inside of me tells me that there is a strong possibility that Kulzak might even be around, and bagging him would certainly send a message to the world that no one fucks with Uncle Sam and gets away with it. I'm a firm believer that anyone who does what Kulzak has done should be drawn and quartered in public and with the cameras rolling for the world to see. Heck, the degree of gore won't be any different than what's already shown in the news today. And while we're at it, we should send each limb to the four corners of the world, tour the head through all terrorist-sponsoring regimes, and feed his limbless and disemboweled torso to ravenous dogs.

But that's just me.

I force myself to pay attention.

Once again, we're splitting up in teams of four, and once more I'm teamed up with Karen. Paul Stone and a guy from the local FBI office who introduced himself as Jerry is also in my team. Like Paul, Jerry also looks like he just graduated from junior high. But unlike Paul, Jerry's eyes have that newness glaze that broadcasts inexperience. I guess Paul is growing up in a hurry.

Field operations will do that to you.

The target is located at the corner of Commerce and Lafayette, in the heart of the Warehouse District. I peek out of a nearby window on the lower floor of one of the few warehouses that were never renovated during the tourist boom of the nineties. In an ideal world we would carry out this raid at night, but time is of the essence, and every second that we wait is another second that the bad guys have to wrap up their work here and move on.

So we chose to make our move first, leaving the ops building armed to the teeth, wired, and pretty much ready to kick ass. Unlike Melbourne, though, we're not in uniforms but wearing the touristy clothes that some woman from the local FBI office picked up for us while we were in the air. I'm showing off my beautiful pale legs with a pair of khaki shorts, a plain T-shirt, and sneakers. No vest. It's just too damned hot, so I'm taking my chances. Karen, also declining a vest, is similarly dressed but looks good enough to eat. Her tanned legs are firmer than I had imagined, though I make an effort not to get caught looking again.

We both have our pieces out of sight, not wishing to alarm the handful of pedestrians—tourists like us—or tip off any spotters Kulzak may have placed around the Hutton residence, which looks more like another warehouse, only gutted out and turned into apartments, one per floor—according to the landlord, who lives down the block. Our man is on the third floor. Three two-car garages flank the entryway, two to the left and one to the right of the entrance.

This time around I insist on being on the first squad to go in. If shit hits the fan, like it did in Melbourne, I want to be able to react quickly, hopefully preventing more deaths. Besides, unlike Melbourne, we can't approach the target from all sides, only through the stairs at the front of the building.

The mid-afternoon sun beating down on us like Moses in the desert, we stroll casually down the street, Karen and I leading, followed by Paul and Jerry about ten feet behind. Unlike Karen and me, the rookies are wearing their vests beneath their touristy clothes, as is the rest of the team, currently out of sight.

I scan the area, counting a couple dozen people aside from our team of four. Most are couples snapping pictures of the beautifully renovated buildings, many dating back to the 1800s. A few appear to be businessmen, walking about carrying briefcases. There's even an old wino heading our way, drinking from a bottle inside a paper bag while pushing a grocery cart packed with junk. His long blond hair falling to his shoulders, he gives us a disinterested glance and continues down the block, disappearing around the corner.

There is a mix of abandoned warehouses, as well as those converted into apartments, restaurants, or shops. Although the crowds on this side of Canal Street are only a fraction of the mob populating the French Quarter on the other side of the wide dividing boulevard, there's nevertheless plenty of innocent bystanders to get hurt if something goes south, which given recent events is a damned likely possibility. But we can't evacuate the area without telegraphing our presence, and we can't guarantee their safety without evacuating the area.

Doomed if we do and doomed if we don't.

TWENTY-FOUR

> > > > >

COMPANY

> "WE HAVE COMPANY," ARES KULZAK SAID WHILE LOW-ering the mobile phone in his hand.

"Who?" asked Kishna.

"Paxton just called and claims one of the tourists outside looks vaguely familiar but couldn't place the face."

Kishna dumped her gear into the backpack and shouldered it while drawing her weapon.

Gary Hutton was still busy behind the desktop computer system in his room. He looked at them over his shoulder. "Almost there."

"No time. Let's go."

"But . . . it may not work as you—"

"Now!"

"Why? Something wrong?"

"No time to explain," Ares replied as Kishna entered the password on the side panel of the large metallic case provided to them by Paxton.

She clicked a button on her digital watch before looking up at him. "Two minutes."

"Two minutes for what?" asked a confused Hutton.

"Can you drive?" asked Ares, staring into Hutton's eyes, which seemed clear of the sedative.

"Ah . . . yeah, sure."

"Then get your keys. You and I are going for a little ride . . . and you are driving."

"What about her?"

"Don't worry about me. I know how to take care of myself." Kishna smiled, producing a pair of two-way radios from her backpack, turning them on, and tossing one at Kulzak. "Channel five. Backup is channel three."

Ares pocketed it, before nearly dragging Hutton out of the apartment and down the stairs leading to his two-car garage, where Ares had parked the rented Lexus next to the millionaire's black BMW sedan.

"Smile, old hacker," Ares said, hearing Kishna's footsteps behind them. "You're about to make headlines."

TWENTY-FIVE

> > > > >

ALLEYS

> WE SLOWLY CLOSE ON THE TARGET WHILE USING A disposable camera to join the memory-making couples in the area. I even take a picture of Karen, who smiles without humor.

But she does grab me by the hand, whispering, "Just play the part."

Boy, she's got a firm grip and very soft skin, and I try not to imagine how supple the rest of her must also feel, starting with that freckle.

We reach the smoked-glass entrance, which is sandwiched by a wrought-iron frame, and I produce the landlord's key, unlocking it before going inside, leaving Paul and Jerry outside waiting for our signal. I don't want any more rookie blood on my hands.

Before going inside, I scan the street one last time. It's a lively afternoon. As lively as San Antonio had been less than a week ago. Wrought-iron panels decorate balconies also adorned with hanging ferns and bright flowers. Apparently this is the first day without rain in over a week and the tourists are out in numbers despite the swollen Mississippi and the possibility of floods.

We face a gray-slate corridor roughly twenty feet long. There are three ornate mail slots to our right, along with a door, which leads to one of the two-car garages. Two additional doors on the left connect to the other garages, providing the tenants of this exclusive three-unit building with the security of getting in their cars and locking the doors before opening the garage doors. Although this part of town has been recently renovated, New Orleans still ranks among the highest-crime cities in America.

We focus on the stairs at the end of the hallway and simultaneously draw our weapons even though I hope to hell we don't have to fire them while inside this brick structure. The amplified report of just one shot would be enough to keep my ears ringing for a week.

I hear a sudden rumbling to our right, through the wall separating us from the garage on the other side—the one belonging to the third-floor tenant.

Shit!

I race toward the door connecting to the garage, but before my hand reaches the handle I hear an engine being gunned, followed by three shots fired in rapid succession.

Losing track of Karen, I press my shoulder against the door while turning the knob, racing into the garage, the smell of engine exhaust and gunpowder assaulting my nostrils. Jerry is bleeding on the sidewalk, and I don't see Paul.

There's a vehicle parked to my left, a Lexus, but it's the back of a dark BMW, just beyond the rectangular opening of the raised garage door, that my instincts focus on.

Leveling the Sig on the spinning tires, partly hidden by inky smoke, I fire four times in rapid succession, the reports hammering my eardrums as the car cuts right.

For a brief moment that seems to stretch into eternity, I see the profile of the man in the passenger seat, see his bearded face as he turns to look at me. Our eyes lock long enough to propel me to another time, to a dusty parking lot behind a rundown church in a place I have tried to forget for so long.

Huevos rancheros.

Although in my heart I wanted to find him, I really had expected to find a soldier, or maybe even one of his lieutenants, but not the general himself.

Professional habits resurface with unparalleled clarity, lurching me forward, forcing me into a run while I hold the Sig over my right shoulder, muzzle pointed at the ceiling, forefinger resting against the trigger guard.

Two more shots, like cracks from distant thunder, echo through the surround-sound ringing in my ears as I reach the sidewalk, my eyes so focused on the departing BMW's taillights that I almost miss Karen standing by the entrance firing her Glock. I also spot Paul Stone to my right. He's sitting up, his back against the side of the building, his face a mask of pain as he clutches his chest.

The BMW's taillights explode before Karen drops her empty magazine and reloads while I open fire, shattering the rear windshield.

And I can't hear a thing except for very faint reports.

I can't hear worth a damn but I can run, and I sure in the hell can fire *while* running, which is exactly what I do, cutting loose the rest of my magazine at the departing vehicle, popping round after round, keeping the front sight leveled on that BMW, which, in spite of all of the pounding, gathers speed, turning left at the corner, disappearing from sight, followed moments later by the remote sound of metal hitting metal.

Pedestrians huddle in isolated pockets along both sidewalks, some run inside businesses, others peek out of doors, windows, and balconies. I keep my charge, huffing and puffing, shoving all of the energy in my out-of-shape body down to my pale legs.

Karen cruises past me, effortlessly racing with those long legs of hers, which blend into a whirl of tanned motion, like in a Roadrunner cartoon. She probably beep-beeped when overtaking me, but I can't even hear my own breathing, just my heart-beat pounding my temples. That probably explains why I can't hear what must be some serious commotion on the operational frequency, or the howls of the innocent bystanders smartly staying out of our way, though I do see their mouths moving violently, obviously screaming, and realize it is the background murmur blended with the incessant buzzing.

I too feel like shouting, and not just because the bastard is getting away. I want to shout out loud that someone betrayed us, that some lowlife, bottom-dweller parasite leaked our presence to Ares Kulzak.

That thought has not even quite formed in my mind when a powerful explosion rocks the building. I feel the vibrations through my feet, my legs, and when I turn around I see a fork of flames shooting out of the third-story windows of the building we had just tried to storm.

Glass, brick, and sizzling debris fall over the street behind me, bathing everyone in sight.

But I have no time for that now. I have seen the face of the monster, and I'm taking him down.

And where's the rest of the damned team?

I feel for the earpiece connected to my left ear but find it dangling from the side of my collar. I pop it back in place but all I hear is a bunch of muffled voices.

Great.

Karen reaches the corner a few seconds before I do, letting another empty magazine drop to the cobblestone floor while replacing it with a fresh one. I see the empty clip skittering over the street as I reach her side but hear no clattering. It's weird to be deaf.

I look at my own gun and realize that I have already reloaded, most likely after firing my last shot. Sometimes my instincts even scare me. It's indeed too bad they weren't fast enough to bag Kulzak before he—

The BMW has jumped the curb, smashing into a post, which cracked in half on impact, the top portion falling right over the roof. Steam from the radiator hazes the front of the German vehicle.

Reading each other's minds, Karen and I split, approaching the vehicle from the sides, weapons pointed at the windows. The airbags have already deployed, cloaking the driver's face, his limp body leaning forward. There is no sign of Kulzak.

Karen leans down, unveiling the driver. My bowels contract upon seeing a man in his forties, clean cut, bleeding profusely from his temples, his lifeless eyes staring at a spot just above me. The face matches the digitized image we have of Gary Hutton, and he's been shot, presumably by the missing passenger, by the monster that has just vanished.

A few pedestrians emerge from around the corner, some walking in a crouch, hands shielding their faces. There're people looking down at us from the balconies. Sirens come alive somewhere out there.

Karen's lips are moving as she looks at me.

"The reports in the garage!" I say, barely hearing myself. "I can't hear very well! Speak louder!"

"Which way do you think the other went?" she shouts, running around the BMW.

"The other's Kulzak!"

"What?" She makes a face. Obviously she either didn't recognize him or didn't see him when the BMW drove by in front of the entrance right after I first shot at it. "Are you sure?"

Just then I spot blood on the door handle, on the ground, the spotty trail moving toward a narrow passage in between buildings. I point it out to her, exchange a quick glance, and we're running in the direction of the alleyway seconds before gunfire cracks around the corner we've turned moments ago.

Although my hearing's hosed, I think the shots originated from the front of Gary Hutton's building.

No time to worry about that. I have to assume that the rest of the team will deal with that. Karen and I have to stay on Kulzak, who has been wounded.

The blood trail becomes more and more sporadic as it continues down the dark and apparently empty alley, trash bins and other junk lining the tall brick walls, the smell of refuse filling my lungs as I pant after the short sprint. Sweat rolls down my forehead, stinging my eyes, which I wipe with the shoulders of my T-shirt.

I hate alleys. Too many places for the bad guys to hide, giving them the upper hand while we have to walk down the middle totally exposed.

I peer down the long corridor of stained concrete and see absolutely nothing but crap to either side and the street at the far end of—

A vehicle pulls up at the other end, screeching to a halt just as a figure emerges from behind a bright-yellow Dumpster a couple dozen feet from the vehicle, and the rear window rolls down.

"He's getting away!" Karen shouts as we both race after him.

"Kulzak!" I scream, weapon aimed at the middle of his back. He's roughly a hundred feet away.

He spins around, grinning, before making a run for the waiting vehicle, but not in a straight line, as an amateur might have. He zigzags, magnifying the level of difficulty for a clean shot.

I fire once, twice, both bullets missing him, the reports threatening to rupture my sore eardrums.

Karen and I stop in unison, taking a knee to steady our fire. As Kulzak is about to jump into the rear window and we're about to cut him in half, I see a bright explosion originating from the driver's window, followed by a smoking object in a parabolic trajectory toward us.

Grenade!

Visions of Kulzak disappearing inside the car mix with those of the canister striking wet concrete, bouncing toward us.

My instincts switch from offense to defense, or actually to survival mode. I double back while extending my right arm, grabbing Karen across the chest, lifting her frame with relative ease, embracing her as I rush toward the side of a nearby Dumpster, diving for cover, turning my body over in midair to avoid landing on top of her.

An earth-trembling rumble hammers the Dumpster, which protects us from the flying shrapnel hammering the metallic side like an army of angry carpenters.

The hard landing has knocked the wind out of me, and once again I begin to get lightheaded, dizzy.

"Tom! Are you all right?"

Her voice muddled up with the buzzing in my ears, I nod slowly, breathing deeply, getting up with effort, with her help, trying to get my bearings.

I told you I didn't like alleys.

A hand on her left ear, Karen speaks into her lapel microphone, but since she isn't shouting, all I hear is a murmur.

I really screwed myself up by firing those initial shots from inside the garage. Now it sounds as if my head's stuck inside a beehive.

There has got to be a better way to make a living than this.

"They won't get away!" she screams, guiding me toward the same end of the alley used by Kulzak to escape. "The NOPD has the area surrounded."

As we reach the street and a black Suburban pulls over to pick us up, I get the nasty little feeling that the police cordon securing the place isn't tight enough to keep someone as slippery as Kulzak from getting through.

T W E N T Y - S I X

> > > > >

P A I N

> ARES KULZAK LEARNED AT A VERY EARLY AGE HOW to take pain, both physically and mentally, starting with the day he was orphaned, then during his uncle's constant beatings, and during the difficult years in military school. Throughout his nomadic existence fighting against Imperialism, he became a master in the art not just of inflicting pain but of taking pain, of embracing it as part of his chosen path through life.

Today, Ares clenched his teeth and took the pain while crawling into the front seat of the Lexus, his ribs throbbing from having bounced inside the BMW when Hutton had panicked, crashing into a post just as they had managed to get away.

Or maybe he was still under the influence of the sedative.

But Ares did not have a choice. He'd needed a driver to shoot his way out of there from the BMW's passenger seat.

Now he had to take the pain of his wounds. Ché had lasted weeks living off the land while being hunted like an animal in Bolivia. Fidel had survived years in Batista's prisons. Ares could certainly bear a few bruises as well as the scrape on his left shoulder, where either a bullet or a shard of glass had nicked the skin.

Ares raised his black T-shirt and used one of his socks to wrap the wound tightly, staunching the blood, before lowering the T-shirt. Completing the improvised field dressing, he checked his silenced weapon, which he had used to eliminate Hutton before running into the alley.

Kishna took them through a series of turns to put as much distance between them and American intelligence forces.

"We need to . . . find another car," he said, clutching his abdomen as they accelerated down a narrow street overlooked by abandoned warehouses.

She gave him a slight nod, keeping both hands on the wheel. Her face was misted with blood, but she seemed to be fine.

Their escape plan had worked, though barely. Ares and Hutton had gotten in the BWM and taken off first, going in one direction to attract the attention of the raid team. Meanwhile, Kishna had hidden in the Lexus, parked next to the BWM in Hutton's two-car garage, waiting until ten seconds before the bomb would detonate, and then also flooring her vehicle in the opposite direction, escaping the blast zone in true movie fashion, and heading in a parallel course that allowed for multiple rendezvous locations. Ares had used his radio to guide her to the end of the alley.

But now they needed a place to hide. The blast would only buy them so much time, and the longer they remained on the streets, the higher the chances of someone spotting them.

They turned into a large public parking garage servicing the opulent Harrah's Casino. She punched the yellow button of the automatic ticket dispenser, removed the brown tag sliding out of the slot beneath, and the gate lifted out of the way. They drove in and found a parking spot on the fourth floor.

She stopped the engine and sat sideways, facing him. "Are you all right?"

Ares frowned. "My ribs, but I don't think they are broken, and a bullet grazed my shoulder. Is that your blood?" He extended a finger and ran it over the side of her face.

"It belongs to the *gusano* I shot when I drove out of the garage." She lifted the bottom of her black T-shirt and wiped herself clean.

He inspected the garage to make sure no one had followed them.

"What is next?" she asked, inspecting her weapon before putting it away, as well as the second grenade resting in between her legs. It had an attachment that fit over the muzzle of her weapon, allowing her to use it as a makeshift launcher, which in this case had probably saved his life back in that alley.

"Did you have enough time to launch the attack against the power grid?"

She raised her narrow shoulders. "We should know in less than twelve hours, when the virus stops replicating itself inside the network and becomes active."

Ares peered out of the window, verifying that they had not been followed. An Asian family of six exited a tan minivan, talking amiably while heading for the elevators servicing this level.

"One of the *gusanos* knew me," Ares said, his strength returning.

The fine features on her dark-olive face tightened. "How do you know that?"

"I saw his face. His eyes blinked in recognition as we left the garage. Then in the alley, before you came, he called out my name."

"Did you recognize him?"

"I am not sure. The face seemed vaguely familiar and so did the voice, but I cannot place him. He is probably the same man who Paxton recognized when he alerted us. But it doesn't really matter. They know it is me."

"Then we should expect a manhunt."

He looked away, wondering what had gone wrong, pondering his next move, making his decision. "We need to leave the car and walk for a while. Take only your weapon."

"It is going to be difficult to leave this city," she said.

"That is the thing, my beautiful Kishna," he replied, staring at her, touching her face, her neck. "We are not leaving."

"No?" she put a hand over his. "But we need to keep moving. Jason Lamar is in Austin, and only he knows the third backdoor password to the military Neurall."

"I know, but we cannot leave just yet."

"Why not?" she asked.

"Because that is *exactly* what the *gusanos* expect me to do."

TWENTY-SEVEN

> > > > >

VANISHING ACT

> "WHERE IN THE HELL ARE THEY?" KAREN SCREAMS into her radio.

I'm munching on my lower lip. We've been circling the area for the last thirty minutes along with a dozen other federal vehicles plus just about the entire New Orleans Police Department, which is also monitoring all exits out of the city for a dark Lexus sedan—though I doubt Kulzak would be stupid enough to hang onto his getaway vehicle for very long.

"They're gone," I say, sinking in the rear seat of the black Suburban, my back throbbing from the crash landing by the Dumpster, my hearing slowly returning to the point that I can hear normal conversations—though accompanied by an annoying background ringing.

Crap.

I can't believe I had the bastard lined up in my sights and let him get away. And he obviously has an accomplice, though that shouldn't be a surprise. We have known for some time that Kulzak operates through the use of strategically located support. The faceless driver that launched that grenade at us could have been from a local contact.

I close my eyes and see the monster diving though that rear window just as the pear-shaped canister tumbles toward us. There really wasn't anything else I could have done. As it was, I had barely managed to snatch Karen and find cover.

"Yep," I say, more to myself than to Karen. "The bastard's gone."

"How can you be so sure?" she asks, half looking at me and half glaring at the streets blurring past us.

"Because I know how he operates."

"But he's wounded. He might need medical attention."

"It doesn't matter. He'll find a way. He *always* does."

She also leans back on the large middle seat next to me, arms crossed. Paul Stone is sitting in the third row of the Suburban, still massaging his chest over the spot where one of Kulzak's bullets struck the vest he had been wearing. Lucky kid—though he is not saying much at the moment. Paul had been standing next to Jerry, who had the misfortune of getting shot in the face.

"So you think he's leaving the city right away?" she asks.

I tilt my head. "An interesting question. That's probably what he thinks we would expect him to do: leave a hot zone immediately. Any reasonable criminal would like to get as far away as possible from the manhunt we're mounting."

"But *will* he do that, knowing that's what we expect him to do?"

"Another interesting question. What makes it more complicated is that we have managed to catch up to him."

"What do you mean?"

"We've managed to break his rhythm, and the Kulzak that I know would be quite pissed at that."

"What are you saying? You think he's going to get personal? Come after you and me?"

"Maybe. All I know is that we've stopped reacting to his moves and managed to close the gap. We have shown him that we're not just a bunch of puppets under his control, acting out his script, like we did in San Antonio and Melbourne. We made him alter his game, forced him to change his plan."

"So what can we do beyond what we're already doing?"

"For starters, we should comb through the city of New Orleans—at least as much as is humanly possible. If Kulzak wants to play the I'm-going-to-do-the-unexpected card, we may just beat him at his own game."

"So, you're saying that we stick to our guns and continue doing what we're doing? Searching the living hell out of this city?"

"Yep."

She gives me a resigned pout.

"However," I say. "You still haven't asked the most important question."

"What's that?"

"Who tipped Kulzak?"

She makes a face. "Who *tipped* him?"

"He knew we were coming, Karen. Someone blew the whistle. Heck, he even had a bomb ready as his getaway diversion."

"Maybe he had a spotter, someone who picked us up."

"Maybe, but if I were playing the odds I'd bet that we were not spotted. We looked like your typical New Orleans tourist couple, down to the cheap camera."

"You think this was an inside job?"

"While this might seem extreme, I think someone very close to this operation, if not *inside* the operation, gave us up."

"Do you realize what you're saying?"

"Call me paranoid, but that's what's kept me alive for so many years. I'm trained to assume the worst of people, and right now that training is telling me someone tipped the terrorists."

Pressing a tight fist against her chin, Karen looks away for a moment as the streets of New Orleans rush by. "You could be right," she finally says.

"They were too ready for us, Karen. Even if someone had spotted us approaching the building, how could Kulzak, Hutton, and the person driving the Lexus have gotten to the garage and into their respective cars before we reached the front door?"

"What bothers me with that theory is that if someone in our team did tip Kulzak, why was he in that building? I would have moved to another location."

"Unless he got the call at the last minute."

She doesn't look convinced.

"Look," I say, the spook in me surfacing. "I realize that there might not be a mole, that perhaps one of his people somehow spotted us and managed to warn him, but what is the downside of *assuming* there might be a rat in our organization, at least until we know for sure how he was tipped?"

"All right," she says, still not convinced about the possibility of a leak in the CCTF but willing to humor me. "*If* there is a spy, how do you propose we catch him?"

"I didn't say I want to *catch* the mole. If there is a spy, he or she is likely to be well entrenched and very difficult to find, as shown in the history of our respective agencies. It takes years, and sometimes decades, to catch a traitor."

"Then? What do you want to do?"

I smile. "What I do best."

"I'm afraid to ask what that might be."

"*Use* the mole to *catch* Kulzak."

"How?"

"I'm not sure yet, but somehow I'm certain that you and Mike Ryan will help me figure that out."

"In the meantime we continue searching the city?"

I nod, wondering how Mike Ryan is doing in his world.

T W E N T Y - E I G H T

> > > > >

T I M E

> "WOULD SOMEONE PLEASE CARE TO EXPLAIN TO ME how two terrorists not only slipped through a net of CCTF and FBI agents and police officers, but managed to kill a handful of them while turning the Warehouse District of New Orleans into a battle zone?" asked President Laura Vaccaro while staring at FBI Director Russell Meek and DCI Martin Jacobs, the men who had joined forces to create the Counter Cyberterrorism Task Force. It had not taken long for CNN and the networks to start broadcasting the disaster in New Orleans, though at least for the time being there had been no mention of Ares Kulzak.

Meek decided to give it a shot and leaned forward, looking at President Vaccaro, who sat at the edge of her desk with her arms crossed while staring at her subordinates sitting on the sofas beyond the embroidered presidential seal on the blue carpet of the Oval Office. Vance Fitzgerald stood in the back, by the fireplace, hands in his pockets as he watched the inquisition.

"Mrs. President, the head of the CCTF, Randy Cramer, is heading to New Orleans as we speak to meet with the lead agents on the case. The message we got up here is that the terrorists were tipped. They apparently knew we were coming, ma'am."

"How?"

They shook their heads in unison.

"Last year alone the FBI's budget was just under four billion dollars, Russ. That's *four* big ones." Then she turned to DCI Jacobs. "Marty, I don't even want to *think* how much we're pumping into the CIA these days, and you are expecting me to swallow that you have no idea how the terrorists knew we were coming to get them?"

"Russ and I have a couple of theories, ma'am," said DCI Jacobs, "but that's all they are until Cramer gets a chance to assess the situation firsthand."

"What theories?"

"One is that we simply underestimated Ares Kulzak again. The man does have a long history of surprising us. He's done it before in Central America, East Berlin, Ecuador, Serbia, and other places. There is a chance he may have had a spotter that somehow saw our team moving in and warned him."

Vaccaro let that sink in for a moment before asking, "What else, Marty?"

"Luck," said Jacobs. "He could have just gotten plain lucky."

"Anything else?"

"I'm afraid not until Cramer gets a chance to debrief the lead agents."

"What is the CCTF's thinking regarding Kulzak's current whereabouts?"

Russell Meek leaned forward and said, "He was wounded during the strike, Mrs. President. We think he is hiding somewhere in New Orleans."

"That's a very big place, Russ."

"I know that, ma'am, but we have an all-out manhunt down there."

"A noble effort, Russ, but if your team couldn't capture him while he was inside a building, what makes you think we're going to find him now that he has a million places to hide?"

Meek looked at Jacobs before lowering his gaze to the presidential seal.

Vaccaro turned around and headed for the windows behind her desk, eyes closed as she struggled to control her temper.

We had him, she thought. *We had him and we let him escape.*

She blocked the thought of how many more innocent lives would be lost because of this blunder.

Turning around, controlling the powerful urge to micromanage these professionals, Vaccaro stuck to the same principles that had gotten her this far: letting the experts do their jobs while understanding that certain jobs, like the capture of a man like Ares Kulzak, were not trivial.

"Gentlemen, I am not going to tell you how to do your jobs. However, I will stress to you both the sense of urgency behind this issue and further encourage you to fix whatever problems you believe you may have in your respective organizations."

"Yes, Mrs. President," they replied.

"Same time tomorrow," she said.

"Yes, Mrs. President," they repeated in unison before mustering out.

"They are good men," commented Vice President Fitzgerald after Meek and Jacobs left. "Very experienced at this sort of thing."

"I know, Vance. I know. But we need results. We need answers."

"And the answers will come, Mrs. President. We just need to stay the course. We have the best of the best on the case. We have to give them time to do their jobs."

The president looked away for a moment before saying, "Time, Vance, is a luxury our nation doesn't have."

TWENTY - NINE

> > > > >

CHEMICALS

> AT DUSK, THEY TOOK A TAXI FROM HARRAH'S CASINO
to Canal Street, where Ares Kulzak directed the driver to Rampart Street, a twisting road that eventually became St. Claude Street for no reason whatsoever,
reminding Kulzak of old European cities, where avenues were arranged in convo-
luted ways.

They eventually took a right on Elysian Fields, then a left on Dauphine Street,
and another left on Mandeville, just as Ken Paxton had instructed him to do on the
phone.

They paid the driver and continued on foot up Mandeville, a tree-lined street of
what his contact referred to as "double shotgun" houses, where one room led into the
next starting at the front of each duplex all the way to the rear room, which led into
a small backyard. These old homes were mostly one-story with narrow front porches
supported by elaborate columns, and with steps coming down to the sidewalk. Once
occupied by whites until the rising wave of crime drove them to the suburbs during
the late sixties and early seventies, this old part of town bordered the French Quarter,
its architecture a reflection of the French influence dominating this section of the
city. Eventually the growing gay population of New Orleans bought some of these
old houses and kicked off a renovation process, restoring them to their original
splendor.

Branches from rows of trees beneath streetlights projected jagged shadows down the block as Ares and Kishna reached the corner of Mandeville and Burgundy. His eyes landed on the St. Peter and Paul complex of buildings on the right-hand side. Once a prosperous elementary school, convent, and church, the massive exodus to the suburbs eroded the parishioner support that kept this Catholic church in business. When the old community vanished, so did the church's income. First the school closed down as parents sent their kids to schools in safer neighborhoods. Then the nuns moved to another convent, and finally the church itself officially shut its doors.

"We will meet him outside the old rectory building," Ares said with some effort, his bruised ribs stinging him every time he took a deep breath. The wound on his shoulder continued to burn.

"How long has it been since you last saw Paxton?"

"El Salvador," he replied. "Near the end of the civil war in the early nineties. He went south after that conflict and joined the FARC, who eventually sent him here to support Cartel operations in the Port of New Orleans."

Kishna gave him a sideways glance through narrowed green eyes beneath her bushy brows. "Do you trust him, Ari?"

"I trust that he will not cross me because of our history together, because of his relationship with the FARC and the Cartel, and also because he has two daughters."

They passed the red-brown brick convent and the tall church, its large front doors chained together at the top of the steps rising from the sidewalk. Beyond it stood the rectory building, its lights off, just like the rest of the buildings since their closure.

A shadow detached itself from a tree bordering the south side of the rectory.

They reached for their sidearms, shoved in their pants and covered by T-shirts, but didn't pull them out.

"Do you know the way to Rampart Street?" Ares asked the dark figure standing a couple dozen feet away from them.

"You are closer to Canal Street than Rampart," replied Ken Paxton, completing the code while walking toward them.

"It is good to see you again," Ares said, first shaking his hand, then embracing him.

"Yes, *hermano*," said Paxton, holding his old friend by the arms. "It's good indeed. I only wish we were meeting under better circumstances."

"Yes, yes," said Ares, regarding the retired mercenary, his hair as blond and long as during the days when they had fought alongside Marxist guerrillas to overthrow the U.S.-backed Salvadorian government. "But the *gusanos* will pay for what they did today."

Paxton turned to Kishna, who gave him a brief nod. "I'm glad you both made it. I apologize for not giving you any more time, but I called as soon as I noticed a familiar face and guessed they could be federal agents."

"Your instincts are as sharp as ever," Ares replied. "I also recognized one of them, though I can't seem to place him. In any case, your timing could not have been better."

"Come, my friend," Paxton said, turning on a flashlight and pointing it at the darkness behind the rectory building. "Let's go inside the church. I have also secured medical supplies to tend your wounds."

They followed him to a weed-overgrown stone path that veered around the back of the brown-red brick building, reaching a tall chain-link fence. Paxton unlocked the gate and creaked it open, letting them through before closing and locking it behind him. Warning signs hung everywhere about this being a private property and violators would be prosecuted.

"I went to school here in my childhood," the mercenary said, the flashlight washing the path with yellow light. "A lot has changed, as I told you over the phone. I bought the whole block for almost nothing two years ago and have been using it as my base of operations for the Cartel since."

"What about the police? They do not bother you here?"

Paxton grinned. "Are you kidding? The police think that I'm trying to convert this place into a youth community center so they help me keep hoodlums at bay. I slip them some money every month as a token of my appreciation for their services."

Ares shook his head at how easy the Americans made it for the Cartel to run operations in this country.

The stone path led them to a large rectangular building across a concrete patio behind the church and convent, their opulent structures hiding it from view of the street. Ares spotted a couple of figures resting against the side of the building.

He froze.

"Relax," Paxton said. "I have over fifty million dollars worth of merchandise in there. I have to keep guards around in case punks decide to come and hang out here. At this moment there are ten armed men patrolling the compound."

"Sorry," Ares said. "I am a little paranoid today."

Paxton patted him on the back. "Paranoia saves lives, *hermano*," he added before pointing at the structure. "This used to be the gym." He trained the yellow beam on the door, and producing another key, unbolted a heavy metal door. Reaching inside, he threw a switch, revealing the cavernous interior. The wooden floor of an old basketball court was flanked by industrial shelves that rose to the rafters supporting the roof. Two yellow forklifts were parked off to the side.

"We keep all of the goods at least fifteen feet above the ground level," said Paxton, "in case of an . . . unexpected flood."

Ares grinned. "How about the lights?"

Paxton closed and bolted the door behind them. "Do not worry," he replied. "Not only is this building not visible from the street, but the windows above the bleachers are painted black."

Ares looked up at the large shelves and said, "Looks like you have taken all of the necessary precautions."

"It is not difficult to do with my operating budget. Let me show you the lab and also the medical supplies."

They walked down the middle of the court toward the rear of the gymnasium. Along the way Paxton pointed out several crates. "The cocaine shipment arrives once a month and I hold it here for weekly distribution. We always change the day and time of our operations to keep from attracting attention, and like I said, the police don't bother us and we also make protection payments to key officials at the local U.S. Customs office."

Paxton unlocked a door labeled LOCKER ROOMS, let them through, and closed it behind them after switching off the main lights in the gym.

Inside they found a well stocked mini-infirmary.

"I have to tend the wounds my guards occasionally incur in the execution of their duties," he said, adding, "to minimize attention."

Paxton, assisted by Kishna, disinfected Ares Kulzak's shoulder wound and stitched it with surgical thread. His old friend then administered an antibiotic shot to prevent infection and also inspected his ribs, deciding that nothing was broken, just bruised.

"You're still a fully operational soldier, my friend," Paxton said. "Now, come. Let's go fill your order."

They left the gymnasium and walked down another stone path to a smaller building a few hundred feet away from the gym, along the way spotting more armed guards.

The smell of chemicals tingled his nostrils the moment they walked in what had once been a science lab. Paxton turned on the overheads and also flipped another set of switches. Extractors in the ceiling began to clean the air in the lab.

He spotted the source of the familiar smell on long laboratory tables. Paxton had set up a lab for the development of the kind of explosives that had saved his life this afternoon.

Paxton had also taken a number of precautions, including the removal of anything metallic in the room, as sparks were one of the most common causes of accidental detonations.

Some of the chemicals needed in the manufacture of nitroglycerin, one of the primary ingredients in plastic explosives, lined the shelves above the worktables. But unlike an industrial weapons manufacturing facility, like the ones used by the military, Paxton had to make do for the most part with household chemicals in order to avoid attracting unwanted attention to the operation.

Unfortunately, all modern explosives were a derivative of a nitric acid base, which meant a base of red fuming nitric acid, for which there was no known household substitute in the required 98 percent concentration. But the chemical could still be acquired through the right connections in the chemical and petroleum industry of southern Louisiana.

"This shouldn't take long," he explained, zipping up a heavy-duty lab coat, slipping his hands into long gloves, and donning safety glasses. "I never start mixing them unless I'm filling a specific order."

"How often do you receive such orders?"

He shrugged. "It varies. Sometimes twice a month. Other times more often. Last week I was asked to deliver fifty pounds of TNT to a pier two miles from here. Word was that the stuff went south, to Haiti. Imagine that," he mused. "Ken Paxton, international explosives manufacturer."

Ares approved of Paxton's precautions when handling chemicals. The ingredients required to make blasting gelatin—a form of plastic explosives—were safe by themselves but became highly volatile after mixing, so Paxton only handled them on request.

"I measured the area of the steel hinges securing the gates to the wall this afternoon, after I received your call," Paxton said. "Each one is twelve inches thick by sixteen inches long. I approximated a diagonal cross-section of around eighteen inches or one and a half feet."

"Or about two and a half pounds of explosives per hinge," said Ares, remembering that to calculate the number of pounds of explosives needed to cut through steel one simply squared the diameter of the steel.

"But I won't have time to tamp it," said Paxton, "therefore I'm cubing the amount, meaning just over four pounds per hinge."

Ares agreed.

"Please," Paxton said. "Take those large ice chests on the next table and fill them with dry ice from the bags in the freezer behind you. Use the gloves over the freezer."

Ares and Kishna complied while Paxton began to pour small amounts of fuming nitric acid into five oversized beakers on a table beneath a large extractor, which sucked the fumes out of the room.

Paxton lowered each beaker into an ice chest, carefully packing the dry ice around it to cool the chemical, and then placed a glass thermometer in each beaker.

The ventilation system humming, Ares leaned closer to Kishna to explain the process as Paxton reached for a bottle of sulfuric acid.

"The key to making nitroglycerin is mixing the right chemicals at the proper temperatures," Ares whispered. "First he needs to get the fuming nitric acid to room temperature. That is when he will add sulfuric acid, which is essentially car battery acid."

They observed Paxton as he added what appeared to be three times the amount of sulfuric acid to the fuming nitric acid in each beaker.

"More ice, please," Paxton requested.

Ares and Kishna complied, stuffing more dry ice around each beaker to cool down the mix below thirty degrees Celsius.

"Stand back now, please," Paxton said, his hand holding a medicine dropper, which he used to suck a milky liquid from another beaker.

"He is now adding the nitrating agent to the mixture," Ares said. "In this case it looks like he is using common starch, but sugar, sawdust, lard, cork, and even mercury will work just as well."

Kishna nodded, her green eyes flashing fear and excitement. She had never seen explosives being manufactured, and Ares knew exactly how she felt. Being in the midst of creating explosives conveyed feelings of power and vulnerability.

Holding a bag of ice, Paxton moved back and forth between all ice chests, monitoring the temperature and adding ice as necessary.

"It's critical that he keeps the temperature below thirty degrees Celsius," he said.

"What happens if he doesn't?"

"*Adios muchachos.*"

She braced herself when realizing that Ares wasn't kidding. This was the most dangerous point in the process as the nitration was an exothermic reaction, meaning it produced lots of heat, but the solution had to be kept below thirty degrees for about ten minutes.

Paxton used each thermometer to monitor the temperature and also stir the hissing brew gently until the nitroglycerin formed a layer on top of the acid solution.

Ares watched the procedure with the detached interest of a pro, well aware that if something went wrong he would not even hear the explosion.

After about ten minutes of listening to the whirling extractors, Ken Paxton removed one of the oversized beakers from its ice bath, walking slowly with it to another table, where very carefully and slowly he transferred the entire solution to another beaker partially filled with water. He repeated the process four more times.

Ares stepped up to the last table and watched in satisfaction as the nitroglycerin settled at the bottom, which allowed Paxton to drain most of the acid solution without disturbing the nitroglycerin.

"He now needs to neutralize the remaining acid in the beakers with sodium bicarbonate, which is just baking soda," explained Ares as the mercenary used an eyedropper to add small amounts of sodium bicarbonate, then checked the pH blue litmus paper, and repeated the process over and over.

"The more acidic the solution the more unstable the nitroglycerin will be," Ares said.

"Amazing," she replied.

When Paxton had achieved the right level of alkalinity, he used a large dropper to suck the nitroglycerin from each beaker and store it in another beaker. At the end of forty minutes he had made roughly two liters of nitroglycerin, enough to blow up a few city blocks.

He then mixed twelve parts of nitroglycerin with eighty parts of starch and eight parts of guncotton in a bathtub beyond the tables.

"And that, my dear Kishna," Ares said when Paxton had finished mixing the black and pasty compound, "is how you make high-quality plastic explosives in the field."

"Somewhere around fifty pounds of it," Paxton said before pointing at shelves housing a variety of hardware, from timers and coils of wire, to electrical blasting caps and batteries. "All we need now is a few more items and we will be ready."

Ares stared at the hardware, his mind traveling back to his days in Central America.

Paxton removed his gloves and patted him on the back. "Just like in the old days, *hermano*. Remember?"

Ares nodded, remembering.

T H I R T Y

> > > > >

T I M E   W H E N

> SOAKED IN PERSPIRATION, ARES KULZAK WORKED
diligently in one of a dozen straw huts hidden in the mountains north of San Salvador. Ken Paxton, his mercenary friend, currently retained by the Sandinista government to train Salvadorian Marxist rebels, assisted him in the delicate final steps of making TNT. The explosives were part of a new offensive against high-profile targets on the capital in the hope of boosting morale among the decimated guerrillas after recent defeats at the hands of the American-backed Salvadorian Army and its most-feared division, the *Guardia Nacional.*

"This makes one hundred and twenty pounds," said Paxton, dressed just like Ares, a plain dark-green T-shirt, jungle camouflage pants, and black boots. And just like him, Paxton also wore a thick belt housing a sidearm, a half-dozen spare magazines, and a black hunting knife.

Wiping his brow with his shoulder, Ares reached down for a canteen on the dirt floor and took a few sips. Even in the middle of the night the humidity made it difficult to work, but he could endure it thanks to his conditioning.

"When are they coming to pick it up?" asked Paxton.

"Before dawn," replied Ares, motioning his friend out of the hut and into a muggy night, though a few degrees cooler than inside the stuffy hut.

They walked by an adjacent hut and knelt in front of a bucket filled with water, which they used to wash their faces. Five straight hours making explosives, and they still had at least another two or three to go before they were finished.

"I guess in the end we had to make it all ourselves," Ares complained, frowning.

"Attrition," Paxton said, shrugging. The locals they had trained last week got killed this week by the *Guardia Nacional*, forcing the two military trainers to do it themselves, especially since they could not find any rebels that seemed competent enough to learn.

Paxton pulled out a pack of cigarettes and tilted it in his direction. They lit up and smoked in silence, until they heard a muffled cry and footsteps coming from one of the other huts.

Getting up, they watched two rebels flanking a young woman, probably in her twenties, her dress in shreds, her face bruised, as well as her thighs and arms. It was obvious to Ares that she had been not only beaten but also raped.

But it was the eyes, however, glistening with anger, that caught his attention.

"*Mis capitanes*," said one of the rebels, calling Ares and Paxton by their unofficial ranks of captains. In reality they could have been generals for all that mattered, as there were no higher ranking rebels in the region after the last sweep made by the *Guardia Nacional*. "This *puta* knows a gringo in the American Embassy that provided intelligence to the *Guardia Nacional* last month, resulting in the deaths of many of our comrades. How should we kill her?"

Ares regarded the battered whore, tall, thin, her breasts exposed through the rags, her brown hair matted with dirt and blood. She reeked of body odor and sex. Blood and semen dripped down the inside of her exposed thighs. Beyond the trio, in the small clearing between the huts, Ares saw two men pulling up their pants while laughing.

"Leave her with us," he said. "She might provide us with an opportunity."

The young rebels exchanged a puzzled glance, obviously not aware of the techniques Ares had been trained in in Cuba, where apprehended enemies of the revolution would oftentimes yield a wealth of information in order to save themselves from horrible deaths.

As Paxton stood by watching with interest, Ares took her hands and gently nudged her to sit by the water bucket, using a cotton washcloth to wipe her face clean, then her shoulders, her arms, her legs. Then he offered her a cigarette, which she accepted. He lit it for her, and she closed her eyes while taking a long drag.

"My name is Ares," he finally said, breaking the long silence. "This here is my associate, Ken. What is your name?"

"Ma-Maria . . . Maria Ramirez," she replied, trembling, her lower lip swollen.

One of her eyes was bloodshot and nearly shut. The other, large and brown, regarded her captors with fear and suspicion.

"Well, Maria," he began. "Looks like you have a big problem."

She nodded, her gaze on the ground as she drew from the cigarette, wedged in between two soiled fingers.

"But we might be able to help you," Paxton offered.

She studied them with her one good eye.

"If you help us," said Ares.

"What do you wish to know, *señor?*"

"Your contact at the American Embassy," Ares replied, well aware that it was probably the CIA, which typically recruited foreign nationals like her to do the dirty work for them.

Dropping her stare to the ground once more, she said, "What would I get in return?"

"My associate here has contacts in Guatemala and Mexico. We can get you as far north as Monterrey. From there you can try to cross the border at Tijuana or any of a dozen other places."

"But that takes money, *señor.*"

Ares was impressed. The gringos knew how to pick their informants.

"If the information is valuable, my friend will also arrange for a coyote to take you across," Ares said, trying to put himself in her shoes. Such opportunity at a moment when she had expected another beating and more sexual punishment would seem like a heavenly blessing.

"He goes by Tommy, *señor.*"

"Do you know how to contact this . . . Tommy?"

"*Sí, señor.*"

"How often do you meet him?"

"About once a month, unless I have important information."

"Can you arrange a meeting this week?"

"If you can get me to the *Estados Unidos, señor,* I can arrange a meeting tomorrow."

THIRTY-ONE

> > > > >

LONG AGO

> "HERMANO? COULD YOU HELP ME WITH THESE?"

Paxton's hands holding blasting caps and wire replaced the scruffy image of Maria Ramirez.

Ares said, "Yes, of course," and took the detonation hardware from him.

"I need six feet of wire per cap."

Kishna assisting him, Ares went to work on a nearby table, fingers moving automatically, uncoiling and cutting wire before connecting the standing ends to the blasting caps.

As he did so, his mind once again wandered, recalling the meeting Maria had set up in that small town outside of San Salvador.

Behind an old church.

Long ago.

THIRTY-TWO

> > > > >

CLOSE CALL

> MIKE RYAN FIRST SAW A GLARE BREAKING UP THE darkness that had swallowed his world. Shadows shifted about in the blurry beyond, but he couldn't make them out. Shapeless figures glided in a glowing fog to the tempo of the pounding behind his eyes.

He blinked, slowly clearing the cloud, forcing his attention beyond the pain, noticing a lattice-like pattern of black-delineated gray hexagons.

Ceiling tiles.

"He's coming around. Get the doctor in here."

A familiar voice. A hazy face framed by cascading hair.

"Honey? Can you hear me?"

Slowly, like a grainy picture coming into focus, Ryan saw the soft features of Victoria emerging through, her eyes finding his.

"Vic? What are you—"

"Shhh. Don't speak."

He felt her hand caressing the side of his face, her touch soothing. "How long have I—"

"Almost twenty-four hours," she replied. "I got here as soon as I heard."

Another face appeared next to her, but the magnified eyes behind a pair of thick glasses could not quite converge on Ryan.

Walter.

"The doctor's coming, Mike," said STG's system administrator.

"Hey . . . Walt," he said with some effort.

A white-haired man displaced Victoria and Walter. He was stolid, eyes lacking emotion while inspecting him.

"Hello, Mr. Ryan. I'm Doctor McKenzie. I need to check a few things," he said, using a finger to gently lift Ryan's right eyelid, flashing a penlight at him, its beam piercing right down his optical nerve.

Ryan jerked away at the white-hot pain.

"Hey!" shouted Victoria Ryan. "Stop that! Can't you see that's hurting him!"

Get them, Vic, Ryan thought, breathing deeply, turning his head as his wife placed herself between the bed and the doctor she had just shoved out of the way. Even seven months pregnant Victoria Ryan posed a serious threat to anyone screwing with her husband.

"But, ma'am. I have to check his reflexes."

"Not *that* way you won't! If that's all you're going to do you might as well walk right back out of here, because you're not coming anywhere near him!"

Beyond Victoria, he could now see very clearly the plump doctor flanked by a pair of nurses. Walter hung somewhere in the background, along with a couple of CCTF agents that Karen Frost no doubt had posted for his protection.

"Please, ma'am, I really need to—"

"Aspirin," Ryan mumbled. "Headache."

That's all he had to say before Victoria started ordering everyone around for the pain medication, which arrived in nanoseconds, accompanied by a cup of water, which she helped him drink.

"Thanks, Vic," he said, breathing deeply again, quickly coming around, managing to lift a finger and placing it over his right temple, slowly making a circle.

Victoria gently moved his finger aside and took over the temple-rubbing responsibility. She smiled at him and he forced the end of his lips to curve up.

"You're in big trouble, mister," she whispered, still smiling.

"But, Vic, I—"

She pressed an index finger against his lips. "Not now. First you get better, then you're going to get it for doing this to us." She took his hand and placed it on her belly. "This baby is not growing up without a father, Mike. You hear me?"

Ryan regarded his wife. She had always been naturally beautiful, but this pregnancy made her radiant, her hazel eyes full of life.

Or full of fire, depending on the situation.

But Ryan also remembered the advice her gynecologist had given them just last week: Cut down on the level of excitement. Victoria's body, although slim and buffed from a lifetime of outdoor sports, wasn't ideal for carrying a baby and the longer she got into the pregnancy cycle the bigger the chance that sudden emotional or physical stress could rupture her water bag and trigger a premature delivery.

"Ma'am? Please, I have to check him. I promise no more bright lights."

She gave Doctor McKenzie an exasperated look before stepping aside just enough to let him through, but remaining within striking distance. In a way Ryan felt sorry for him.

"All right, Mr. Ryan. Try to follow my finger," he said, holding an index finger about a foot from Ryan's face and slowly shifting it around in every direction.

"Good, Mike. Very good. Now, could you move your toes for me?"

Ryan did, or at least he thought he did. He lacked the strength to lift his head and see them for himself.

"Very good, Mike. Now, can you tell me your full name?"

"Michael Patrick Ryan," he replied. *Does he think I'm brain dead?*

"And what month is it?"

"April . . . look, pal, I'm okay. Just have this nasty headache."

He felt fingers applying light pressure against the bottom of his wrist and saw the doctor checking his watch, then nodding and saying to Victoria, "He's out of his coma alright, but not out of the woods. He could drift away any moment."

"*Coma? Drift away?*"

"Look, honey," Victoria said. "Whatever happened to you when you were plugged into the computer halted part of your normal brain activity, at least according to the tests they ran. Now we need to make sure that everything is ticking up there again." She patted the side of his head with two fingers.

"I'm telling you I'm fine," Ryan insisted.

"Do you remember what happened before you passed out, Mr. Ryan?"

Ryan remembered *exactly* what had happened. He had been too careless while walking through a digital mine field and was lucky to be anything but a vegetable following the EMP strike. His only guess was that MPS-Ali must have somehow absorbed part of the pulse that had nearly reformatted his brain. Measuring his words to avoid giving away any specifics to the case—per his agreement with Karen Frost—Ryan told them enough to get this doctor off his back and also appease Victoria's obvious concerns, but without revealing anything confidential to the case, adding at the end, "I guess a digital EMP nailed me before I could jack out."

Dr. McKenzie gave Victoria a brief nod. "Well, I'm going to run some tests later, but on the surface he appears to be okay. You're a lucky man, Mr. Ryan."

"Great, Doc, thanks," Ryan said, managing to sit up, his strength quickly returning—as well as the realization that the cyberterrorists were still at large. He was more determined now than ever before to nail them, especially for trying to fry his noodle. "Now, could you excuse us for a moment, please. I need to speak to my associates in private about a real-time problem."

At that moment Walter and the agents stepped forward.

The doctor got the message, gave Ryan a brief smile, and said, "Be careful, Mr. Ryan. You might not be so lucky next time." And he was gone, along with the nurses, leaving Ryan with Victoria, Walter, and the CCTF contingent.

Wearing a green hospital gown, Ryan shifted to the side of the bed, placing his feet on the cold tile floor. He took his wife's hand and gently nudged her to sit next to him, telling her with his eyes that a personal chat would have to wait until he had taken care of business. She understood and complied, sitting by his side, resting an arm over her belly while facing the trio overlooking them. For a moment Victoria reminded Ryan of a lioness protecting her small pride.

But wasn't that the job of the male lion?

Ryan shrugged and said, "Say, Walt, is the power grid okay?"

"So far so good," replied Walter, his bulky glasses hanging on the ridge of his long nose, his eyes looking at everything but Ryan even though he knew the guy was supposed to be staring straight at him. "Your mock attack worked beautifully, Mike, certainly getting SWOASIS's attention and forcing them to shut down all external passwords. What in the world possessed you to do that at the last moment?"

Ryan looked at Victoria before lowering his voice a few decibels while grinning. "Can you keep a secret, Walt?"

"Yes, of course."

"I used to be quite the hacker myself, until this lady here forced me down the straight and narrow."

"Well," the middle-aged computer scientist said, "I'm glad you're on our side now. The SWOASIS network has been spared the horror of San Antonio."

"For now, Walt. But let's not claim victory yet."

The crossed eyes, magnified by the Coke-bottle glasses, shifted about in apparent confusion. "What do you mean?"

"When I was jacked in, I saw what appeared to be a dormant virus being deployed. They may have managed to inject the network with this virus, which could be just in an incubation stage," Ryan said, glancing at Victoria, before shifting his gaze back to Walter and frowning. "It could be stealthily replicating as we speak and we wouldn't know it until it struck."

"But, Mike, the last report we received thirty minutes ago from SWOASIS indicates no unusual reduction in disk space at the servers of the utility companies."

One of the telltale signs of a virus invasion in a hard drive is a reduction in space due to the virus gobbling it up during the replication process.

"I know at least a half dozen viruses that will read the time stamps of data files in a system and compress them to make room for cloning, thus avoiding raising any alarms."

"All right," Walter said. "I'll have them check for that."

"There are also viruses that will replace part of a data file with themselves, thus avoiding the requirement for compressing files altogether. They avoid detection by also altering the files that haven't been used in a while."

"Can they be found running a DIFF between the current data files in the network and an archive from a week ago?"

DIFF was a Unix command to compare two files and report any differences. By comparing the existing data files in a network, which were suspect of a virus corruption, with files from a week or so ago, before the virus attack, the result should produce the virus itself—along with any valid changes made to the files since that time.

"Maybe," said Ryan. "But the viruses may have also affected the system's applications, including programs like DIFF, meaning the results you get could be misleading, and even then you will still have to comb through the report to eliminate all legal changes done since the last archive before you can be sure that you have isolated a virus."

"Well, Mike," Walter said, throwing his hands up in the air. "What other options do we have?"

Dropping his eyebrows and lightly grimacing while briefly glancing at Victoria, Ryan said, "I would have to rebuild MPS-Ali and jack in again to really gain—"

"*What?*" barked Victoria.

"Well, honey, there is no other way to—"

Her eyes filling with anger, she added, "Perhaps you *are* insane! Maybe part of your brain *is* dead after all!"

"Leave us for a moment, please," Ryan said.

The trio backed away in a hurry.

Victoria slit her eyes and looked ready to devour him.

"Vic," Ryan calmly said, holding her hands in his. "I have no choice in the matter. If those bastards are successful and manage to bring down that grid, it will be a disaster. Imagine for a moment the kind of havoc such a blackout would cause in a metropolis. The body pileup; the wounded; the property damage. It will be out of this world. The criminals would turn a city like L.A. inside out in twenty-four hours."

She wasn't anywhere near convinced. "The damned government has plenty of programmers, Mike. Why can't *they* worry about that? Why in the *hell* do we pay these bastards so much tax?"

"That's the thing, Vic," he said in the most soothing and reassuring tone he could muster. "Their tools are limited at best, and in many cases antiquated. Their programmers, unfortunately, are really not of the caliber of those in the private industry, and especially of the quality of the criminal hackers employed by these cyberterrorists. We can't just sit still and let them do it to us, honey. The stakes are way too high. I mean, have you *seen* this town?" He extended a thumb over his right shoulder at the window behind them, from which the smoldering Alamo City could be seen clearly.

Her eyes, wet with anger, darted toward the window.

"We're at war, Vic, just like back in 2001," he continued. "And like it or not, I happen to be one of the poor bastards with the right combination of weapons and skills to land in the front lines. This is no different than our boys in Vietnam or Desert Storm. We're fighting a new wave of tech-based terrorism . . . call it *tech*rrorism if you please, and I'm one of the best soldiers we have."

Lowering her gaze to the white tile floor, she said, "But why does it have to be you?"

"Because I happen to be so damned good at it."

"Obviously not *that* good, or we wouldn't be having this conversation."

"It's all part of the game, Vic. You can't win every battle, so you take your licks, learn from them, and go on."

Victoria dropped her fine brows at him while crossing her arms. "It's *not* a game, Mike. According to Dr. McKenzie, you came this close." She spaced the thumb and index finger of her right hand a quarter of an inch apart and shoved that in front of his face. "*This* fucking close, from . . . from . . . *damn* you, Mike. I don't deserve this. Our *baby* doesn't deserve this!" A single tear ran down the right side of her face. She brushed it away while taking a deep breath, lips compressed as she burned him with a green laser stare.

Mike remembered what the gynecologist had said about stressing her out during the next couple of months. At the same time, he could not just let these terrorists go for a cyber joyride across America. Arranging his face into a mask of compassion, Ryan said, "Look, Vic, it's like this. I either put my life on the line and do this, or people will die. And make no mistake about it. There *will* be many deaths, just like it happened here, or in New York in 2001. I'm talking kids of all ages, adults, the elderly. I'm talking about mothers losing their children, about kids being orphaned. I mean, have you taken a look at the death roster yet?"

She slowly nods.

"It's quite sobering, isn't it, and the worst part is that it makes the terrorist strikes against the World Trade Center and the Pentagon look like the appetizer. Almost twenty-seven thousand people got incinerated in this town, Vic. Do you realize that?"

She nodded again.

"Twenty-seven thousand people, Vic. It has a way of quickly changing your perspective, your priorities. And now Melbourne is part of this mess. I sure as hell plan to do anything—*absolutely anything*—to prevent another San Antonio. So, that's what it boils down to. That's why I took a leave of absence. That's why I'm putting my life on the line. And that's why I'm asking you, as my wife, as the mother of my baby, to *please* support me on this."

Victoria stood and went up to the windows. Ryan watched her eyes staring into the beyond, standing still, like a wax statue, brown hair falling below her narrow shoulders, hands beneath the tiny protuberance holding their gift from God.

"There's something else," he said. "I have reason to believe that the agent that attacked me was intelligent."

She turned around. "Intelligent?"

He nodded. "As in a direct violation of the Turing directive from the Department of Defense. The AI construct was under a digital spell from one of MPS-Ali's viruses but it managed to break free, and when MPS-Ali hit him again, the construct had already learned how to make itself immune to it. It looks like there's a supercomputer out there running loose without our inhibitor software. If that's the case, I have to find it and kill it. I also need to contact the Society to report this violation, though there isn't much they can do without more information—which I can only get by jacking back into the network."

"All right, Mike," she finally said in her deep voice. "But if you get hurt again, you better *pray* you become an eggplant because if the terrorists don't kill you, *I* will for putting me through this hell."

THIRTY-THREE

> > > > >

REAMING

> NO ONE LIKES TO HAVE HIS RIGHTS READ, ESPE-
cially the way we've been busting our asses, but that's exactly what my old CIA boss
Randy Cramer is fixing to do as he steps into the small conference room in the company of a couple of aides. The CCTF has taken over part of the fourth floor of a federal building in downtown New Orleans, where our FBI brothers—probably out of
pity—provided us with a dozen offices, plus fax machines, phones, and computer ter-
minals to help us set up a temporary base of operations to find the missing terrorist
and his accomplice driving the getaway car, whom an agent described as a dark-
skinned woman with closely cropped blond hair and light-colored eyes.

I haven't seen the old bastard for some time, ever since he masterfully washed his
hands from the *huevos rancheros* disaster and we went our separate ways—him to pro-
motions, fame, and fortune, and yours truly to a penalty tour of the lesser regions of
our planet.

Almost as tall as me but thinner, Cramer walks in dressed in a dark double-
breasted suit, shiny black shoes, and a designer tie—a hell of a contrast to our stained
shorts and T-shirts since we have not found the time to change after Kulzak turned
that section of the Warehouse District into a war zone.

Karen and I have been swamped with police reports, false sightings, questions
from the media, and even a call from the governor, who held the CCTF, and in par-

ticular its parent agency, the FBI, accountable for the likely decline in tourism in the coming months.

A full head of silver hair crowns a well-tanned face showing only the handsome damage of too many weekends sailing in Chesapeake Bay. Rumor around the Agency was that he owned a forty-foot schooner. Although he is around ten years my senior, meaning mid-fifties, the well-groomed—and probably even tweaked—asshole looks my age.

"Tom," he says in his patrician voice, his feeble attempt to try to sound like a Kennedy. "It's good to see you again."

Before I know it I'm shaking this guy's hand—though I make a mental note to wash before supper.

"Agent Frost," he says dryly with a single nod.

"Mr. Cramer," Karen replies with matching warmth.

Then there's that awkward silence that comes from the knowledge that a reaming is near, kind of like the calm before the storm. Cramer motions his aides to wait outside.

And then there were three.

Sitting down across from us at a rectangular table, Cramer crosses his legs and rests his hands on his lap. "Quite a mess you've got here," he finally says.

Warning, warning. He is using the *you* instead of *we*, meaning he's already distancing himself from our activities.

"Mr. Cramer," Karen says. "We were very close today. We took as many precautions as we—"

Cramer raises an I-don't-want-to-hear-it open palm at her, then adds, "I'm afraid we're beyond that now, Agent Frost. This situation has deteriorated to the point that serious consideration is being applied to courses of action that display statistically higher probabilities of success."

"In *English*, Randy," I say.

Cramer shoots me a look, which I bounce right back at him. Face it, people, compared to the way he has fucked me in the past, there's little more this man can do to me, so I don't need to be nice to him.

"We're considering new leadership for the CCTF field operations," he says.

"Last time I checked you didn't get to make those decisions, sir," said Karen in a gutsy move that gained my instant admiration. "Is Director Meek aware of your intentions to replace me?"

"*And* me," I add, before I proceed to remind him of our last conversation right after the Melbourne fiasco. If Karen is out, so am I.

Karen looks at me in a way that I hope Cramer didn't notice.

If he did he doesn't reflect it in his stare as he replies, "I informed Director Meek and also Vice President Vance Fitzgerald, whom the president has appointed as White House liaison to this investigation, that it was my intention to come down here and get a firsthand sense for the ongoing operation before I felt comfortable in making any recommendations to them."

"Meaning you haven't made any changes yet?" I ask.

"Correct," he replies. "But make no mistake about it. If at the end of this conversation, which, I have to admit, has already started on the wrong foot, you fail to convince me that you know what you're doing, I will get you both replaced . . . just like that." He snaps his fingers, and I feel like snapping his aristocratic neck.

After a moment of silence, in which I take the time to count to ten and say a little prayer for self-control, Cramer says, "Now, why doesn't one of you start filling me in on what took place from the moment you landed in New Orleans this morning?"

Karen takes the lead, covering in great detail our arrival and initial meeting with the FBI and the local police. She explains how forces were deployed around the target's third-floor apartment, how we approached it, and how things went to hell a moment later.

"And he just vanished?" Cramer asked.

"Just like that," I say, snapping my fingers while slitting my eyes at him.

He ignores me and turns to Karen. "How much does the press know about this?"

"Not a thing," she replies, "though I did promise them a statement before nine so they can have something ready for the ten o'clock news."

"No one talks to the press but me," Cramer says in a tone that left no room for negotiation.

"Just be sure they leave our names out of it," I remind him, not wishing for Kulzak to know who we are, though he might already if there's indeed a mole in our ranks.

"I know how to do my job, Tom. The question is, do you still remember how to do yours?"

"We know how to do our job, Randy. The question you should be asking is how in the hell did Ares Kulzak know we were coming?"

Cramer drops his eyelids at me.

Before he can reply, I add, "As Karen described, everything was done by the book. No one but those with a need to know were aware of what we were up to. Not even the cops on the scene really knew who we were going to arrest, or the exact house. But Kulzak knew we were coming. The bastard knew, Randy. Someone tipped him off."

"What are you suggesting, Tom?"

"I'm not suggesting anything. I'm telling you that it sure smells as if he has someone on the inside, and that someone warned him about our move."

Cramer crosses his arms and looks away before saying, "If I remember correctly, exactly eight people knew about Mike Ryan's breakthrough—aside from Ryan and his associate at STG, of course. We are three of those eight. The others are the heads of the FBI, the CIA, the NOPD chief, the vice president, and the president. Which one of those are you suggesting is the mole, Tom?"

I shrug.

"Could it be possible that Kulzak had a spotter out there and saw you coming?"

"We were dressed like tourists," says Karen, "down to the shorts, T-shirts, and cameras." She points at her clothes and then at mine. "I really don't see how."

"How long was it from the point you stopped in front of the building to when you went in and heard them in the garage?"

"Thirty seconds tops," I say, having been asked that question about a dozen times by the FBI and the NOPD today.

"Certainly not enough time to pull together such an elaborate counterattack," says Karen.

"For your average crook, perhaps," says Cramer. "But we're dealing with Ares Kulzak."

Well aware that anything I say here will most definitely not only be used against me but twisted and taken out of context if it meant career advancement for Cramer at the price of my demise, I say, "It still feels like an awfully short amount of time to go from Hutton's apartment, down the stairs, and into the garage."

"But is it physically *possible* to do?"

I close my eyes, realizing exactly where the guy's going with this: trying to prove that we blew it by tipping him of our presence, giving him time to counterattack.

Cramer adds, "The reason why I'm asking these questions is because if your mole theory was correct, I don't see why Kulzak would take such a chance and remain in Hutton's apartment if he knew you were going to pay him a visit."

Which is the same argument Karen made when I first told her about the possibility of a mole. For a moment I begin to question my own opinion of why things went to shit.

"Maybe he got the warning a few minutes before we struck," I say. "Maybe there was a delay in his communications channel."

"I see," says Cramer. "So, let me get this straight. You believe that one of the people who knew about the Gary Hutton connection, say someone very close to the office of the director of the FBI, heard the news and leaked it to Kulzak a few minutes before you arrived."

I don't reply, realizing that it does sound pretty thin, but then again, I don't see how he could have possibly spotted us until we stopped in front of the building.

"I think I've heard all I needed to hear from you two," Cramer says. "Let the CCTF graveyard shift and the NOPD continue looking for Kulzak. In the meantime, I will review all of the information available and also chat with the NOPD chief and a few other people before I catch my plane back to Washington in two hours. Tomorrow I'll issue my recommendation to the FBI director and the vice president."

"What about a statement to the press?" asks Karen.

"Hold them until tomorrow," he says. "I want to keep a lid on things until I get the chance to—"

"Lid on things?" I say. "Wake up, Randy. The lid's been off since Kulzak smoked the Warehouse District this afternoon! We *have* to tell them something. Otherwise they will *make up* something."

"I'll think about it." He gets up and leaves the room without another word, closing the door behind him.

I turn to Karen, whose face is the color of a boiled crab.

"Let me buy you a drink," I tell her. "Give us both a chance to vent a little."

She gets up, looks at the door, at me, and back at the door, her nostrils flaring as she breaths very hard. Then she closes her eyes and nods.

"A drink would be great, Tom. Just *fucking* great."

THIRTY-FOUR

> > > > >

GETTING PERSONAL

> I'VE HAD TO WAIT OVER SEVENTY-TWO HOURS FOR this, but I have to admit that the wait has been worth it. Karen and I are having drinks at a small corner table in the bar of the Royal Orleans, an old French Quarter hotel. Our team continues to comb the city, but as I have suspected all along, Ares Kulzak is gone, vanished. We eventually found the missing dark Lexus sedan on the third level of the Harrah's Casino parking garage. The NOPD plus some of our agents spent the following hour evacuating the garage as well as the adjoining casino before allowing the bomb squad to approach the vehicle. Fortunately, the car wasn't wired, sparing us the horror of another Melbourne—though our boys came close to getting lynched by a mob of angry gamblers.

I sipped my scotch and water, my lips tingling with delight.

"It's almost pornographic," Karen says, pointing at me with the cigarette she had just lit. Up until a minute ago I had no idea the woman smoked. Maybe our two failed raids, the session with Cramer, plus the two glasses of wine that she has already consumed got her into a smoking mood.

"Pornographic?" I ask, regarding her over the rim of my glass. I guess I'm going to miss that freckle as well as those eyes, which are growing glazy from the alcohol.

"Your face. The way you're holding that drink," she replies, wedging the cigarette between the index and middle fingers of her right hand. "You'd think you're . . . I don't know, doing something else."

I take another sip from this heavenly drink, my throat and chest warming up. "A stiff drink and catching people like Kulzak are the *only* things I have left that provide me with some level of stimulation." I glance back at the bar and catch the young waitress who served Karen her first drink looking at me. She smiles and I smile in return.

"Well," Karen says after observing my silent exchange with the blonde. "And silly me thought that all spooks engaged in plenty of . . . *extracurricular* activities."

I stare at her brown eyes, and I'm not sure what I see. The woman sure is attractive, though a bit on the harsher side of the spectrum, and she does know how to control her facial expressions. One moment you can almost read what's on her mind and the next she just locks it all away.

I shrug, too damned tired to care. I'm going to finish this drink and maybe another one, and then I'm heading up to the plush king-size bed of my hotel room on the third floor of this expensive joint. For once Uncle Sam spared no expense. With luck, a comfortable bed, plus the exhaustion, combined with the alcohol and the remaining humming in my ears, will mask the jazz flowing out of a dozen clubs plus the constant chattering of the crowded streets, and send me on my merry way to deep sleep. I could use the earplugs I always travel with, but the alcohol is more fun.

"So," I ask. "What do you think is going to happen next?"

"You'll probably head back to Langley."

"And you?"

"Who knows," she says. "Maybe it's time to move on. I'm too damned old to be chasing bad guys."

"I doubt that seriously."

"What do you mean?" she asks, sipping more wine. "We screwed up, Tom. We had him and we blew it. He escaped our trap and managed to do so while also killing two of our guys and wounding several others, and don't forget the blast. It's got the city of New Orleans up in arms."

Despite my warning, Cramer didn't allow us to release a statement to the press. Just as I warned him, lacking any input from us, the press did what it always does in such situations: made up something, which in this case wasn't too far from the truth. They spun a story on the ten o'clock news about organized crime and international terrorism operating in New Orleans. City officials, claiming that tourism—this town's bread and butter—would decline because of the explosion, wanted to sue the CCTF, which means suing the FBI, for negligence. Somehow one of the stations got ahold of my name as well as Karen's and decided to include them in their report, which was also released to the news wire thirty minutes later. Now Kulzak knows who we are. That article made us targets for life.

"How long you say you were in the Bureau?" I ask.

"Over twenty years."

I continue sipping my first drink and my gloomy mood suddenly brightens up a bit. I think the blond waitress has something to do with it. Although I would never engage in carnal pleasures with someone so young, the knowledge that she has found me attractive has cranked up my ego a notch or two. Maybe returning to my hole in Langley after this stormy three days is all for the best. Perhaps I'm still marketable enough to have a shot at a relationship.

"Why do you ask?"

"Just wondering what kept you there for so long."

"What kept me here so long," she says, almost to herself, her eyes distant. She reaches down for her glass of white wine, takes a sip, lightly smacks her lips together, and says, "What kept you at the CIA for two decades?"

"That's been asked and answered. Besides, didn't your mother tell you it's impolite to answer a question with a question?"

She sips more wine and says, "I didn't think I would get out of answering that so easily. Then again, what would you say if I told you that was none of your business?" She takes a final drag of her cigarette and crushes it in a round brass ashtray.

I lift my half drained glass at her, swirl the ice a bit around to mix up this heavenly brew, and take another sip. Perhaps the alcohol is quickly thinning my elephant skin. Normally nothing gets through my hide, but right now, after saving her little ass from being blown to pieces by Kulzak's grenade *and* using my own body to cushion her fall, I have to admit that I am taking that remark a bit on the personal side.

"I always make an attempt to learn as much as possible about the person I'm risking my life with," I finally say. "A little knowledge about how someone thinks can go a long way in a situation. Then again, after today's snafu I doubt we'll be sharing any more exciting moments." I drain my glass, set it down, and flag the cute waitress for a second one as she briskly trots by.

A long silence follows, and I don't mind it. After all, the ball is in her court. I'm just waiting for my drink, which arrives just as the taste of the last one starts to leave my mouth.

"My husband and I were working a case a long time ago," she says the moment Blondie leaves us alone, "a conspiracy between the private sector and elements of the Pentagon. The bastards planted a bomb in his car. There was very little left for me to bury."

As I just stare at her, Karen drinks the remaining half of her wineglass in one long swig before using it as a signaling device for Blondie, who comes rushing down with the bottle, pouring her another one. Then she grabs her pack of cigarettes, lights up, and adds, "They skipped the country."

"Where did they go?"

"Colombia."

"Drug related?"

Somewhere between alternating sips and drags she says, "It actually wasn't, but they thought they were going to find a safe haven there after I cracked their operation in the States. They were wrong."

"How long ago was that?"

"Over ten years ago." She stops dragging and intensifies the sipping.

This little chat is obviously upsetting her, but she doesn't seem to be in any hurry to end it, so I decide to press a little more. "I'll take it that the FBI was able to work out an extradition deal with the Colombian government?"

The sips are quickly turning into swigs, which drain her fourth glass. She flashes it at the waitress. At this point I'm beginning to get a little concerned about her. Those brown eyes are rapidly losing focus. I can handle three scotches before my body mass starts to feel it. I get shit-faced at around the fifth or sixth one. She probably weighs less than half my weight and has already passed me.

"No deal," she says, her voice slurring. "We didn't try to get one, and to tell you the truth I wanted no deal from the Colombians. Bastards always want something in return, even after all the aid we give them."

"But I thought you said you nailed them."

"You bet your ass I did." Fire glows brightly behind the alcohol haze as she works on her fifth glass, her lips as red as a cherry and quite moist. She looks about her, says, "Man, it's hot in here," and proceeds to roll up the sleeves of her blouse to her elbows, then unbuttons the top two buttons down to her cleavage, revealing the white-lace bra I had noticed before.

"How did you do that?"

She looks at me blankly. "Do what?"

"Nail them."

"Oh, that," she stares into the distance for a moment. "I took a leave of absence from the Bureau. Four weeks. I did it in two and then had me a long and relaxing Caribbean cruise."

"Karen," I say, leaning forward, resting my elbows on the table. "*How* did you do it?"

"Tracked them down. You can buy anybody's cooperation down there . . . with the mighty dollar," she says, her pupils dilating. She's beginning to glide through her words, almost singing them, skipping a syllable here and there. "And when that doesn't work . . . there's the almighty Beretta. That'll get you all of the . . . assistance you need."

"Where did you find them?"

"Mountaintop villa . . . used to belong to some drug dealer."

Dreading the answer, I ask the question anyway. "How did you kill them?"

"Two shots each," she says casually, though her slur is definitely gaining on her ability to articulate. "First one in the balls and then another one . . . in the head . . . though I let them squeal for a while . . . like pigs . . . had to make sure they knew who was killing them." And with that the fifth glass of wine is also history.

I sit there holding my drink, watching the ice slowly melt into a shot of scotch I no longer feel like drinking. This woman went on her own to a foreign country, tracked down her husband's murderers, and paid them back in kind.

Boy, you don't hear that every day. I raise my glass at her. "To swift justice."

She glares at me, her eyes filled with pride and that something else I'd rather not think about. I also have another rule: No sex with a drunk woman, and Karen Frost is already well past that point in my book.

"Cramer," she says. "He's going to crucify us tomorrow, right?"

I set my glass down and lean back on the table, dreading to tell her what's on my mind.

"You can be honest, Tom. Please . . . I need to know."

"All right," I say, looking straight into those glistening brown eyes, seeing through them. She is scared, man, and I don't blame her. Over twenty years with the Bureau and now a thing like this. "First thing Cramer is going to do is find a way to distance himself from the actions committed by us here. When did you notify him of our exact plans in New Orleans?"

"Well, he knew that we were headed for New Orleans while we were still in Melbourne."

"No, I mean, when did he learn that we had pinpointed Gary Hutton's home?"

"Oh, two hours before the raid. I called in to let him know that we had a break-through and were about to act on it. He said he would report the finding to his superiors and wished me good luck."

"Was there a written exchange?"

"Nope."

"I hate to tell you this, but unless there are written records—transcripts—of his communications with us, or we can find a witness, the content of any conversations you two may have had could be slightly adjusted to show that you were acting according to the on-site responsibility granted to you by the CCTF."

"But he knew what we were going to do because I told him, and he gave me his blessing, his *sanction*, as you would call it. Otherwise he should have called it off."

"That may have worked in the FBI, but you forget that Cramer is CIA, or *former* CIA, but nevertheless a spook at heart, and I know what's going through his mind right now. Trust me, Karen. He's going to sell us out big time. I've been his fall guy before. I know a holiday sale when I see one and this one is going to be bigger than the day after Thanksgiving."

"I feared as much," she says. "I guess I had higher hopes that the CCTF would . . . ah, fuck it." She holds up her empty glass for the world to see.

Blondie walks down the nearly deserted bar in her cute little black outfit holding the bottle of wine. She winks at me.

Great. Here I am, with two women signaling like I'm some sort of landing jet-liner, but one's too young and the other's too drunk.

Blondie reluctantly pours Karen another glass before strategically retreating to the counter.

Karen pulls out another cigarette but her thumb keeps slipping off the lighter, her motions becoming sloppy, uncoordinated.

I take the lighter from her hands and flick a flame on the first try. Cigarette in mouth, she inches toward it, struggling to hold the tip steady, missing the target a couple of times, finally lighting up before drawing in deeply, exhaling through her nostrils.

"So, Tom . . . what are my choices?"

"From where I'm sitting, I see two. You could resign immediately, before Cramer has his discussion with the FBI and the White House tomorrow. That would signal an honorable acceptance of your mistake and most likely guarantee you full retirement benefits."

"Dammit, Tom. I'm . . . I'm only forty-three!" she shouts, slapping the table. "I'm too fucking young to retire!"

People at the other end of the quiet bar stare in our direction. I wave a hand in silent apology before saying, "All right, but let's keep it down. You asked me for options, right? I'm going to give them to you, but you need to behave. Deal?"

She exhales heavily, pushing out her lower lip, ruffling the bangs hanging over her forehead as she looks away. "Okay, okay. I'll keep it down. What's my other option?"

"You fight back. You go to the FBI director and present your side of this and then let the chips fall where they may. The risk here is that if you lose you could get fired from the CCTF without any benefits. You would be essentially on your own."

She crosses her arms and legs and tosses her head to the left, toward a courtyard beyond the glass window next to our table.

"Terrific," she says, eyelids half closed while drinking more wine in between drags. "There isn't a . . . *third* option by any chance . . . is there?"

I sure can't think of one. She finishes her wine and signals the waitress for another one.

Blondie is about to pour but stops when realizing that Karen can hardly keep her head up. The young girl looks at me for direction.

You know you got to be hopelessly shit-faced when a bar in the French Quarter doesn't want to serve you more booze.

I shake my head before telling Karen, "Bar's closed, boss."

Blondie gets her answer and walks away.

"Now," I add. "Why don't we head on up?"

Karen refuses to accept the fact that she has allowed herself to get drunk and makes a failed attempt at getting up. It's certainly a sight to see. I catch her on her way down, keeping her from bruising herself against the table and slate floor. And just like that I'm holding her in my arms, like a newlywed couple.

"Twenty-two years, Tom," she whispers, her breath reeking of wine and the raw oysters we had before the booze. "Cramer is going to . . . fry me tomorrow, isn't he?"

I really hate to tell her the truth at this point, especially with her emotions already coating her sleeves. What's even worse is not what Cramer might do tomorrow, but what *Kulzak* is going to do to us after Cramer and his allies in the government are through chewing us out.

I choose to keep that to myself, deciding that this woman has had enough to worry about as it is.

"Yep," she says. "Fry me . . . and . . . and . . . there's . . . there's nothing I can do."

"You need some rest. I'll take you to your room," I say, heading out of the bar, ignoring a few curious stares, praying we don't stumble upon someone from the CCTF or the Bureau.

The more I hold Karen Frost the sorrier I feel for her. In the eyes of Washington she was the one in charge of field operations, and the mistakes in Melbourne and New Orleans are all hers. Cramer will see to it that that's how it goes down. I was blamed for just one screwup with the *huevos rancheros* incident and look at what happened. They're not going to give her another chance.

But then again, when it comes to bagging Ares Kulzak, you need a heck of a buffer because the bastard's as slippery as those damned oysters back at the bar, and guys like Cramer—and the folks in the White House for that matter—just don't appreciate what we're up against.

"What . . . am I . . . going to do . . . Tommy?"

Tommy? Only my closest pals at the Agency call me that.

Her eyes are closed.

"You go on," I say, realizing she won't be remembering any of this tomorrow but choosing to dispense the advice anyway. "You don't let those bastards get to you. Trust me, I know what I'm talking about, having lived through one of Cramer's witch-hunts."

"CCTF agents . . . have . . . died on my watch," she murmurs. "And they were all so . . . young."

I was waiting for that one to surface, and the sad thing is that it will continue to surface for the rest of her life. To this day I still have nightmares about Jerry Martinez.

"They would still be alive if they had gotten the chance to *learn* something," I say. "Problem is the Bureau, lacking enough seasoned hands, throws these kids at the wolves way too soon. I'm amazed Paul Stone has made it this far."

"I would also be . . . dead . . . if it weren't for you." Karen is now drooling while talking. A string of saliva makes a diagonal bridge from the corner of her mouth to the collar of her blouse.

Flattery always makes me nervous. I'd rather get reamed than praised. At least with a scolding you know where you stand, but a compliment could be given for any one of many reasons, the least of which being a true commendation.

She throws her arms around my neck. "You saved . . . my life."

Before I can reply she finds my mouth just as we get into the elevator. I taste the alcohol, confirm that those lips are as soft as they have looked for the past few days. I take a moment to savor the freckle while my finger reaches for the control panel, stabbing the button for the third floor.

"Karen," I say, pulling away, the reality of what I'm doing sinking in. "This is not a good idea. You're not only my boss, but you're also—"

"Wasted?"

"I think you might be even past that."

"I know you . . . want me, Tom. I saw that . . . look in your eyes." She pats my back as her head lands on my chest. "It's okay . . . I like you too . . ."

Well, her energy shields are certainly down. Too bad I can't bring myself to fire my photon torpedo.

By the time the elevator door opens she is in deep sleep, slobbering all over my shirt. Lucky me.

I guess technically she is trying to exchange bodily fluids, just not quite in the way I had envisioned it. But my landing gear is certainly reacting to her nearness. Perhaps I should go find Blondie after tucking her in, and just land my roaring jetliner on her tight little runway. Heck, the oysters might even help me do a couple of touch-and-goes.

Either that or I can always take matters into my own hands. I don't have a rule against that.

Well, I do leave Karen in her bed—fully clothed, of course—before heading to my own room a couple of doors down the hallway and crawling into bed.

But I'm too worked up to sleep.

Unlike Karen, I only got the chance to drink one and a half scotches, which is better than none, but not nearly enough to offset what that woman did to my system in the elevator, leaving me in limbo as I stare at the slow-turning ceiling fan. So no booze, no Karen, and no Blondie.

That just leaves the job, so I try to think objectively about today's events. My mind quickly replays those critical seconds in that alley. It's amazing how certain moments stick with you like bad heartburn. Today I definitely made enough of those lasting memories, and of a wide variety too, including the good, the ugly, and the bizarre. And just as it happened during previous encounters with Kulzak, I begin to doubt my ability to catch him—not that we're likely to get another chance to do so. Cramer is going to nail Karen tomorrow—and yours truly right behind her. He's got the stake and the hammer. He just needs the final blow. Maybe I should flap my wings and vanish before sunrise.

Seriously, though, anything Cramer can do to us is a walk in the park compared to what Ares Kulzak will do when he gets his hands on us.

And trust me, he will.

Maybe not tomorrow, or next month, or even next year. But he will. One day in the not-so-distant future, maybe after I'm retired—or forced to retire—a van will pull up alongside me in some street in some town, and I will know.

Which is why I have no choice but to get him first.

But how? After tomorrow Cramer is going to make sure that Karen and I don't spend another second on this case, or maybe even on the government's payroll. If we have failed to catch him with all of the resources of the U.S. government behind us, how could I possibly bag him on my own?

The thought of setting a trap and using yours truly as bait crosses my mind, but I immediately see the futility of such a tactic. Kulzak would smell the trap from miles away and find a way to turn the tables.

Or would he? Maybe a well-disguised bait combined with his lust for revenge could give me the edge I need to get him before he gets me—that's assuming, of course, that he does the job himself. He could delegate the task to a subordinate, in which case my one-time trap would fail to eliminate the real threat.

I get up and walk up to the curtains, peeking at the street below. People walk about, half of them holding a drink, all of them partying in spite of the dangerous water level beyond the concrete walls surrounding the city.

Man, if someone really wanted to screw this place up all he'd have to do is . . .

I freeze, wondering if Kulzak would actually try to do something like that in retaliation for this afternoon.

I stare at the joyful crowd.

What's on your mind tonight, Ares Kulzak?

Are you in the area, or have you already skipped town, perhaps on your way to terrorize another city?

Maybe you do have something in mind for the Crescent City after all. Perhaps a way to teach us a lesson about interfering with your plans?

The NOPD and dozens of agents are still on the hunt, trying to find him, but given the size of this place our net is way too coarse.

But what can we really do? Karen is out of commission, and I'm already halfway there.

Before I know it I'm calling Paul Stone, whom we left roaming the streets in the hope of getting lucky.

"Paul," I say when he answers his mobile phone. "Tom Grant. How are you holding up?"

"Lots of work but nothing to show for it."

I grin. Less than two days with me and he's already taking like a veteran. No small talk, just the facts. What he probably doesn't realize is that he has already experienced more field operations excitement than most veterans.

"In that case, call the team over to the Quarter," I say, "and also notify the cops to join us as well."

"Excuse me?"

I frown. Perhaps he still has a thing or two left to learn. I repeat the request.

"Why the French Quarter?"

"I think I know what his next move is going to be."

THIRTY - FIVE

> > > > >

WET AND WILD

> THE CITY OF NEW ORLEANS, IN PLACES AS LOW AS eleven feet below sea level, was kept from flooding by a complex system of earthen levees, concrete walls, and gates that held back the nearly bursting Mississippi River as well as the swelled Lake Pontchartrain, where the Bonnet Carré Spillway dumped Mississippi water at the maximum rate of 250,000 cubic feet per second. From there, the water flowed through the marshlands of the Atchafalaya basin and into the Gulf of Mexico.

Sandwiched between the river and the lake, the flood-protection scheme was arranged in two concentric circles. The earthen levees provided the outer protection ring. In case the river or lake water managed to spill over the edge of these levees, city officials had built ten-foot tall concrete walls as a second protection ring, separated from the levees by as much as a few hundred feet. It was along this concrete wall, which enclosed all of the city, that huge steel gates were kept open to allow traffic in and out of New Orleans, but were closed during high-water emergencies to hold back the overflowing river or lake, as was the case tonight.

However, the well-engineered system, already stressed by rains and melted snow from the north, had been pushed to the breaking point by the recent tropical depression, which had remained stationary over the Crescent City for several days before drifting east, but not before dumping over two feet of water in the area. All the while, the flood relief system struggled, cubic foot after agonizing cubic foot, to pump the water away from a metropolis on the verge of disaster.

The Crescent City lay there ripe, vulnerable, well below the boiling surface of the river, of the adjacent Pontchartrain, kept alive by an overloaded siphoning system, living on borrowed time, like a terminal patient hooked to a life-support system. It was only a matter of time before nature reclaimed this land, this Atlantis on the Bayou, slowly sinking, dropping lower and lower under its own weight, methodically being erased by the forces of nature.

And Ares Kulzak prepared himself to accelerate the process, to achieve in minutes what would have taken nature centuries to accomplish.

Dressed in a blue jumpsuit with an embroidered MR&T logo in black over his breast pocket, Ares pretended to be just another technician of the Mississippi River and Tributaries Project, the multistate organization chartered with providing flood protection for the alluvial valley between Cape Girardeau, Missouri, and the river's delta.

Followed by Kishna Zablah, also dressed in an MR&T uniform, he clutched a duffle bag while climbing the ladder leading to the control room of the largest floodgate in the New Orleans floodwall system, the seventy-foot long gate by the entrance to the New Orleans Airport holding back a monstrous wall of Lake Pontchartrain water. The gate had been closed over a month ago, when the lake, swelled by the Mississippi water being diverted through the Bonnet Carré Spillway, poured over the earthen levee and reached the concrete wall built years ago for days like today to protect the airport and a highly developed section ten miles west of downtown New Orleans.

According to Paxton, now busy setting up charges at smaller floodgates by the concrete wall surrounding the French Quarter area, only two security guards manned the control booth—a glass and metal structure—at this late hour of the night. Ares could see both guards beyond the glass door staring at a small television resting over the control panel.

Ares let Kishna go first as they neared the door. She held a silenced gun behind a notepad.

The guards, both in their forties, very large, and sporting beards, jumped to their feet when she tapped on the glass, obviously not believing their eyes. Kishna's suit, one of several Paxton's associates had stolen from the local MR&T warehouse a few hours ago, was a size too small, snugly wrapping around her provocative figure, the focus of the technicians' hungry stares as they unlocked the door.

She shot them both in the face without fanfare, blood, brain, and chunks of skull spraying the glass window behind them. Their lifeless bodies dropped over the metal floor like rocks.

Ares set the bag down and helped her drag them out of sight, inspecting the quiet streets below as he closed the door behind them. Blocks and blocks of homes extended beyond the tall gate, backdropped by the outline of Kenner and Metairie in the distance, two large suburbs west of the city. From this vantage point he could see to the north the traffic flowing across IH-10. The vast expanse of concrete of the New Orleans airport projected south of the interstate, amidst the moving lights of jetliners taxiing to and from the runway. Behind him, on the lakeside, the angry swells of the Pontchartrain clashed against the gate's thick steel plate just a few feet below the edge. He judged that the water level stood roughly a dozen feet over the deserted street.

While Kishna pushed the television unit aside and sat behind the small panel that controlled the gate's motion, Ares rushed downstairs and hauled three large boxes, which he left on the small landing. Then he went back inside and opened the duffle bag, removing a charge on a remote-controlled detonator. He fastened it to the upper track that guided the steel gate when it was retreated. Then he watched Kishna do her high-tech dance.

The panel seemed quite simple, the levers controlling the motors clearly identified, just as Paxton had explained. But the controls could not be used until she had bypassed the safety feature built into the control system that prevented any gate motion while the humidity sensors on the lakeside of the gate signaled the presence of water.

Her fingers worked automatically, without wasted motion, skillfully splicing the wires coming from the water sensors and connecting them to the leads of a six-volt battery, tricking the computer-control system into believing that the water level had receded below the bottom of the gate, meaning the gate could be safely slid back.

She then pressed a series of green buttons across the top of the panel, disengaging the dozen magnetic locks clamping the gate in place, breaking the watertight seal.

Ares watched in satisfaction as the gate shifted a fraction of an inch under the enormous pressure, leaking water down the narrow gaps between the gate and the concrete wall.

"Ready, Ari?" she asked, standing next to him, excitement flashing in her eyes.

"Open it," he said.

With the same lack of hesitation with which she had shot the two security guards, Kishna Zablah activated the electric motor and engaged the drive mechanism. The massive gate began to slide out of the way on tracks built on the water side of the wall.

The narrow spray of water widened, inch by inch, its sound steadily increasing from a light drone to a rumble, growing to a roar as a torrential flow clashed down the street with dam-bursting power, flipping their parked car like a toy, throwing it against other vehicles down the block, before sweeping them all right through the first row of houses. Roof lines tilted, collapsed under explosions of brick, wood, and sparks, all drowned by the soul-numbing, bellowing growl of the broadening wave, by the swells and foam boiling down the neighborhood, sparing nothing, leveling everything, crashing down the fence separating the airport grounds from the city.

The vibrations propagated across the receding gate, onto the concrete wall, and through the booth bolted to it, rattling the glass, threatening to crack it.

Ares flipped a switch on the RC unit that Paxton had given to him, and a small explosion added to the havoc.

The gate, still blocking part of the gap between the concrete walls, ripped off the upper track, screeching while twisting in the direction of the cascading water, also dislodging from the lower track and disappearing beneath a torrential madness of black water and silvery froth.

The Americans will not be able to block the opening so easily now.

From the safety of their booth, Ares observed the surreal sight, the dreamlike front scattering across the large expanse of airport grounds, reaching the tarmac, splashing against the landing gear of jetliners. He saw ground crews running for higher ground, some reaching it, others washing away in the waist-high current.

He watched the sight with growing delight, this being the first time he had seen the product of his work, of his vision, real-time. Against Kishna's advice, Ares stepped outside, wishing to fully immerse himself in the experience, feeling the mist on his face, hearing the crushing rumbling of water clashing against concrete, against stone, its thundering growl rattling his soul.

He filled his lungs with the wetness of the moment, let the misty haze caress his face as he looked toward the north. The impact damage progressively lessened as the waterfront stretched out across dry land, like dark fingers reaching deep in between rows of houses, flooding but no longer demolishing.

Ares and Kishna went to work, opening the boxes on the landing outside the booth. One contained a self-inflating raft made of multiple layers of black plastic to merge them with the night. The second was a trolling engine, small but sufficiently powerful to prevail against the current. The third contained two marine batteries—enough to get them where they needed to go.

Wondering if Paxton had been successful in the French Quarter, Ares grinned at the boiling surface as Kishna headed down the top of the concrete wall, away from the opening, to find a stable place to inflate the raft. He followed her.

Their mission in New Orleans complete, Ares Kulzak headed to his next destination: Austin, Texas.

THIRTY-SIX

> > > > >

HIGH-TECH COWBOY

> RYAN SHOT THROUGH LAYERS OF THE BINARY LATtice belonging to the SWOASIS firewall, each denser than the previous one, intended to slow down illegal users, depleting speed, momentum—if there were such things in this world.

The borders of the innermost tiers of this multilevel shield jumbled as he approached them, sharpening as he skirted past while broadcasting the correct accessing sequences at the precise times. A nanosecond in error in either direction and he ran the risk of becoming an eggplant, even if MPS-Ali, playing wingman, managed to absorb the digital EMPs that Walter and the sys admins at SWOASIS had warned him about. They could not afford to lessen their security protocols to let Ryan have an easy run through their matrix—not while the threat of an incubating virus loomed over the entire computer-controlled power grid.

A psychedelic maze of pulsating pixels surrounded the core of the system, where the powerful search engines resided, as well as the logs for all of the recent functions performed by the master operating system.

Ryan issued the final password, a string of letters and numbers so long that he had to rely on MPS-Ali to do the complex broadcast. Not only did the floating alphanumeric characters have to be issued in the proper order, but each character, in itself a unique eight-bit field of binary data, had to be embedded in a waveform of varying frequency according to a program governed by the melody of Beethoven's fifth symphony, played in D minor.

Alphanumeric characters embedded in digitized music.

The possible combinations of this nested password were astronomical. It didn't surprise Ryan that the terrorists had kidnapped the genius behind the defensive shield. No hacker—or AI for that matter—however brilliant or innovative, could crack it within a human lifespan.

So they grabbed Gary Hutton and forced the info out of him.

Ryan frowned, though his seamless face, as reflected by the pixel-mutating cocoon surrounding the core shell, remained impassive. This went to show that no network, however well protected, was safe from a determined cyberterrorist, particularly one relying on real-world actions to bolster his high-tech skills.

While the surface of the nucleus altered its color from pink to purple and back to pink in cycles of ever-increasing frequency in response to the password, Ryan and MPS-Ali orbited it, probing for gaps. They did this carefully, systematically, searching for weaknesses in the glowing strata of a sphere that grew progressively translucent, until the shell became as clear as glass.

His cyber agent reported no external anomalies. From the outside of the core all seemed normal. He couldn't detect any viruses left behind by the cyberterrorists.

Now it's time to check the guts of the system.

They plunged inside, through a vast ocean of orbs of assorted neon colors according to their time stamps. The dark end of the range marked the directories with the oldest time stamps, some from as far back as a week, the last time the system was fully backed up by the IT group.

The lighter end of this glowing spectrum indicated directories accessed as recently as a few nanoseconds ago. The interior of the core was certainly much larger than what it appeared to be, judging by its outside shell—as was usually the case in Ryan's virtual-reality world.

Thanks to the expeditious work of Walter and the SWOASIS boys, MPS-Ali housed a link to the week-old archive copy in its real-time storage databanks, accessible on demand.

The search-and-destroy algorithm that Ryan invoked, and which had earned him a patent during his Stanford days, armed him with a localized digital laser—or LDL, as he had called it in the patent application. It empowered him with the ability to selectively alter the state of the ones and zeroes in the machine code belonging to the files of the SWOASIS network. MPS-Ali carried out the search portion of the task, performing an advanced DIFF between the contents of the existing files in the network with those from a week ago. But unlike the SWOASIS network's resident DIFF program, which Ryan suspected of being corrupted by the same virus infecting the rest of the network, his DIFF program was clean, protected by MPS-Ali.

The cyber pugilist went to work, simultaneously shifting the data from both the active file and the archive into a sterile buffer. It then performed the desired comparison of the given file and posted any mismatches onto a bulletin board that was accessed by a series of artificial intelligence engines that analyzed them in parallel according to a variety of parameters, including the time it was altered, the length of the difference, the location of the difference, and the type of change made, the latter of which was categorized as being either an instruction or actual data.

In a matter of milliseconds—oceans of time in the cyberworld—MPS-Ali interpreted the results for Ryan, discarding the true random changes in data that resulted from normal network activity from those changes that tried to disguise themselves as random, but which, when grouped together according to the cataloguing parameters used by the AI engines, showed the expected propagation patterns of a computer virus. This particular virus was quite naughty. The time stamp showed a progression that was anything but linear and could only be predicted with a complicated Fourier transform. In addition to the complicated time component, the virus also changed size from mutation to mutation according to yet another Fourier transform, in essence nesting the two. And to make matters even more complicated, the location of the alien string within each data file varied according to a third transform. A classic operating system would have never recognized such elegant intrusion until it had gone active.

But not today.

So far the virus had contaminated roughly 15 percent of the files scanned, and according to the time stamp it was progressing at the rate of one percentage point every hour, and even that seemed to be changing according to another formula that Ryan didn't need to spend computing cycles calculating. Between the three parameters—time, size, and location—he had all of the required information to begin the second portion of his mission.

Destroy.

Actually, the task was a little more complicated than that. Ryan had to return the files to their unaltered state, but in such a way that the virus didn't realize it was being attacked. Otherwise, Ryan ran the risk that the virus, sensing his assault, could launch a premature strike, which could still be devastating to the system. The only way Ryan knew of achieving such a stealth hit was by reversing the order in which data was altered according to the FIFO principle: First In First Out, meaning he had to start with the earliest-altered file and move his way to the most recent one. An analogy of Ryan's approach would be to attack a single line of marching soldiers by silently killing them one by one starting from the rear of the line, without alerting the soldiers in front.

The files, now represented as long, DNA-like strings of data, unrolled in front of Ryan, projecting outward in all directions, the origins hovering all around him, forming a sort of sphere.

Assisted by MPS-Ali, Ryan went to work, riding the strings like a high-speed surfer, searching for the illegal sequences, which were marked by different colors from the rest of the strand. Cyan against magenta. Neon green against metallic blue. White against chocolate brown.

And he had to go through each one, firing the LDL at the alien strings, marking them for MPS-Ali and his array of AI engines, which followed behind him reversing the effect of the virus, cleaning out the code. Like a ground operator painting a difficult target with a laser to guide a bomb dropped by a plane, so did Mike Ryan stain the illegitimate bits of data, identifying them for mutation.

And he did it over and over in a high-tech marathon that lasted almost five hours.

As the system issued a full-eradication confirmation message, MPS-Ali reported a runner departing the network.

Another messenger!

Guessing that the runner was headed to its owner to report that the virus had been destroyed, Ryan went in pursuit of the silver figure while MPS-Ali stained it just as it reached the neon-green conduit of a T1 line. They followed it through a jadish blur of digital acceleration before spilling into the starred expanse of an Internet Service Provider, jagging past pulsating suns and their orbiting worlds, across an asteroid ring of aging hardware, and into the emerald portal of another T1.

His stomach churned from the twisting path of this tunnel of hazed green light as MPS-Ali executed a series of impossible maneuvers, before they shot into another galaxy, repeating the process dozens of times, cruising through ISPs tagged with physical addresses in Wichita Falls, Reno, Sacramento, Hartford, Winston-Salem, and Memphis, before arriving at an ISP in Austin, Texas.

Austin?

Ryan remembered his two-month adventure in the Texas capital, where his generous new employer had turned out to be in the middle of a conspiracy that reached the halls of power in Washington, D.C., a conspiracy that had nearly ended the life of Victoria—and his own.

Ryan followed the silver figure as it changed patterns, just like in his previous chase the day before, approaching not a constellation but a cavernous enclosure of blinding white light, a wireless holding station. This time, however, he could not tell just how big the place was. The light and the spherical shape made it appear as if the station went on forever.

The glistening runner rushed across it at great speed, diving into a charcoal cloud that slowly swirled out of nowhere, like a twisting cyclone, growing darker as Ryan and MPS-Ali neared it.

Sheet lightning flashed across its surface as the digital squall line propagated toward them. Embedded in the haze Ryan saw code, but it wasn't Assembly, or Fortran, or Pascal, or C++. Ryan was staring at a colossal cloud of a much higher-order language.

BACK OFF NOW.

The message flashed across his field of view, a warning from MPS-Ali, who shot a scarlet fog, representing a paralyzing virus, at the angered storm.

Like a pilot ejecting out of a damaged fighter jet, Ryan accelerated backward, away from MPS-Ali at sickening speed, triggering memories of videos recorded by cameras mounted on rockets as they shot away from Earth.

As he distanced himself from the threat, as his cyber agent held back the boiling cloud of angry code, Ryan recognized strings of instructions and data that didn't belong in this networked environment.

Ada.

Ada code?

In the distance he watched this cloud rumble past MPS-Ali's virus block. The expert system fired a second burst of red gas but it had no effect on the incoming threat.

It adjusted! It's learning!

MPS-Ali vanished amidst bolts of lightning, but not before dispatching a final message to his master.

JACK OUT IMMEDIATELY.

As the storm accelerated in his direction, threatening to swallow him whole, and thunder rumbled in his ears, Ryan grabbed the HMD and ripped it off his head.

The shot of electricity stabbed his hands, making him drop the head-mounted display, which crashed on the tiled floor of the STG computer room. The glass enclosures housing the miniature plasma screens shattered on impact.

Sweet Jesus!

His hands trembling from the electric shock that would have certainly lobotomized him, Ryan glanced over at Victoria, hands holding her belly, peacefully snoring on the couch that Walter and the boys had brought in before he'd jacked in.

Damn, he thought, checking his watch. Almost midnight. *What in the hell just happened?*

Breathing heavily, realizing how close he had come to becoming a vegetable, Ryan knelt down and inspected his HMD, smelling burnt plastic from the darkened printed circuit board of the microelectronics that managed the virtual-reality experience.

And what an experience that was.

Thoroughly exhausted, his face filmed with sweat despite the chilled air blowing out of overhead vents, he stood and stretched his limbs.

It would take him some time to fully assess the damage, which, in addition to cooking his VR hardware, probably had erased the loaded version of MPS-Ali. But amidst the acrid odor tingling his nostrils from the barbecued equipment, Ryan also sniffed food.

His stomach grumbled in spite of his near-death encounter.

He eyed a box of pizza and another one filled with doughnuts on the table next to the couch. The junk food had not been there when he had plugged into the computer matrix.

Ryan sighed. Pregnant women surely had some bizarre eating habits. A couple of weeks ago Victoria had woken him up in the middle of the night and dispatched him to the grocery store to get her a half dozen cream-filled doughnuts after claiming to have had a dream about dancing doughnuts calling out, "Eat me, eat me."

Weird.

A few months ago Victoria would have never touched the stuff. Now she seemed to eat them on a regular basis but somehow had managed to keep her weight down, probably thanks to her naturally fast metabolism, though she had already started to watch her salt intake after she began retaining fluid, particularly in her feet.

Ryan grabbed a slice of pizza; cheese, pepperoni, and anchovies. He loved the latter as much as Victoria hated them, the reason only half the pizza had them—the half that wasn't touched. Of course, her half had an interesting combination of pineapple and grilled chicken that Ryan had never seen her eat before.

He chewed while examining his system's monitor. As he had suspected, the VR hardware had taken the brunt of the attack, acting as a surge protector for the rest of the system. The computer was still operational, though certain partitions of the primary drive were corrupted, including a container roughly half the size of a shoe box, packed with the Flash memory cards where the code of MPS-Ali resided.

Leaning back, he exhaled, trying to put things in perspective. At least he had blocked the attack on the power grid and had obtained a possible new lead for his CCTF associates. The runner had gone to a wireless holding tank servicing the Austin area.

He only wished he had also gotten ahold of the cyberterrorists' next target, which would have helped him focus his defenses rather than spreading them to thousands of potential targets across the Internet.

But he didn't have time for wishful thinking.

Ryan needed to contact Karen and Tom and relate what he had found. Then he had to reload MPS-Ali from CD-ROM and pick up where he'd left off—though he admitted that the mysterious dark cloud had puzzled him. Ryan had never seen anything like it, in size, level of aggressiveness, immunity to attack, and just plain sheer devastating power. It took revolutionary software and hardware to generate a pulse that would fry the hardware at the other end of the line.

We're definitely not talking about a virus here anymore but a very intelligent system, he thought, determined to figure out what sort of AI had launched such a nearly fatal attack.

Certainly an AI that doesn't have an inhibitor.

And from what he was able to tell, the AI interface that he experienced wasn't coded in C++, like MPS-Ali and so many other AIs, but in Ada, a higher-order computer language used mostly in embedded commercial, industrial, and military systems. An embedded application was a system that ran without the need of being interfaced to a network, like the guiding system of a rocket, or the autopilot of a jetliner, but not as the backbone of a networked artificial intelligence system. He wondered if the AI itself was actually coded in a more classic language but had an interface to Ada so it could talk to the millions of embedded systems out there programmed in the same language.

Shelving that thought for the time being, he gave his VR gear another disappointed glance.

Definitely toasted.

At least he had brought extra hardware, though at this rate he would literally burn through it in a couple more sessions—that's assuming he didn't get roasted first.

Ryan frowned. There had to be a better way to improve his odds. His gear, albeit among the best in the industry, still did not provide adequate protection. He needed something more powerful, more robust, more capable of withstanding the harsh environment he was trying to crack. Ryan needed tools that were still not available in the open market, in universities, in commercial research labs. Ryan needed to gain access to the advanced military research projects at Los Alamos and other Pentagon-sponsored facilities and see what was available that would help him in his cyber battle against Ares Kulzak and the highly intelligent system backing him up—a system that was in clear violation of the Turing directive.

At that moment Walter and his Coke-bottle glasses walked into the lab holding two cans of soda. He noticed the smoked hardware and then stared at Ryan, though it was difficult to tell exactly where the man was looking.

"You missed the fireworks," Ryan mumbled.

"What happened?" Walter asked with concern.

Ryan brought a finger to his own lips before pointing at Victoria. Walter nodded.

"Just had a rough session," Ryan whispered. "I did find and eradicate a virus. The power grid is safe."

"I was talking about you," said Walter in a low voice. "Are *you* okay?"

"Close call, but I'm fine."

"But," he said, setting the drinks down before touching his right temple with an index finger. "Your temples . . . they're all . . . red."

Red?

Ryan felt them with his finger and cringed as he touched warm flesh. The pulse had reached him after all, though certainly quite attenuated.

"Never mind that," Ryan said. "And not a word of this to Vic. The network is safe but I'm afraid the crooks are headed to their next target."

"Where?"

Grabbing one of the sodas, popping the top, and taking a swig to wash down the pizza, Ryan said, "Austin, Texas."

"Austin? Why?"

"My educated guess is that they're going for the second largest high-tech hub in the nation. Now, help me find Karen Frost's cell phone number," he said. First he had to warn Karen. Then he needed to contact the Turing Society and report this violation. Then he would call his contacts in the Pentagon.

THIRTY-SEVEN

> > > > >

BLASTING CAPS

> ON DECATUR STREET, ACROSS FROM ST. LOUIS
cathedral, in the heart of the French Quarter, Café Dumonde thrives with latecomers, mostly tourists weary of the rowdy clubs on Bourbon Street. Here they get to enjoy some of the best coffee with chicory in the world—along with an order of beignets covered in powdered sugar—while a lone street musician pours his heart into the melody streaming out of his shiny saxophone. The hat by his feet displays the generosity of the evening's crowd.

But I'm not sightseeing.

I'm trying my darnedest to keep *others* sightseeing in this city for a long, long time.

Paul Stone and I are inspecting the gate behind the fountain just to the right of the famous café. His features have tightened since I first met him a few days ago. There's something about nearly getting killed twice—and also seeing others get killed—that has a way of hardening a person. If you don't believe me go ask all of the survivors from the terrorist strikes of 2001.

Stone's ice-cold eyes, and low, hissing voice are but two signs that this rookie is rapidly maturing in front of my eyes. I'm not kidding you. The kid looks like he could eat stones in his breakfast cereal. Tonight I've used the hell out of his newly found charismatic trait—plus my own NYPD charm—to convince two dozen overworked CCTF agents and twice as many cranky NOPD cops to patrol the perimeter of the concrete wall surrounding the city. I even got the cops to throw in a six-man team from the local bomb squad, standing by in an alley a few blocks away.

We're actually focusing more on the steel gates than the wall itself. The thinking here is that a blast of C4 has a greater chance of success against the six inches of steel in the gates than the wall's five feet of reinforced concrete. In addition, the gates are being held in place by two hinges on one side and a lock at the other. A well-placed blast against either could dislodge the entire gate, which would pretty much flood the entire downtown area.

Ironically, I almost became the first casualty of the evening, but not from a terrorist strike. I nearly impaled myself when I accidentally sat on one of a few bronze pigeons adorning the knee-high edge of a fountain. The bird's beak went up my ass, making me jump and scream while holding my sore butt, drawing laughs from Stone and a handful of cops.

I glare at the menacing street artwork and realize there are several such bronzes along the side of Café Dumonde, from Decatur to the concrete wall. Sizes vary from the small winged proctologists to a life-size boy and girl holding hands on a bench. There's even one of a sax player leaning against the railing of the steps connecting the street to the sightseeing platform built over the wall. On a normal day you're supposed to walk down the other side, over a pair of railroad tracks, across a visitor parking lot, and up to the earthen levee for a view of the Mississippi and its slow-flowing traffic. But today the experience ends on top of the platform, where the concrete wall marked the current left bank of the river. The earthen levee has not been visible for weeks now, ever since the river spilled over.

From the looks of it I would guess it's going to be a while before the waters recede to their normal level. In the meantime the city, albeit vulnerable, is quite safe.

And it's my job to make sure it stays that way.

"Nothing abnormal here, chief," Stone says pointing down the barrier in the direction of Jax Brewery. "Shall we?"

I give him a brief nod, my rear end still throbbing. We have about a half a mile of wall left to cover. We started way back, where Esplanade Avenue dead-ends into the river, and are working our way toward the Warehouse District, by the wharfs. We've got four NOPD uniformed cops with us to get some respect from the half-drunken crowd, not that an old hand like me needs it, but it never hurts to have extra muscle around in case things get ugly.

And when it comes to Kulzak, things *always* get ugly.

Stone has volunteered to be our scribe, using a grease pencil to cross off the gates on his laminated map after we check them. At the end of the round, which I'm estimating at another hour or so, we're all going to get together back here, at Café Dumonde, and compare notes. The goal is to have checked all of the gates along the entire perimeter, as well as the wall itself.

At least the night is cool and there's a breeze blowing from the river as we proceed along the wall. The gap between the barrier and the back of the establishments varies from a few feet to a few dozen feet—space that in some cases is being used as a parking lot, though most of it is poorly illuminated.

"Next gate is another two hundred feet straight ahead," says Stone, using a penlight to read the glossy map.

The area in question is an alley right behind the old Jax Brewery building, now a multilevel shopping center.

I flicker my flashlight and aim it at the ten-foot-wide passage, torching its darkness, scaring off a handful of rats roaming over a rusted Dumpster. Dozens of large bugs take off, one of them buzzes in between Stone and me. I swat it with the flashlight and send it into a death spiral.

"What in the hell was that?" asks Stone.

"Roaches," one of the cops says behind me.

We turn around. The stocky policeman—a middle-aged man who, like so many other people in this town, should be spending a little more time at the gym—is grinning.

"Roaches?" I say.

"Yep."

"I didn't know they could fly," says Stone.

"They do here, pal," he replies.

We move on, washing the wall with our flashlights, seeing nothing but stained concrete mixed with some graffiti until the next green gate, where we once again pause and check for plastic explosives. The place, which is essentially an alley, smells just as bad, reminding me of this afternoon's encounter.

I frown, wondering why it always has to come down to dark alleys, which I hate with a passion.

"Clear," says Stone, marking his map while the cops make a semicircle around him. "Next is just down this alley, before reaching the main parking lot on the other side of Jax Brewery."

I point my flashlight in that direction and catch a figure with shoulder-length blond hair standing by one end of the gate a hundred-some feet away, his hands pressing something at chest level against the spot where the gate meets the concrete wall.

At first I think I'm staring at the bronze of a woman, but then the bronze moves and looks in my direction, and I realize that it is neither a bronze nor a woman. In another second all beams converge on him.

"Freeze!" I shout, instinctively breaking into a run, weapon already in my right hand, pointed at the stranger.

While holding the flashlight like you would a microphone, but with the beam trained on the target, I press my left wrist over the right one, making a horizontal cross that keeps both the gun and the flashlight locked and pointed in the same direction—a trick I learned long ago in New York.

The man starts racing away from us, his movements fluid, like a trained athlete.

Having gotten trained in a police department where you only warn once before you shoot, and then going to a government agency where you shoot first and *then* ask questions, I instinctively drop to one knee, firing twice, aiming for the legs.

Four reports whip the night, echoing between the wall and the rear of the three-story building, stinging my still-sensitive eardrums. I realize that Stone has mimicked my moves and also taken two shots at the stranger before the NOPD cops have even drawn their weapons.

When it's this dark, the muzzle flashes tend to contract your pupils a bit, which explains the spots that have emerged in front of my eyes, though our powerful flashlights help offset that.

A brief eye contact with my protégé to commend him on his timing, and we're sprinting over wet asphalt, the beams from our flashlights crisscrossing before zeroing in on the figure sprawled on the alley, legs thrashing as he attempts to get up.

Stone gets ahead of me just as we're halfway to the potential terrorist.

There's youth for you.

In spite of the way I'm holding my hands to keep the weapon and beam trained on the target, I do manage to outpace the well-fed NOPD officers, whom I direct not toward the stranger, who, albeit wounded, isn't screaming, but in the direction of what I fear are the plastic explo—

Another shot cracks down the alley, its muzzle flash originating from Stone's gun, illuminating the fallen stranger by his feet.

"Paul!" I shout, nearly out of breath. "We need him alive!"

Without replying, Stone kicks something away from the stranger, who is now holding his right wrist.

I suddenly understand.

Stone must have spotted a gun.

I focus my flashlight on the black object Stone had kicked.

It's not a gun.

The silver antenna coming out of one end tells me it is a remote controlled transmitter.

My gun and flashlight still held in a horizontal cross at eye level, I finally reach Stone, breathing heavily, already breaking a sweat in spite of the breeze.

"Is that what I think . . . it is?"

Keeping his eyes on the target, who looks like a man well into his fifties, if not early sixties, Stone says, "Looks that way, chief."

"Stay with him," I say, a bit puzzled at the quickness of such an old man.

Turning toward the cops, who have reached the wall, I say, "It's a bomb. Don't touch anything!"

The bastards part like the Red Sea and are all too happy to get away from it and go fetch an ambulance, the bomb squad, or even stretch yellow police tape at both ends of the alley—anything but doing what I'm doing—standing next to what looks like enough explosives to cream my sore ass.

While Stone covers the aging terrorist and the NOPD cops conveniently stay out of my way, I take a moment to inspect the bomb. I train the beam on the bulk of gleaming black plastic explosives almost an inch thick enveloping the entire top hinge, which itself is almost a foot tall and half as wide. Three blasting caps embedded in the mass connect to wires running down to a second block of plastic explosives covering the lower hinge. The wires bundle up and disappear in a backpack resting by the foot of the wall. Pressing an ear to the nylon pack I hear tiny beeps at regular intervals of about two seconds each.

Terrific.

The timer appears to be ticking but it seems steady, probably still moments away from the final countdown, which my experience tells me will be marked by a reduction in the interval between pulses.

So we have time to disarm it.

I look at the blasting caps in the explosives. Three per charge. Typically, the triggering device inside the backpack would set off the small charges in the blasting caps, which would in turn detonate the main charges.

One way to disarm them is to pull the blasting caps off the plastic explosives. But if I know Kulzak, unless the caps are all removed in unison, the triggering mechanism might detect that and detonate the caps. If that happens when any of the caps are within a foot of the plastic charges, there's a pretty darn good chance that they could also go off.

I glance at the array of wires coiling into the backpack and wonder if we should just cut them. But again, it could be booby-trapped. If one wire is cut before the others, even by a fraction of a second, it could be enough to set off the charges. And as far as the backpack itself, I'm willing to bet one of my cushy government paychecks that the slightest motion will set it off. Either that or by using the remote control that Stone so timely shot off the old fart's hand.

Leave it alone, Grant. Let the experts deal with it.

I walk back to them, kneeling by the aging terrorist, whose face is lined with age—though there are solid muscles beneath the wrinkled and spotted skin of his exposed forearms. He looks like a retired body builder, but it's the fact that he has yet to utter a single sound even though he's been shot twice in the legs and once in his wrist that tells me we're dealing with a pro.

And that's when I remember.

The wino outside Gary Hutton's building this afternoon!

Son of a bitch!

But a lifetime of espionage work has taught me to keep such discoveries to myself for the time being. The man appears to know how to take pain—a skill taught only in selected places in the world, like the Special Forces and the Navy SEALs, along with other such elite fighting forces—plus your usual assortment of terrorist organizations.

Yep. We're definitely dealing with a pro.

"How are you holding up?" I ask the man who warned Ares Kulzak of our raid this afternoon, in the process blowing my mole theory since I saw him at least a couple of minutes before going inside, certainly long enough for Kulzak to react in time.

The aging terrorist keeps his stare on the hand holding his wounded wrist, which he's doing not out of pain but to staunch the blood loss, just as he has got his right calf pressed over his left thigh, the two places where we wounded him. He's slowing down the blood loss through well-applied pressure, which tells me I'm not dealing with a suicidal fanatic but more with a survivalist, giving me hope that we might be able to work out a deal.

"We can help you," I add. "But you need to help us first. Where is Ares Kulzak?"

He closes his eyes and breathes deeply through his nostrils. Then he opens his eyes and stares at the end of the alley, like he's waiting for something.

Leaving him in the hands of my skilled pupil, I train the flashlight on the remote-control triggering device, roughly the size of a box of cigarettes with a tiny keypad and an LED display in front showing battery level and the word LOCKED in front.

Shit. It's encrypted, and not only that, but it's likely to give you no more than a couple of chances to enter the access code before signaling the backpack over there to play "Goodbye Yellow Brick Road."

I search the stranger while Stone keeps his gun steady on him. As expected, the man's clean. No weapon, no ID, nothing that would reveal his identity.

I stand just as the bomb squad gets here. The team leader introduces himself to me by a name that sounds like hors d'oeuvres but it's spelled on his name tag HORDVEAUX.

I extend an index finger toward the bomb and explain to him that we will all become finger food if he screws up. Failing to appreciate my dark humor he goes straight for the bomb, followed by his teammates.

Sirens now blare in the distance. I guess the ambulance is on the way for Mr. No Name, who continues to stare toward the parking lot beyond the alley.

My spook sense once again starts tickling the hairs on my ass.

"Stay here, Paul," I say. "Don't take your eyes off of him."

"Where are you going?"

"Where's your map?"

"I dropped it back there. Why?"

"How many gates between us and the Warehouse District?"

"Two, maybe three. Why?"

"I'll be right back. Just make sure he doesn't get away."

The bomb squad has set up a couple of large floodlights, bathing their area of interest with intense white light, which reflects off the concrete and creates a twilight in the alley.

I holster my piece and flick off the flashlight, but hang on to it. It makes an excellent club. I'm not kidding you. I saw a cop once beat the crap out of two knife-bearing punks in Queens with only his flashlight.

I flag two of the cops guarding the alley's entrance. "Back my man up over there," I tell them. "He's covering a professional terrorist, who's just as deadly wounded. Don't let him out of your sight and go with him to the hospital. Got that?"

"We got it," one of them replies. "Where are you going?"

"To check something out," I say, ducking under the police tape and running toward the parking lot on the other side of the brewery building.

"Tom!"

I check my rear without breaking my stride.

Well, what do you know?

It's Karen Frost, back from the dead.

She's talking to some cops about a half block away, and they're pointing in my direction.

"Wait up!" she shouts.

I let her catch up before picking up my pace again. She looks pretty ragged: wrinkled clothes, messy hair, smudged mascara circling her eyes. What happened to the sexy babe I deposited in her room a few hours ago?

"I'm out for . . . just a little while . . . and you have the entire task force looking for . . . *bombs?*" she asks, out of breath, her bloodshot eyes looking for mine in the twilight of the parking lot.

"Got bored," I replied, wiping my brow without slowing down. "What happened to you? Couldn't sleep?"

I know she's shooting me one of her looks but I don't turn my head to give her the pleasure. She finally says, "Mike Ryan woke me up. Says the cyberterrorists are in Austin."

"Austin? As in Texas?" Now I look at her.

"Yep."

"Interesting," I say.

"Mind telling me where we are going?"

"Oh, it's a pretty night for a jog."

"Tom!"

"All right, all right. We found a terrorist placing a bomb on the gate behind the brewery. I think there's more than one of these crackpots setting up bombs."

"Is he alive?"

"Shot him three times but he's still breathing."

"*Only* three times?"

"I'm slowing down in my old age."

"Where is he?"

"Back there. Stone and a couple of cops are guarding him 'til an ambulance gets here."

We keep running under the curious stares of a few bystanders. Off to the right the festivities are still in full swing despite the late hour, the gunshots, and the sirens. People come to the Quarter to party, even with the high crime and the river threatening to spill over, and nothing short of a hurricane is going to send them home. Heck, some of them—especially the most inebriated—are already snapping pictures of the cops swarming to the area like they're part of the local tourist entertainment.

We reach the other end of the parking lot in silence, all the while inspecting the wall, spotting nothing abnormal. More buildings flank the far side of the lot, along with the expected alley in between the back of the row of buildings and the wall.

The wall.

I find myself running to the rhythm of an old Pink Floyd tune. I'm about to mention it to her but choose against it, deciding she's probably too hung over to handle that.

Sliding the switch on my flashlight I direct the yellow beam at the wall.

"Paul told me there's a few more gates between us and the Warehouse District, which is being covered by another team," I say, my lungs burning, as well as my legs.

Damn. I'm really out of shape.

We press on, past Dumpsters, piles of paper, empty cardboard boxes, and more rats and mutant flying cockroaches. The deep horns from nearby vessels rumble over the river, mixing with the clicking sounds of our shoes and my heavy breathing. If one of Kulzak's bombs doesn't kill me this run just might. My heart is pounding in my chest like a pissed-off gorilla and my limbs feel like they're being pricked by a million needles.

"Over there, Tom," she whispers, pointing to the next gate, a small one for pedestrian traffic.

And there it is.

Another charge.

Kulzak's got this place wired. Karen brings her radio to her lips and checks with the rest of the teams, but no one else has found anything, not even the team covering the Warehouse District.

My heartbeat pounding in my temples, my mouth drier than cotton, I stare at the black plastic explosives covering the hinges, glistening in the yellow light. At a glance it looks like the same drill as the first one, except that the smaller charges require just one blasting cap apiece, both connected to wires leading to another backpack.

Great. I'm some lucky alley cat, standing once again by yet another charge, smaller than the first, but still quite capable of sending yours truly to Headstoneville.

Taking a knee, I slowly place the left side of my face over the front of the backpack, gently pressing my ear against the nylon.

I hear the beeps, only these ones are closer than in the first bomb, about a half second or so apart . . . maybe even less than that, and I think they're actually getting closer and closer.

It's at times like this that I wish I had stuck to the bouncing business back in Manhattan.

"There isn't much time," I tell her. "Check the next gate. Hurry."

"What about this one? Shouldn't we call the bomb squad?"

"There isn't *time* for a bomb squad!" I bark. "Now go check the next one before this fucking place ends up ten feet under water!"

She gives me the look and then she's off.

Sorry, girl. I don't want you around with what I'm about to do.

"All right," I whisper the moment her footsteps vanish in the night. "Let's see what we have here."

I listen once more, and the beeps are almost on top of each other. I'm out of time. The city is out of time. I suddenly realize that if this charge goes off, then the torrent that will follow is going to move the charge in the other backpack, setting it off, which explains why Mr. No Name was calmly staring in this direction. He had no intention of talking because he was just waiting for the blasts to try to escape.

If I had a pair of wire cutters I could probably snip the two small wires at the same time, but I don't have any such tool in my possession, and even if I did I don't think I would use them. As I explained before, it's impossible to cut them at the *exact* time. The circuitry of the triggering mechanism would detect the change in resistance between the cut and the uncut wire for the millisecond between the first and second cut, sending the pulse through the uncut wire before I could snip it.

On the other hand, I could pull out the blasting caps with synchronized firm tugs. Although that would not alert the resistance-sensitive circuitry of the bomb's electronic brain, the brisk motion could shift the contents inside the backpack, triggering the electrical pulse. By then I hope to have the blasting caps far enough away from the charges that they will not go off. Of course, I'll be holding the damned things when they pulse the detonating electrical spike, but what other immediate choice do I have?

Getting a firm grip on the top cap with my left hand and the bottom one with my right, I lean into the charges.

Crap.

This is going to hurt.

Praying that Karen Frost has the sense to do something similar should she find another charge, I glance up to the star-filled night and catch a half-dozen river rats, each the size of a small cat, looking down at me from the top of the wall, their curious red eyes glistening in the darkness.

Not exactly the kind of rats I would like to take with me on a suicide mission, but I count from one to three anyway.

In one swift motion I jump back while plucking the electrical blasting caps out of the charges, throwing my arms up and behind me, like an Olympic gymnast performing a back flip, only I don't recall ever reaching the floor again. Nor do I remember any applause from my unexpected audience overhead.

My arms feel like they've been immersed in a vat of molten lead. The white-hot pain is so intense that I can't even scream. Colors explode in my brain before all goes dark.

THIRTY - EIGHT

> > > > >

INCENTIVES

> PRESIDENT LAURA VACCARO LEARNED A LONG TIME ago that when it came to fighting terrorism there was never any such thing as a true and final victory. Every American president going back to the colonies had to deal with some form of terrorism, and despite an administration's finest efforts to eliminate it, terrorism always found a way to spring right back into the headlines. The names of terrorist leaders came and went, some remaining in our memories more than others, like Osama bin Laden and his coordinated strikes in 2001. But their acts were all the same, the fear inflicted on the population never changed, and the overwhelming anger and frustration that descended on those charged with the protection of a nation only worsened over time.

The president watched the video feed from New Orleans, where a minor victory had been achieved just hours ago by the quick thinking of the agents leading the case, in particular by Tom Grant, the CIA officer who had had previous encounters with the terrorist still at large. The CCTF agents had also captured a suspect, who was being flown to Washington for questioning.

But the local team had not been able to prevent the flooding of the airport area, where the loss of life and property damage would likely rank it among the worst man-made disasters this nation had ever experienced, second only to San Antonio and the destruction of the World Trade Center.

And it happened on my watch.

"How is Tom Grant?" Vaccaro asked, aware of what the agent had done to disarm the bomb.

"In stable condition, Mrs. President," replied Randall Cramer, whom Vaccaro had summoned here tonight along with Russell Meek and Marty Jacobs. Fitzgerald, as always, remained in the background listening to the conversation. Defense Secretary Davis was at the Pentagon, and the Secretary of State remained in Moscow. "He suffered minor burns on his hands but is awake and eager to pick up the case and follow the new lead in Austin."

"I only wish we had more agents like him," Vaccaro said. "Perhaps then we wouldn't be in the trouble we are today."

Cramer didn't say anything, which Vaccaro found peculiar.

"That's why he is where he is," said Meek, filling in the silence. "Along with Agent Karen Frost, who was responsible for disarming the third bomb."

"Yes," the president replied. "Make sure they get anything they need in Austin. *Anything*. Is that clear?"

Heads began to bob at the executive order while Meek, Jacobs, and Cramer all joined in a choir and said, "Yes, Mrs. President."

"All right," Vaccaro said. "Now, tell me about the lead in Austin."

Cramer explained how Mike Ryan had come upon it, just as he had stumbled onto the New Orleans lead during a previous Internet excursion.

"Amazing young man," he commented. "Make sure that he and his wife are being looked after carefully."

"That actually brings me to his request, Mrs. President."

"Request?"

"Yes," said Cramer, crossing his legs. "For protection."

Vaccaro made a face. "Aren't the Ryans under your protection already?"

"After seeing the way Kulzak killed our agents, Mr. Ryan is getting nervous and has requested Secret Service protection."

Vaccaro almost chuckled but managed to contain it. "Isn't that a little *extreme* and . . . well, unusual?"

"It is, Mrs. President," said Cramer. "But that's what he has requested in order to continue assisting us. He fears for his life as well as the life of his wife, who is pregnant."

"I see," Vaccaro said, crossing her arms. "Russ? What do you think?"

"Plain and simple, ma'am. If it wasn't for Mike Ryan, the CCTF would still be combing through the rubble of San Antonio looking for clues. He's the man who gave us the Melbourne lead as well as the one in New Orleans and now Austin. We need him a hell of a lot more than he needs us. If the kid wants Secret Service protection, then he gets Secret Service protection. I've already made arrangements to utilize one of our safe houses in the Austin area."

Vaccaro glanced over at the director of Central Intelligence. "Marty?"

"I'm with Russ on this one, Mrs. President."

"Vance?"

Fitzgerald said, "I think it's just a matter of how many agents Mr. Ryan wants."

"Very well," the president said. "Send the protection, but let's make sure he continues to earn it."

"Speaking of earnings, Mrs. President," said Meek, the orange freckles on his face moving as he frowned. "Mr. Ryan had a second request."

"Really?"

"It's regarding his contract with us. He wants to renegotiate in light of the increased exposure to danger to himself and his wife."

President Vaccaro looked away in exasperation. Whatever happened to citizens wanting to serve their country for the simple sake of *serving* their country? JFK would be rolling over in his grave at the brazenness displayed by this new generation, where it seemed that everyone down to the janitor was a businessman.

"Fine," she finally said. "You have my authority to do whatever it takes to keep him focused. Protection, money, bonds, a car, a house, even a damned tour of the White House. Just make sure you catch the bastard who is destroying our cities!"

THIRTY - NINE

> > > > >

NOT ENOUGH

> FROM BEHIND THE TINTED GLASS OF A BLACK
sedan, Ares Kulzak watched the myriad of boats crowding Lake Travis, just west of
Austin, Texas. They waited on the outer edge of the parking lot of a restaurant called
Carlos and Charlie's, by the shores of the manmade lake, created decades ago by
damming the Colorado River as it flowed through the hill country. The lake was over
forty miles long but not that wide as it followed the twists and turns of the river that
created it. Walls of chalky limestone projected upward from the water's edge to meet
wooded crests dotted with luxurious homes overlooking the lake.

Kishna sat behind the wheel drinking from a can of soda, her honey-colored skin
glowing as much as her sunglasses. The restaurant shared this waterfront with the
Emerald Point Marina, its many docks projecting onto the water like fingers, housing
boats of varying sizes in covered or open slips. A third business utilized this well-
developed marina, a place called Just for Fun, which rented all kinds of water craft,
from personal watercraft to speedboats and party barges.

From his vantage point, Ares watched speedboats, cruisers, yachts, sailboats, and
the smaller PWCs roam about. Some pulled skiers, others tugged inflatable rafts
packed with kids. In the distance one of those two-level party barges slowly cruised
down the middle of the lake.

"Looks like fun," said Kishna.

Ares watched his reflection on her glasses, dropping his gaze to the prominent cleavage of the bikini top she wore to blend in with the lake crowd. She smiled and threw him a kiss. Perhaps after this mission they would head for the Cayman Islands for a well-deserved vacation.

But business must precede pleasure, he thought, lowering his gaze even further, to the newspaper spread between them, its front page showing the picture of the same man who had come after him in New Orleans, the one who had called out his name in the alley: Tom Grant, senior agent of the Counter Cyberterrorism Task Force. There was a second agent mentioned, the leader of the field team, Special Agent Karen Frost, as well as the head of the CCTF, Randall Cramer.

CCTF AGENTS PREVENT FLOOD IN DOWNTOWN NEW ORLEANS.

He had read the article this morning, after driving all night on IH-10 out of New Orleans, through Baton Rouge and other southern Louisiana cities, and then on to Texas, where they went straight through Houston and then up Highway 71 to Austin, where Neurall had already been hard at work locating their next target. They had taken turns driving, reaching the Texas capital at around ten in the morning.

According to the article, the CCTF agents working in conjunction with the New Orleans Police Department had managed to disarm the three bombs deployed to flood the French Quarter and most of the downtown area. A suspect was apprehended while setting up one of the bombs and was being held in custody at an undisclosed location. His name had not yet been released.

Ken Paxton, Ares Kulzak thought.

His comrade in arms had failed him, but he knew that Paxton would not say a word about his knowledge of Kulzak's operations or his involvement with the Cartel. The man had two daughters. At this moment, while his drug operation was likely being moved to another location in New Orleans, Cartel connections were probably contacting one of their law firms to defend him.

He will never talk, Kulzak thought, and that meant that the Cartel would leave him alone to serve his jail term if found guilty, or allow him to live in peace if found innocent by the American court system. Based on recent history, a case like that could drag on for years, long after he had accomplished his primary mission with Neurall.

Of more immediate importance was that Kulzak made an example of the CCTF agents, in particularly Randall Cramer, the head of the CCTF, and his star agents Frost and Grant. His Colombian sponsors had practically invented the concept of going after government officials charged with leading the fight against drugs as a way to kill their commitment. Ares intended to use the same demoralizing tactic here. The Americans had been foolish enough to allow their names and pictures into the newspapers, which called them heroes and praised their instincts and efforts, including the severe electrical charge that Grant endured while disarming one of the bombs with his bare hands.

Ares sighed.

Heroes.

In a way Ares admired Grant's courage, however misplaced.

Tom Grant.

Ares felt he had met him before, and strangely enough, so had Paxton.

But where? When?

He shook his head. Perhaps it would come to him later.

Ares studied the man's picture once more, deciding that the mysterious Grant was a frontline soldier fighting for what he believed in, unlike the *gusanos* that sneaked into Cuba under the cover of darkness so long ago, killing everyone he had ever loved.

But he still had to be eliminated—along with Cramer and Frost—and in the worst possible way. In order to insure success Ares wondered if he would have to do it himself.

Ken Paxton was too old, Kulzak thought. *I should have never asked him to assist me beyond the manufacture of the weapons.*

Ares felt certain that had he and Kishna been the ones setting up those charges, downtown New Orleans would have been underwater by now, just as the airport and lakefront areas were at the moment.

"Do not feel bad, Ari. We inflicted a devastating blow in New Orleans," said Kishna, apparently noticing the anger he felt boiling inside of him. She drummed a fingernail on the second article of the paper's front page. "Over three square miles of homes and businesses, plus the airport is under seven feet of water. Over two hundred drowned and tens of thousands homeless, plus the damage is estimated in the tens of billions. Not bad for a night's work."

She rubbed his left shoulder. "Three American cities in less than one week, Ari. It is unprecedented, even as measured by the strikes of 2001. Our sponsors must be quite pleased."

"It is not enough," he replied, disappointed not only in Paxton's failure, but also because a series of wide canals, walls, and creeks had contained the water damage to that section of the city, sparing the rest. According to the article, crews were also already hard at work plugging the gap in the retaining wall and starting the draining process. Another article described how parts of San Antonio were already coming back on-line only six days after the attack. "The Americans are too resilient," he said, remembering just how quickly America had also rebounded following the hijacked jetliner crashes several years back. "We have to hit them harder."

Kishna set her drink on the console. "And we will, Ari. Remember that the attack on SWOASIS accomplished its primary objective. They did find the virus, but the inhibitor alteration was not detected, just like in San Antonio. The supercomputers controlling the network are now getting smarter, but anyone checking for Turing compliance will not know it. So let them think that they prevented a virus from shutting down the network. It would have been nice if our smokescreen had created havoc in Los Angeles, like it did in San Antonio, but let's not lose sight of our real task, of the reason we embarked on this critical mission. We have two of the four required passwords to access the biggest and most sophisticated supercomputer in the world, the twin to our dear Neurall, and once we obtain the other two backdoor passwords, we will control the crown jewels of the Americans, and they will not even know it until it is too late, until we order Neurall to fire missiles at their own cities. So forget San Antonio, Ari. Forget New Orleans. The best is yet to come."

She was right, of course, but Ares Kulzak still enjoyed watching Americans suffer now, and was disappointed that Los Angeles had not been turned into a chaotic wasteland by now.

"That said," she added, "there are some changes that I will have to make to our approach. Not only did someone spot and eliminate our virus diversion, but that same someone tried to follow my runner as it came reporting back to us. Neurall, charged with guarding the path of the runner, would had reacted quicker but at the time I was adapting it for our next attack by interfacing it to an Ada module. It took him a moment to detect the intrusion, before going after the intruder, who was armed with an expert system and also virtual-reality hardware. Neurall formatted the expert system before blasting the hacker, who should have been flat-lined."

Ares listened to the explanation while observing a large yacht approaching the marina.

"Instead of just keeping Neurall protecting the path to my system, I should have left her guarding the virus until it struck," she added. "I will not make that mistake again, even if it further exposes the AI."

The more exposure Neurall had to the frontlines, the larger the risk a hacker could find a link within Neurall that pointed to its inner sanctum in the Colombian mountains. But the Americans' cyber defenses were more formidable than originally anticipated, forcing him to take more risks. San Antonio had been easy thanks to the element of surprise. And Melbourne had also been a snap. But the enemy was aware of their strategy now and measures had obviously been taken to deter further strikes.

The yacht decelerated as it steered around the breakwater, further slowing down when reaching the slips. The grumbling sound from its engines was carried over by the breeze sweeping across the parking lot, mixing with the rustling inside the small cardboard box holding the two mice Kishna had purchased at a pet store earlier today. The box, along with a metallic ice bucket, small blowtorch, and other interrogation essentials, lay in the rear seat, along with two backpacks—courtesy of Paxton—each housing enough explosives to level a small building.

Pressing the rubber ends of a pair of binoculars against his eyes and fingering the adjusting wheel, he brought a man with silver hair and two attractive women into focus. They stood on the open bridge; the man behind the wheel, the women flanking him. All wore bathing suits and smiles.

He handed the binoculars to Kishna.

"Is that him?" he asked her.

"Yes," she replied a moment later. "That's Jason Lamar. Still the womanizer he was back at MIT."

After docking the vessel in one of the larger covered slips, the trio walked down the short gangway and into the parking lot. There, the ladies kissed him before stepping into a sedan and driving off. The man waved them off before walking to a black Porsche.

Jason Lamar, an MIT associate professor of advanced software development, had made his fortune during the late nineties by launching a short-lived but highly profitable dot.com. During his tenure at MIT, in addition to codeveloping Neurall for the Department of Defense, Lamar had contracted for the Commercial Airplanes Group within the Boeing Company during the development of the Boeing 777, the world's first commercial jetliner to be fully controlled by software.

By software coded in Ada.

"Let's go get your old colleague," said Ares.

Kishna replied by starting the sedan.

She waited until the sports car pulled out of its parking spot and headed for the lot's exit.

Then she began to follow.

FORTY

> > > > >

HEROES

> LIFE IS A PENDULUM.

One day you're considered an idiot, your career is going down the drain, and you're about to lose your job, and the next day you're a hero.

Today, sitting in the rear of the Bubird heading for Austin, I'm not feeling much like a hero but more like an electric-chair survivor. My hands continue to tingle from the shock and they look a tad sunburned, but I least I *have* hands.

Karen Frost is up in front talking to Paul Stone, who is to be commended for the way he handled himself last night. And even Karen did all right, nailing the last bomb by herself by simply opening the backpack and disconnecting the battery.

I'll be damned.

She'd just *disconnected* the fucking battery, which is also what Sergeant Appetizer and his bomb squad did to disarm the first bomb.

I guess I've always had a knack for doing things the hard way.

The blue skies over southwestern Louisiana extend as far as I can see from my window seat, dotted here and there with low-hanging cumulus clouds.

It actually doesn't really matter *how* we prevented the flood as long as we did, though I wish I could say the same about the handful of square miles around the New Orleans International Airport that were swallowed by Lake Pontchartrain. And just like in San Antonio, it's one thing reading about it and watching CNN, but this morning's boat ride over the flooded section of Interstate 10 before reaching the

Huey P. Long Bridge and getting in a car to go to Baton Rouge and catch this plane had served as a harsh reminder of what happens when we lose a battle to the monster.

Emergency crews are sealing the hole in the wall before starting the long process of pumping the water out of the area and rebuilding, starting with the airport itself, which went out of commission when the first wave struck.

But in spite of it all, the media just loved my last-minute deployment idea and more so the fact that I nearly killed myself to save the downtown area and the historical French Quarter—not to mention the hundreds of thousands of tourists jam-packed in those few square miles of hotels, restaurants, bars, and shops.

So, with that clout behind me, the first thing I made sure of was that Karen continued to be the big cheese around here. And don't get me wrong. I did it not because but *in spite* of last night's elevator episode. I happen to think that she really has what it takes to run the field operation, and having her in charge of all of the overhead associated with our job allows me to focus my own resources much more efficiently.

Now, it's all fine and dandy that Cramer didn't go through with his threat and allowed Karen and me to keep our jobs, but not for the sake of a steady paycheck. I still believe we are the best chance our country has. If anyone is capable of catching Kulzak, it is this team. We have proven that we can survive his counterstrikes while getting closer to him. All we need now is a way to change the rules of the game, to stop reacting to his moves.

Unfortunately, I'm not only fighting Kulzak but also our own government politics.

Remember the old guy with the long blond hair we caught last night in New Orleans? Well, although I'm sure that he only has limited knowledge of the whereabouts of Mr. Kulzak, he could still provide some insight into the case. You never really know what fragmented pieces of intel might transpire into a break in the investigation, so you pursue all possible avenues.

Therefore, I wanted a round with this guy to put my old interrogation skills to work and short-circuit the information-gathering process. But Cramer nixed it, claiming that the CCTF would not lower itself to the level of terrorists by resorting to such savage methods, and explained that the suspect—which was all he was until a jury found him guilty—was already in Washington in the company of his lawyer.

Now, how's that for good old American justice?

Through my ingenuity, and a little luck, we have captured one of Kulzak's soldiers, and now my own government won't let me interrogate him.

Sometimes we deserve to get crapped on.

So, that potential avenue slammed shut by those who think they're on our side, I try to tell myself that perhaps the *suspect* was indeed a dead end because the Kulzak I know would never be stupid enough to confide in what appears to be a foot soldier. I chose not to fight that battle, opting instead to follow Ryan's latest lead in Austin.

Karen walks down the narrow aisle holding two cups of coffee. She smiles without showing her teeth as she hands me one before taking a seat next to me. "We'll be there in an hour. Mike Ryan will be waiting for us at the terminal. He has a couple of theories he'd like to discuss with us."

I just nod and take a sip of coffee. It burns my lips, but that's how I like it.

She thumbs open a small plastic bottle of aspirin, popping four pills in her mouth, and washing them down with a few sips of coffee. She actually looks pretty good for the morning following a serious consumption of alcohol, though her eyes are still a bit red and the skin around them looks a little swollen. But her lips are moist and that freckle appears as delicious as it tasted last night.

She's wearing her hair pulled back tight and secured with a silver and turquoise barrette, which matches the bracelet hugging her right wrist and the buckle of her leather belt. Now that I pay more attention I realize that in addition to wearing black jeans and a black denim shirt, she is also wearing her black boots.

Yee-haw.

I guess we're going back to Texas. The cowgirl even has a gun strapped to her belt. Maybe I can convince her to ride the big Grant bull.

"How are you feeling?" she asks. With her hair pulled back, Karen's exposed forehead gives her a serious, businesslike look, further strengthened by her Western clothes. Her whole appearance, combined with her harsh voice, broadcasts a don't-fuck-with-me image that I'm sure would be quite effective on anyone who wasn't with her in that elevator last night.

"Been worse," I say, putting the elevator scene out of my mind while flexing the fingers of my left hand and taking another sip. In my own sick way I'm actually glad that the current surge in those electrodes knocked me out for about six hours. At least I finally got some uninterrupted sleep.

"Your hands still throbbing?"

"The ibuprofen is helping, but it feels as if my skin is covered by ants."

"That was a very brave thing you did back there, Tom."

"Brave? I think *stupid* is a more appropriate term."

"I know the difference between bravery and stupidity. What you did is as brave as they come, just like the way you shielded me in that alley."

There we go with the flattery again. I glance at the freckle before forcing my gaze away from any part of her anatomy.

"How are *you* doing?" I ask, changing the focus of the conversation.

"Still employed," she says while holding up her cup.

I lift mine up to hers and the paper rims touch. We smile at the same time.

"I guess they'll hang onto us," I say, before adding, "which is better than being *hanged* by them."

She chuckles before sipping coffee.

Hey, that's the first time she actually laughed at my dark humor.

"We kept most of the city from getting flooded, Tom, thanks to your initiative."

"If I recall correctly, you handled one of the bombs yourself."

"*Tom*," she says, lowering her voice. "I was out of commission in my hotel room when you pulled this spontaneous search party together. And I wouldn't have joined you had Mike Ryan not called me and woken me up with news about the Austin lead. Heck, I don't even remember *getting* to my room."

Up to this point we've been too busy to discuss the aftermath of her drinking extravaganza at the Court of Two Sisters.

"I took you to your room," I say, deciding to level with her. "And I also tucked you into bed."

My words rips away her Texas-tough mask like a tornado. She almost spills her coffee. "You *did?*"

"Relax. I was a gentleman the entire time . . . and no one knows what happened."

For a brief second a mix of gratitude and relief flashes in her eyes. "Everything got hazy after the fifth glass of wine."

Her perfume tickles my nostrils as I inhale while leaning over and whispering, "Karen, *I* would have been plastered with the amount of alcohol that you consumed, and you're less than half my weight. You tried to get the waitress to pour you another glass but I convinced her not to. Then you pretty much collapsed right there, so I had to carry you."

She crosses her arms while swallowing and looking around her to make sure no one is in listening range before also dropping her voice to a mere whisper, her face just inches from mine as she says, "You *carried* me?"

"Either that or you were going to sleep on the floor of that lounge. Again, no one relevant saw you. We went up the elevator, and I did have to search in your pockets for the room key."

She is staring into my eyes as if I'm from outer space.

"I pulled the bed covers, set you down, covered you back up, and left."

"And that's it?"

I lift my right hand and extend the ring, middle, and index fingers. "Scout's honor."

She leans back on her seat. "I guess I must have been dreaming."

"Dreaming?"

"In the elevator . . . I thought that—never mind."

"Oh, well, *that* wasn't a dream, Karen." I wink.

"Oh, God," she whispers more to herself than to me, placing a hand on her mouth, color coming to her cheeks. "Did I . . . ?"

"Yes, but you didn't know what you were doing, and again, nothing—absolutely nothing—happened beyond an innocent kiss. You have nothing to be ashamed of."

She closes her eyes for a moment. Who knows what's going through her mind. When she finally opens them she whispers, "I'm truly, *truly* sorry for putting you in that situation, Tom. I'm not a lush and I'm definitely not a . . . slut. I'm not sure what came over me."

I grin and pat her on the wrist. "I never thought you were either one."

She drops her gaze to the carpeted floor, obviously embarrassed.

"Look," I add. "We're both under a lot of pressure and are bound to release steam now and then. Yesterday was your turn, and I took care of you. Tomorrow might be mine. I sure hope you don't leave me plastered in some alley sleeping it off."

I get that perplexed stare again, like I'm this alien from a distant galaxy. I've been out of the dating game for some time now, but the last time I checked there was still something called gallantry, right? The rules about interfacing with members of the opposite sex haven't changed that much in the past decade, have they?

"Besides," I say at her silence. "Whether you realize it or not, we're both now on the same boat."

"What do you mean? We've *been* on the same boat."

"No, Karen. We have been on the same *investigative team*. Now we're on a boat that's gone beyond the point of no return, thanks to the media. I'm talking about Ares Kulzak. He knows who we are and by now also where we live and the model of car we drive. We can't go back to our normal lives because he will be waiting for us. If we're lucky we will die in an explosion or by a bullet in the head when we least expect it . . . *if* we're lucky."

She stares at me for a moment, then says, "Tom?"

"Yeah?"

"Have I told you how much I'm enjoying your cheery personality?"

She waits for an answer and when I just shrug she says, "We really can't stop hunting him, can we?"

I finish my coffee and pop a stick of gum in my mouth to help me with the pressure building up in my ears, still sore from yesterday. "Not if we want to live to a ripe old age. We have to find and eliminate the bastard—with or without the sanction of the CCTF. We're on his black list now, and there're only two ways to get off of it. He'll either kill us or we kill him. There's no in between."

"Well," she says. "For what it's worth, this isn't the first time I've found myself in such a bind."

"Good, then the next question might not be so hard to answer: Do you have any close relatives, anyone you care about?"

"None," she says, even though the look in her eyes tells me there is someone she does care about, and based on last night's elevator episode, that someone is likely to be yours truly. "Everyone died a long time ago. There's nothing that man can take away from me or threaten me with."

She didn't say it, so I, in turn, can't also confess that the unspoken feeling is very mutual. Instead I reply, "That makes two of us."

"All right," she says, her tone of voice stiffening, conveying business. "Let's review the plan for when we land in Austin."

FORTY-ONE

> > > > >

FLASHBACK

> DÉJÀ VU.

The feeling overpowered Michael Ryan as he rode alongside Victoria in the rear of the Secret Service sedan through the entrance to a subdivision in Lakeway, a city bordering the south shore of Lake Travis.

"It's like we never left, Mike," Victoria whispered as they proceeded down the main street of the exclusive neighborhood, where home prices progressively increased as they neared the water, climaxing with waterfront properties.

The dark sedan, followed by a Suburban packed with Secret Service agents, continued down the gentle incline as the street sloped down to the lake, turning into the driveway of an opulent Mediterranean-style mansion. Towering stucco walls, a clay tile roof, and lots of windows stood beyond the wrought-iron gate blocking the entrance.

The gate slowly slid out of the way, and they continued down a cobblestone driveway that ended in a circular driveway in front of the mansion, adorned by a beautiful fountain in the middle and three Secret Service agents in dark suits standing about, dark sunglasses concealing their eyes.

"Pretty weird being here," said Ryan, remembering the last time he had visited the home of his former boss, Ron Wittica, now serving two life sentences at a federal prison after being convicted on charges ranging from money laundering and treason to first-degree murder.

"Never thought I'd see this place again," she said as the driver shut off the engine. "Though it is somewhat poetic this is now a government safe house."

Ryan regarded his wife, remembering how close he had come to losing her back then, and how he'd sworn to never—ever—get dragged into another government task force. Yet, here he was again, years later, in the middle of a new case. Visiting places like this one brought back those old feelings, making him question his commitment to Karen Frost.

But another voice boomed within him, repeating the same phrase over and over. *Remember the Alamo.*

Ryan closed his eyes. The recent cyber strike had certainly given new meaning to the old slogan. He couldn't walk away and let Kulzak rape and pillage this nation at will, especially given that it was Ryan's own data, however painfully extracted, that currently steered the direction of the investigation. Without him, the CCTF would be operating in the dark.

Karen had requested that Ryan meet her in Austin—which happened to be the most likely place to bump into the cyberterrorists—for a face-to-face discussion of their options. He had agreed to the meeting but only if two stipulations were met. The first was that Victoria and he were kept in a safe house surrounded by as many Secret Service agents as the Department of the Treasury could spare, which in this case was eleven—all flown in from Washington early in the day to protect the life of the man who might be able to deliver Ares Kulzak. The second—and he had not received Karen's response yet—was to increase his compensation package for the extreme risk the government was putting his family and himself under.

Ryan didn't feel the least guilty about using taxpayers' dollars, particularly for the protection of his family. Not only did he feel he'd earned it, but he was determined to take zero chances. Victoria had been abducted by the enemy the last time Ryan had agreed to assist Karen Frost right here in Austin, and only his quick thinking—plus a lot of luck—had kept Victoria from ending up at the bottom of Lake Travis. She couldn't afford to go through the same level of excitement in her current condition.

Johnson, the agent sitting next to the driver, planted an elbow on the back of his seat while turning around to address his passengers. He was the leader of the security detail. "My men will help you set up your equipment. The refrigerator and bar are already stocked, courtesy of the CCTF. We will be patrolling the grounds twenty-four seven. You and your wife will be safe here."

Ryan nodded, though having been around the block once, he was all too aware that there was no such thing as being *truly* safe. If heads of state could be assassinated in this age of high-tech executive protection, so could they by a determined terrorist.

But at least he had increased the odds in his favor by bringing in the Secret Service.

Followed by Agent Johnson, Ryan held Victoria's hand as he stepped away from the vehicle and headed for the front door, already guarded by two agents wearing sunglasses and earpieces, both African-American in their thirties, their bulky muscles defining the shape of the dark suits they wore. The clean-cut agents smiled politely, and one of them opened the door for them.

"Looks the same," said Victoria as they stepped into the foyer.

"Your dossier states that you've been here before," said Agent Johnson from behind. "You did your country a great service back then, Mr. Ryan. We'll take good care of you and your wife."

"Thanks," Ryan said while surveying the large living room beyond the entryway. "Please, call me Mike."

"Sorry, Mr. Ryan. Agency rules."

Ryan shrugged and inspected the interior of the mansion, which looked just as he remembered it. Even the furniture hadn't changed. Beyond the French doors lining the back of the living room, manicured lawns sloped down to a boathouse, backdropped by the bright-blue waters of Lake Travis. He'd forgotten just how darned big houses were in Austin compared to Silicon Valley. The boathouse alone could enclose his house in Mountain View.

But he had little to complain about in that department. During his cyber excursions into the guts of the money-laundering ring he had helped Karen Frost crack way back when, Ryan had leaked funds from one of many overseas accounts into a numbered Swiss account under his name—and Victoria's. The few million dollars were never noticed in the shuffling of billions, his unwritten payment for the suffering that Victoria and he endured during that case. In addition, Uncle Sam had given them a healthy financial reward. Though nowhere near what he had kept for himself, it had been enough to purchase a home in the overpriced market of Silicon Valley. The government, of course, had kept all of the criminal ring's assets, from dozens of bank accounts to high-dollar properties like this one sprinkled across the country. This time around, Ryan had requested an even larger reward for his troubles.

"According to the brief, this place was kept pretty much intact after appropriation," reported Agent Johnson, who, like the other Secret Service agents, didn't seem to have a first name. For a moment he wondered if that was even his real last name. Johnson was as tall as Ryan but wider, and not from fat. The man belonged in the line of scrimmage on *Monday Night Football*. He was dressed in typical Secret Service fashion, dark suit, lapel microphone, and a flesh-colored earpiece with a wire coiling into his suit behind the right ear.

"Is the security system working?" Ryan asked, remembering the state-of-the-art monitoring system that Ron Wittica had installed. It included at least a dozen cameras plus laser and infrared sensors.

"It's been improved in the past few years, Mr. Ryan. Two of my agents are already manning the control room. There's no one getting anywhere near this place without us knowing about it."

"What about the boats?" Ryan asked, pointing at the structure by the shore, whose architecture matched the house, down to the clay roof and stucco exterior.

"A yacht, a ski boat, and two personal water craft, all in working condition and part of our evacuation plan in case the streets are blocked."

"And the T1 in the library?" Ryan asked, remembering Wittica's broadband connection.

"Ready for you, sir. Is that where you want your gear delivered?"

"Please. There should also be a few packages arriving later on today from Los Alamos and the Pentagon. Just have them delivered to the same room."

"Very well, sir."

"By the way, where are we sleeping?"

"The master bedroom upstairs is already set up, sir. If it's all right, I'll have my men deliver your suitcases there."

"That will be great. Thanks," Ryan replied.

While Johnson went to work, Ryan and Victoria walked to the covered patio beyond the French doors.

"How's that for service?" Ryan said, winking.

The lake breeze swirled her hair and pressed her loose summer dress against the front of her body, accentuating her belly. She looked lovelier than ever, standing against the light wind, chin up, hands beneath her growing baby.

She looked at him and frowned, fine facial features tightening, hazel eyes giving Ryan a glance of concern. "That's *just* how things started the last time, Mike. All was great and then everything went to hell."

"Things are different this time, Vic. We are under government protection. The Secret Service is looking after us, for crying out loud. It doesn't get any safer than that."

"I'm just worried, Mike, about the baby, about you, about us."

Ryan didn't respond. He simply held his wife and prayed.

FORTY-TWO

> > > > >

ADA

> THE TRIP FROM THE AIRPORT TO THIS LAKE HOUSE was uneventful, at least until we tried to get past the Secret Service agents guarding the wrought-iron gate.

I sigh.

Damned Secret Service.

If you think CIA officers are all hush-hush, then multiply that by ten and you'll get a picture of what it's like to deal with the Secret Service when you're not the one being protected. They are the most egotistical, royal pain-in-the-ass people you'll ever deal with. Even after we showed them our credentials and they matched them to their log, they still didn't let us through. They first called Washington, got approval, then rummaged through our stuff and came this close from performing a cavity search before waving us through.

You'd think the president was living here. But when you think about it, they are guarding someone just as important. Without this kid we would be deeply screwed.

Now, ten minutes later, we're sitting on the patio of this mansion by the shores of Lake Travis sipping iced tea, which isn't doing a damned thing about my growing hunger.

I have not eaten a damned thing since those oysters last night, and given that there's no meal service on the Bubirds, yours truly is one hungry son of a gun, which explains why my stomach's growling like a baboon in heat.

But my lack of nourishment woes aside, I have to admit that this is some fancy joint, with awesome views, nice furniture, lake access, and primo boats, including a serious yacht.

According to Ryan, sitting across from Karen and me, this place was once owned by his old boss, until the government took it over following the investigation where Karen and he first hooked up. Maybe Uncle Sam will turn it into a retirement home for CCTF agents one day.

"Hey, Mike," I say, unable to help myself. "I would have asked for this place as a reward way back when. With the money they recovered from that case Uncle Sam should have even thrown in those boats over there." I stretch my thumb toward the huge boathouse.

Ryan looks amused by my comment. Karen, however, decides to drive the heel of her boot onto my bruised left instep. I'm sure she meant it in jest, but I happen to have one hell of a bruise there from the other night.

Damn!

She might as well have kicked me in the balls. I nearly piss on myself while holding back the tears threatening to burst out of my eyes.

"Tom, are you all right?" Karen asks.

Oh, sure, so nice of you to be so concerned!

"Got a bruise on that foot," I say, my voice about to crack as I take a deep breath while shooting her an I'll-get-even-with-you-for-this-later look. She's lucky I have this rule about not hitting women.

"Sorry," she whispers.

Apparently unaware of our game of footsy, Ryan gives me an embarrassed smile and says, "I really can't complain about the deal I got, Tom. The government was quite generous."

Crossing my legs and massaging my instep, I ask, "Your wife doing okay?"

"Tired. She's upstairs, sleeping. She asked me to wake her up when you guys got here." He checks his watch, then says, "We'll have lunch in a little while. I'll get her up then."

Lunch? Food. My stomach rumbles again.

"When is she due?" asks Karen.

He rubs his chin a moment before saying, "About two months to go."

"Well, Mike," Karen says. "I'm glad that you have chosen to continue to help us out, especially in light of your recent experiences in cyberspace. I'm also pretty sure that Victoria wasn't very happy about them."

Ryan rolled his eyes while leaning back and crossing his arms. "That doesn't even *begin* to describe how she felt when she heard that I was in a coma."

Karen looks at me before shifting her gaze back to Ryan, almost as if she's hesitating to say what's on her mind. "I know we made a deal with you at the beginning, but now, in light of what's happened, I've run your request by my boss and the FBI director, and they have agreed to increase your compensation for the risk you and your family are taking by assisting us."

Increase his compensation?

Hello! What about *my* fucking compensation for nearly frying my *cojones* last night?

The pain from my instep and the tingling in my hands vanishes in the wake of the drowning feeling of being totally, utterly unappreciated around here. Maybe if I wasn't working for the government, maybe if I was a *consultant*, like Ryan, my compensation package would also get adjusted.

Heck, maybe then the bastards would even feed me three meals a day.

Chill out, Grant. You're not doing it for the money.

You never have.

And that's true. You don't join the CIA with the hope of getting rich and famous. For that you become a lawyer, a politician, or a TV evangelist.

You do it for your country, for democracy, for freedom.

Or so I tell myself as I park my tongue while Ryan inspects the sheet of paper that Karen slips across the table. The whiz kid glances at it, smiles, nods, and places it under the thick manila folder in front of him.

"Victoria will like this," he finally says, "especially with the baby coming and all."

I'm not jealous by nature, but sitting across the table from someone twenty years my junior who apparently has it all—a beautiful wife, a kid on the way, a job he's awesome at, and plenty of dough—does have a way of staining my heart the color of the bile I feel like puking.

I mean, c'mon, I've been busting my ass for over two decades doing everything from walking the beat in New York to getting beat in San Salvador. And all for what? So that people like Mike Ryan can live the American dream?

And have I really made that much of a difference anyhow? Would world history have been any different had Tom Grant stuck to the bouncing business while attending NYU and gotten that international business degree? I was getting pretty decent grades, you know?

I half listen as Ryan gets Karen up to speed on his life in California, my mind trying to find the point in time when I stopped caring about school and turned to the streets. Then I remember the cop who spoke at my social deviant class during my sophomore year. He had impressed that nineteen-year-old kid sitting in the back row, the one who'd worked nights as a bouncer in a Manhattan club to pay for school and make ends meet, the one who had been on his own since high school because his father beat his mother to death and sent the kid to the hospital for a month.

I remember dropping out of college and joining the force before I realized it. Soon after, I was stepping into the middle of dozens of domestic disputes every month, trying to make a difference, trying to keep other kids from ending up like I did, first in a hospital and then in an orphanage. My early twenties seem like a big blur now, as I rapidly climbed up the ladder in the NYPD before the spooks recruited me following a high-profile terrorist case that I cracked as a first-year detective.

I do remember now all right.

But it's not Ryan's fault. It isn't anyone's fault, not even my abusive old man, a hell of a mean drunk who'd beaten us for years until the cops took him away for bashing my mother's head with a hot iron and for breaking four of my ribs and cracking my skull when I'd gone to her rescue, as I always did.

But I had failed her. I had let the monster kill her, just as I had let Kulzak kill Madie.

I really have no one to blame for the way my life has turned out but myself. I'm the one who has to live with the constant second-guessing game that one half of my brain likes to play—particularly late at night—to torture the other half.

"All right, Mike," I hear Karen say while I'm in the middle of this unexpected daydream. "What have you learned?"

Looking toward the lake, spotting a pair of sailboats in the distance, I flush those memories out of my mind and focus on the upcoming discussion. Underpaid or not, I'm a government agent and this is the most important case of my life, if anything because failing to solve it could mean death by Kulzak—the kind of death that would make my dad's beatings feel like a slap on the wrist.

Ryan starts to explain what had taken place. How he had followed a runner through the Internet, taking him straight to a service provider in Austin.

"The last runner was the one that pointed to New Orleans, right?" I ask.

"Correct," Ryan says, sipping iced tea, before proceeding to explain the storm-enshrouded digital entity that had nearly killed him.

"What do think that storm cloud was?" Karen and I ask in unison.

"I don't think it was a *what* but a *who*."

"Kulzak?" Karen asks.

The kid runs a hand through his short dark hair. He reminds me of what's-his-name from the old flicks, *Platoon* and *Wall Street* . . . Charlie Sheen. That's it. With the intense but somewhat mischievous eyes and a desire to do the right thing.

"No," he says. "I don't think it was a person, but an entity of some sort."

"Like MPS-Ali?" I ask.

R . J .   P I N E I R O

"Right, but much more advanced and powerful . . . and deadly. Do you remember what I told you about the Turing Society?"

I nod, and so does Karen, obviously aware of this secret club of propeller heads. I offer, "You make sure the computers don't get too smart by using some kind of inhibitor."

"Correct," he says. "This thing that attacked me was too intelligent. It was a real-life artificial intelligence construct."

"According to the Turing test?" I ask. Look at me, talking like a pro.

He slowly nods. "We fired a virus at the AI, which made it slow down while we tried to get away. However, it learned how to counter the virus and make itself immune to it—all in a matter of a few seconds. No human could have done that. This machine is in direct violation of our Turing doctrines, and it's armed with very sophisticated technology—some of which I didn't know existed. The digital EMP it fired at me pretty much fried the electronics of the HMD I was wearing."

Karen shakes her head. "I thought that you had the latest and greatest gear."

"That's coming this afternoon," he says. "Directly from Los Alamos and the Pentagon. But I can assure you that even that equipment could not create a pulse like the one I saw and felt."

"Then," I ask, confused, "how is it possible that the United States, the smartest high-tech nation in the world, doesn't have such technology but some cyberterrorist does?"

"It's the nature of the machines, Tom."

"What do you mean?"

"If a sophisticated supercomputer is allowed to teach itself, to learn from its mistakes, it will do so at an exponential rate, much faster than humans can. This system has apparently done just that, making itself far smarter than our computers. My guess would be that it is at least ten years ahead of us in software complexity."

"Why can't we do the same and catch up?" asks Karen.

"Because of the danger that if we allow our systems to teach themselves, they will quickly outpace the human rate of learning, meaning they will get smarter at a much faster rate than their creators."

"And they could then turn against us," I say, finishing Ryan's train of thought.

"All I can hope for is that the military hardware and software help me bridge the gap between our machines and this thing running loose out there," Ryan says. "That's one problem that myself and my colleagues at the Society are dealing with. Another issue is the fact that this uninhibited AI appears to be partially coded in Ada, not in C."

"What kind of language is Ada?" I ask, aware of the other computer language.

"It is the name of a language used mostly in embedded applications."

I happen to know what an embedded application is from the Y2K scare. Embedded systems are those that operate in stand-alone fashion, like elevators and traffic lights. What I didn't know is that most of them shared a common computer language called Ada. I ask Ryan where the name came from.

"The software was named after an English lady by the name of Ada Byron," he begins, his voice taking on the tone of a lecturing professor. "She was the daughter of Lord Byron, though the famous romantic poet had nothing to do with his daughter's upbringing as he divorced Ada's mother and left England soon after she was born in 1815.

"Ada had a clear gift for mathematics and studied under Augustus DeMorgan, who is today famous for one of the basic theorems of Boolean algebra, which forms the basis of modern computers. Ada eventually connected with Charles Babbage, who built one of the world's first differential engines, a mechanical calculating machine, the predecessor of the computer. She worked with him for the rest of her life. Ada believed that mathematics would eventually develop into a system of symbols that could be used to represent anything in the universe. In her notes she suggested that the analytical engine could go beyond arithmetic computations and become a general manipulator of symbols, and thus be capable of almost anything. Ada even suggested that such a device could be programmed with rules of harmony and composition so that it could produce what she referred to as scientific music."

"Scientific *music?*" My Texas two-step partner and I say at the same time.

"A term to express technical harmony," Ryan explains. "Software and hardware working as one, which is the essence of artificial intelligence. Ada foresaw the field of artificial intelligence almost two hundred years ago. Most of her work was captured in her life's work titled, *The Sketch of the Analytical Engine*, which became the definitive work on the subject. This is the reason why this software, which is used in many complex embedded applications, is named after her."

"What are we facing here, Mike?" asks Karen.

Ryan leafs through the loose sheets of his folder, mostly pages with scribbled notes plus a few printouts from Web articles. He stops halfway through the thick pile. "All right," he starts. "I surfed a few sites last night, after I called you, to get a better feel for how many applications out there are using Ada, and I have grouped them into six major categories." He lifts his gaze from the papers and shifts it between Karen and me.

The kid might be smart and much richer than *moi*, but he would fail miserably as a government agent, especially as a spook. His face says it all.

We're in deep shit.

"Go ahead, Mike," says Karen. "We can handle it."

"It's pretty ugly," he says, surprising me. "Let me start with the easiest: banking and financial systems. Ada is used by Reuters, by many Swiss bankers, and also by other financial institutions throughout Europe."

"I thought you said that Ada was used in embedded systems. Aren't banks networked in this day and age?"

"They are, but they still use Ada."

"How?"

"Take automatic teller machines, for example. They need to operate like an embedded system, autonomously dealing with a client in the field, checking passwords, taking a picture of the user, issuing cash, et cetera. But yet, they need to be networked to the main branch to check balances and other account statistics in order to complete the transaction."

"What about banks in the U.S.?" asks Karen.

"No. We're still using Cobol and are transitioning to C. Wall Street is mostly C based, as well as most American financial and brokerage institutions. Now let's get into the scarier ones. The second category is a combination of communications and space exploration, since satellites are a vital part of our ability to . . . reach out and touch someone."

I stare at this kid and for once don't appreciate the humor.

He gets our silent message and continues. "The ultimate embedded systems are satellites, required to perform on their own for many, many years with no direct support from Earth. Ada truly excels in these situations and therefore is used in a variety of satellites. NASA, for example, uses Ada on its TDRSS ground stations, which handle all of the communications with the shuttles. There's the INMARSAT, a satellite used for voice and data communications for ships at sea. NSTAR is used by the Nippon Telephone and Telegraph. Our own Coast Guard's GPS receivers are running Ada code. Also the Ariane 4 and 5, the primary rockets used by the European Space Agency to launch satellites run with Ada. Hughes has a couple of models of communications satellites running Ada. The International Space Station is run mostly by Ada software. And so on."

I'm speechless. Any of those systems would make an awesome target for someone like Kulzak.

"The good news," Ryan continues, "is that by their nature, embedded systems are not directly networked, meaning a hacker can't just get on the Internet and click his way into them, like the cyberterrorists did in San Antonio, or tried to do at the SWOASIS. The terrorist would have to physically reach the target system and then find the proper way to interface into it to alter its operation."

"Wait a minute," I say. "If a terrorist is going to go through the trouble of getting to the system, why bother interfacing to it? Might as well just strap a charge of C4 and blow it up."

"Right. That's what doesn't make sense about an artificial intelligence system based on Ada, unless the terrorists have figured out a creative delivery method."

"All right, Mike," I say. "So far we've covered banks and space vehicles. What else do we need to worry about?"

"The third category is railways."

I feel as if I've just swallowed molten lead.

"The metro systems in dozens of cities around the world, from Athens, Paris, and Hong Kong, to Caracas, Budapest, Mexico City, and London. They all use Ada for the control systems of the cars as well as the master traffic controller. The famous TGV, the French high-speed train, is solely controlled by Ada software, as well as the new automatic control project of the New York City subway system and the Swiss Federal Railway System. The big problem I see here is that most of those systems, like the ATMs of a bank, operate in independent fashion but are linked to a centralized system."

"And that centralized system is tied to the Internet," Karen says.

"What isn't these days?" I add.

"Now," Ryan says, his face becoming grimmer. "The fourth group is commercial aviation."

Oh, no. I look at Karen and find her already staring at me, her brown eyes glistening with the concern that matches the turmoil in my stomach. We all still remember the air traffic shutdown of 2001.

I no longer feel like eating.

"Go on, Mike," she says for the both of us.

"Ada is used in anything from cockpit navigation and flight control systems to communications, onboard entertainment, and even brake systems. Boeing, for example, uses Ada in their line of 737s, 747s, 767s, and most extensively, in their 777, which programmers call the *Ada plane*, with nearly all software in Ada. Other jetliner manufacturers like Airbus, which competes directly with Boeing, use Ada in their most popular models, the 320, 330, and 340 commercial jets. Then there's the Fokker F-100, a midsize jet used extensively by American Airlines. There's also a host of other jets, Russian, Dutch, Canadian, and Swiss."

"But again," I say. "The fact that they are embedded systems means that the delivery of a virus is complicated."

Ryan tilts his head. "Yes and no. The modern-day traveler carries a laptop computer on the plane. In some models of aircraft there might be ways to access the plane's digital backbone through the connection feeding each foldaway TV monitor in the business or first-class sections. With the right interface and protocol software a virus could be injected into the system and kept dormant for twenty-four hours, or perhaps timed according to the flight schedule of the aircraft so that it's activated while the plane is over the Pacific, hours away from any viable airport. Or worse, it could disable the jet seconds after takeoff over a heavily populated area."

Karen and I exchange a glance, wondering how in the hell to block that short of prohibiting the use of laptops—or any other electronic device—aboard a commercial flight.

"What's worse," Ryan adds, "is the extensive use of Ada in Air Traffic Management Systems by just about every country in the world, including the United States."

"You mean the software in the control towers, Mike?" I ask.

He nods.

"And that software isn't as isolated as the one aboard aircraft, right?"

Another nod.

"So," Karen says. "What's the connection between Ada and Austin? Why does it require Kulzak to be in Austin?"

"Before you go there," Ryan says. "I think you should know what else is controlled by Ada."

Karen and I lean back in our chairs. Had I known Ryan was going to be such bearer of good news I would have stolen the little bottles of scotch and whiskey from the minibar at the Court of Two Sisters. I sure could use them now.

"The fifth category is general industry, in particular nuclear power plants in Belgium, England, and the Czech Republic. There's other places, like the Volvo automotive assembly plant and Mitsubishi Electric."

We have no comment to that, though memories of the Chernobyl incident do flash in my mind. "What's the last one, Mike?"

"The military."

I'm speechless, and so is Karen, as we stare at this kid while going through the denial phase.

"Let's start with our air force. Just about every fighter jet, troop carrier, bomber, and helicopter has Ada code in some capacity, from the F-16 fighter to the B1-B and B2 bombers. On the army side we're talking tanks like the M1A2, our main battle tank, the Apache and the newer Comanche helicopters, and the Patriot Missile System. The navy uses Ada in its submarine combat systems, in the legendary Tomahawk missile as well as the SM2 and SM3 missiles, fire support systems, engine control, and close-in weapons systems. It's fair to say that without Ada the navy would be reduced to a large collection of vessels with World War Two fighting capability. And last, most of our continental missile warning systems and counterstrike launch control computers are programmed in Ada."

I stand and face the lake, arms crossed, my stomach no longer grumbling. A large white sailboat is being propelled by a blossoming sail of vibrant colors. Two Secret Service agents patrol the shoreline. Two others are strolling by the fenced property line to my left. A third pair roams the edge of the woods marking the right side of the property.

What's the connection between Ada and Austin? My investigative nose tells me that the bastard, just like he did in New Orleans, is here trying to break someone into yielding a password, a code—something—to gain access to a network of some sort that's a bridge into one of these embedded systems Ryan just described.

"What are you thinking about, Tom?"

I tell her without looking back.

She agrees, adding, "I could have the boys compile a list of all possible corporations and individuals in the Austin area that are in any way related to Ada development efforts."

"That's a start," I say, turning around, facing them. "Though I doubt he will be staying at the place of business or residence of whoever he's trying to break. Kulzak will not make the same mistake twice."

"What about the terrorist you caught last night in New Orleans?" asks Ryan. "What have you guys learned from him?"

I stare at Ryan and then just look at Karen, before looking back at the lake. The words are choked in my throat.

"He is in Washington, Mike," says Karen. "Apparently he has gotten himself a team of lawyers, who claim that he was just an innocent bystander and victim of police brutality."

Ryan shakes his head before mumbling, "That's . . ."

"Amazing, isn't it?" I finally say. "In a way we deserve this shit, you know. We have become a society that protects the rights of the bastards who are trying to eliminate it. You'd figure that we would have learned our lesson back in 2001."

"So I doubt we will be getting anything from him anytime soon," says Karen. "What else can we do with the information we have?"

"I have an idea," Ryan says.

We both look at him. He takes a moment to explain.

"Mike," I say, after he is through. "You're brilliant."

"Or suicidal," he adds, "depending on your point of view. Let's just hope that the gear that arrives today is as cutting edge as the folks from Los Alamos claim it is."

FORTY-THREE

> > > > >

PMAS

> THE BOEING 777, DESIGNED TO FILL THE GAP
between the smaller 767 and the legendary 747, was first delivered in May 1995 as
the -200 model, capable of carrying 328 passengers for 5925 miles. Three years later,
a new derivative, the 777-0, provided seating for 394 passengers in its stretched fuse-
lage. Over four hundred Boeing 777s had been built to date for airlines all around
the world, starting with domestic carriers American, Delta, Continental, and United.
In the Asian-Pacific Rim, Air China, Cathay Pacific, China Southwestern Airlines,
Thai Airways, Korean Air, Japan Airlines, Malaysia Airlines, and Singapore Airlines
all had vast fleets of 777s. On the European market, 777 customers included Air
France, British Airways, and Aeroflot. And across Middle Eastern sky, Egypt Air,
Emirates, El Al Israel Airlines, and Kuwait Airways proudly flew their advanced Boe-
ing 777s.

And Ada software controlled most of its systems, starting with the Airplane Information Management System (AIMS), the largest central computer on the jetliner,
consisting of over 613,000 lines of code. Two AIMS boxes handled the six primary
flight and navigation displays, pitch, roll attitude, direction, air speed, rate of climb,
and altitude. AIMS also served as the primary maintenance device to which the 777s'
other computers reported, feeding the data into a centralized maintenance system for
repair logging. Other AIMS functions included thrust management and flight data
acquisition. Ada also ran in the communications modules mounted on the 777s' seats

and offered passengers a variety of services, from in-flight movies and video games to flight information updates. Ada managed the 777s' brake control system, fuel management, and even cabin pressurization, auto-pilot, and auto-land systems.

The Ada plane.

Ares Kulzak reviewed the information displayed on Kishna's laptop computer screen as he sat by her side in the rear office of an old warehouse in North Austin. Jason Lamar lay fully sedated on a mattress in the corner of the room, by the door leading to the commercial construction equipment storage area, almost four stories high. Bulldozers, cranes, dump trucks, backhoes, and other equipment he did not recognize occupied most of the available space. According to a local contact associated with the Cartel, the place had not been used in several months, ever since the local economy became saturated with commercial developers.

The interrogation had gone much smoother than Gary Hutton's in New Orleans. Jason Lamar had no tolerance for pain, and the mere mention of the cauldron and of Kishna's mice had been enough to insure his full cooperation. The passwords to access Boeing's technical Web site had been accurate, gaining them access to the primary parameters of the 777s' third-generation Portable Maintenance Aid. The PMA-III was an interactive maintenance tool that allowed mechanics and engineers to analyze and solve airplane problems at the worksite, in the hangar, in the shop, in the office, or even at the flight line. Improvements from the first two generations of PMAs included the capability to interface directly to the 777s' digital backbone and run diagnostics prior to every flight in the time that it took the jetliner to deplane and pick up another load of passengers. Boeing had advertised the tool as a maintenance marvel guaranteed to boost the 777s' already pristine record by performing in a matter of minutes the same inspection that usually took dozens of mechanics several hours to complete on other aircraft.

"Monthly inspections before every flight," Ares said, reading the slogan at the top of the PMA-III's Web site.

Kishna nodded as she clicked the mouse to advance to the next page of text.

When not used to monitor the vital signs of the 777s, the PMAs were connected to their docking stations, which, in addition to recharging batteries, interfaced them to Boeing's central PMA station, where software updates were automatically released by Boeing's Digital Division in Seattle, Washington. Mechanics around the world got product updates and troubleshooting techniques directly from Boeing, as well as Ada software revisions that they could in turn download into their respective 777s.

"Here," Kishna said. "This is the directory for PMA software revisions. Changes are sent from this location, through the Internet, to every customer site on the globe."

Ares grinned. "Where they get downloaded into the 777s during their next airport stopover. Incredible."

"It is efficient and smart," she said. "Cutting the cost of expensive field upgrades by application engineers and personnel training. PMAs provide mechanics and engineers with quick, easy access to the guts of the 777 through on-line manuals, fault isolation aids, advanced system diagnostics, illustrated parts catalogs, and other critical information. And any required updates are obtained real-time while docked to their stations. Boeing claims that if its preflight procedures are followed by its clients, Ada software upgrades released by their Digital Division would make it to the entire fleet of 777s worldwide within forty-eight hours."

"Two days," Ares mumbled. "How long will it take you to prepare Neurall and coordinate the multiple strikes?"

She pouted, extending a thumb over her right shoulder at the sleeping scientist. "With his help probably within the hour."

He kissed her on the cheek. "Then get to work, *mi amor*. If all goes well, before the sun goes down we shall turn the entire fleet of Boeing 777s into our very own guided missiles." Inspired by those jihad strikes of 2001, Ares planned to also crash jetliners into high-profile targets, but doing so without relying on unpredictable hijackers, airline crews, and passengers by bypassing the human factor altogether. Machines behaved just as they were programmed. For them, software was software, regardless of whether it directed a jetliner to a safe landing or into the United States Capitol.

"And most important," she said, trying to put things in perspective for him, "is the fact that after today, we have obtained the *third* backdoor password to the Pentagon's Neurall. The checksum matches the other two passwords we got from Littman and Hutton."

Soon, Ares Kulzak thought, staring at the woman he loved. *Very soon.*

FORTY-FOUR

> > > > >

CODE-TO-CODE COMBAT

> THE VIBRANT NETWORK PAINTED ON HIS NEW helmet-mounted display carried a resolution Michael Ryan had never seen before. The amazing fluidity of the images and the high-definition graphics created a degree of virtual-reality immersion that truly impressed Ryan as he wore a nine-pound back-top computer developed by Los Alamos for the army. The lightweight HMD connected to the main system, which Ryan wore as a backpack, and which interfaced him to his workstation via a wireless high-speed Ethernet connection that was good for up to a thousand feet from the source.

The hacker in Ryan, however, had already customized a few aspects of the system, designed to interface with a new generation of tactile gloves and boots, plus a microphone connected to a voice-activation program. Ryan had kept the interface, but had loaded his own VR software, which responded to his eye movement and which also interfaced him with his cyber agent, MPS-Ali.

The last twelve hours had been quite busy for Ryan, making the modifications not just to the army gear but also to MPS-Ali. Along with the hardware, the scientists at Los Alamos had also released to Ryan a directory of highly virulent code plus the antidote shields, which he used to develop counterstrike routines for MPS-Ali. The programs, mostly Trojans, had originated from a number of sources, including arrested hackers, classified university projects, and government-sponsored software development at Los Alamos in conjunction with the Pentagon's advanced weapons division. Two of the deadliest Trojans, one called DROWNDEEP and a second titled NUKER2, were brand new developments, meaning their chances of working against anyone coming near Ryan and MPS-Ali were greater than average.

While Ryan was told that they were powerful enough to neutralize the intelligent system that had come close to flat-lining him on his last run, he had decided to augment their chances by lacing the viruses with Ada code. His argument was a simple one: If the intelligent system is going after Ada coded systems, its chances of being fooled by the Trojans were increased if they sported the same type of code. In fact, even Ryan and MPS-Ali coded themselves with Ada just to be on the safe side.

Ryan took off next to MPS-Ali, surfing through the T1 line out of the lakefront mansion and bursting into a nearby ISP, a familiar constellation of networks and users that seemed unusually crisp, as if he had 20/15 vision or was using a pair of binoculars, only without the tunneling effect.

Ryan dispatched MPS-Ali in a search-and-tag mission, looking for all networks that held Ada code in their servers. Ryan's plan was to surf through every ISP in the greater Austin area and report on all companies using Ada, and report any programs roaming through any ISP that contained Ada. Ryan saw it as the equivalent of roaming the streets at night looking for trouble, hoping to stumble into the same bully who beat him up the last time—only this time around Ryan was better armed to fight the rogue AI.

While he waited for the information to arrive, Ryan decided to test drive the new wireless security cameras he'd had Agent Johnson install around the house. The feed from the twelve new cameras could be viewed one at a time, or in a mosaic-like fashion. Ryan could stare at any one of the small screens, blink, and the screen would magnify immediately. But the system also had some level of intelligence. Created by Los Alamos for the future soldier, it constantly monitored the information displayed on the screen and had a huge memory bank to store up to forty-eight hours of imagery per camera. The intelligent host could compare the newly acquired images to the saved ones and highlight an anomaly from the pattern of the past two days. Since the cameras had only been in operation for less than twelve hours, half of them were outlined in red, indicating anomalies. Ryan briefly reviewed time-lapse versions of the cameras, watching Victoria and himself in the dining room earlier this evening, then strolling by the shores of the lake, then relaxing in the large family room upstairs, before heading down to the library. Other cameras showed Karen and Tom having a chat up in front, before getting into the rear of a sedan at around six and then returning at eight in the evening. Secret Service agents roamed the inside and outside of the mansion at various times. Eventually, the intelligent system would recognize the patterns and put the rest of the cameras on green status. The folks at Los

Alamos claimed it usually took between twelve and twenty-four hours. From that point forward, there was little reason to monitor the cameras unless the intelligent host flagged a zone, in which case Ryan would don his portable pack and jack in to view the reason for alarm and take evasive action if needed.

Ryan hated to break it to Agent Johnson and his boys, but the Los Alamos system provided far better information than the two agents manning the control room staring at the ten hardwired cameras installed way back when. The pager-size warning device clipped to Ryan's belt would alert him of an intrusion before the Secret Service agents spotted the breach. And the entire system had instant battery backup, from the wireless cameras to the interface to his computer, which worked off an Uninterrupted Power Supply capable of keeping him on-line for up to six hours following a blackout.

A map of the property hung over the mosaic screen highlighting the location of the user as well as of the cameras and providing alternate paths to avoid the enemy in a battle situation. In his case, Ryan saw himself as a green figure in the blue outline of the house layout. Victoria sat nearby in the room reading baby magazines. Infrared sensors on each wireless camera provided a count of all warm-body creatures of a weight larger than eighty pounds. The system went as far as mapping the specific mass of each individual, tagging them as "friendly" blue figures. The cameras, eight outside and four inside, covered roughly 70 percent of the property and currently displayed nine of Johnson's ten agents. Karen Frost and Tom Grant sat in the back porch reviewing a stack of reports cluttering the round wrought-iron table.

Ryan had sensed some energy between those two earlier today but couldn't put his finger on it. He knew very little about Tom Grant beyond his CIA dossier, but had plenty on Karen Frost during their last case right here in Austin. He had always felt bad for the middle-age female agent, especially after the loss of her husband, killed by one of the criminal rings she had been trying to crack. He respected and even admired Karen for figuring a way to pull it all together following that tragedy and keep chipping away. Ryan wasn't certain he would have had the strength to do the same should something similar have happened to Victoria, especially with a baby on the way.

Forcing focus, Ryan decided to test-drive the helmet-mounted display's translucent feature, activating it.

An instant later the library where he physically stood materialized around him but as a background only. The digital representation of the ISP remained in place on the translucent dual screens in front of his eyes, but the backdrop had changed to the real world.

Now this is cool, he thought, turning to face Victoria, sitting in a reclining chair flipping through the pages of a magazine with a bored expression on her face.

The scientists at Los Alamos had really struck gold with this happy marriage of the physical and virtual worlds, allowing the foot soldier to see the terrain around him—which was quite vital in battle—but without giving up the overlay of the real-time intelligence feed from headquarters.

It was a little weird to see both of them at the same time, but Ryan quickly learned that depending on which one he focused on, the other had the tendency to fade away some, like shifting to his peripheral vision, just to come alive again the moment he tried to focus on it.

Pretty serious technology, he decided as he continued to look at his wife while MPS-Ali's report began to fill a window floating off to the right of the monitors.

The whole scene was surreal. He was used to windows superimposed in a VR run backdropped by his software's interpretation of the network he was visiting, which he typically represented as a constellation of some sort with a black surrounding to simulate space. Now that blackness had become the physical world.

Enough sightseeing. Get to work.

Leaving the translucent option enabled, Ryan began to review the information gathered by Ali on the networks supported by this ISP. So far only three had returned with any resemblance of Ada code. In two of them the code had not been changed in over twelve months and the last one had gone through a revision less than a month ago. All three sites supported field controllers in the oil industry. None of the corporations reported any observable anomalies in the past couple of days. All employees had reported to work as usual.

Before he could finish thinking it, MPS-Ali once again flew wingman and they shot at amazing speed through a sea of flaring suns toward a wall of green T1 spaghetti at the other end of the galaxy, surrounded by the blurred bookcases of Wittica's library. Getting used to navigating while keeping tabs on the real world and also monitoring the status of the wireless cameras, Ryan taught himself how to shuffle multiple balls at once, a task made simpler by his combination of eye commands with hand and foot motions. He understood why it was vital to keep the outside world in perspective when he came close to kicking a chair while turning, an action that drew a curious look from Victoria.

"Sorry, honey," he said while briefly disabling the voice-activated mike. "Keep reading your magazine." The acceleration through the T1 made him take a side step, kind of like being in one of those IMAX theaters where the moving image tricks the body into sensing motion when there is no real physical motion beyond what's projected on the screen. The conflicting forces, however, knotted his stomach.

"How do you know I'm reading a magazine?" she asked, confused.

"I'm in both worlds, Vic," he responded while checking that MPS-Ali didn't get too far ahead of him as the jade neon-laced conduit twisted and turned through cyberspace.

They exited the T1 and plunged into another ISP constellation, pulsating suns and orbiting planets encircled by a myriad of green connections.

MPS-Ali headed off to hunt for Ada code, leaving Ryan by his lonesome once more, though he wasn't quite alone. He could talk to Victoria, who wore the same sundress as this morning but was barefoot and her hair was pulled up with a barrette. For a moment Ryan wondered how she would handle motherhood, especially since this wasn't a planned pregnancy. The Ryans had wanted to get their careers going for a few more years before having kids, but the baby growing inside Victoria's womb was a silent testament that birth control methods aren't 100 percent guaranteed. In the past few weeks, she had hinted at wanting to stay home and become a full-time mom. Ryan had been surprised at first that Victoria Ryan, Miss Career Woman, would consider giving it all up for the baby, but it was obvious that her maternal instincts were far more powerful than her historical desire to play the financial rat race.

Another screen in the mosaic turned green. The Los Alamos intelligent security system was slowly learning the video pattern it was monitoring. Data also began to flash on MPS-Ali's update window indicating no detected Ada activity on this service provider.

And off they went, ISP after ISP, cruising through the multiple galaxies forming the digital spine of the Austin network, making their way east from the Lakeway area, located west of Austin, reaching the west side of the city, across the downtown area, and onto the multiple ISPs servicing the industrial community north of town.

While waiting for MPS-Ali to complete its scan in the second-to-last ISP in the Austin area, the sound of an invading network abruptly hissed in the HMD's headphones. Planets and suns blurred for a moment, losing focus, then resolved in shades of gray while the half sense of someone reading over his shoulder flickered and vanished, before color returned to the constellation.

What in the hell was that?

Then Ryan saw a smudge of clear mass traveling across the ISP, temporarily distorting the fabric of the matrix as it followed a course that kept it on the periphery of the planets, bordering the flaring apertures of the T1s.

Still cloaked by the Ada shell, Ryan went after it, following it from a respectful distance even though in this place space was irrelevant. The colorless blotch could double back in a flash and fry him.

The window from MPS-Ali returned with mounds of Ada code.

The ISP was flooded with it.

What does that mean?

His right hand ready to trigger the release of DROWNDEEP while his left kept NUKER2 in backup mode, Ryan ordered MPS-Ali back to his side. Violating the laws of physics, the expert system almost materialized by Ryan, similarly shrouded.

LAUNCH SURFACE SCAN. NO RETURN QUALIFIER.

MPS-Ali complied. The scan, like a shoot and forget missile, materialized just inches from MPS-Ali's flawless body and propagated toward the amorphous haze, reaching it a moment later and spreading a blue stain across its surface.

The blur slowed down while the scan completed its pass. The stain lifted from the translucent shape but didn't return to MPS-Ali with results. Doing so would have telegraphed their presence. Instead the stain contracted into a ball before trembling and exploding, sending particles in every direction. The laws of probability dictated that some particles would reach them, and he was right. A few bytes' worth of compiled machine code traversed him and MPS-Ali, as if they weren't there, continuing to the middle of the galaxy.

Ryan made a copy of the passing binary debris, verifying that it was indeed Ada, at least on the surface.

The blur became milky. Interior streaks of chalky white danced within the amorphous edges of the construct, like monochromatic holograms, turning silver, then platinum, then bright white. Very bright.

The blinding shape began to expand, sheet lightning forking across its boiling surface, just like the last time. The AI was obviously pissed that it had been forced to show itself because of Ryan's little trick.

Remember me, buddy? Let's see what you've got locked in there.

RELEASE DROWNDEEP.

The Trojan, like arc light, bolted straight toward the middle of the thundering construct, piercing the surface, plunging inside.

Initially Ryan saw no difference. Then slowly, the lightning disappeared. Surface movement became sluggish, turning bronze, developing a patina. DROWNDEEP, a simple virus by itself, possessed two deadly components. The first was its incredible ability to replicate exponentially, spreading across the entire network in seconds. The other component was its prejudicial attack against the system's real-time clock, the pulses that allowed the billions of transfers of information in any system, including this construct. Without a clock the program could not execute its lines of code, could not compute information, could not launch a runner to alert its master that it was being violated.

But there was a catch. Most programs began to self-destruct when the clock stopped, like oxygen-starving brain cells. Ryan had limited time to scan the information inside the rapidly darkening block before it bled into the lattice of the matrix and was lost forever. Also, many constructs were expected to report periodically. The lack of an update would trigger an alarm at the master's location, resulting in the likely dispatch of sentry constructs.

Followed by MPS-Ali, Ryan tore into the heart of the paralyzed AI, scanning everything and anything that still held a charge, that had not yet drained its logical state. The depleting memory banks still contained thousands upon thousands of undocumented lines of code, but unlike the surface, the heart of the construct was not all Ada. The primary control system, the heart of the machine, was programmed in C, and it was still pumping. DROWNDEEP had halted the pulses supporting the Ada code but had not altered the C code.

Ryan reached this core, still glowing white, and felt its energy, the hissing charge cracking hollowly in its sudden vastness. Again, the laws of physics didn't apply. Albeit very small from the outside, once immersed in it, the cloud seemed infinite, overarching, and it was allowing Ryan to visit it. Perhaps it was the Ada shell he wore, or maybe that when the Ada core froze it somehow altered its overall defense mechanism.

But Ryan sensed the raw power. It vibrated beneath him like a subway train rushing below the street, only there was no street, no ceiling, no walls, only floating sheets of white soaked with binary code inside this high-energy echoing chamber, which MPS-Ali decoded at lightning speed.

The information formed in space, at first as if viewed through frosted glass. Then MPS-Ali's algorithms cleared it, adding definition, stringing data one bit at a time on taut grids of gleaming memory, like an artist splashing talent onto a canvas, one stroke at a time, transforming pallid hues into essence, filtering through gigabytes of jumbled data, extracting, distilling, translating machine code into ASCII characters, into words, which soon emerged, one by one according to Ryan's assigned priority. First the construct's target. Then its origin.

TARGET: THE BOEING DIGITAL DIVISION.

ORIGIN: 367 COR&$%$^&#

A siren dopplered in the distance.

A lilac neon laser sliced through the wounded construct with savage power, lavender smoke spiraling as it cut through the pulsating core, halting its operation. Help from the master AI had finally arrived, meaning it was time for Ryan to bail.

MAXIMUM REVERSE.

Ryan and MPS-Ali shot into warp speed, backing up fast, reminiscent of old *Star Trek* episodes, propelling straight into the doorway of a T1 tube, and continuing to rush backwards through repulsive twists and turns.

A green glow surrounded them as they dashed away from the glowing security construct dispatched to check on the satellite when it had failed to respond following Ryan's attack.

Boeing Digital Division.

The words formed in Mike Ryan's mind as the green glow of the T1 enveloped him fully, as MPS-Ali dragged him through the ridiculously twisted conduit.

A purple glow washed out the emerald hues of the T1 just behind him. The AI had tagged them, just as MPS-Ali had stained the runners in previous sessions.

He fired another copy of DROWNDEEP, but the blue haze fizzled as it touched the lilac surface, like water droplets on a hot skillet. Just as he had feared, the AI had already digested the virus, decoded it, and made itself immune to it.

Ryan was still holding on to NUKER2 but didn't want to release it. These Trojans could only be used once against a complex construct.

The violet glow closed in, gleaming with the power of a thousand amethysts in direct sunlight.

OUT. OUT. OUT.

A hardwired relay in the interface mechanism of the back-top system unplugged Ryan and MPS-Ali from the network.

"Are you all right?" Victoria asked, setting down her magazine.

Ryan blinked and took a deep breath, slowly giving his wife a nod. "I think I may have figured out what the terrorist's next target is."

"You did?" She stood.

"Yeah," he said, swallowing spit, feeling as if he had just finished running a marathon. "Let's go find Karen and Tom."

FORTY-FIVE

> > > > >

PLEASURE

> ARES KULZAK EMBRACED HER TIGHTLY, LIFTING HER light frame off the table by the glowing computer screen, which had just reported a successful release of the virus across Boeing's Digital Division, plus confirmation from Neurall that the core supercomputers of the large corporation were now in rapid learning mode after removing the Turing shackles.

At this moment, as she shivered while wrapping her legs around the back of his thighs, her deadly virus propagated down the backbones of the PMAs used by thousands of aircraft mechanics around the world to perform their obligatory Boeing 777 preflight diagnosis checks, which would appear normal. Then the planes would begin to fall, begin to crash, focusing the attention of the CCTF team on that aspect of the case rather than on the subtle changes done to the supercomputers, which, through Neurall's coaching, would already be smart enough to keep their growing intelligence a secret from their creators. And most important, the attack would hide the fact that Jason Lamar had provided them with the third backdoor password to access the military version of Neurall.

Her back pressed against the wall, Kishna removed his shirt, then her own, letting Ares mouth her nipples while her hands fumbled with his belt buckle, before she pulled down his trousers.

This woman knew how to please him, how to give him the kind of physical and mental satisfaction that took everything away, the anger, the frustration, the months of planning, propelling him to faraway places, to streamlined jetliners taking off in the dark, to their shadows rising higher and higher in a star-filled sky, to their inescapable fate in the night. That was just their smokescreen, but one that brought him immense satisfaction, far more than the strategic nature of their mission. The falling jetliners would give Ares instant pleasure, just as Kishna did now.

Ares found her lips, her tongue, kissing her as intense as his desire for revenge against the Americans, against the CCTF. He grabbed her buttocks and pushed himself hard against her, his mind already savoring the blow that would be inflicted against the head of the CCTF in Washington. Sever the head and the rest will go into disarray.

Ares closed his eyes, feeling Kishna's body against him, remembering the first time he had been with a woman and the satisfaction that he had extracted not just from Marta but from his uncle's demise, which had propelled him to the life that was rightfully his.

They moved in unison for minutes, letting it all go, immersing themselves in the pleasure they extracted from each—

A steady beep invaded the room.

Kishna opened her eyes and tried to move away but Ares held her in place, climaxing a moment later, releasing inside of her.

The beeping intensified, signaling an anomaly in the constructs.

He let her go, shuddering while exiting her, fumbling for his fallen trousers before following her back to the table.

"What . . . is it?" he asked,

Naked, her chest heaving, Kishna sat on the chair and began to click keys. Windows opened and closed. Information flashed across the screen.

"They intercepted us again?" he asked, buckling his belt, catching his breath, ignoring the wetness in between his legs.

Kishna shifted her eyes from the screen to Ares Kulzak. "They have not intercepted my virus yet. They stumbled across a sentry construct and managed to inject it with a virus that allowed them to penetrate it."

Ares tightened his fists, forcing self-control. "*And?*"

"I think they might have figured out our target."

"What . . . *else* did they figure out?"

"Maybe the physical origin of the sentry construct, which in this case is our current physical location."

"But . . . *how?* I thought you said anyone coming near the AI would be immediately flat-lined, and those who managed to survive would be sent on a wild chase of ISPs around the globe."

"I know, Ari," she said, her dark lipstick smudged across her cheeks and chin. "But that all ended when the strangers pierced the fabric of the construct with a brand new Trojan virus, something I have not seen before, and against which the construct had no defense. Fortunately for us, the wounded construct sent a digital S.O.S. to Neurall, who extracted a sample of the virus, developed an antidote, and dispatched a second sentry construct, this one immune to the virus. The intruders, whose signatures, by the way, match the ones who intercepted the SWOASIS strike, tried to get away. And they did, but not before we extracted their ISP, which with further probing yielded a T1 connection billed to an address in Lakeway."

"Lakeway?" said Ares, crossing his arms. "That is by Lake Travis, yes?"

"Correct."

"I see," he said, a plan quickly forming in his mind. "And you believe they could know our current location."

"Yes."

"What about the modifications to Boeing's supercomputers?"

"Still intact, as they should be."

"Any indication that they have figured out what we're really after?"

"No. There has been no abnormal activity reported at the Pentagon. The *gusanos* have no clue what we're really after."

Ares stared into the eyes of the only person in the world who mattered to him. Everyone else was expendable. Everyone else obeyed him out of fear or greed. But Kishna loved him unconditionally, just as his mother had once loved him, without strings, willing to do for him anything he wished.

And right now Ares Kulzak wished revenge against whoever was interfering with his strikes, even if such attacks were just the distraction to keep the CCTF away from their real mission.

The enemy was getting too close. If Kishna was correct and the CCTF had learned of the attack against the jetliner manufacturers, then it was just a matter of time before the warning reports were distributed around the world. Less than six hours had elapsed since the initial virus deployment, meaning a high likelihood that a small percentage of the world's fleet of 777s had been infected and were back in the air. Kishna's virus was set to strike not at an absolute time, but at a time relative to the coordinates read by the onboard computers, which would then direct the jetliners to new destinations.

Ares narrowed his dark eyes.

Time.

It always came down to a race against time, now compounded by contests in both the real world and the virtual world.

Contests he intended to win tonight.

Picking up the phone, he dialed a Washington, D.C., number he had long ago committed to memory. He listened to the greeting of the answering machine before leaving a short but concise message.

"I hope this does not backfire, Ari," Kishna said when he hung up.

Ares frowned, once again having violated his cardinal rule about not relying on others besides himself and Kishna. But he had no choice. He had to deliver a devastating blow against the CCTF to get them off his back, and that meant severing the head *and* the legs of the American counterterrorism team, eliminating targets in two cities simultaneously. The only way he could do it in a single night was by relying on his Russian contact and former brother-in-arms, now a prominent figure of the Russian mafia in Washington, D.C., to handle that hit while he took care of the agents in Austin.

The Counter Cyberterrorism Task Force.

Ares stared at his hands.

Tonight I shall bring you to your knees.

FORTY-SIX

> > > > >

AIRBORNE VIRUS

> FLIGHT 33 WITH SERVICE TO TOKYO-NARITA INTER-national Airport left Los Angeles International Airport at 6:15 P.M. The flight crew, longtime airline employees, was formed by two pilots with a combined experience of forty-five years and over twenty thousand hours of logged flight time, and by a seasoned navigator. The trio worked this route twice each week, hauling passengers from L.A. to Tokyo and back very safely, mostly due to the strict security procedures that were instituted by the FAA in the weeks and months following the terrorist strike of 2001, including a new armored cockpit door, capable of insulating the crew from potential terrorists.

What impressed the captain most about the 777, in addition to the extensive security measures, was its glass cockpit. CRTs had replaced the arrays of gauges and dials that crowded the cockpit of most jetliners in the world. Two screens monopolized the space directly in front of the captain. The Primary Flight Display provided information of all the parameters required for flight path control, from attitude, altitude and speed, to angle of bank, and vertical speed.

To the right of the PDF was the Navigation Display, which, like the name implied, provided the flight crew with navigation information, route, traffic, and weather. A similar set of displays spread out in front of the 777's first officer. In between them was a fifth CRT, the Primary Engine Display, providing control and monitoring of all engine parameters. Sandwiched in between the PED and the captain's ND, were three small displays, the only resemblance to older cockpits. The top one displayed attitude, the middle one airspeed, and the bottom one altitude. The console between the captain and his first officer was still traditional, with side-by-side throttle controls and arrays of switches and buttons for communications, plus three Control Display Units, one for the captain, one for the F/O, and a third, larger one in the middle for both. The CDUs aided the flight crew in managing such items as navigation, in-flight performance optimization, fuel monitoring, and flight-deck displays.

All of the information was there, of course, in colorful detail and presented in an easy-to-read format, from basics like altitude, speed, and heading, to the status of its two engines.

Below the surface of the seemingly orderly display of information, a virus had been replicating in exponential fashion the moment mechanics at LAX performed their preflight diagnostic check.

The attack occurred very suddenly at exactly four minutes after takeoff.

The captain first noticed a problem when the plane began to level off at two thousand feet over the ocean and turn back toward the mainland.

The pilot tried to regain control of the plane, but the fly-by-wire computer, responsible for translating his commands to the 777's engines and control surfaces, kept the plane on its new course.

The first officer tried to call LAX to inform them of their situation, but the governing communications software had long ceased to function.

Holding the mike in his hands, listening to the static humming from the overhead speaker in the cockpit, the first officer stared at the captain, the futility of their situation reflected in his wide-eyed stare.

The nose began to drop as the autopilot pointed the jetliner toward downtown L.A., its many buildings alive with lights as the sun began to set on the dusky horizon.

The captain, growing aware of what could happen, remembering those jetliners crashing into buildings back in 2001, performed an emergency fuel dump. If they were going to crash, they would do so without any fuel to burn to minimize the destruction.

But the onboard computers did not relay his command.

Oh, dear God, the captain thought, as downtown L.A. grew in size, as they headed for a tight cluster of office buildings south of the airport.

The captain tried everything to force his vessel away from the oncoming skyscrapers, his ears listening to the screams in the cabin as passengers realized what was going on.

But nothing worked. The systems would not respond, would not convey his inputs to the flight surfaces.

Visions of glass and steel filled his windshield before flames enveloped him.

FORTY-SEVEN

> > > > >

SWAGS

> THE LIST WASN'T VERY LONG. ACCORDING TO THE on-line Greater Austin Phone Book directory, the partial address that Mike Ryan had extracted, 3467 COR, could have been 3467 Corona Drive, Corporate Drive, Corporate Street, Coral Drive, Cordoba Street, Corinthian Boulevard, Cornell Drive, Corral Street, Cortez Lane, or Cory Drive.

Yeah, tell me about it, but at least that narrowed our search from an entire city down to ten blocks.

Of those ten, eight of them didn't have street address numbers greater than 2000. So we narrowed it to two. The first one, Cortez Lane, was a residential neighborhood. The second one, Cordoba Street, was deep in the industrial sector of north Austin, matching the location of Ryan's ISP search.

So here we are, at 3467 Cordoba Street, just three hours after Mike Ryan and his wife came rushing out of the back of the house with the info on Boeing's Digital Division plus this partial address. While we left a team trying to find any Austinite who may have worked—or still worked—at Boeing, Karen and I went off to pursue this lead, which we considered far more meaningful. After all, even if we come up with the name of a former Boeing employee or contractor, the chances of him being at his home address after the Gary Hutton incident are next to nil. This street address, however, marked the point of origin of the attack against Ryan while he was poking around the network and caught the cyberterrorists with their hands in the virtual cookie jar. I can only hope that the time it took to find the place and get it surrounded wasn't long enough for Kulzak to react. Of course, both Karen and I are making a paramount assumption: that Kulzak is physically at the point where the attack originated.

Anyway, that's the best lead we have, so we're running with it.

Standing behind a pair of dump trucks parked in the alley next to the warehouse, I begin to second-guess the plan of attack that Karen and I have devised.

I'm not sure what was running through my mind when I volunteered to be the first to go into this place while the rest of the force—a mix of CCTF agents and APD officers, two bomb squads, six fire trucks, two ambulances, and even a pair of police helicopters—stood by waiting for my signal. In addition, APD snipers dominate the roofs of every building around the warehouse plus there are three SWAT teams standing by. Believe me, it wasn't easy talking the SWAT guys into this at first, but once I reminded them of San Antonio, Melbourne, and New Orleans, they agreed to give me three minutes inside the building before they came in full gallop.

Now I'm having second thoughts.

Too late, Grant. Play it out.

And I do, hauling an aluminum ladder courtesy of the fire department while moving toward the southeast corner of the building in almost total darkness thanks to the night-vision goggles the SWAT team loaned me, which transform the night into palettes of green.

I take my time, measuring my advance, well aware that all it would take is one misjudgment on my part, and the last thing that might go through my mind could be my asshole as my body is torn into a million pieces by one of the bastard's booby traps.

The entryway I have selected is a window roughly ten feet above the wet concrete facing a parking lot and another warehouse at the far end. I can see a half dozen emergency vehicles and lots of people in front of that structure, roughly a football field away—hopefully far away enough should anything blow up.

But don't think I'm just a lone and idiotic crusader here. There is logic behind my apparent desire for an early cremation. According to my best estimates, Ares Kulzak has been in Austin for less than a day, and we caught his operation in progress around three hours ago. I keep telling myself that's not enough time for Kulzak to mount an elaborate counteroffensive, like the one he put together in Melbourne, when he had days to plan and execute.

So I'm making a couple of serious wild-ass guesses, or SWAGs. The first is the assumption that any expected raid on the place would come from the front, where the offices and the large garage doors are. The rest of the warehouse is nothing but walls and these small windows. The second assumption is that, assuming my first SWAG is correct, I would have time to spot the bomb and find a safe entry point for the bomb team.

While a part of me tells me that's probably wishful thinking, I set down the rubber-soled bottom of the ladder about five feet from the building and slowly let the top end rest against the corrugated-metal wall without making any noise.

I pause to catch my breath, relaxing my burning shoulders from hauling the ladder. At this point in time, in spite of my best logical reasons why breaking into this place isn't an insane thing to do, I make the sign of the cross like a good Catholic boy, start reciting my favorite psalm—and also reach for my Sig. Tonight my piece is sporting a bulky silencer just in case I come face to face with a devil while walking through the valley of the shadow of death.

Silently praying that the Good Lord guides my steps, I head up, rung after rung, wondering if my feet will ever touch the ground again while still attached to my legs—and the rest of me for that matter.

I opted to wear a vest tonight, though my perspiring body is already protesting the decision.

I reach the third-to-last rung, my head leveled with the bottom of the window.

Slowly, very carefully now, I press the sole of my right sneaker against the second to last rung and hoist myself just enough to try to peek inside.

The goggles are awesome, providing me with a clear view of the otherwise pitch-black interior. I see nothing but tons and tons of construction equipment, mostly heavy stuff, like bulldozers, backhoes, cranes, and a large number of dump trucks like the two parked down the alley.

Just as the SWAT team had indicated.

All right, Grant. Check the window.

Locked.

Of course.

I reach into my side pocket and produce a diamond-tipped glass cutter and a small suction cup attached to the end of a handle. I've done this many times during my field operative days, and tonight is no different.

I press the suction cup against a section of the glass and cut a circle roughly six inches in diameter. Then gently—very, *very* gently—I wiggle the suction cup's handle, dislodging the circular piece of glass, which I leave attached to the suction cup dangling from the side of the ladder with a lanyard.

Reaching in with my left arm, I unlock the window and slowly slide it up. The police had checked with the alarm company, and this warehouse only has alarm sensors in the front by the large garage-style doors used to move the oversized construction machines. A thief would not be able to steal much through this window.

I climb through and feel lucky that not only am I still hanging on to all my limbs, but that a large bulldozer happens to be parked right by the window, making it easy for me to climb down to the floor.

"I'm in," I whisper into my lapel microphone. The clock has started ticking.

"Careful, Tom," says Karen through the earpiece I have shoved in my right ear.

The smell of rubber, engine oil, and dust tickling the hairs up my nose, I drop to a deep crouch and start moving sideways along the length of the bulldozer, reaching what I thought would be the scooper but instead finding what looks like a gigantic mechanical claw.

Beyond this odd appendage stands another bulldozer, which I guess is yellow but to me everything is as green as the acid squirting in my stomach for having come here alone. Nothing like the strong possibility of going up alone against the monster to drive a wedge right through your courage.

I like huevos rancheros.

Focus!

Blinking away the sight of an emasculated Jerry Martinez, I try to subdue my rocketing heartbeat, once again hammering my chest like the hammers from hell.

Hell.

I start to wonder if that's just where I have descended when I reach the front of the warehouse, by a pair of closed door offices hugging this corner of the building. According to the quick external survey I did of the place, both offices also have doors facing the front parking lot.

Next to the offices I see the three large garage doors lining the balance of the front of this structure. There is no sign of bombs anywhere.

And also no sign of Kulzak.

My eyes shift between the two office doors, wondering which one has the prize I seek.

Maybe both.

Maybe none.

"One minute mark, Tom," says Karen through the earpiece shoved into my right ear. "Everything okay?"

Since I'm currently equating being okay with still being in possession of the Grant family jewels, I tap my mike once.

My silenced Sig leading the way, I make up my mind and go for the second door, the one farthest away from me, slowly resting my ear against the side, hearing nothing.

So far my theory has panned out. There are no apparent booby traps anywhere in the building. But there could be one inside one or both of the offices.

And so, I say to myself: What would *you* do if you were Kulzak and had to rush off because the gringos were coming?

Being Kulzak I'd certainly like to leave behind a smelly turd for my fans, but not a very elaborate one—just good enough to crap on them the moment they came knocking on the front door.

But what about the *back* door of each office, the ones facing *moi*? Would I have had time to booby-trap those? And how would I had left the office once I had booby-trapped the front doors?

"Two minutes, Tom. Are you okay?"

Another tap.

I decide that had I been Kulzak, I would have wired one of the outside doors, then gone through the back door of that office, and into the adjacent office, and then out the front door, meaning only *one* front door would be hot. If this theory of mine is true, then I shouldn't expect to be turned into a well-done New York strip by opening either one of the two rear office doors.

Inhaling as if I'm taking my last breath, I go for the closest door, turning the brass knob while promising God to be a good boy for the rest of my life.

You wouldn't believe the kind of shit that suddenly floods my mind as I finish turning the knob and contemplate inching the door open. I think of my mother sprawled dead on the living room floor with half of her forehead bashed in. I think of my old man holding a blood-stained iron, his eyes glinting with animal rage. I see him turning toward me; watch in horror as he raises the iron over his head. I see my mother's hair, blood, and brains layering the edge of the weapon that became the primary exhibit during the murder trial. I can feel that first blow, just above my left temple, knocking me down, my vision tunneling as I tried to get up, as he kicked my torso, cracking my ribs, before pounding my head again with the iron. The only thing that saved my ass was the fact that I had—and still have—a very hard head.

Yeah, I know. Pretty weird stuff to be thinking about right before I open this door. Madie also comes into the picture, and I wonder if that's because I'm about to join her as well as my mother.

Concentrate, Grant, or you will *join them.*

On the count of three.

I frown.

Three!

I push the door and stare at a desk, a couch, and two chairs—along with a black backpack case wired to the front door.

Bingo.

I check the next door and find the office clean—aside from some poor bastard strapped to the couch staring at the ceiling with lifeless eyes and a hole in the center of his forehead.

Cautiously, I open the front door and stare at a number of lights across the street. "Found one bomb and one body," I say into my lapel microphone. "Get the bomb squad in here. Only come through this door."

"Good job, Tom," says Karen. "I guess all of those prayers did pay off."

Was I praying out loud?

Standing in the doorway waiting for the bomb squad I begin to get an uneasy feeling about how straightforward this has been. The Kulzak I know *always* surprises me. Every time I think I know what he is going to do, he manages to pull one over on me. This time it looks as if I was able to get into his mind.

Or did I?

The job next door certainly looks like it was done in haste, just something to leave behind while trying to get somewhere else in a hurry.

Trying to get somewhere else in a hurry?

Then the thought hits me with the force of a hundred Melbournes, and I'm suddenly dialing my mobile phone to reach the main number at the Lakeway mansion.

"C'mon dammit," I curse as the phone takes its own sweet time to make the connection.

Acid squirts in my stomach when I get a busy signal. I try Agent Johnson's mobile phone but it directs me to his voicemail.

FORTY-EIGHT

> > > > >

HOUSE CALL

> ARES KULZAK MOVED SWIFTLY, QUIETLY, WITH PUR-
pose under a crystalline sky, his predatory eyes watching another American agent
drop to his knees unable to signal for help, unable to make the most primitive of
sounds after a silenced 9mm caliber round tore open his neck, exiting just above the
shoulder blades, nearly severing the head.

Wearing the last of the explosives backpacks, Ares glided past his last victim while
making his way up the left side of the mansion. Kishna, with Neurall's assistance,
had already taken care of the high-tech side of the attack from the safety of their
vehicle parked across the lake, disabling the phones as well as paying the security system company a cyber visit, forcing the installed base of monitors to replay the video
recorded in the previous hour while she gained access to the real-time feed, which she
then used to guide him through the grounds.

Kishna had also tapped into the mansion's phone line to perform a smart cut,
which allowed a dial tone but any phone number dialed from the mansion would
result in a busy signal. Likewise, anyone dialing the mansion would get a busy signal.

There were still cellular phones and radios, of course, which once again made
time his enemy. He needed to eliminate the external guards before the ones manning
the interior of the mansion—and in particular the two parked inside the control
room—realized that they were under attack and could use their cellular phones to
call out for help.

"All outside agents have been neutralized," Ares said into his hands-free wireless headset connected to the cellular phone strapped to his belt.

"Confirmed. Proceed inside," replied Kishna.

Six agents neutralized in under three minutes, and none of them saw it coming, all dying before realizing what had hit them. In a way, Ares had been disappointed at the relatively mild state of alertness of this security detail. Most were young, inexperienced, relying on their muscular physiques, their weapons, and their high-tech gear to do the work for them.

Kulzak had caught them off guard. One of them had even had his eyes closed and his head resting against a wall. He never opened them again.

The front of the mansion reminded him of an old Italian villa, with a circular cobblestone driveway and a fountain in the middle. He stepped over the bodies of his first two victims this evening and reached for the front door, which was, as expected, unlocked.

The spacious foyer led to a large living area, matching the layout of the mansion Kishna had downloaded from the security company.

"I'm in," he said.

"I see three people sleeping in the living room," she said. "All wearing business suits. Looks like more agents."

He went straight for them, his silenced Heckler & Koch MP5 submachine gun leveled at the closest figure.

Without hesitation, he fired once at the head before switching targets, firing a second time, switching targets, and firing at the third agent just as he began to sit up, the force of the gunshot pushing him back down.

Then silence.

"The last two guards are in the control room," she said.

Ares headed their way.

FORTY-NINE

> > > > >

WAKE-UP CALL

> THE VIBRATION ON HIS WAIST WOKE HIM UP.

Ryan took a deep breath, sitting up in the king-size bed of the second floor's master suite wearing nothing but a pair of jogging shorts and the beeper linked to the wireless security cameras.

He blinked to clear his vision, checking his watch.

One in the morning.

He had fallen asleep just an hour ago, exhausted after spending most of the day and night in cyberspace, including two hours with the system administrators at Boeing's Digital Division. The flash alert had been broadcast around the world within the hour to ground the 777 fleet until a thorough virus scan could be performed on the onboard software.

His mouth feeling dry and pasty, Ryan verified that his beeper was indeed vibrating, signaling that one or more of his cameras had picked up an unusual pattern.

Without turning on the light to avoid waking Victoria, Ryan stepped out of bed and donned his backtop computer, tactile gloves, and HMD. He'd left the mobile hardware hooked to an AC outlet by the sofa on the side of the large bedroom. The battery charge on the system didn't go beyond ninety minutes—a problem the military contractors had to solve before the unit could be useful to the soldier in the field.

He powered up.

Cyberspace blurred, then resolved, revealing the mosaic-like windows of the twelve wireless camera feeds. Half of them had pulsating red frames, indicating a change from the recorded pattern of the last twelve hours.

His heartbeat rocketed at the sight of Secret Service agents sprawled on the lawn, on the driveway. The wireless cameras clearly displayed their lifeless eyes, their shattered skulls.

Shit!

Fully awake now, Ryan invoked MPS-Ali and got him to loop on the video clips that had triggered the alarm. The cyber agent complied, and Mike Ryan witnessed the assassination of several Secret Service agents by a hooded figure. According to the time stamps on the video clips, the last agent had been killed just a minute ago.

"Vic!" he hissed, enabling the translucent option of the HMD, watching his wife stir in bed. "Vic, get up."

As Ryan dispatched MPS-Ali to alert the security company of this impending breach and also to dial Karen Frost's cellular phone, he witnessed the assassination of the two agents manning the control room, their faces exploding in crimson clouds. Add to that the three dead in the living room plus the six outside, and that brought the number to eleven.

"*Vic!*" he hissed again.

"Wh-what?" she mumbled, hugging a pillow while rolling away from him, beyond the superimposed fabric of the computer matrix, currently displaying the blue rectangle of the mansion's security system company. MPS-Ali, dressed in silver and purple, was pinging it with the access code.

"Keep it down," he said. "The mansion is under attack."

He had not seen her move so fast in years. Dressed in a long pink nightgown with the words BABY INSIDE stenciled across her abdomen, she jumped out of bed and staggered to his side.

"What's going on?" Victoria asked.

"*Karen Frost,*" he heard through his headphones when the CCTF agent answered her cellular phone. There was a loud rhythmic noise in the background.

Signaling his wife to hold on, Ryan said into the HMD's microphone, "We're in trouble, Karen. By my count all eleven agents are down."

"*What?*"

"All dead, and we'll be following them very soon unless we get some help right away."

"*We're on a helicopter heading your way. ETA in another ten minutes.*"

"Ten minutes!" Ryan protested, struggling to keep his voice down. "This thing is going to be over in ten *seconds.*"

"Hide, Mike. Hide yourself and Victoria. We'll be there as soon as possible. We've also alerted the Lakeway Police."

While his cyber pugilist gained access to the security system network and punched in the hostage code, Ryan carefully made his way to the door leading to the front balcony. He opened it before doubling back to where Victoria stood.

"Why did you do that?"

"Trust me," he said, leading her into the large walk-in closet beyond the white-tiled bathroom.

A figure rushed by one of his cameras' field of view, the one covering the foyer and the staircase. Ryan caught him again with the camera placed at the top of the stairs: a hooded man holding a large gun heading his way.

Fear twisted his intestines.

In the same instant Ryan heard the distant thunder of an AI in the vicinity of cyberspace. The surround sound had emanated from inside the security company's network, and that made sense. What better way to break inside the mansion than through a dual cyber and physical attack?

Like a pair of comic-book superheroes, Ryan and MPS-Ali shot past exterior layers, hovering above the core of the security company's system. The AI's cube-shaped cloud floated off to their far right, waves of sheet-lightning layering its surface while mating with the spherical network hub. A broad arc of blinding light interfaced it to the guts of the system, as if performing a glistening high-tech copulating act through a broadband connection pulsating with streams of data transfers. MPS-Ali reported that the frequency of the digital transactions matched those from the mansion's video monitoring system.

Bastards have broken into the security system.

As he watched this high-tech display, an idea suddenly formed in Ryan's mind, a way to turn the tables on the intruder.

While circling the spherical representation of the security system's network, MPS-Ali shot a blue laser containing a request to tap into the mansion's cameras at the network's core. The cyber agent steered the request clear from the luminous construct to avoid disturbing it, though Ryan felt certain the AI would not bother them while in the midst of its cyber copulation, as it was directly linked with the assassin's ability to maneuver at will inside the mansion.

From this angle, though, the AI looked more like a parasite than a mate, a leech sucking data from its unaware host.

An instant later, the feed from the requested cameras appeared just above the mosaic of the wireless videos. Through multiple cameras, both his own as well as the mansion's, Ryan watched the hooded figure burst into the upstairs guest room.

I see you, he thought, as his idea rapidly developed into a counterattack plan.

The assassin left the guest room and rushed down the corridor connecting it to the master suite.

The dark shape of his wife huddling against the corner of the closet forming the background of his cyber world, Ryan ordered MPS-Ali to access specific segments from the video captured by his wireless cameras shortly after dinner.

"Mike," she whispered. "Who killed the guards?"

"I'm not sure," he replied, leaning down in the closet, out of the way from the doorway. "But I'll be damned if he's going to hurt us."

His cyber agent returned with the requested MPEG video clips.

As the assassin reached the door to their bedroom, Ryan gave the order, realizing he would only get one shot at this.

F I F T Y

> > > > >

I L L U S I O N S

> ARES KULZAK KICKED THE DOOR TO THE MASTER bed-
room. It swung open, fanning him as he cruised through, before bouncing against
the wall and swinging back in the opposite direction, missing him by inches.

His silenced MP5 swept past sofa chairs, panning beyond a television and bookcases, zeroing in on the unmade bed, on the pillows that had fallen on the floor by its
sides. Someone had been sleeping here, and that someone had gotten up in a hurry.

So far Ares had eliminated Secret Service agents. But where were the persons that
they were protecting?

His peripheral vision caught something moving to his right, and he pivoted while
dropping to a deep crouch, lining the MP5 with the source of the motion: the door
to the balcony swinging in the lake breeze.

He ran to it, past it, stepping into the cool but humid night.

The balcony stretched almost fifty feet to a second door, the one leading to the
guest bedroom he had just searched. But that door had been locked from the inside.
He had checked it.

Ares verified that it was still locked.

"There's movement outside," Kishna reported. *"A man and a woman."*

"Where?" he asked, rushing back inside, glaring at the empty king-size bed, not
understanding how they had gotten past him, the only explanation that made sense

being that the couple had managed to get across to the guest room via the balcony, unlocking the door with a key while he had been in transition from there to this room.

"They are headed toward the boathouse."

Cursing his luck, Ares hurried back to the balcony hoping to get a clean shot from his second-story vantage point.

A heartbeat later he was in position, leaning into the iron railing, the MP5's metal stock pressed against his right shoulder, left hand holding the bulky silencer from beneath, right forefinger resting on the trigger casing while he searched for his targets.

"Where are they?" he complained when failing to spot them.

"Off to the right of the boathouse. They are staring at the lake now," replied Kishna.

He peered into the darkness beyond the reach of the estates' floodlights, which grazed the lakeshore structure with wan yellow light, throwing a shadow where Kishna claimed the runaway couple stood—too dark to see from his position.

Deciding that the mansion's cameras must have superior low-light capability, Ares said, "Don't let them out of your sight! I have to go down there myself!"

He raced back inside, through the bedroom, down the corridor, reaching the round staircase. His legs protested the effort as he leaped down the steps three at a time, landing on the foyer, running through the living room, past the still figures of the dead agents.

He approached the French doors, his gloved hand grasping the nearest doorknob. Locked.

He tried the next one, but it was also locked from the inside with a key, and Ares understood why. A thief could easily break a glass panel, stick a hand through the opening, and unlock the door—unless the mechanism required a key from the inside as well as the outside.

Wondering how the pair by the boathouse had gotten outside, Ares turned sideways to the door, recoiling his left leg before extending it toward the frame, striking it just above the doorknob with the heel of his shoe while keeping his toes pointing down.

Wood cracked.

He hit it again. The frame splintered, gave. The door swung open, some of its panels shattering, but Ares was already dashing down the thick lawn, eyes pegged on the upcoming boathouse, searching for the silhouettes he knew would be there.

"I do not see them!" he protested a moment later, stomping over the lawn flanking the one-story structure. A bird shrieked in the distance.

"They are gone now . . . wait. I see agents!"

"Agents? That is . . . *impossible*," he said, breathing hard. "I killed them all . . . unless more have come."

"Two of them wearing suits on the north perimeter, heading your way. No weapons in sight."

His gaze shifting from the boathouse to the left side of the mansion grounds, Ares made his decision to meet the incoming threat head-on, particularly if the American agents had not had the sense to draw their weapons.

"Where?" he asked, his knees protesting the way he pushed himself back up the shallow hill. "Where are they?"

"At the rear corner of the house. They are just standing there!"

Sweat running down his chest, Ares felt a knot forming in the gut of his stomach. He did see two agents—the ones he had *killed* on his initial run.

There was no one else in sight.

"Kishna, do you see the dead guards?"

Silence.

"Kishna!"

"I . . . I do not see dead guards anymore . . . where are they?"

"*Mierda!*" he screamed, letting his frustration get the better of him.

"What is happening?" she asked.

"We have been tricked," he said, his logical side calming him down. He could not fight the enemy with emotional outbursts. He had to remain professional, focused.

"Tricked?"

He did a three-sixty, convincing himself he was alone—alone with the lifeless guards she could not see through the security system's video monitors. "Someone is feeding you the wrong video. Check for strangers roaming the security company's network and then unleash Neurall on them."

FIFTY-ONE

> > > > >

BUYING TIME

> THE VIDEO PATCH HAD BEEN THE EASY PART.

MPS-Ali had seamlessly diverted an earlier recording into one of the mansion's live video feeds, showing Victoria and Ryan taking a stroll by the lakeshore after dinner.

The last-ditch effort had paid off. Ryan watched the displays as the hooded assassin ran downstairs and out the back.

MPS-Ali had then altered a second live video feed, replaying two agents patrolling the side of the property, which had prompted the assassin to head in that direction.

Confusion.

Ryan had to create as much confusion as he possibly could to buy himself and Victoria time.

But just as he had feared, the cyberterrorists were catching up to his trick. While the AI continued to ride the security company's network, a second construct materialized next to it, like a clone, but with far more intense lightning flashing on its data-rich skin.

MPS-Ali immediately broadcast a message to Ryan.

BACK OFF FAST.

Ryan complied, leaving MPS-Ali engaged with the security system. Since he could not remain by his cyber agent's side and formulate new strategies based on the assassin's reaction to his trick, Ryan removed the Turing inhibitor from MPS-Ali to give it the chance to learn and adapt should the cyberterrorists change the rules of the game.

Taxing his mind by acting in both the cyber and the real worlds, Ryan stood and took his wife's hand after verifying that the assassin was still roaming outside. "Let's go," he said. "We're getting out of here."

"Where is the assassin?" she said, getting up with difficulty, a hand beneath her belly.

The second construct got closer to Ryan, who was essentially on his own. Pulling out his copy of the NUKER2 virus while also retreating, he lured the unsuspecting AI to a trap. In the distance he saw MPS-Ali still performing his duties while the first AI remained coupled to the network, meaning the assassin was still getting the wrong video. He would be able to keep this up as long as he remained jacked in, which would be as long as he could stay ahead of the second AI, whose job it was to catch up to Ryan and flat-line him with a digital electro-magnetic pulse.

The backdrop to the inevitable high-tech skirmish shifted as Ryan and Victoria moved from the closet to the bedroom and then toward the door leading to the corridor and the stairs. His attention shifted from the real-world surroundings—as seen through the translucent HMD—to the video screens of his cyber world, to the incoming digital storm cloud and its lobotomy-capable flashes of lightning.

"Mike? Where is the assassin?" she asked again.

Keeping track of his own location, the location of the assassin, and the damned AI construct trying to turn him into an eggplant required all of his attention. He had little bandwidth left to answer his wife's questions. "Just follow me. I can't—"

The AI shot forward at fulminating speed. Ryan hit the MAX REVERSE option and shot out of the security system's network through a pulsating emerald-green T1. Unfortunately, without MPS-Ali he couldn't execute the twist and turns as fast as he would have otherwise, and the AI caught up to him an instant later.

Lightning flashed, followed by a thundering roar that struck too close for comfort. He knew the next blast would hurt.

As Ryan exited the T1 onto the galaxial vastness of an ISP, and as the rumbling construct threatened to swallow him, Ryan released NUKER2.

A bundle of neon magenta filaments shone at the AI, spreading across its angered surface like psychedelic angel-hair pasta, enveloping it in swift fluid motions. Bolts of lightning forked through rapidly closing gaps as the strings swelled deep into the AI's fabric before crystallizing, before paralyzing the trembling construct.

The AI momentarily disabled, the assassin still wandering outside the house, Ryan led Victoria down the stairs to the foyer and off to the left, by the control room, trying to avoid tripping on something while focusing in and out of both worlds. He watched one of his wireless monitors display the assassin going inside through a French door and stand in the living room inspecting the bodies of the dead Secret Service agents.

The AI sentinel cracked under the overpowering pressure of the NUKER2 virus, exposed its core, its essence, written not in Ada but in C, in the preferred language of the latest-generation constructs.

Rather than running away from the wounded AI, Ryan turned the tables and dove inside it through a jagged tunnel of magenta icicles and frozen lightning.

As he did this, Ryan also pinged MPS-Ali for an update. The cyber agent replied with a digital thumbs-up, having detected an attempt by the cyberterrorists to gain access to Ryan's wireless cameras. Free from the Turing inhibitor, MPS-Ali had processed the attack, running it through its logical loops, and generated, all by itself, a counteroffensive by changing the access passwords and locking the cyberterrorist out of their system.

In just a matter of seconds MPS-Ali was quickly becoming a true AI construct, only this one was on Ryan's side—at least for now. The Turing Society believed that if allowed to become too intelligent, machines could eventually turn against their creators. He made a mental note to reformat MPS-Ali after this.

Ryan and Victoria reached the control room and saw the two agents dead on their desks, blood pooling around their shattered skulls.

"Mike . . . one of them is Agent Johnson."

"I know," he said, closing and locking the door behind them. The assassin was heading upstairs again, randomly checking the house, apparently no longer believing the information MPS-Ali was feeding his cyber associate inside the security company's network.

Ryan and Victoria could take their chances and use the second door in the control room, the one leading to the servant's quarters and out the side of the house, but once outside they would be exposed, and in Victoria's condition they would be unable to run fast or far. The mansion was adjacent to a wooded hill—a hill Victoria could not climb.

The assassin rummaged through the master bedroom, crossed the corridor into the upstairs guest room, and then headed downstairs.

Time, Ryan thought. *I need to buy us more time.*

While Victoria grabbed one of the dead agents' pistols, Ryan ordered MPS-Ali to momentarily release control of the hardwired cameras back to the cyberterrorists to give them the illusion that they were back in control with the idea of then starting a second round of confusion. Amazingly enough, his cyber agent replied that such action was already being executed.

Ryan, who couldn't use a gun while wearing the delicate tactile gloves, spent thirty seconds explaining to Victoria how to release the safety and check that there was a round in the chamber. Then all she had to do was point and shoot at anyone coming through the door while he continued to work in cyberspace.

Looking behind him in the virtual world, through the gleaming ice of the frozen construct and the dim jadish glow of the enclosing virus, Ryan shivered at the exponential speed in which MPS-Ali was learning without its Turing shackles. For the moment he was glad he had removed them. He had to do everything and then more to keep the assassin guessing until help arrived.

"Quick," he said to Victoria, who was clutching the large black gun with both hands. "Let's hide out of the range of that camera."

"Why?"

"Because MPS-Ali is about to turn them back on."

"Why?"

He pressed a forefinger against his lips and checked the digital readout on the bottom left-hand side of his stereoscopic field of view, realizing that only eleven minutes had elapsed since he had woken up. He whispered to Victoria that they had to keep quiet because once MPS-Ali yielded control of the cameras to the cyberterrorists, they would be able to hear their conversation even if they were out of the camera's visual range.

Huddled against a corner of the control room, the coppery smell of blood filling his lungs with every breath, Ryan forced himself to keep up with this tiring pattern of multiplexing between the information on the screens, the real world around him, and anything he could learn while rummaging through the digital entrails of the immobile construct. He felt certain that somewhere buried inside the millions of lines of code was another clue that Karen Frost and Tom Grant could use to bring this madness to an end.

FIFTY-TWO

> > > > >

ROUND TWO

> "IT WORKED!" KISHNA REPORTED THROUGH THE EAR-
piece.

"How can you be sure?" Ares Kulzak replied, inspecting the modern kitchen, including three separate sinks, two automatic dishwashers, a large closet packed with all kinds of food, and a well-stocked refrigerator.

It appears that we managed to eliminate the user blocking the video feed. I can see you in the kitchen and also all of the dead pigs in the living room, the control room, and all around the house.

"In that case," he said, "where is the fugitive couple that was sleeping upstairs?"

I do not see them on any of the screens.

"Then I will check every room again, one by one."

FIFTY-THREE

> > > > >

BRILLIANT

> THE SELECTION OF VIDEOS HAD TO BE DONE VERY carefully. Ryan watched while MPS-Ali played movie director, channeling the live video stream from all cameras, including the one in the control room, while altering just one, but doing so without creating any conflict in the information previously displayed.

MPS-Ali waited while the assassin checked the downstairs area, before running a brief clip of the Ryans staggering from the master bedroom into the closet just as the assassin was about to reach the control room.

Brilliant, Ryan thought. *Absolutely brilliant.*

FIFTY-FOUR

> > > > >

PERSONAL EFFECTS

> CURSING UNDER HIS BREATH, ARES KULZAK STOPPED halfway to the control room and headed back upstairs when Kishna reported the brief sighting of the couple rushing into the master closet. He had already exceeded his time budget for this assault. By now he was supposed to be away from the mansion and on his way to meet up with Kishna.

The same determination that had driven him all these years filling his veins, Ares moved swiftly inside the master suite, the MP5 aimed at the door leading into the closet.

"Can you see me?" he whispered.

"Yes," Kishna replied.

I have got you now, he thought, rushing inside the large closet and firing two three-second bursts. The silencer absorbed all the reports, except for the metallic clinks of the firing mechanism set in full automatic fire. The silenced rounds struck wood and plasterboard with the sound of a dozen pounding hammers. But there was no one here. He saw no bleeding bodies, no figures shifting in the dark, no cries or screams.

Just silence.

A silence that ripped through him like those bullets had torn into the walls, like the trouncing of his heartbeat against his temples.

He breathed, realizing that once again he had been tricked. Someone out there was making a fool out of him, was mocking him, and his instincts told him that it was the same hackers who were interfering with his strikes—the *pendejos* who would pay dearly for such insult.

"It's empty!" he protested. "There is no one—"

Alarms suddenly blared across the mansion and all lights came on.

Instead of rattling him, the wailing noise served as his wake-up call that it was time to retreat, to live to fight another day.

"I'm heading out," he said into the small microphone. "Wait for me at our rendezvous point."

A final glance at the empty closet, Ares Kulzak turned to leave, but his eyes landed on the closest nightstand adjacent to the bed.

A man's wallet.

He picked it up, opening it, staring at a California driver's license.

Michael Patrick Ryan.

You will be sorry, my friend.

He turned his head toward a faint noise in the distance, echoing off the hills.

Helicopters.

He pocketed the wallet and hurried out of the room, climbing down the stairs, dropping a small backpack loaded with three pounds of Paxton's explosives between the foyer and the living room, an impact switch activating a five-minute timer.

I will get you one way or another, Mr. Ryan.

Rushing out the back, Ares moved like a shadow toward the same wooded hill he had used to reach the mansion.

FIFTY-FIVE

> > > > >

BLOWN COVER

> "HE'S GOT MY WALLET," RYAN SAID IN DISBELIEF, feeling as if he had just swallowed molten lead.

"What?" Victoria asked.

"I just saw the son of a bitch snatch my wallet from the nightstand upstairs. Damn!"

"Oh, God!" she said, a hand covering her mouth. "Now he knows who you are . . . who *we* are."

Ryan watched the assassin run into the woods flanking the southern edge of the property. At the same time, he noticed movement in two of the other cameras. Police cars. He also heard the whop-whop sound of nearing helicopters.

Ryan ordered MPS-Ali to once again blind the cyberterrorists by unplugging them from the video system to keep them from watching the approaching cavalry.

At least they had managed to stay alive. Flipping the master alarm switches on the control panel behind the desk had done the trick. He had read once that nothing frightens a burglar more than noise and lights.

Victoria took a deep breath, hands beneath her stomach. "This was too close, Mike. And now he has your wallet. He knows where we live. What are we going to do?"

"We're going to fight back," he said, switching off the alarm but leaving the estate's lights on. He dialed Karen's mobile phone number.

"We're almost there!" she shouted over the deafening rotor noise.

"He's running away!" Ryan shouted. "Get him. He's got my wallet! He knows who I am."

FIFTY-SIX

> > > > >

PEA SOUP

> "DROP US OFF OVER THERE!" KAREN SCREAMS AT the police helicopter pilot after listening to Ryan, who still had the intruder in sight on one of his cameras. I'm about to lose the Chinese meal we all had a few hours ago because of the bumpy flight at the hands of this former navy pilot, but manage to hold it all together while sharing the front seat of the chopper with Karen and this Topgun renegade. Three guys from the SWAT team armed with everything from assault rifles to night-vision goggles sit behind us. Paul Stone is also back there with them.

I also don't particularly enjoy being enclosed in a bubble of Plexiglas while hovering so damned close to the treetops that I wouldn't even have time to kiss my ass good-bye should the rotor fail.

Stop bitching, Grant, you ain't doing it for the money, right?

"There!" Karen shouts, pointing at the woods south of the estate. "Get over there!"

The pilot cuts in that direction in one of those guts-in-your-throat maneuvers that he probably thinks are cool but leave landlubbers like me longing to execute a kick-your-balls-up-your-throat maneuver on him.

Before my quavering stomach gets a chance to adjust, he drops the craft down on the grassy field by the tree line, cushioning the landing with a last-second burst of rotor power.

The SWAT guys are already out and running toward the spot where the dark silhouette of the man I hope to be Ares Kulzak disappeared into the thicket just before we landed.

I think I'm going to puke all over myself, but Karen, apparently immune to rough flying, is already pushing me out of the door.

"Go! Go!" she screams, the mobile phone in one hand and the Glock in the other."

I grab my Sig and jump out, clenching my teeth while peering at the moonlit woods, watching the SWAT trio gallop in a straight line after the intruder.

Paul Stone gets ready to follow us, but fearing that the house is booby-trapped, we tell him to back-up the SWAT team. Although disappointment flashes in his young eyes, he nods, draws his weapon, and follows them.

Sorry kid, I think. *You'll be safer with them than with us.*

We hustle in the opposite direction, the downwash of the helicopter weighing down against us while the pilot takes off to make room for the next craft, packed with more assault troops.

I realize a moment later that running and nausea don't mix. My gut tightens and up shoots partially digested Chinese rice, sesame chicken, and sweet and sour pork to my gorge, erupting a moment later with the power of fifty Old Faithfuls.

The world freezes around me as I'm doing the Linda Blair thing, puking all over my shoes, tears clouding my eyes as every last freaking muscle in my body tenses. The stench of Chinese food and bile rakes my nostrils as I let it all out.

Damn!

"Tom!" Karen says, somewhere to my right. "Are you okay?"

Dizzy, bracing my aching gut, smelling the acidic reek crawling up my nostrils, I step away from the white-speckled pea soup puddle I've just vomited. At least my head isn't spinning yet.

"Are you all right, Tom?" she asks again.

What kind of stupid-ass question is that anyway? Does it look like I'm fucking A-okay? Do I smell like I'm just having the time of my life? Does it look like I'm enjoying this Technicolor yawn?

"Let's go," I finally mumble, wiping my mouth with a sleeve, breathing deeply through my mouth, the pressure in my stomach momentarily lessening, the moment passing as we head for the mansion, toward Ryan and Victoria, who claim to be fine.

But you're *never* fine with Kulzak. The bastard *always* has a way of leaving little booby-trapped presents behind, especially after the way Ryan tricked him.

Keeping the phone pressed against her right ear, Karen instructs Ryan to remain in the control room. I inform my stomach that I've officially blocked all exit points.

The last two choppers don't offload their teams on the lawn but fly toward the top of the hill. Half listening to the conversation through the earpiece while I was tossing my tacos, I've learned that the cops in the other choppers are heading there to try to cut the assassin off. More cops are trying to seal the area in cars and boats.

But why, oh why, do I still have a feeling that, just as my obstinate stomach is threatening to launch another batch of green power brew through my clamped jaw, the slimy Ares Kulzak—if that's indeed who the assassin is—will also find a way out?

That's because I'm not sure what to expect, which is why I'm going after the Ryans rather than the figure that rushed into the woods, who could be a diversion. Mike Ryan is my priority. He's the guy who has gotten us this far, who has managed not only to block some of the attacks, but has actually retaliated. I know no one else who has done that against Kulzak and lived to tell—a realization that makes me kick even harder as the rush of adrenaline fills my veins once again when nearing a place where Kulzak has potentially been just moments ago.

The mansion is still a couple hundred feet up the same gentle hill I strolled around earlier this afternoon pondering on my next move against the monster without realizing that once again I was acting out another scene of a script written by the little devil.

The flashing lights of police cruisers pulsate in the night in front of the mansion, but everyone is under strict orders not to enter the place as it could be wired. I want the cops and the Ryans to sit tight until I get a chance to look around, which I plan to do as soon as I can haul my out-of-shape body to the rear of the mansion, the place where Ryan saw the assassin leave.

"Feeling better?" Karen asks, her hair and her breasts bouncing as she trots next to me like some award-winning mare at a horse show, without the slightest sign of stress or sweat.

It is at Kodak moments like this when people who are physically fit have a tendency to piss me off, especially when I'm soaked in perspiration, my throat and nostrils are burning, and there's green puke on my gun and my shoes.

"Yeah," I say. "I'm feeling just dandy."

FIFTY-SEVEN

> > > > >

GUT FEELING

> WHILE WAITING FOR THE GREEN LIGHT FROM THE
CCTF agents, Ryan kept a close watch on the activity displayed by the monitors in
his cyber world. Help was definitely on the way, but Tom Grant and Karen Frost
had just requested that they remain inside the control room until the mansion was
swept for bombs—something that didn't give him or Victoria a warm and fuzzy
feeling.

*If there was the chance of bombs inside the house then why in the hell are we being
requested to stick around?*

MPS-Ali reported that the AI interfaced to the network was terminating its link
and retreating. The cyberterrorists were bailing not just in the real world but also in
cyber land.

Ryan considered his options. The same people who were telling him now to stay
put while they swept for bombs were the ones who had *assured* him that he was safe
in this place.

He also wondered if he should send MPS-Ali in pursuit of the AI but decided
against it as it was in clear violation of the Turning law to release an uninhibited construct into the Internet.

Instead, Ryan ordered it to join him here, deep inside the frozen construct that
NUKER2 held in place for them, securing it down so that Ryan could perform his
desired cyber surgery in an effort to find out more about these cyberterrorists. The

stakes had just gone up significantly for Ryan and his wife. The terrorists knew his name, and using their high-tech resources they would soon know everything about the Ryans, from place of employment to the last time he used his Visa card.

Focus.

An instant later MPS-Ali appeared, and Ryan noticed that the cyber agent had shed its former silver and purple suit for a gold and black one, just like the one Ryan wore.

Deciding to deal later with that apparent claim of equality with humans, Ryan also put aside the lost wallet and the near-death encounter and concentrated on directing MPS-Ali to attack the iceberg that had become the immobilized construct and salvage as much data as possible. Like the brain of a person who has stopped breathing, the digital banks of the captured AI were also being methodically erased.

MPS-Ali drilled deep into the construct's framework with appalling speed, gobbling up and transferring mounds of memory space, some containing already corrupted data and others storing partially intact information. The sorting of the cyber loot would come later, after MPS-Ali had salvaged any byte of memory that had a chance of containing information.

When his cyber agent finished scanning the construct's outer layers, Ryan instructed it to probe deeper. Most AI constructs were modeled after the human brain, and like an oxygen-starved mind, the less critical areas would die first, like long-term memory and reasoning skills. The sections controlling voluntary and involuntary muscles and organs would go last. The human body was programmed to try to remain alive for as long as possible, even if it meant surviving as a vegetable. Likewise, the construct's innermost lattice, the one that controlled its basic functions, the one defining its true essence, its digital DNA, would be erased last. And it was this semi-frozen layer of the construct's structure that MPS-Ali focused on, copying as much of it to Ryan's backtop hard drive until the AI construct finally ceased to operate, becoming just an icy block of random ones and zeroes.

Glancing at the readout on the lower left-hand corner of his digital field of view, Ryan checked that four minutes had elapsed since seeing the assassin leave the mansion. A glance at the monitors revealed that Tom Grant and Karen Frost were about two-thirds of the way up the hill. He didn't feel like hanging around what would be at least another ten or more minutes by the time they got here and checked around the house.

"Mike," she said. "I don't feel very good." She grimaced while setting the gun on the floor and bracing her stomach.

Ryan struggled to control his growing anger. The government had promised him they would be safe, yet here they were, surviving on their own after the security detail had been eliminated. Should he trust them yet again by staying put?

Making up his mind, Ryan leaned down. "Can you stand?"

"It was a cramp," she said, breathing deeply before nodding. "It passed."

He helped her up while watching MPS-Ali off to the side busily deciphering and cataloguing the gigabytes of data it had copied from the construct. Ryan had prioritized the digital DNA of the construct first in an attempt to get a clue regarding its origin. If he could find the creator, Ryan felt certain he could find the mastermind behind this mess.

"We're leaving?" she said, wiping her brow. She was sweating, the stress obviously getting to her. Her hands felt clammy and her face seemed a bit pale.

This was bad. Real bad.

Her doctor had warned them about the dangers of an early delivery given her slim physique and had insisted on no stress for the last two months in order to give the baby more time to grow in her womb.

"We're getting out of here, Vic."

"But Karen said—"

"Let's just say I have a bad feeling about sticking around too much longer. Call it a hunch."

He slowly guided her to the metallic security door leading to a small covered patio on the left side of the house. From there they slowly headed toward the front of the mansion, where police cars were arriving in numbers.

He spotted some of Karen's subordinates and waved at them. The CCTF agents recognized them and rushed to their side with a pair of blankets while also flagging two paramedics, who placed Victoria on a stretcher and took her inside one of the air-conditioned ambulances parked off to the left of the driveway, a safe distance from the mansion.

Ryan glared at the emergency vehicles and the crowd of cops and agents gathered around them—all far away from the house.

This alone fueled Ryan's anger to a new level. Everyone out here had been warned of the risk of a bomb inside the house and had kept a respectful distance, yet he had been instructed to remain inside.

He swore to himself at that moment to never—ever—place his safety, and the safety of his wife and unborn child, in the U.S. government's hands.

FIFTY-EIGHT

> > > > >

THE MOHICAN

> THE SWAT TEAM AT THE TOP OF THE HILL IS NOW IN place and combing through the forest heading downhill. With luck they will sandwich the man responsible for what I now see when reaching the rear patio.

The bodies of two Secret Service men are sprawled on the limestone terrace, limbs twisted at unnatural angles, dark pools of blood around their heads.

A brief sigh is all the respect I can afford them until I know the area is clean.

I proceed slowly through a French door that had been kicked open—judging by the cracked frame and splintered wood beneath my shoes.

The place has more lights than I can count, and they are all shining on the three agents inside, all unfortunate enough to have been on their break sleeping. They never had a chance, executed just like the pair outside, their craniums blown open, blood and brains staining the light fabric of the sofas. All of them have emptied their bladders. One smells like he has voided his bowels.

From the information we had gotten earlier from Ryan, I knew the agents had been slain, but it's only now, after seeing them and smelling the acrid stench of blood, urine, and excrement that raw anger displaces my nausea, inducing the exact opposite effect it would on normal people. I begin to get *really* pissed—an emotion I can't allow to overtake me, lest I have a strong desire to end up like them.

Or worse.

Karen is right beside me, hands busy with the cellular phone and the gun. She doesn't even flinch at the gory sight. This is what separates the rookies from the old hands.

"The Ryans," she whispers, pocketing the phone and clutching the Glock with both hands. "They left the house."

"They *what?* When?"

"Just a moment ago."

"How?"

"The control room has two doors. One to the inside and one to the outside. They're with the police up front."

Doesn't anyone follow orders anymore? Why do I fucking bother? The door to that control room could have been wired. The whole damned place could have gone up in smoke with all of us inside!

Resisting the temptation to scream, I decided to let that go and focus on the job at hand, inspecting the kitchen first, finding nothing but empty cartons of the take-out Chinese we all had feasted on a few hours ago—the spotty pea soup I regurgitated down the hill. Ironically, the smell of Chinese food makes my stomach grumble far more than the stench from the dead agents.

"Kitchen's clear," Karen says, stepping into the foyer. I'm right behind her but bump into her when she stops abruptly.

She lands on her knees in front of me and looks back over her shoulder.

"Sorry," I say. "Why did you stop like that?"

She frowns and points at the corner where the foyer meets the living area.

I stare at a familiar black backpack wedged in between the legs of a small, round, marble table topped with some kind of local artwork of metal, turquoise, and—

"Please tell me that's *not* what I think it is," Karen says, making a face.

I quickly kneel by it and try to listen.

The beeps are so close together that they almost sound like a steady tune. My stomach tightens. We have to get out of here.

I stand and pivot away from it as if I've stepped on a nest of scorpions, snatching her light frame along the way.

"Tom—"

"No time! Let's go!" I scream, keeping her by my side, my left hand clasping her right arm as we dash across the living room, past the dead agents, through the open doorway, and onto the terrace, our shoes thudding against the limestone.

We jump over a dead agent, his lifeless eyes staring back at me, as if trying to tell me something.

And that's the last thing I see before an arresting force punches me in the back. I only have time to pull Karen closer to me, embracing her as the back of the house erupts in a thundering, ear-piercing crescendo of gushing flames, broken glass, and smoldering wood.

The vest takes the brunt of the impact while I'm holding her small frame from behind, tight, very tight, feeling as if a giant hammer is pounding my back.

Burning debris shoots past us like a shower of flaming meteors. I try to scream as the intense heat envelopes me, as billowing smoke blinds me, but the blast has taken the wind out of me. I try to breathe but can't, feeling as if my lungs have collapsed, as if my legs can no longer support my weight.

Falling.

I'm falling, sinking, unable to control my body, unable to shout for help, my arms no longer holding Karen Frost, my eyes shielded by a thick veil of smoke, but the smoke isn't swirling like it did a moment ago. And the pain is suddenly gone, vanished, along with the noise and the pressure.

I stand and stare in half shock at the destruction around me, at the smoldering rubble across the street, at the smoke sizzling skyward.

People run about me screaming, crying, shouting as I stagger toward the demolished structure, toward the remnants of the building where my team is, where Madie . . .

Smoking ruins surround me as I climb over mounds of debris looking for her, for the only woman I have ever—

There. On that concrete slab just to the right of the collapsed roof.

She's laying face up, eyes closed, arms by her sides, her face as angelic as on those long nights where I'd just stayed up watching her sleep, holding her as she stirred, as her body sought mine in the dark, as our bodies became one. Close. Very close. Reaching a unity I never thought possible.

A perfect bond abruptly severed by the monster.

I'm kneeling by her side, feeling for a pulse, detecting none, clearing her airway, placing a hand under her neck, gently inching her head back while I take a deep breath before pressing my lips against hers and exhaling, trying to force life into her, trying to hang onto the dream, to the promise, to a life beyond the uncertainty of field operations.

But she's not responding, her face draining of all color, her body turning cold, stiff.

Madie is slipping away from me, away from my world, just like the smoke spiraling up to the clear skies, slowly fading with the blue expanse, slowly becoming a part of something else. Kulzak has stolen her, has prevented me from—

Her eyes open, dilated pupils on a ghostly-white face staring at me while her frigid hands clasp the sides of my head like a vise and pull me down.

No, Madie. This is wrong. Your body was never found! You do not exist!

I try to resist, but my arms no longer respond, hanging uselessly from my shoulders as her lips cover my mouth, as her warm breath rushes deep inside my body, warming my core.

And I'm falling again, dropping into a bottomless cave, losing all perspective of up or down, of life and death. Only her steady breaths now, one after another, hissing deep inside of me, stretching my lungs again and again, awakening my muscles, lifting the veil around me, returning the pain on my back, the heat, the wailing sirens of emergency vehicles, the smell of smoke and singed hair, and—

I stare straight into her brown eyes as she's giving me mouth-to-mouth, the gift of life, a hand beneath my neck, her fingers pinching my nostrils to force the air into my lungs.

Lips parted, Karen Frost pulls back as I cough, as I breathe on my own, as I cringe in pain while expanding my chest.

I cough again, tears in my eyes, a stabbing pain in the pit of my stomach.

"You are crazy, Tom Grant," she says, smiling while touching my face with an open palm as my breathing becomes steady, as the abdominal pain recedes. "You have to stop shielding me like that. I don't break that easily."

"Jesus," I mumble. "Did . . . I . . . ?"

She nods and checks her watch. "Almost two minutes. For a moment there . . ."

I nod, realizing just how close, once again, I've come to becoming Kulzak's latest victim, and for a moment I wonder if I have feline blood running through my veins.

She helps me sit up and we just stay there a while in silence watching the surreal spectacle that Kulzak has once again created.

"The man sure knows how to make an exit," she comments.

Her hair, damp from perspiration, sticks to the side of her face, darkened by the smoke.

I'm slowly coming out of my near-death experience and just watch as fire trucks surround the blaze beneath a rising cloud of glowing ashes. Two dozen firemen are already setting up their gear. A moment later bright streams of water project over the fire, amidst an ocean of red and blue flashing lights.

There are people who are thought to have the Midas touch. Kulzak has just the opposite gift. Everything he touches turns to shit.

Amidst the firemen and patrolling cops I see a pair of paramedics—a man and a woman in their twenties—hauling large silver cases while running in my direction. More police cruisers reach the area, sirens wailing.

Let the party roll.

I tell the young pill peddlers that I'm all right, but they insist on taking my blood pressure, checking my heartbeat, and shining lights into my eyes. I get a little nervous when I see them slipping on latex gloves but they stay away from any body cavities.

A group of cops are headed our way.

"Don't go anywhere," Karen tells me, kissing me on the cheek and winking while cupping my chin. "These two will take care of you. I'll be right back." She stands up and goes to meet them.

Did you see that? She just kissed me on the cheek and gave me one of those slow female winks. What does that mean? As much as I can get inside the mind of terrorists, I'm pretty pathetic about understanding the opposite sex.

Karen is leading the conversation, pointing at the house, at the woods, at her watch, and then at me. I want to hear what they're saying but the roaring inferno, the rumbling fire engines, and all of the background shouting and sirens drown their conversation.

Everyone stops and turns to the fire when there's a secondary explosion inside the house, followed by a skyward burst of sizzling debris and a column of flames. Two exterior walls collapse inward. More searing ashes light up the night like fireworks. The pillar of yellow flames continues to gush upward, for a moment reminding me of those oil fires in Kuwait. I can feel the heat from where I'm sitting. A growl that sounds like a tiger going for the kill rumbles from the flickering inferno.

"Gas line!" someone shouts in the distance. "Cut the gas line!"

This is quite the spectacle. Firemen rush to one side of the property and pull up the cover of a manhole, reaching inside. A moment later the blazing column vanishes, but there's still plenty of fuel for a fire that the multiple water streams can't seem to quench.

Karen and the cops resume their conversation. The Dynamic Duo also goes back to work, removing my shirt and then my vest, and begin to check my back for wounds or burns. It looks like the vest saved my ass, stopping the household shrapnel that shredded my shirt. The back of my head, neck, and arms, however, are another story. And I know what the smell of singed hair means, though I put it aside for now.

The male medic, named Stan, is roughly half my size. He works on the scrapes down my left arm while the lady paramedic, a cute pixie blonde named Stacey, cleans a minor cut on the back of my neck before applying an antibiotic cream and bandaging it.

Stacey and Stan.

I'm too tired to conjure a smart-ass comment about that.

Anyway, they're telling me how lucky I am to have survived with just superficial injuries.

No offense, but at the moment I don't feel lucky and also don't feel like chatting.

The little medics realize their big patient is not in a talkative mood and proceed to chat among themselves about an upcoming UT game as they keep patching me up.

The smell of burnt hair is now getting to me and I put a hand to the back of my head, grimacing when feeling a large patch of hairless scalp on the back and the sides of my head. I cringe in pain when I touch it.

"Don't," Stacey tells me in her high-pitched voice, a bit on the nasal side. "It's only a minor burn but still could get infected. Be grateful that you had thick hair. It served as a buffer to keep your skull from enduring a more severe burn." She starts applying another kind of cream to my exposed skull.

I turn around and stare at her, catching a grin on her lips.

"That bad, huh?"

"You can probably start a new trend," she says, holding back a wider smile.

"Yeah," says Stan. "At an Indian reservation."

Tom Grant, honorary Mohican. I guess all paramedics go to comedian school in this town. Or perhaps, just like me, they also use humor to shave the edge off the realities of their profession.

But I did survive to fight another day, and just as I'm actually beginning to feel alive again despite my cosmetic problems, I see Karen reaching for her mobile phone and closing her eyes as she makes the face she always makes when Washington is at the other end. I really can't wait to hear what Cramer is going to say about this one. The bastard is likely to claim he had nothing to do with setting up the Ryans at this mansion. And what will annoy the hell out of me is that his superiors will probably let him get away with that even though he's the one ultimately in charge of the CCTF. I mean, you either are in charge or you're not. You can't have it both ways, but Cramer seems to always find a way to manipulate a situation to his own advantage.

She hangs up and heads my way.

"All right," I say. "What does the asshole have to say about this?" I wave at the fire and the bodies.

"Nothing."

"Nothing?"

"Nope."

"Why?"

"Because he's dead, Tom."

"*Dead?*" I try to stand but the young couple playing doctor behind me scream at the same time and force me to sit down. "What happened?"

"Car bomb. Happened just thirty minutes ago. There wasn't much left of him. I'm guessing Kulzak was trying to kill the CCTF's investigative team by chopping off the head."

Well, what do you know? Cramer always wanted to be a hero. He finally got his way. He became a hero all right.

A dead one.

And please, don't ask me to feel too sorry for him. Remember Jerry Martinez? Remember the shit jobs I got after that for the next decade? That was his doing. So he got killed. Well, so did eleven Secret Service agents tonight and yours truly for that matter—for a couple of minutes anyway.

For a moment my sick mind wonders if the devil didn't feel like dealing with Cramer and me on the same night and had to kick one back up here, and since there were pieces of the old bastard spread across two city blocks, I got the lucky break.

Karen kneels by my side and starts inspecting my head while the paramedics continue to patch me up.

She raises one of her fine brows while trying to contain a grin.

"I know," I say. "I feel like Tonto."

Her smile widens. "I think you look very handsome without hair."

"I think so too," replies Stacey.

"Me too," says Stan, smiling.

As I sit there wondering how to reply to that, one of the cops calls Karen back. She gives me another wink and runs back to talk to them.

I suddenly feel lonely, but not for long. Ryan is heading my way.

"Check that out," I say to the paramedics, tilting my head in his direction. Ryan looks like a character from a low-budget sci-fi movie with the cyber helmet under his arm, weird-looking gloves, blinking computer hardware strapped to his back and chest, and even wires coming out of his ass.

"Welcome to our planet," I say, giving him the Vulcan sign from *Star Trek*. The paramedics laugh.

"Good one," says Stacey.

Ryan doesn't find it amusing, and I don't blame him. The Ryans are damned lucky to be alive. Actually, luck probably had little to do with it. Mike Ryan single-handedly *saved* his family despite our recent foul-ups.

"How's Victoria, Mike?" I ask, turning serious.

"How do *you* think? She almost went into labor in that control room!"

"Where is she?" both paramedics ask in unison while standing up.

"Your friends in the other ambulance are looking after her," he replies.

"Look, Mike," I begin to say. "I'm really sorry for—"

"Save it," he says. "I thought you guys were on the level with me. You've withheld key information on the AI."

I'm about to reply but can't discuss the case in front of the young bonesetters, so

I do the only thing I can: politely tell them to go take their comedy show elsewhere. This patient will survive without any more creams and Band-Aids and bad jokes.

Annoyed, they pack up and leave.

"You sure have a way with people," Ryan says as they walk away.

"What's on your mind?" I ask.

"Whatever it is you're keeping from me, Tom. *That's* what's on my mind."

Before I can reply, Karen comes back and joins us. "Just got a report from the SWAT teams. Bad news. No sign of the assassin."

"Great," says Ryan. "Next time maybe I'll install a couple of laser guns on the walls and take him out *myself*. Lord only knows I did just about everything else!"

We both look at him. The guy's all stymied up, and he's got reason to be, but at the same time it's not like we've been sitting around with our thumbs up our asses.

Although I'm tired, scraped, burnt, and even scalped, I decide to let the comment go, and so does Karen, who adds, "We have over forty people on that mountain and enough police cruisers blocking the area to start a Fourth-of-July parade. The lakeside is also blocked off with police boats."

"Then where is he?" Ryan demands to know.

"Look," Karen says. "I'm really sorry that you and your wife—"

"You let him get away."

"Mike, we don't yet know if—"

"Jesus, Karen! You don't get it, do you? The bastard has my wallet. *My wallet!* He knows who I am, where we live. Our lives are *fucked* again, Karen, just like the last time I helped you!"

"Mike," she says, obviously upset. "I—"

"You *promised* me this wasn't going to happen! You guaranteed our protection!"

"C'mon, Mike," I say. "We're doing the best we can under the circumstances. We brought in the best there is to protect you and—"

"You call that the best protection you can provide?" he says, pointing at the inferno and the dead bodies. "Those agents, rest in peace, might have been terrific at what they did, but obviously weren't enough to handle the terrorists, and now those terrorists know who has been screwing with them in the cyber world."

"You don't know that, Mike," I say. "All they got was a wallet. They don't know how you are involved in—"

"Oh, *please*! How stupid do you think I am? Or the terrorists for that matter? They will dig, Tom, and they will put two and two together and connect me to the person responsible for blocking their work."

"Mike, please. Calm down. We will work this—"

"Don't tell me to calm down! You're the one who told me to stay put, to remain in the house with my pregnant wife while everyone else was staying far away!" He touches my chest with the helmet. The kid is really pushing it.

"Look—" I start.

"You told me to stay in the control room, Tom!" he continued. "Jesus Christ, man! The only reason Vic and I are still alive is because we didn't listen to you! Because we got the hell out of there before the bomb went off! I mean, look at you. You could barely take care of yourself!"

"Mike," Karen starts. "We are all in the same—"

"That's the other thing," he shouts, cocking a finger at both of us. "We're *not* on the same team."

"What do you mean?" she asks.

"You're withholding information that I could have used in the past two days!"

Karen opens her mouth but nothing comes out.

"You mentioned that before, Mike," I say, choosing to remain in the adult state despite my throbbing scalp, "but I still have no idea what you're talking about."

"I'm talking about the AI, Tom. The construct that nearly lobotomized me . . . twice!"

"What about it?" Karen asks.

"MPS-Ali just reported that amidst the bits and pieces of digital DNA extracted from the AI construct I neutralized tonight there was a signature, a code, that can only come from one place in the world."

"A code?"

"An intelligent encryption program to serialize software and hardware in a very secretive way so that if the stuff is ever stolen someone running the proper scan can detect it and realize it's been stolen."

"Who creates this code for serial numbers, Mike?" I ask, for some reason fearing the answer.

"The Department of Def—"

His words are cut short by a thundering roar from the woods, near the lake, followed by the agonizing screams of men.

FIFTY-NINE

> > > > >

PATIENCE

> ARES KULZAK PRESSED A BUTTON ON THE SIDE OF
the depth meter strapped to his right wrist and a light illuminated the dial, informing
him that he was just below twenty feet. A compass secured to his forearm confirmed
his heading: north, away from the exciting side of the lake.

But even while holding this depth and estimating that he had already swum a few
hundred feet, he could still hear the rumbling of the Claymore mine he had set up to
cover his getaway. Hundreds of lead pellets shot simultaneously by a charge of C4
pretty much guaranteed stripping the commitment right out of any search party.

He also heard the screws of the search boats. Once in a while a boat would get
very close to his position, even cruise right over him, but searching the water for bubbles would be fruitless. Ares didn't wear SCUBA gear, like that used by sports divers,
because such open-circuit apparatus emitted bubbles and noise, which under his current predicament would be deadly.

Ares relied on the same type of underwater apparatus used by the U.S. Navy
SEALs, a closed-circuit rig also called a re-breather. The oxygen flowed from a bottle
strapped to his chest, through a regulator, and into his mouthpiece. When he
breathed out, rather than creating bubbles like in a SCUBA system, the re-breather
directed this exhaled mixture of oxygen and carbon dioxide through a canister of
baralyme, which absorbed the CO_2 and let the purified oxygen back to the mouthpiece. Since only the consumed oxygen needed replacement, which was a very small

amount every time he breathed, Ares was only required to haul a small oxygen canister to stay underwater for as long as a SCUBA diver wearing large double tanks—and he did it while remaining totally quiet.

Navigating in complete darkness, guided only by his dimly lit instruments, he maintained his course, slowly kicking his legs, the large fins propelling him forward at a steady pace. He didn't need to hurry as he had no one following him, and the blast would confuse them even more.

But the night had not been a victory. Ares had managed to terminate a number of Secret Agent *gusanos*. However, his primary target had escaped alive. He could only hope that the attack in Washington against Cramer had met with success.

Staring into darkness, Kulzak thought of Karen Frost and Tom Grant, the two agents he had hoped to surprise tonight. Instead he had stumbled onto a third individual and an unidentified woman.

Michael Patrick Ryan.

Ares carried the wallet in a waterproof pouch secured to the re-breather with a short lanyard. It would take Kishna less than an hour to learn everything about this man, whom Ares suspected had not only blocked some of his efforts but had also confused Kishna and Ares during the raid. That would certainly explain all of the Secret Service protection. The Americans were guarding the person capable of fighting Kulzak in cyberspace.

Another formidable enemy, he thought. *Worthy of my skill.*

But an enemy that he nonetheless had to eliminate, just as he had to kill Frost and Grant.

Patience.

In the depths of this lake, while escaping the enemy, Ares remembered his instructors covering the subject of patience in many ways. His Cuban and Russian trainers had stressed to him the power of patience, a weapon far more powerful than the firearms he already handled so proficiently.

Patience.

It came in many ways. Sometimes it meant waiting for an enemy to make his move. Other times it required him to hold back until a situation had settled down before striking again.

"Patience on your part will drive the enemy insane, forcing it to act prematurely, to make a mistake," an instructor had once told him at the officer's school in Havana.

And so Ares Kulzak continued to kick his legs, continued to get away to fight another battle on another day.

Despite the evening's disappointing results, his primary agenda remained intact. While the CCTF, with the likely help of this Ryan, had been successful in blocking some of his strikes, they had not yet caught on to the fact that more important than the mere death of a few thousand *gusanos* and the destruction of buildings were the backdoor passwords to access Neurall's twin.

Such thoughts accompanied Ares Kulzak as he kept his pace for another two hours. By three in the morning, after he had not heard any propellers for some time, he injected oxygen into his buoyancy control device, which he wore around him like a vest, inflating it just enough to break his neutral buoyancy and head up to the surface, feeling certain that the enemy would not be waiting for him.

Darkness.

He looked behind him and saw the distant lights on the water, on the ground, and up on the hill, as well as the glowing structure that had been the mansion. Flashing beacons from emergency vehicles still glared in the hazy horizon.

He had covered what appeared to be around two miles in record time. His old Cuban instructors would have been proud.

Ares swam toward his rendezvous point with Kishna on a lakefront property for sale several hundred feet away, finally approaching the shore but remaining immersed except for his face.

Slowly, he reached for a small flashlight strapped to his waist and flickered it twice toward the dark water's edge.

A moment later he saw four dim flashes.

He inched closer to the limestone rock delineating the property until reaching knee-deep water, at which point he sat and removed his fins and mask.

"Ari?" a voice echoed from the woods beyond the rocky shore.

"Yes," he replied, getting up and walking onto solid ground. "I have made it."

Kishna emerged from the tree line dressed in black. He handed her the fins and mask.

"Is our flight on schedule?" he asked. They had chartered a jet out of Austin for a one-way trip to the West Coast.

She checked her watch. "It leaves at ten. We need to hurry."

Ares removed his re-breather unit and slipped out of the wet suit before heading toward the woods. "The bastards tricked us," he said.

"I know . . . I'm also afraid that could have created a serious problem," she said. "About Neurall."

As Kishna explained how the physical location of the AI might have been compromised, Ares Kulzak turned to face the water, gazing into the darkness beyond the shallow swells lapping against blocks of limestone. He peered at the opposite shore, at the blow he alone had delivered against a much more powerful enemy, inflicting many casualties.

But it wasn't enough.

It was *never* enough.

The enemy always found a way to fight back, to resist, to force Ares to conceive new strategies, to accelerate his itinerary. And now the enemy might have found a way to really hurt him. If Neurall was compromised, so was the location of the large processing lab of the Cartel.

If the Americans attacked and destroyed it, his life wouldn't be worth the river stones on which he walked. But that was all part of the life that fate had chosen for him on that beach in Cuba.

His eyes drifted skyward, focusing on the bright star just beneath the quarter moon.

It's a planet, not a star, Ari.

My planet, my life.

He remembered his mother's words, remembered the story of Ares, the brave god who had many enemies but still managed to prevail, to survive.

And I will continue to survive. Even if the Cartel chooses to turn against me.

You see, Mami, Ares thought, tightening his fists. *With these hands I will change the world, even if it takes a lifetime, even if the enemy grows stronger.*

He had promised to do so on the sands of his homeland a long, long time ago.

S I X T Y

> > > > >

C L A Y M O R E

> "GET THE FUCKING PARAMEDICS OVER HERE!" I shout at the top of my lungs while Karen and I help a member of the SWAT team haul the bleeding body of Paul Stone from the brush.

My stomach is once again doing cartwheels as we set him down on the ground. According to one of the SWAT guys the kid got the brunt of what looked like a claymore mine on his lower body.

"My legs . . ." Stone mumbles, eyes closed. "I . . . I can't . . . feel them . . ."

I stare at Karen, whose eyes are filled with tears. For some reason I also feel like crying but manage to hang on to my professional face. This is a field operation, dammit, and people get hurt. I can't let this get to me, especially now. I need to keep my—

"Tom . . ." Paul mumbles, shaking. He is going into shock.

Where are the damned paramedics?

I look up and see Stacey and Stan running my way. They set their silver cases on the grass next to my boy and move us out of the way while she starts cutting off his pants with a pair scissors and he snaps open one of the cases and rips through the plastic wrapping of a syringe.

"What's his name?" Stacey asks.

"Paul," I say.

"Paul," she says, leaning down, trying to get Stone to look at her. "I'm Stacey, Paul. Can you hear me?"

"My legs . . . can't feel them," he mumbles again, his head moving from side to side, his eyes closed.

"Paul," Stacey insists. "Listen to me. We're going to take care of you. You're going to be all right, but you need to help us. You need to fight, Paul. You need to help us help you."

Stone manages a slight nod while moaning in pain.

"Good, Paul. Very good. We're going to take good care of you, all right?"

As he nods again, Stan stabs him in the arm with the syringe and injects a clear liquid. A moment later Stone stops trembling and he becomes visibly relaxed, closing his eyes and breathing regularly. The medics strap an oxygen mask to his face.

Hang in there buddy, I think to myself while standing off to the side with Karen, who takes my hand. She is crying, though no one can really tell because she is right next to me and her hair flanks her face.

This is exactly why I try to avoid learning the last names of rookies. It's easier that way. Once you add last names, they become part of your immediate family, and it just rips you apart to see them hurting.

The female paramedic finishes removing the trousers and we all get a glimpse of the kind of damage the sizzling-hot pellets of a claymore can do from a short distance.

Karen looks away in obvious disgust.

I feel like I'm going to puke again, images of Jerry Martinez flashing in front of my eyes as I stare at the kid's exposed groin and see just torn flesh and cartilage and exposed entrails where his genitals should have been.

Huevos rancheros.

I'm having an out-of-body experience.

Stone's mangled groin suddenly pulsating at the end of this long tunnel, I find myself leaning against Karen to remain standing. She senses my downward shift and helps me remain on my feet.

Oh, dear God. This can't be happening again!

But it is, and the deafening howls of Jerry Martinez slap me across the face as he writhes in pain on that dusty parking lot while Ares Kulzak and the other terrorists laugh and piss on him and call him a faggot.

A moment later and a few deep breaths, and I'm standing unassisted again—though my mind remains in a state of havoc.

The damage is far too extensive for the paramedics to handle here. Kulzak has maimed him to the point that they can't do anything beyond stabilizing him prior to a helicopter ride to a nearby hospital.

In addition to hooking him to IVs, the medics apply bandages to the disfiguring wounds and a handful of tourniquets to quench the blood loss from the severed arteries in his thighs. Then they place him on a stretcher.

The reverberating sounds of a StarFlight helicopter rumble in my chest as the medics, two cops, and Karen and I all help to get him to the landing craft.

And just like that they are gone: the choppers, the medics, and the noise. But the medieval sight has etched itself in my mind forever.

Huevos rancheros.

As the helicopter's flashing beacon disappears in the darkness, as the cops head back uphill leaving me alone with Karen, my thoughts not only go to Paul Stone and my old pal, Jerry Martinez, but also to a young bride somewhere in Iowa who will be getting a phone call in the next twenty-four hours informing her either of the death of her husband or of the crippling wounds he has sustained.

Wounds that will scar him for the rest of his life.

SIXTY-ONE

> > > > >

TOUGH CALLS

> IN THE OVAL OFFICE, PRESIDENT LAURA VACCARO stared at the TV screen as it displayed scenes from downtown Los Angeles, where a fully fueled jetliner had crashed into the city, evoking visions from 2001.

Visions we vowed never again to allow on American soil.

Vaccaro turned to the disconcerted faces of Russell Meek and Martin Jacobs, along with Secretary of Defense Malcolm Davis, and the ever-present Vice President Vance Fitzgerald.

"Let's start with Cramer," she said. "What do we know about that?"

"One bomb and three shooters, Mrs. President," said Meek, dressed in a typical dark-blue FBI suit, white shirt, and yellow tie, his freckles moving about his face as he frowned. "All with automatic weapons. They killed all four agents in the car chase following the explosion. Two D.C. police cruisers happened to be in the neighborhood and came rushing to the scene, opening fire on the assassins, killing one of them. The other two got away."

"What do we know about the dead assassin?"

Meek, who apparently had all of the facts memorized because he never opened the folder on his lap, said, "Although he didn't have any ID on him, a fingerprint match identified him as Aleksei Russinof, a Russian immigrant with no prior arrests. A search of Mr. Russinof's home on a three-acre property in West Virginia an hour ago, however, revealed a large cache of automatic weapons along with enough chemicals to manufacture a dozen pounds of explosives. We also found the names and addresses of a number of his Russian associates, including a few who are already in our files as suspected members of the Russian Mafia in this country."

"So," Vaccaro said, crossing her arms. "Am I to assume that Mr. Kulzak is being backed by the Russian Mafia?"

"Yes, Mrs. President," replied Meek.

"How many members of the Russian Mafia is the FBI currently tracking, Russ?"

"We have sixty-three suspects being followed. Of those, we currently run phone taps on fifty-one."

"What about in prison?"

"Seventy-seven men and five women currently serving anywhere from six months up to life. Two of them are on death row."

Vaccaro stared into the distance before closing her eyes. The time had come for her to show what she was really made of. The time had come to stop playing by the rules. The time had certainly come to stop listening to those who didn't have the interest of the nation at heart—a group that included those who made a living out of critiquing every decision she made.

Making her decision, President Vaccaro proposed a plan of attack that shocked her audience.

"Some people will claim this approach is unconstitutional, Mrs. President," warned Russell Meek.

"Russ, let me remind you that as far as I am concerned, we are at war. The enemy has so far attacked three of our cities—four if you want to count Austin—and this is our way of retaliating. I don't care what the press says, Russ. I don't care what the opinion polls have to say about my plan, which, by the way, I take full responsibility for. At the end of the day what I care about is putting a stop to the madness, even if doing so gets me impeached. Are we clear?"

"Crystal, Mrs. President."

A silence descended on the room, and Vaccaro couldn't help but wonder how many other leaders before her had had such a straight talk with their subordinates. There was a chance that she could get in trouble for taking such bold action, but if she was indeed going to have to throw herself at the mercy of the Congress, Vaccaro would much rather have the basis for the impeachment being her fight for the welfare of the nation than the basis for the impeachment of one of her predecessors.

"And for the record, gentlemen, this meeting is being videotaped. Now," she said, "tell me about the situation in Austin."

SIXTY - TWO

> > > > >

COMMITTEES

> FUNNY HOW THINGS WORK. SINCE CRAMER IS NOW
dead, we reported Ryan's finding to the director of the FBI, who called up the vice
president, who called the president, who called the Pentagon.

Next thing we know, there's a horde of people arriving in Austin by presidential
order. The scientists from MIT who developed Neurall, the artificial intelligence that
sported the coded serial number that Ryan found last night, arrived by mid-morning.
Then the brass started showing up right before noon along with a couple of scientists
from Los Alamos and even Ryan's old professor at Stanford, who also happens to be
one of the founders of the Turing Society. To mediate this eclectic body, the president dispatched the vice president, who arrived just after lunch in the company of a
another installment of Secret Service guys.

And this is all dandy, except that there's now way too many cooks in my kitchen,
and the more people who show up down here the more depressed I get.

Don't kid yourself. The only reason why we have managed to stay on Kulzak's tail
is because of our nimble CCTF team, which allowed us to make real-time decisions
fast, without the need to run everything through a committee—which is exactly
what I watch taking form in this conference room at Austin's Four Seasons hotel, our
new home after Kulzak remodeled the last one.

Not only do I hate committees because they always slow things down, especially at
a time when we have to accelerate them, but most of the folks sitting here were

nowhere to be found when we had to make our real-time field decisions and therefore see themselves in a position to question everything that we have done, especially the unavoidable screw-ups that are a part of life in my business.

I'm sitting next to Karen at one end of the long conference table. Ryan sits across from us, his eyes on occasion shooting a brief glance at my new hairdo—or perhaps I should say a *lack* of one. I just couldn't get used to the Mohican look, so I shaved it this morning in my hotel room upstairs. I think Karen likes it.

Ryan has MPS-Ali with him—though in the real world he is just a fancy-looking shoebox packed with FLASH memory cards. According to him the cyber agent has developed into an AI construct in the few hours since Ryan removed the Turing inhibitor to try to even out the playing field when doing high-tech battle with this rogue AI called Neurall that Ares Kulzak somehow has managed to control—an AI that was first conceived and developed by the Pentagon in conjunction with a number of professors from the venerable Massachusetts Institute of Technology.

With the help of MPS-Ali, Ryan has managed to piece together a very comprehensive report on what has taken place since the government drafted him out of his stable California life. Like most everyone in the room, I have spent the past hour reading it while the White House mediator arrived, and I've got to tell you, this MPS-Ali is one pretty darn smart hunk of silicon, detailing everything that took place in San Antonio, Melbourne, New Orleans, and Austin in far more detail than even I remember—and I remember a lot. I sure wish I'd had access to this construct during my NYPD and CIA days. As good as I am at remembering facts and then applying them in an investigation, writing reports to my superiors has always been one of my shortcomings.

Vice President Vance Fitzgerald, looking just as he does on TV, is dressed in a gray business suit and a red power tie. He probes the audience with his deep-blue eyes on a face lined with the stress he's endured as a four-time senator, then Speaker of the House for one term, before landing in second place to Vaccaro at the last convention.

Sitting at the opposite end from us, the Viper brings the meeting to order and briefly goes over the accomplishments of the CCTF in the past few days. Ryan, who later apologized to Karen and me for his emotional outburst following the explosion at the mansion, managed to e-mail a copy of the report to Fitzgerald while the Viper was in the air, and the man has obviously read it and memorized it because he is now summarizing it and drawing logical conclusions. Pretty impressive.

The brass is sitting on both sides of Fitzgerald: a general from the army, another one from the air force, and a navy admiral. They are here to represent the interests of their respective branches of the armed forces. Though I don't know them, I do know the second army general in the room, the man sitting by the MIT professors. His name is General Malcolm Davis, the Secretary of Defense, and previous director of the Defense Intelligence Agency, the military version of my beloved CIA.

You know the old saying is true, that military intelligence is a contradiction in terms. The DIA was always the subject of jokes at the CIA. We always felt the DIA didn't know its head from its ass, and if you don't believe me then explain why is it that the DIA, which has twice the number of employees and three times the budget of the CIA, produces far less results than us.

In addition to our friends in the military, there are also contingents from the civilian side who arrived with Fitzgerald: the director of Central Intelligence, Martin Jacobs, who I know from the old days, and the director of the FBI, Russell Meek. Karen seems to think that Meek is all right, and I tend to agree. It was Meek who ordered Cramer to include me in the CCTF. He has now taken over the CCTF until a replacement can be found—though I doubt there will be a lot of volunteers after the way the terrorists roasted Cramer's ass.

I count about forty people in the room, including six Secret Service guys standing around, two right behind the Viper.

In my opinion there's about thirty-seven too many people and they all should head back to whatever place they came from and let us do our job. Just throwing more bodies at the problem isn't going to solve it any sooner. If anything, it's going to slow things down at a time when we need to be picking up the pace.

But that's just me.

Fitzgerald goes around the room introducing everybody but I can't keep up with the new names. Perhaps someone should have taken the time to handwrite either name tags or something else to know who is who, but I guess that's asking too much. One thing I do notice is that the seating assignments were done with rank in mind, meaning the big fish sit by the Viper and the lowest forms of existence gather near us at the other end.

Fitzgerald wraps up his introduction with a statement that the president herself has given him full authority to oversee this investigation. He also promises that all suggestions will be considered and that no question will be deemed stupid. I write that down and show it to Karen, who elbows me.

Fitzgerald adds that there is a highly mixed set of skills present here today and that means there would be many questions required to clarify points.

Said differently: The meeting is going to be very fucking long, consuming tons of time.

Time we didn't have.

Meanwhile, Kulzak was out there running loose, lean, and mean without the benefit of a committee steering his decisions. But I promised Karen I would behave, and

I do, quietly sitting there while the nation's vice president gives the floor to Defense Secretary Malcolm Davis, the man responsible for the creation of Neurall during his DIA days.

General Davis stands so everyone can see him. The man is in his late fifties, nearly bald, and sporting a barrel chest and tons of glittering medals. Although we always laughed at his former military intelligence agency, Davis does project an image of someone who knows what he's talking about.

"Seven years ago," he starts in a booming voice, "under the coordination of Professor Arturo Corrado from MIT," he waves his hand at the gentleman in a suit sitting next to him, "we worked on a project focused on the development of software capable of self-evolving, of mutating, and in the process making itself smarter. Dr. Corrado, currently heading the MIT Artificial Intelligence Lab, will now share the details of the project."

Davis takes his seat and Corrado gets up. He's as thin as a twig, with unkempt hair, tiny round glasses perched at the tip of his nose, and wears an ill-fitting gray suit. He clears his throat and says in heavily accented English, "Ladies and gentlemen, over a half century ago, a mathematician named von Neumann came up with a way to realize the concept of self-reproducing computer programs. Up to that point scholars had discussed the possibility of machines replicating themselves but they could never get past the problem of infinite regress."

Infinite what?

"Could you explain that term for us nontechnical types, please," asked Fitzgerald, reading my mind.

Corrado stared at the vice president for a moment, almost in disbelief that he was not familiar with such a concept. I'm about to join in and claim ignorance as well but Karen grabs my hand when she sees it leaving the table and forces it back down.

Ever since New Orleans I get the strange feeling that she's treating me with post-coitus confidence even though we still haven't parallel parked, unless she took advantage of me during my recent unconscious episodes. But if we have indeed done the belly to belly hustle, I hope my other bald head had a great time because my recently shaved one doesn't remember.

Corrado finally says, "A program might try to create a clone using a blueprint, but the problem is that this blueprint, or self description, is a part of the original program, so what describes the description, and what describes the description of the description? That's the concept of infinite regress."

While that explanation might work for his highly educated MIT students, this poor New Yorker who barely made it through high school is still out in left field.

"In *English*, please," says Vice President Fitzgerald.

No shit, José.

"Ah, excuse me, Mr. Vice President," says Ryan. "Why don't I take a stab at it?"

The Viper looks down toward the bottom-dweller end of the table and slowly nods, probably amazed that someone on this side of the tracks has an opinion at all. "Very well, Mr. Ryan. Please enlighten the common folk."

"All right. I think the concept of infinite regress solved by von Neumann can be best explained with an analogy. Say for example that you ask an architect to make an identical copy of his own studio. The blueprint used by the builder would have to contain a miniature version of the blueprint, which would have to contain a miniature copy of the blueprint, and so on. Without this data the builder would not be able to re-create the study perfectly. There would always be this blank space where the original blueprint had been. Von Neumann came up with a way to break out of the problem of infinite regress by proposing that the self-description—the blueprint—could be used in two distinct ways. First, as the instructions whose interpretation leads to the construction of an identical copy of the original, and second as data to be copied, uninterpreted, and attached to the newly created clone so that it will also have the ability to self-replicate. In the architectural analogy, this two-step process would include instructions for building a photocopy machine. Once the builder completes the copy of the architect's studio and the photocopier is built, the builder would then simply run off a copy of the blueprint and put it into the new studio."

"Thank you, Mr. Ryan," says Fitzgerald.

The MIT scholar gives Ryan an approving nod before continuing with his dissertation.

"This is the same transcription-translation concept used by living cells," Corrado says. "They use their blueprint, called genotype, in the same two ways. In the transcription step, DNA is copied mostly unexplained to form mRNA, which is then interpreted to build proteins, thus completing the cloning process.

"Since then, programmers working in the field of artificial intelligence have taken von Neumann's concept and developed it in various directions. Our colleagues at Brandeis University, just outside of Boston, for example, have created a colony of tiny machines that evolve and give birth to other machines without any human guidance. Granted, so far these robotic life forms aren't very advanced, made up of bundles of tubes resembling randomly linked sausages that creep, slither, and even roll across lab bench-tops. But mind that while their sole talent, movement, is quite primitive, so were the first creatures that appeared on our planet hundreds of millions of years ago."

Corrado takes a moment to review his notes, and I take a moment to ponder on these robotic life forms.

Captain, Captain, the spaceship engineer has just reported robotic life forms crawling out of his ass.

I chuckle and get a look from Ryan across the table and another elbow from Karen.

I glance at Fitzgerald, who is looking at Defense Secretary Davis as if saying, *this guy had better make his point quick. We're here to catch a terrorist not receive a lecture from an MIT nerd.*

Corrado finds his place and continues. "While the artificial intelligence department at MIT focuses both on software as well as hardware, the former, unbound by the mechanical limitations of the physical world, makes forward progress at a faster rate than the latter. Software development is not restricted by the relatively slow advances in the robotic fields of microengines and nanolithography. We therefore have been able to borrow the Darwinian evolutionary concept and create a new class of computer programs with the ability to self-evolve, to quickly learn from the mistakes of the previous generation and create a smarter new generation of code. Our AI computer programs would alter, or mutate, primitive subroutines and algorithms and choose the fittest mutants, those showing the potential for learning according to certain parameters, while discarding the others. Our AI engines would become quite adept at solving specific tasks, like avoiding mistakes at assembly lines, or inserting circuits, or painting cars, and a host of other repetitive tasks. However, we always limited the capability of the artificial intelligent systems, working with other institutions around the country, including our colleagues at Stanford, who first came up with the concept of the Turing Society."

Corrado points toward Ryan and his old college professor, both of whom return a slight nod before Ryan stands and clears his throat. "As Dr. Corrado indicated, we all became aware that given enough memory space and microprocessor speed, these systems could evolve into truly thinking machines. Also, given the explosion of the Internet during the late nineties and the beginning of this century, we came to the realization that the potential existed for certain supercomputers—not all, but definitely a concerning growing number—to learn at an exponential rate and perhaps even form an alliance of machines networked by the same links used by their creators."

"Mr. Ryan, Dr. Corrado," says Fitzgerald. "What you are saying is that our technology has advanced to the point that there are some systems out there with the capacity to become intelligent?"

"Correct, sir," replies Ryan. "Just as Dr. Corrado indicated, computer programs can develop the capability to use the Darwinian concept of evolution and natural selection—survival of the fittest, if you will—to evolve, to adapt, to survive, just as life on this planet. Take the example already presented on the colony of self-evolving micromachines. While it took nature millions of years to develop the first organisms capable of moving over land, it took a supercomputer just a few days to go through the millions of mutations, or generations, discarding the weak ones and selecting the stronger ones, and repeating the process over and over, creating a variety of mechanical concepts, some obvious ones and others not so obvious but that still were capable of moving across a lab table. In other words, the computer generated workable designs on its own, and given enough mutations those robotic life forms got faster and stronger. The same computers have already developed mechanical concepts that would take our scientists years to build and test. Some of those computer-aid design concepts have been used in aviation, in the automobile industry, and even aboard the space shuttle, and they would have been impossible to conceptualize without the use of computers. Now, the Turing Society advocates the use of computer for such tasks, as they improve the quality of life and further advance our world. What we are against, is allowing those same systems to mutate on their own, to become smarter than the task for which they were originally designed. That's why we came up with the Turing Inhibitor, a program that acts as Big Brother inside a computer system, monitoring its activities and flagging any hint of increased intelligence. Now, two days ago I encountered an artificial intelligence roaming loose in the Internet. As I have indicated in my report, this AI is assisting the cyberterrorists in their attack against this nation. I managed to capture one of its satellite constructs and upon dissecting its digital DNA found it to contain the kind of encrypted serial numbers used only by the Department of Defense. And you know the rest."

Yep, we sure do.

"Thank you, Mr. Ryan," says Fitzgerald, turning back to Dr. Corrado, who was still standing.

Realizing that was his cue to pick up where he left off, the MIT professor says, "As Mr. Ryan has indicated, we had enough evidence way back when to be concerned and thus helped sell the Turing Inhibitor concept to the White House and then to Congress, which made it a requirement for all computers with the potential for developing intelligence. While this was going on, word of our AI research reached the Pentagon, and they sponsored a large-scale software development project. The military was interested in MIT's digital version of the natural selection process, which by then we had combined with a concept from the University of Michigan called cybersex."

That draws a chuckle from some, including me. I glance at Karen, grinning, but she isn't laughing.

"Which," Corrado adds, "is *not* what some of you are thinking. Cybersex is the concept of allowing parent programs to pool their best features, algorithms, and subroutines into their offspring rather than using mutation alone for improvement. We have also taken concepts from Swiss researchers who have created computer models of the nervous systems of cooperative insects like ants and bees, and found their software models spontaneously working together in the gathering of food, the building of hives or nests, the selection of queens, and so forth. The Pentagon requested that we take all of our AI concepts and develop a large-scale system capable of becoming smart through mutation, cybersex, and also structure it along the lines of a bee colony. We named the project Neurall."

Fitzgerald turns to Malcolm Davis. "General, why don't you share with everyone in the room the primary purpose of this system?"

I'm guessing by that comment that the Viper has been aware of the existence of Neurall.

Leaning forward, resting his forearms on the table, General Davis says, "Neurall runs many aspects of the Pentagon computer network, including firewall security, communications encryption, and e-mail traffic monitor. One of the primary reasons why we implemented it, however, was to handle the real-time management of our missile-early-warning system, response protocols, damage assessments . . . those type of tasks. The development, which was done in conjunction with MIT and then Los Alamos, who took over the project before full deployment a year ago, was fully approved by both the White House and Congress."

"The project included control of the launch codes, right?" asks the vice president.

Davis nods. "Yes, sir. That was part of the product specifications given to MIT along with the research grant. We needed a hacker-proof system intelligent enough to constantly change the launch codes while keeping all of the missile silos, nuclear subs, and the football in sync. That process used to be highly manual and error-prone, which from time to time jeopardized our ability to retaliate effectively should an attack have occurred."

"And why was there a need for this system to have such a high level of intelligence?" asked Fitzgerald.

"If the chain of command got severed during an attack, Neurall would be fully capable of launching a retaliatory strike. This was a feature requested by both the White House and the Pentagon."

There is a moment of silence in the room, and I see it as my opportunity to ask an obvious question. "Did Neurall have one of those inhibitors installed to make sure it never got too smart and perhaps decide to turn against us?"

"Of course," says General Davis. "The Turing Society sanctioned the project.

Neurall wasn't a loose cannon, ladies and gentlemen. Neurall was carefully designed and put into operation with all the appropriate precautions and monitors, *exactly* as described in its product specification, which was audited by a number of independent contractors and agencies, including the Turing Society."

I look at Ryan and his old professor. Both of them nod.

"All right," I continue. "Then how do we explain the version of Neurall that Mr. Ryan stumbled upon?"

Dr. Corrado looks at the guys from Los Alamos, who look at Secretary Davis, who is looking at the vice president, who is looking at the MIT guys. I follow the eyeball chain twice in search of my answer.

Davis says, "There were two versions of Neurall."

"Why?" I'm on a roll now.

"Backup," Dr. Corrado replies before Davis gets a chance to do so. "Every software development effort has to be regularly backed up in case of a corrupted disk, power failure, or a host of other computer-related problems. We couldn't afford to lose years of development to a glitch. We *had* to make at least one backup."

"Where was it kept?"

"At our lab in the Artificial Intelligence department," says the MIT professor, "and in total isolation in a vault. It was not hooked up to any networks. We essentially kept it in its box, just like Mr. Ryan's AI over there."

"How could it be stolen?"

"Very cleverly, I'm afraid. It was replaced by an identical box of FLASH cards, only this one was empty."

"And?" I ask, realizing that's what happens when nerds decide to play the security game. "What did you do when you realized that the backup was missing?"

"We immediate reported this security violation to General Davis."

"Who else did you report it to?" I ask.

The look-around game is about to start again, but General Davis squashes it by replying, "No one else. The Pentagon felt that it was in the interest of national security if this incident went unreported while the DIA investigated it."

Don't you just love these military types, always thinking that they are so special?

Well today I'm in no mood for their bullshit, so I say, "Now, *that's* a bunch of crap."

That gets me another elbow from Karen plus a burning stare from the defense secretary. Ryan closes his eyes, and so do Meek and Jacobs. I know I'm out of line but screw it. Getting some passion into a discussion always has a way of short-circuiting the process of getting to the bottom of the problem and then onto possible solutions.

"This was a *military* operation, Mr. Grant, and it remained under *military* jurisdiction."

"Very well, then," I say. "Why don't you tell us how the DIA went about recovering this stolen military equipment?"

Davis just glares back for a long while before replying, "It was never found, but we did figure out who stole it."

Well, that's more than I thought the DIA was going to be able to accomplish. "Who is that?"

Secretary Davis looks at Corrado, who says, "Her name was Kishna Zablah, one of our Ph.D. candidates. She vanished the same day that the Neurall backup disappeared from the vault."

"I take it that she was involved in the development of Neurall?" I ask, knowing what the answer is going to be.

Corrado nods. "Very much so. She spent two years at MIT working on several modules, including programming of the top-level neurology."

"So it's safe to assume that she could have removed the inhibitors from her copy of Neurall."

"That's a possibility, yes," says Corrado.

I look at Secretary Davis, who is staring at the table.

"So," I say, to recap in my own words. "This Kishna steals a copy of the most advanced AI we have ever created. She has the knowledge not only to remove the Turing Inhibitor, but also to nurture the AI, to set up the right environment for it to learn, to develop. Now she is using it against us to level our cities, and the DIA, choosing to go solo in this investigation rather than enlist the help of its civilian sister agencies, has not been able to find her or the AI construct. Does that pretty much wrap it up?"

"All right, Tom," says Director Meek, who obviously has to say something since he is our boss and I am rapidly becoming a royal pain in the ass. "I think you have made your point."

But I'm not even warmed up yet.

However, before I can fire my next career-limiting question, Davis offers even more revealing information about the case.

"The development of Neurall was essentially run by four former MIT professors, plus a handful of handpicked graduate students and Ph.D. candidates, like Kishna Zablah. Three of those professors were Dr. Herbert Littman, Dr. Gary Hutton, and Dr. Jason Lamar."

I feel as if someone had just fired a bullet smack in the middle of my chest.

"What . . . what does that mean?" Karen asks, but she is looking at me.

I quickly recover from the initial shock and say, "I think it means that in addition to gaining access to STG, SWOASIS, and Boeing, Ares Kulzak was also after something that had to do with Neurall."

"What could that be?" asks Fitzgerald, looking at both Dr. Corrado and Secretary Davis.

Both shake their heads, but Corrado offers, "Maybe they wanted additional insight into the development of the military Neurall. If I have my dates correct, Kishna left about a full three months before we released Neurall to Los Alamos. My guess is that she was trying to catch up on any improvements done to it so she can in turn make them to her stolen version."

Makes sense, but my spook sense is screaming at me that there is something else there. I, however, can't think of it just yet, so I decide to accept that explanation for now. Instead I ask what I think is the next logical question. "Dr. Corrado, you mentioned there were four professors who developed Neurall. Who is the fourth?"

"That would be David Foulch."

"Then that would seem like the next best logical place to go, unless Kulzak already got to him." I check my watch. "After all, it's been over twenty-four hours since Lamar was reported missing."

Corrado looks at General Davis, who frowns while saying, "Mr. Foulch left MIT under less that desirable circumstances. He was . . . how should I put it? He was having sex with a number of undergraduate female students in exchange for passing grades. There was quite a scandal on campus that year. He didn't leave a forwarding address. I started a nationwide search last night with the assistance of the FBI."

We look at Meek, who returns the stare while nodding once.

Okay, so Foulch is missing in action and for all I know he might even have changed his name in order to escape the embarrassment of getting caught screwing college girls. My only consolation is that if we have a hard time finding him, so would Kulzak—or so I'd like to believe.

Karen is ready to move on. "How long ago was this backup of Neurall reported missing, Mr. Secretary?"

Davis regards my boss before replying, "Six years ago."

"Mr. Ryan, Dr. Corrado," Karen says. "Given what you know in the field of AI, could you project how much intelligence capability could be developed by Neurall in this time frame?"

"A very interesting question," the MIT professor says. "A question that myself and my colleagues have been asking ourselves for some time. A key factor in developing Neurall is knowing how to power it up, how to keep the resident hardware running in optimal condition. Take the small construct that Mr. Ryan has and imagine a system a hundred times larger and with the capacity to be enhanced as FLASH memory and microprocessor speed increased in the past several years. Given that, and also assuming that it landed in the hands of someone competent, like Kishna certainly was, Neurall would have developed into an entity that's tens of years ahead of us."

"And," adds Ryan, "the only reason why it's only *tens* of years and not more is because the software will still be bounded by the physical limitations of microprocessor speed and memory size."

"Correct," says Corrado. "We're estimating that at the stage that we lost the backup of Neurall a good capable team might be able to make it learn at a rate anywhere from three to five times that of humans. Given that it's been missing for six years translates into eighteen to thirty years ahead of us."

"Which means that it's still not smart enough that it can't be defeated," comments Ryan. "But it does learn very fast from its mistakes, as I have personally witnessed."

There is a moment of silence in the room.

"All right," says Fitzgerald. "Now that we have established where this AI comes from, I would like to move to the topic of damage assessment."

Damage assessment?

I think I'm having another out-of-body experience.

I close my eyes and pray that the Good Lord provides me with the control to keep my mouth shut and my temper in neutral. Kulzak is out there running loose and these clowns want to tie everybody down with a damage control exercise. Doesn't anyone realize that unless we get back in the saddle again what we have seen so far will just be the appetizer?

The Viper goes on to say, "The reports from San Antonio, Melbourne, New Orleans, and L.A. have already exceeded a combined one hundred and fifty *billion* in damage. All four areas have been declared federal emergency zones."

Now, please don't get my last comment wrong. I do care about the victims. I mean, I really, *really* do. But at the same time, I can't afford to stop and spend too much time feeling sorry for them while the bastard who caused the pain is still at large.

Failing to read my mind, Fitzgerald continues. "I received a report from the FAA on the way down here indicating that in addition to the 777 crashing into downtown L.A. last night, there were two others. One was lost somewhere over the Pacific on its way to Singapore and a second one in the Swiss Alps. The rest of the fleet is grounded until technicians can scrub the software system. Still, it looks like about eight hundred dead or missing."

I close my eyes, trying to imagine what those people went through, but a single word flashes in my mind.

Snacks.

As horrendous as those disasters were, they are just Kulzak's snacks. I'm certain that we haven't seen the main course yet, but we will if the politicians don't let us get back to work. If Neurall was programmed to control our nukes and Kulzak has a copy and somehow manages to hook it up to the Pentagon's Neurall, it could all be over in fifteen minutes.

Fitzgerald spends ten of those fifteen minutes going over the damage, including the three dead cops and four injured from last night's attempt to catch the assassin in the woods next to the mansion. One of them was Paul Stone. Last time we checked, the kid had survived the operation with both legs intact, but there was no mention of his genitals—although based on what I saw last night only a miracle would have saved them.

Poor kid.

More and more I'm believing that it was Kulzak himself who did the deed. It takes a special talent to kill eleven Secret Service agents and then successfully get away without a trace.

And I mean without a fucking trace.

While the Brady Bunch arrived this morning, Karen and I spent the better part of the morning alongside a number of CCTF and FBI agents, plus a small contingent of really pissed-off local cops, looking for clues around the area.

We found none. *Nada.* Zip.

Ditto on the warehouse and also at the house of Jason Lamar, the poor dead bastard I found in one of the offices.

So, no clues. No trails. Nothing.

I lean back while Fitzgerald and his aides are discussing press releases on the dead and injured. Pinching the bridge of my nose while closing my eyes I once again begin to wonder if we're ever going to catch the bastard.

You know how people often tell you to get back in the saddle? Well, what if you've gotten back on the horse a dozen times already, just to get thrown back off, and half the time the horse stomps on your head and kicks you in the balls? Do you still try to get back on? How much is enough?

In my case, as well as Karen's and Ryan's, we don't really have a choice, and we all know it.

Kulzak knows who we are. If he could get to Cramer, who had a security detail following him everywhere, even to the john, then we are dead as well.

Unless we get to him first.

The Viper concludes his assessment speech and finally gets to what we all need to be thinking about: the future.

He says, "Well, people, everything up to this point is history. The question on the table is: What do we do to move forward?"

Funny thing. The higher beings at one end of the table stare at one another for a while and suddenly find themselves looking down the food chain at Karen, Ryan, and I, who happen to know something they don't, something Ryan had figured out through the fragmented digital DNA that MPS-Ali had pulled out of the dying AI.

Within the hour the three of us, along with Victoria, Vice President Fitzgerald, FBI Director Russell Meek, and DCI Martin Jacobs are aboard Air Force One on our way to the nation's capital.

SIXTY-THREE

> > > > >

JET PLANE

> ARES KULZAK LOOKED OUT THE SIDE WINDOW OF
the learjet he and Kishna had chartered out of Austin. His contacts in the Cartel had
explained to him that the second-safest way to travel in America was by chartered
flight, which, unlike commercial jetliners, didn't require him to go through an airport terminal where contingents from the FBI, the CCTF, and the APD could be on
the lookout for him.

Kishna sleeping next to him, Ares leaned back in his leather seat and tried to relax
while his mind explored his options. The CCTF was getting too close. He no longer
operated with the same freedom as before, and that was expected. What wasn't
expected was the level of intensity with which the Americans have fought back in the
cyber world, not only blocking his strikes despite having an AI like Neurall on his
side, but also turning that against him, particularly last night.

He gazed out the window once more and stared at the snowcapped mountains.
The pilot had already announced that they would be touching down at San Jose
International in another forty minutes, and from there they would go straight to a
rental car already reserved for them under a fake name by members of the local Chinese Mafia, his third sponsor on this mission across America.

Ares closed his eyes at the compromises he had to make. Under normal circumstances, he would have requested that the pilots drop them off in a city along the
way, like Phoenix, Denver, or Las Vegas, where they would steal a vehicle to get to

the nearest town with an airport and charter another plane to take them the rest of the way, thus making it harder for the CCTF to follow their footsteps. But time was definitely running out for him, meaning he was being forced to take shortcuts.

If what Kishna said about Neurall was true, then it was once again a race against time before the CCTF located the AI in the mountains of Colombia. He had to obtain the fourth and final backdoor password and connect the two Neuralls for long enough to achieve his final objective, the final phase of a plan that would not only bring America to its knees, immensely benefiting his sponsors, but also achieve the level of revenge that would secure him a place alongside the great fighters against American Imperialism.

SIXTY-FOUR

> > > > >

FLASH

> ON THE THIRD FLOOR OF THE J. EDGAR HOOVER building in Washington, D.C., Ryan inserted another FLASH card into the new back-plane of MPS-Ali, gently pressing both ends of the credit-card-size unit to make sure it sat snugly in its edge connector.

"Like, how long will it take you to upgrade this AI? And what's the total memory capacity that you would like to get to?" asked Charlie Chang, the computer lab manager, whom Russell Meek had assigned to work with Ryan as soon as they arrived a few hours ago.

Ryan didn't feel like explaining every step of the process to Chang, though he had to admit that the Asian-American had been quite helpful in pulling together the required hardware in record time.

They had landed at Dulles International Airport just before nine in the evening and arrived here shortly after ten. Part of the deal Ryan had made with the government was getting Victoria the ultimate protection possible. Vice President Vance Fitzgerald then invited her to spend the night in the Lincoln Room of the White House, the safest place on the planet. Now Ryan could focus on the task he had signed up to do—a task that meant putting everything on the line to get just one shot at killing this illegal version of Neurall, which according to the bits and pieces of data MPS-Ali had extracted on their last run appeared to be operating somewhere in the eastern region of Colombia, based on the ISP signature he had decoded.

"It'll probably take another hour to get the construct upgraded," Ryan finally said, going through the remaining steps in his mind. "I'd like to get MPS-Ali an additional five gigabytes of memory."

"How much did you start with?"

"Three gig." Ryan had requested permission from both the vice president as well as the Turing Society to not only continue running MPS-Ali without an inhibitor, but also to enhance its potential for this upcoming run, and that meant adding more memory since the AI had already consumed all three gigabytes soon after Ryan removed the inhibitor on his last run through the cyberspace.

Memory limitations, in a way, limited MPS-Ali's ability for further learning even without an inhibitor. Albert Einstein would have stopped learning if he had reached the limits of his ability to store information, and that's exactly what had happened to MPS-Ali, a limitation Ryan was about to relax in order to have the smartest possible AI on his side.

Sipping a diet soda, Chang nodded while pushing his thick glasses up the bridge of his nose with a forefinger. "That's a lot of memory."

"It takes memory to learn," Ryan said, plugging in another FLASH card. MPS-Ali was definitely growing in the physical world, but Ryan still planned to keep the AI construct mobile so he could interface it to the backtop computer that had saved their life in Austin. The new box for the AI resembled a three-inch binder but with the sides protected. Once closed, the box would fit inside a harness that Ryan could strap to his chest during a run, hooking it up to the backtop computer and the battery charge through a bundle of cables running across his right torso. But the extra couple of pounds of memory would be worth it, expanding the construct's ability to learn. The compromise had come in battery life, dropping to less than thirty minutes because of the AI's increased electrical power demands. That, however, should not be a problem as Ryan wasn't planning on leaving this computer lab during the entire run, thus remaining plugged into the AC outlet of an uninterruptible power supply. A UPS was definitely needed given the critical nature of the run. He would only get one shot at this and didn't want a power glitch to screw it all up.

"What are you planning to teach it?" Chang asked.

Ryan had not discussed his plan of attack with anyone except the vice president, Russell Meek, Martin Jacobs, Karen Frost, and Tom Grant, each of whom was responsible for a piece of the plan. Everyone else didn't have a need to know, even the resourceful Charlie Chang.

"For one thing those new viruses," Ryan replied, pointing to a stack of floppy disks containing the FBI's most recently acquired computer viruses, half of them confiscated from hackers before they were released on the Internet. "Especially the Brazilian one you were telling me about."

"That's a mean one," Chang said. "Wiped out a couple of networks down in Rio. You sure you want to mess with it? I mean, if it gets loose around here . . ."

Ryan smiled. "The real question is, will it be mean enough for the job that I intend to use it for."

"Well, the fact that I renamed it *Medusa* should tell you just how deadly it is," said Chang.

"Medusa?"

"Everything that even looks its way turns to stone. And I mean stone, man. There ain't nothing that can be done for the attacked software except reformat."

"That's mean," Ryan said while inserting another FLASH card. "Sounds like what I'm looking for."

"So what exactly is it that you intend to do after jacking in?"

"Sorry, pal. I'm not allowed to tell you."

Chang frowned and dropped his gaze to the floor. Ryan had already had to tell Chang to step outside during the long meeting he'd had with a couple of scientists from the Pentagon an hour ago on the methodology for interfacing with the military Neurall operating from the core of the Pentagon's network.

Feeling sorry for the FBI computer analyst, who'd been asked just to follow orders without asking questions, Ryan said, "But I'll tell you this. Hang around and keep an eye on that monitor after I start my run. You're about to witness a pretty intense cyber battle, which reminds me, what do you have for me in the area of personal computer protection?"

Chang smiled. "We're the FBI, man. We've got nothing but the best."

SIXTY-FIVE

> > > > >

HEART TO HEART

> I THINK THIS EVENING WE'RE MAKING UP FOR THE
wasted day. Karen and I march out of the elevator and down a hallway in the basement of the CIA headquarters in Langley, Virginia, to do something the CIA hasn't
done ever since Clinton got struck with that case of morality I told you about and
halted some of our unsavory but highly effective practices.

Since my transfer paperwork officially moving me from the CIA to the CCTF
hasn't gone through yet, my badge still works at all of the electronic security check-
points and doors, and therefore we don't need an escort to move about the building.

This is a huge place, easy to get lost in. The compound houses over half of the
CIA's twenty-two thousand employees in two main buildings on a property of over
two hundred acres along the Potomac River in Fairfax County. We're in what's considered the new CIA building, though it was finished way back in 1988. It has over
one million square feet.

Like I said. Huge. In all of my years at the CIA, I may have seen less than 20 percent of the place, and I seldom made it to the old CIA building next door.

After landing at Dulles, Ryan headed for Fedland and Karen and I came to
Spookville, where the flag up front is at half mast because of all of the recent deaths,
which I'm sure includes Cramer's—though I've yet to find anyone at my level who
liked the old bastard.

Anyway, we arrived about an hour ago. We got Karen all signed in, went through a briefing on the suspect, who had been delivered here within the hour following the president's approval of my plan this afternoon, and then we went on to carry out our portion of the plan, which, if it goes as we hope it will, could solve this within the next twenty-four hours. And that's a good thing because yours truly isn't likely to last much longer than that, and neither is Karen, whose bags under her bloodshot eyes are challenging mine.

"Are you sure you're okay with me playing the straight man?" she asks.

I remember her story in Colombia and say, "If what you said took place in Colombia was for real I think you're going to do just dandy leading this thing."

"That was a long time ago. I'm more civilized now," she says, smiling.

"Yeah. I've noticed."

"Are you sure this tactic will work?" she asks.

I nod. "Paxton is an American. He was in the Special Forces before he went bad. I've seen his kind before. They're all first red-blooded patriots, but after some time in the field—particularly in a place like El Salvador—they become disenchanted with America, and frankly I don't blame them because I too became tired of my superior's head-up-his-ass decisions. They eventually leave the military to use their skills and contacts for profit, doing anything and going anywhere they can to make money."

"Mercenaries," she says.

"Exactly. And unlike fanatics like Kulzak, mercenaries don't have a strong sense of loyalty to anyone in particular and can be turned with the proper incentives."

We continue down the long corridor, plain white walls overlooking a sickly looking pastel-colored vinyl floor, all beneath evenly spaced fluorescent lights.

Not a lot of activity at this late hour in the basement of the most powerful intelligence agency in the world, but that's because this area is mostly reserved for storage, mechanical, and air-conditioning rooms, mainframe computers driving the labs upstairs, and a handful of *very special* rooms. The bulk of the activity running operations around the globe takes place upstairs, where large teams of officers work in shifts twenty-four/seven to try to keep America safe from loonies.

We're heading toward one of those special rooms, the clicking of our shoes echoing hollowly down the corridor. Karen, who will act as the lead interrogator, carries the subject's folder under her left arm.

One more turn at the end of the next hallway and we spot the guards standing by the door, armed, hands free by their sides. In their thirties, they look in our direction while reaching for their holstered weapons. Even deep within the protective fences and walls of the CIA, these guys are paranoid.

Good.

They should be when dealing with anything remotely associated with Ares Kulzak.

"Gentlemen," I say, extending my badge at them. "CIA Officer Tom Grant and FBI Special Agent Karen Frost to see Mr. Ken Paxton."

This should be of no surprise to them since DCI Martin Jacobs himself arranged everything on short notice, including this security detail, but being the professionals that they seem to be, the guards check our badges very carefully, making a face when comparing my new bald look with the picture on my ID.

He finally decides that we're the same guy and lets us in.

The place brings back memories from the old days, when we would bring in suspects and run them through the wringer to obtain information, or to turn them, or simply to scare the crap out of them—whatever got us what we needed from them at the time. My NYPD background had come in handy during those initial years with the Agency, before I was officially trained and shipped off to exotic destinations around the world. Of course, these rooms were then officially closed during the Clinton years.

A man in his mid-fifties with bleach-blond hair down to his shoulders and a face that belongs to a retired prize fighter sits behind a metal table in the middle of the room. He stares back at us with a pair of the coldest eyes I've seen in some time. He's well built, just as I remember during the brief moment I saw him in that alley in New Orleans after Paul Stone shot him in the legs. He looks like he recovered from his gunshot wounds just fine. I can't see his legs but I do spot the bandage on his right wrist.

Two CIA guards are with him, standing with their weapons ready a few feet behind him in the back of the room. To my left there's a large one-way mirror, behind which Jacobs, Meek, and a camera crew are settling down to watch the show.

Live, from Langley, it's interrogation night!

"I want my lawyers," Ken Paxton says, his hands in tight fists, his wrists anchored to a pair of handcuffs bolted to the heavy-duty table, which is in turn bolted to the floor. Mr. Paxton isn't going anywhere tonight, at least not until we get what we need from him.

"Dead men don't need lawyers," says Karen, dropping the folder in front of him but out of his short reach.

He blinks once, confusion momentarily glazing those light-blue eyes.

"They killed you, remember?" she says, sitting down while I stand by my assigned place on the side of the square table, between them, arms crossed, looking big and mean.

"Killed me?"

She nods while opening the folder and extracting a sheet of paper. "Just got the report an hour ago from the D.C. Police Department. Looks like someone dressed as a cop managed to get inside the station, where they were holding you overnight pending your hearing in the morning, doused you with gasoline, and set you on fire inside your cell." She ran a finger across the middle of the report as if pretending to read it. "You burnt to a crisp before the guard on duty could get the door open and put out the fire. According to the medical examiner who did the autopsy at Georgetown University Hospital, you died en route."

I shake my head. "A pisser of a way to go, pal. It must have really sucked."

Now we play the staring game as he shifts his gaze back and forth between us.

"This . . . this is an outrage!" he shouts. "Where am I? I demand to see my lawyers! I know my rights!"

"Guess you haven't been listening to the lady, lamebrain. Dead men don't have rights."

"Damn it! I'm not dead! You can't do this to me!"

"Scream all you want, shit-for-brains," I reply, slapping him hard in the back of the head.

"Hey! That's police brutality! I will sue you for—"

I whack him again, shoving his head forward.

"Dammit! You can't do this to—"

Whack!

He finally shuts up. It usually takes three for his kind to start to get the message that the rules of the game have been changed.

"If I were you," I say, grabbing a mane of hair and forcing him to look straight into my eyes. "I would pay *really* close attention to what that lady has to say. It's your *only* ticket out of here." Then I let him go.

"Mr. Paxton," Karen says, playing her role. "It looks like despite our best efforts to protect you, Ares Kulzak got to you first."

"But don't feel lonely, asshole," I add. "You're not the only one that the bastard has barbecued in the past day. He also cooked our boss, Randall Cramer. Left him well-done."

Karen fishes out a set of black-and-white photos with today's date and a time stamp of just thirty minutes ago. It's indeed amazing what can be done with computers these days. She sets three of them in front of him.

"These were taken by a hidden camera in your cell. I mean, that is you, isn't it?" She taps an unpainted fingernail against one of them. The sequence of pictures shows Paxton standing in the middle of the cell, then backing away to the rear, then someone wearing a police uniform—with his face appropriately shaded—emptying the contents of a bucket on him.

"This next set can be a bit upsetting," she adds, "especially for you. This must have really hurt, Mr. Paxton."

Karen places three pictures of a burning figure inside a cell on the table. One standing, one on its knees, and one on the ground.

She follows with pictures of a police officer with a fire extinguisher and photos of paramedics hauling him away. The final picture is a face shot of a grossly-burnt Paxton with the hair and most of the ears missing, bloated lips and singed brows and eyelashes, but it is definitely him—or at least a computer version of what he would have looked like.

"We're really, *really* sorry we failed to protect you against your former employer, Mr. Paxton. It's obvious to us that he simply didn't trust you alive after you fell in our custody."

Damn. I feel like I could just reach over and kiss her for such an award-winning performance.

Paxton stares at the last photograph, his fists so tight that I see the knuckles turning white. "They . . . they would never . . ." he stopped.

I grin at Karen, who says, "Who are *they*, Mr. Paxton? *Who* would never have done *what*?"

"Never mind," he says. "This useless trick will not work. You don't get another word from me until I see my lawyers."

"We will be notifying your next of kin of your death in the morning," Karen says matter-of-factly.

Paxton stares at her before mumbling, "You bitch."

I slap him on the back of the head again. "Watch your tone with the lady, dipshit."

Karen slips the photos back into the folder and pulls out a report we got from a combination of IRS records and the FBI. "Kenneth Thomas Paxton, Junior, age fifty-eight, only child born to Kenneth and Virginia Paxton of New Orleans, Louisiana. Parents passed away in the seventies. You joined the army after high school in 1973. Five years later, you applied and got accepted to the U.S. Special Forces and operated as a military advisor in El Salvador during most of the eighties before coming home and retiring from the military. I show you leaving the United States in 1991 via Mexico and not returning until 1997, settling back into your hometown of New Orleans. I show a marriage record for a Kenneth Thomas Paxton, Junior to one Melissa Daniels in 1976, while stationed with the army in Fort Hood, Texas. You have two children, both girls, Jane and Gale, in their twenties but living under different last names even though neither one is married."

Ken Paxton is speechless, his breathing a bit erratic as he closes his eyes.

"The record also shows a divorce," Karen adds in a monotone voice, "between

Kenneth Paxton and Melissa Daniels Paxton in 1978, the year you joined the Special Forces."

"How do you know so much about me?"

"It's part of the FBI's job to know everything about everyone," Karen replies, before asking, "so which family member would you like us to notify of your death in the public obituary, Mr. Paxton? We were thinking both daughters."

He shakes his head. "You can't do this! They will kill them!" He tries to get up, kicking back his chair, but the handcuffs hold him in a crouching position.

I lean down and grab his mane of hair behind the neck with one hand and the chair with the other, yanking the head back and forcing his ass back on the chair.

When I let go, Paxton drops his face into his palms, mumbling, "You . . . you don't understand."

"Try me," Karen says. "Why would Kulzak kill your family?"

"Kulzak? Jesus, you don't get it, do you?"

"No, Mr. Paxton. Why don't you explain it to us?"

"I work for the Colombian Cartel, lady. I'm helping Ares Kulzak because my superiors asked me to—the same superiors who arranged for my lawyers."

The Cartel?

Ryan's claim that Neurall is operating from somewhere in Colombia starts to make some sense.

Karen doesn't skip a beat. She says, "You think the Cartel, not Ares Kulzak, will kill your family if you betray them?"

"It's not Kulzak I'm afraid of," he adds. "Though you don't want to get on his shit list because sooner or later he will come after you. I know the man all too well, but the immediate worry is the Cartel."

"So as long as you keep your mouth shut, you will be left alone by both the Cartel and Kulzak."

"Look, lady. It's just like in the Mafia. Loyalty and services are rewarded with financial compensation. But along with that comes the knowledge that double-crossing my people would result not just in my death, but in the death of my daughters—and they won't die from a bullet in the head. They have special ways of dealing with traitors and their families. If I uphold my end of the deal with them and just go to jail if found guilty, then I continue to be in their good graces. But if I cross them . . ."

"I guess you've got a hell of a problem, then, buddy," I say, "because we're releasing this story to the press tomorrow."

Momentarily confused, Paxton looks at Karen, who nods. "But . . . if you do that they will know it is a trick and my daughters . . ."

"People die," I reply.

"But . . . but they're *innocent!*"

"So were the people that Kulzak killed in San Antonio, Melbourne, and New Orleans, Mr. Paxton," says Karen.

"Or the hundreds who died last night when those jetliners fell from the sky," I add.

He sits back. "What do you want?"

"What everybody wants, Mr. Paxton. Information."

"If I help you," he begins, "what's in it for me and my daughters?"

Karen and I exchange a rehearsed glance, and I give her a slow nod per the unwritten script we worked out on the way up here.

"You will hang yourself in your cell," Karen says. "Your body will be examined by a coroner in the presence of your lawyers. All you have to do is play your part. We'll take care of the rest, including making you look dead."

"How?"

"That's our little secret," I reply, winking.

"You will remain in custody," explains Karen, "until we apprehend Kulzak, at which point we will give you the option to participate in our witness protection program or go out on your own with a yet-to-be-negotiated amount of cash. We will also offer to bring in your daughters and provide them with new identities."

"Take it or leave it, Blondie," I add. "This is your only chance to save yourself and your girls while doing your country a service."

Ken Paxton closes his eyes and slowly nods. "Ask your questions, though I'm sure you're well aware that my knowledge of his operations is limited."

"Let us decide what's important, Mr. Paxton."

"Where would you like to start?"

Karen is about to reply but I cut in. "Why don't you tell us a bit about yourself, maybe starting with the first time you met Ares Kulzak."

Looking into the distance, Paxton says, "That would be El Salvador, during my days as a military advisor with the U.S. Special Forces."

I exchange a brief glance with Karen before she says, "Go on, Mr. Paxton."

He does, telling us how he had personally profited from that long civil war through shadowy deals with the Marxist guerrillas, which eventually led him to Kulzak. Just a few minutes into his confession, and I'm ready to snap his neck. The bastard wasn't only there, among the hooded guerrillas surrounding Jerry Martinez, but he was the one who castrated him!

Jesus Christ, I'm feeling dizzy and have to step back while Paxton continues.

I like huevos rancheros.

Kulzak's words echo in my mind, over and over, along with the agonizing screams from my old CIA buddy and the monotone confession of this mercenary.

Mustering savage control, I shove my emotions aside and step back to the table while listening to an old familiar tale, pretending it was the first time I've heard it. Then Paxton shifts gears and briefly covers his clean break from the military before heading to Colombia to join the FARC, where he remained for many years, until his contributions earned him the confidence of the Cartel and a post in New Orleans, where he has remained since.

"I got word from my people that I needed to support the efforts of Ares Kulzak during a mission in the New Orleans area," he adds, covering the Hutton incident and a meeting with Kulzak and his computer accomplice, Kishna Zablah, later that evening. Together, they manufactured the explosives we found him deploying that night, as well as the two Kulzak took with him to his next mission, plus the claymore that maimed Stone and the weapons and ammo he used to murder the agents.

I realize then that one of those bombs was the one he used last night to create the bonfire at Lake Travis, meaning he still has at least another one in his possession.

As the mercenary goes over detail after detail, my mind shifts to Ares Kulzak, wondering where in the hell he went after Austin.

SIXTY-SIX

> > > > >

VPS

> "WHAT DOES THAT MEAN, ARI?" KISHNA ASKED, SIT-
ting up in the queen-size bed while watching the television set in their San Jose, California hotel in the heart of the Silicon Valley. She had her computer on her lap and
the VR interface between them.

He tried to understand what the reporter had just meant by the comment that the
CCTF was undergoing an internal reorganization following the murder of its director, Randall Cramer, the night before. More announcements were expected in the
next forty-eight hours.

"I think it means just what it means, that they are reorganizing. The termination
of Cramer caused a larger ripple effect than I had anticipated," he replied.

Then the news broadcast switched to the situation on the Boeing 777 front, starting with a statement from a public relations spokesman from the Federal Aviation
Administration that the fleet remained grounded while technicians removed the
infected programs. All other planes would continue to fly.

The screen changed to an aerial view of Los Angeles, where the jetliners had triggered the destruction of three large office buildings in a manner all too familiar to
the 2001 strike.

Dressed only in his underpants, Ares exhaled deeply through his mouth. He had
accomplished something totally unprecedented: the virtual hijacking of a jetliner,
plus turning it into a guided missile just as those Arabs had done way back when.

But smartly, without the need for suicides.

But Michael Ryan had managed to figure out his target and sent an alert, preventing most of the intended damage.

Michael Patrick Ryan.

Ares stared at the sheet of paper Kishna had given him earlier, after running his name through a number of on-line detective services.

He is barely twenty-four years old, Ares thought, glaring at the information. *Yet, he has caused so much trouble for us.*

Ryan had a wife, Victoria, the pregnant woman Kishna had spotted with him on the videos.

Mike and Victoria Ryan.

He would deal with them just as his Russian associates had dealt with Cramer, just as he planned to deal with Karen Frost and Tom Grant, the mystery man whom both Paxton and he had recognized but were unable to place.

But there was a far more pressing issue at the moment, and it had to do with Neurall. Kishna feared that sometime during last night's mission, one of Neurall's constructs might have gotten attacked by a virus and its core digitally dissected. If that was the case, then there was a strong possibility that the physical location of the primary ISP in Bogotá, Colombia's capital, used by Neurall may have been identified.

Although the *gusanos* may have narrowed Neurall's physical location from anywhere in the world to the seven hundred square miles serviced by the ISP, Ares felt that the AI would remain safe long enough for Kulzak to track down the last password required to interface Neurall to its military twin in the Pentagon.

Then it will not matter.

"Has Neurall compiled the addresses?"

"Almost there," Kishna replied, tapping the keyboard for another minute before acquiring the home address of David Hill, formerly known as David Foulch, the fourth MIT scientist responsible for the creation of the original Neurall. "It had not been that difficult for Neurall to find him, given the proper search parameters, plus a brief hacking trip into the legal firm that he used to change his name after leaving MIT."

David Hill, who had managed to shed his scandalous past, was currently living in the residential hills of nearby Palo Alto, California with his new wife and newborn son. He was a vice president at a local software firm.

SIXTY-SEVEN

> > > > >

FOREVER

> SO CLOSE TO HOME AND YET SO FAR AWAY.

That's the story of my life, and as we drive from Langley on the George Washington Memorial Parkway, which follows the Potomac straight into the nation's capital, I take a moment to glance across the river at Bethesda, Maryland, where my new house is.

I silently curse those damned reporters in New Orleans for making it impossible for me, or Karen, who happens to live about a mile away from me, to go home.

Karen sits in the passenger seat of the rental car Russell Meek got us at Dulles so we can get around since we also can't use our own vehicles, lest we have a strong desire to end up barbecued like Randy Cramer. We could have gotten a security detail courtesy of the FBI, but we declined it and instead decided to become each other's bodyguards. The last thing either one of us wants is more blood on our hands. We're both professionals and are armed and dangerous. If Kulzak wants to come after us, let him. We will not go down without a fight.

Needless to say, both Meek and Jacobs urged us to remain at either the FBI or the CIA headquarters for our own protection, a precaution we also decided to decline for the same reasons. I refuse to live my life in fear and so does Karen.

Constantly checking my rearview mirror, I follow the speed limit as we head into D.C.

"Anyone following us?" she asks.

"Not that I can see."

"Feeling better?"

"Yeah," I reply. "After all these years I finally find the bastard who physically cut off my friend's balls and I can't touch him." In addition to cooperating with us on Kulzak, Ken Paxton gave us a world of information on FARC and Cartel activities in Colombia and the United States—information that would soon make its way through the FBI and the military to guide domestic and offshore strikes respectively.

Life is indeed full of little surprises. I'm glad I didn't find this out about Paxton until tonight, otherwise I can't promise that my forefinger wouldn't have slipped when I had my piece pointed at the bastard's head in that dark alley. Of course, my killing him back then, as good as it may have felt at the moment, would have prevented us from turning him and gathering so much intel. Now our president has at least one clear target to go after in retaliation for San Antonio, Melbourne, New Orleans, and now Los Angeles.

"So," Karen says, yawning, stretching her arms. "Where are we going?"

I shrug. Ryan called from the FBI about thirty minutes ago, right after we finished up with Paxton, and reported that he's ready to do his thing but has to hold his cyber attack until the navy vessels get into position off the coast of Colombia, which is going to take another six hours, meaning Karen and I get to hang loose in the area at least until then.

The problem, however, is that it's past two in the morning and all of the bars I know are closed, which leaves just a few roadside motels on the outskirts of town. Without an advanced reservation you can kiss off the chances of finding a decent hotel within a five-mile radius of the White House.

So I propose heading south, toward IH-95, which borders the southern end of Alexandria in the hopes of finding a motel that can takes us for the night.

"I always suspected you were a classy guy, Tom," she says, cracking the window while she lights up a cigarette from a pack she'd just bought at a convenience store. The wind sweeps back her shoulder-length hair, fluttering against the headrest. "I guess all I'm worth to you is a fifty-buck motel room."

"I meant to *sleep*." I'm so tired I doubt Mr. Johnson is going to wake up and smell the coffee.

She draws on the cigarette and exhales toward the slit between the top of the glass and the window frame.

"By the way," I say. "You did really good back there."

She gives me a strange sideway glance, and I realize this is the first true compliment I've given her since we met. "Thanks," she says.

"Do you think it's going to work?"

"I'm not sure about anything anymore, Tom. But I'll tell you this, of all the crazy ideas I've heard in my two decades with the Bureau this one tops them all. I doubt even Ares Kulzak will see it coming."

"On the other hand, it may not make any difference at all since we're still operating in the dark here."

"What do you mean?"

"We still don't know why Kulzak is killing the creators of Neurall. There is an agenda behind the killings and behind the disasters we have seen. Like I said before, I believe now more than ever that they were just a smoke screen. And we still have no clue where this David Foulch went. For all I know he is already six feet under somewhere in this great country of ours."

While thinking about my own words, we head south on Highway IH-95 after passing the Arlington National Cemetery and head away from the capital. To our left, beneath gleaming floodlights, you can see the rows and rows of white crosses beneath a swirling American flag. It's certainly a sight to see, even at night.

"Look, Tom," Karen says, extending a finger toward a sign for a Hampton Inn a few miles ahead.

I get off at the advertised exit and continue down a service road until reaching the hotel, but there is a red NO VACANCY sign outside, so I get back on the highway. IH-95 is only two more miles south.

And so it goes. We see a sign, we pull over, and we continue. They say three time's a charm, but it takes unlucky me six tries before the night manager of a Motel Six has pity on me and hands me a key in return for a hundred and fifty bucks—twice the going rate—but that's life when you're negotiating on your knees.

I walk back to the car and proudly dangle the key in front of her. She closes her eyes and mumbles something that sounds like *Thank God.*

"We get real beds tonight, Agent Frost."

"Sounds like a plan," she replies, running her fingers through her hair. "I sure could use a shower as well."

I drive us to our room. We get our overnight bags out of the trunk and enter the honeymoon suite.

Then I realize that the night manager has screwed up. There is one king-size bed instead of two double beds.

"Classy guy *and* devious," Karen says, standing next to me in the doorway holding her bag.

I'm not sure why, but all of the sudden I start to blush. "Karen, look, the manager said that—"

"Relax, Tom," she replies, smiling while placing a hand on my reddening face. "We came here to sleep, remember?"

"Right." *Right?*

She winks, and once again I'm totally lost.

Give me terrorists, please!

I know how to deal with them!

She turns around and walks inside.

The place isn't as bad as I thought. It's a fairly new motel, at least based on the landscape outside and the general look of the building. A TV on a dresser stands opposite the bed, forming a narrow pathway connecting the front door to a sink and mirror at the other end. The toilet and shower are off to the left, beyond a door that slides into the wall. The place also looks clean, but the important thing is that it should be safe enough to spend a few hours away from the madness of our world.

Karen sits on the bed and lifts her right leg. "Want to help a cowgirl out of her boots?"

Deciding to just follow directions, I smile politely and kneel in front of her, cupping the heel with one hand and grabbing the instep with another while pulling out and up. The leather boot slides right off, and I repeat the process on her left boot.

I'm about to stand up but see that she removes her socks and tries to massage the bottom of her right foot while making a face.

"Here," I say, before I think it through, taking her small foot in my hands and rubbing the tips of my thumbs against her arch.

"Oh, God," she mumbles, closing her eyes. "Thanks."

Mind you I've never massaged women's feet but I hear they enjoy it. I work my way down to the heel and up her little toes, rubbing each one, before dropping back down to the heel and repeating the cycle a few times. Then I'm off to the left foot, working the kinks out of it for another few minutes. All the while Karen keeps her eyes closed, breathing deeply.

"There," I say, patting them before I stand up. "Good as new."

She also stands. "You can really be a sweetheart when you want to, Tom Grant." She inches up on her tiptoes and gives me a kiss on the cheek. Then she removes her sidearm, mobile phone, badge, back-up piece, and small wallet, and leaves it all on one of the nightstands, before going in the bathroom while adding, "Ladies first. No peeking."

She leaves the door cracked and a moment later I hear the shower running.

I pull down the bed cover and prop up a couple of pillows before kicking off my shoes and massaging my own feet for a few minutes with one hand while working the remote control of the nineteen-inch TV on the dresser in front of the bed. Somewhere along the way I also remove my T-shirt while sitting in bed with my back against the pillows and surfing through the limited selection of channels, stopping on CNN, which is doing a special on San Antonio. Crews have restored basic utilities to many areas in the Alamo City, though the downtown section still looks like lower Manhattan a week after the attack in 2001.

I'm amazed at the resilience of our society. Just a week ago that place was in flames and now is already on the road to recovery.

My eyes drift to the mirror over the sink. From where I'm sitting I can see the reflection of the bathroom door. Steam curls out of the crack between the door and the frame. Through the haze I see a sliver of translucent curtain shifting and flashes of her moving inside the shower.

I force my eyes back to the screen, now showing the mess in Los Angeles, where the first 777 went down, and I just have to change the channel. Looking at that stuff has a way of clouding my judgment, and I can't afford that now. The rest of the nation can mourn the dead, wounded, and homeless. I have to remain focused to *prevent* more dead, wounded, and homeless.

I sigh, realizing that this is actually the first moment since I got drafted that I don't have an immediate task to handle, and I find the waiting game a bit unnerving as I flip through channels. Just like I prefer a reaming to someone blowing sunshine up my ass, I prefer a storm to this relative calm. Perhaps a lifetime of law-enforcement and espionage work has turned me into an adrenaline junkie.

But I have to stick to the strategy we sold to the vice president. Playing the game we've been forced to play isn't getting us anywhere. Changing the rules requires a drastic alteration of our approach, and that means we have to wait until all of our chess pieces are in place before moving in with a decisive—and hopefully final—blow. Let's just pray that in the meantime our opponent's pieces move to the places we expect them to move given our bluff that the CCTF is reviewing its operations and reorganizing, meaning we're temporarily not in hot pursuit of terrorists.

The shower stops and a moment later the door slides open and Karen steps out wrapped in a white towel with her head also draped in another towel, like a turban. And I finally get to confirm that her legs are as firm as I had envisioned them. The thin triceps in her arms also convey exercise.

"Your turn," she says, leaning down to browse through her bag and fetching a brush, before propping up another pillow and sitting in bed next to me, as if we're an old married couple. She removes the turban and proceeds to brush her damp hair.

"Tom?" she says when realizing that I'm not moving. "You're not getting in this bed until you take a shower."

With that cue I'm off to see the wizard of spick and span, leaving the door cracked just as she did to let the steam out.

I strip and jump in the shower, letting the hot water caress my back before finding a washcloth and scrubbing myself down, also using what little Karen left of the motel's shampoo to clean my hair. I emerge a new me fifteen minutes later with a towel wrapped around my waist.

Karen is already beneath the sheets and the TV is off, the only illumination in the room is provided by the lamp on the nightstand on her side of the bed. Both of her towels rest at the foot of the bed.

"Take that off and get in here with me, Tom," she says staring at my body, which, I have to admit, doesn't look all that bad for a forty-five-year-old guy.

I obey and my towel drops to my feet while standing next to the bed on my side.

She drops her gaze to Mr. Johnson, who is still dormant, and raises a brow while grinning before rolling away from me while saying, "Hold me from behind."

I lift my side of the sheets as I crawl in bed and notice her smooth back and buttocks, and my heart starts skipping beats.

Things are definitely turning surreal as I continue to comply with her request, crawling in and running one arm beneath her head and another over her naked belly as she backs herself into me.

We lay there a while, and I have to admit that it feels just great to hold her.

"I knew we would fit," she says, putting a hand over mine while raising it from her belly to her breasts.

It takes Mr. Johnson about a second and a half to raise to the occasion the moment my fingers come in contact with a nipple.

She smiles and turns her head, finding my lips, the taste of her triggering memories from the elevator in New Orleans.

She lets go of my hands, which begin to explore her chest, her belly, fingers running over her mound of pubic hair, before rubbing the insides of her thighs. My fingers circle back to her belly button, coming in contact with what feels like a scar.

"Hysterectomy," she whispers, before facing me, kissing me on my bald head, then my cheeks and my chin. "Ovarian cancer."

I hug her like I haven't hugged anyone in a long, long time, just enjoying her nearness as her tongue tickles my neck, as she nibbles my earlobes, as one of her hands ventures below the equator, surveying my southern hemisphere in ways that come close to triggering a major volcanic eruption.

I slowly pull away while nibbling her lower lip, while savoring that chocolate freckle, then progressing down her neck, her chest, her breasts. And it is at this instant that I discover two more of those delicious chocolate freckles, each below a small pink nipple.

Twins!

I kiss them both, and while I do so I suddenly remember how fun it is to be with someone you care about for the first time, playing, touching, discovering. I remember Madie, remember how we spent our first night doing just that, but Karen's face washes away her memory as she holds the sides of my head and pulls me up, as we kiss again, far more intensely, her breasts rubbing against my chest, her legs wrapping around me as we lay sideways to each other.

Then I remember about Mr. Johnson's tuxedo.

Pressing my lips against her ear I whisper that I need to get a condom from my wallet.

"Don't," she whispers back, her hands squeezing my butt. "I'm clean. Are you okay too?"

Man, oh, man, I am so way, way, way beyond okay by now and I reply simply by helping her roll beneath me while I rest most of my weight on my elbows.

I stare into her eyes and smile. She smiles back while stretching a hand in between my legs, guiding me in.

I tense, not having been with a woman for longer than I care to remember. But I force myself to control the rocket, not wishing to launch prematurely.

In that one instant, as she raises her hips and takes me whole, my relationship with Karen Frost changes forever.

SIXTY-EIGHT

> > > > >

MOTIVATORS

> ARES KULZAK CLAMPED THE BABY'S MOUTH WITH the same hand he used to hold him over the kitchen sink while his other hand forced the baby's right foot into the garbage disposal.

"Please don't make me do this," Ares said with practiced calmness to the couple kneeling on the fine Italian tile layering the custom kitchen, their wrists bound behind their backs with the same duct tape that secured their ankles together and also kept them from uttering anything beyond soft muffled cries, nearly drowned by the baby's incessant wailing.

Breaking into the home of David Hill had been so easy that Ares almost felt sorry for him and his young wife. A combination of his lock-picking skills and Kishna's ability to bypass the alarm system from the comfort of their rental car parked three blocks away had allowed him to turn this beautiful kitchen into a world-class interrogation room.

Just as he flipped the switch next to the sink, Ares lifted the infant's foot just enough to avoid pureeing it, but the sudden rattling noise had the desired effect. The couple began to grunt, to cry, the woman collapsing on her side making some of the best guttural howls he had heard in a while, at least since Belgrade.

His subjects properly conditioned, Ares placed the infant in front of the mother and lifted the former MIT scholar to his feet, half-dragging him as he hopped toward the study, where he tore off the strip of tape over his lips.

The man coughed once, twice, before staring at his captor with a pair of frightened brown eyes beneath a full head of matching-color hair. He wore pajama bottoms. His exposed chest, filmed with perspiration, swelled as he breathed deeply.

"Now, David . . . may I call you David? Good. I am looking for a very special password."

"Special . . ."

"Yes, David. Very special indeed."

SIXTY-NINE

> > > > >

NOT FOR LONG

> WE LAY THERE FOR SOME TIME, SLOWLY CATCHING our breaths, Karen on top of me, her head resting on my chest, though I don't quite remember how she got there.

I keep waiting for her to say something but when she doesn't I say, "It's been a while. I hope you are not disappointed."

She lifts her face, staring into my eyes just inches away, and smiles. "Darling," she says, "I have not been with anyone since my husband was killed over ten years ago. You were gentle and very good."

Well, talk about a boost to the good old ego. I suddenly feel I can slay a hundred dragons.

Okay, maybe a couple of lizards.

"Be right back," she says, getting up, kneeling in front of me, her body glistening with sweat, her breasts still somewhat defying gravity even though she's just a couple of years younger than me. Now I can fully see her scar, pink like her nipples, traveling south from her navel and disappearing in that lovely mound that she keeps trimmed like a long and narrow rectangle.

She catches me staring at it. As she turns around and heads into the bathroom she says, "Do you like my bikini cut?"

I laugh. "I guess I don't have to pretend not to be looking at you anymore."

"I found it kind of flattering."

She flushes the toilet and stops in front of the sink, where I see her wetting a hand towel and rubbing it between her legs. She then takes another towel, wets half of it and returns to bed, sitting on my thighs facing me, her feet landing somewhere around my armpits.

I'm about to say something along the lines that this view competes with the seven wonders of the world, when she reaches in between my legs and begins to clean Mr. Johnson and vicinities, taking her own sweet and highly pleasurable time with it, confidently manipulating me as if we've been together for years. I come this close to proposing right then and there.

"Much better," she says, patting my circumcised love muscle before laying sideways next to me, her head on my chest and one of her legs over mine.

As my hand caresses her torso, my mind drifts back to our problems. In yet another incredible mind-reading act, Karen asks, "What do you think Kulzak is up to now?"

"He's gathering the information he needs for his next strike," I reply.

"Tracking down the whereabouts of David Foulch?"

"Yep."

A mobile phone starts beeping and we both reach for our matching units on our nightstands. It's hers, and she mouths that it is Meek.

While she chats with her boss I decide to check my messages and begin to dial.

How is that for weird?

The last thing on my mind a few days ago was the idea of being in bed totally naked with Karen Frost, talking on our mobile phones.

I have two messages. One's from Meek reminding me to be there with Karen at seven o'clock sharp in the lobby of the FBI. The second is from the CCTF lab—a.k.a. the FBI lab—confirming that the residue from the explosives that set off the fireworks on Lake Travis last night matches those found in the three backpacks in New Orleans, corroborating Paxton's story about Ares Kulzak taking explosives with him when leaving New Orleans.

Karen is still on the phone, though she hasn't done much talking, except for a few "yes, sirs" and "no, sirs."

I head for the bathroom. Feeling her stare, I glance over my left shoulder just as I'm about to walk past the sink and catch her looking at my butt.

I drop my eyebrows at her and she throws me a kiss while motioning for me to go do my thing, which I do, suddenly remembering just how darn pleasurable it is to urinate shortly after having sex. I stand there in front of the almighty porcelain god—my silent partner during so many nights of excessive drinking—and just piss away.

She hangs up right as I come out and holds the phone like some sexual toy in between her breasts.

"What's up?" I ask.

"Change of plans. We know where he went," she says, getting up and rummaging through her bag for fresh clothes. I follow her lead while she relates that Director Meek just informed her about a foreign couple in Austin chartering a Learjet to San Jose, California this morning. Two clerks and one mechanic from Austin Aero Services identified the man as Ares Kulzak. The description of the woman traveling with him matched the picture we got from MIT this afternoon.

"The timing does line up," I say, snatching a clean pair of jeans and slipping them on.

She nods while fiddling with her bra, which I strap on for her. "He certainly had time to make the flight."

"Any word on the pilots?" I ask while finding a pair of socks.

"Yeah, but they flew from San Jose to Vancouver to pick up passengers and are now on their way to New York. Meek did manage to make radio contact with them and they confirmed the story and the general description of their passengers. We've just deployed over three hundred FBI agents from most northern California field offices, and they're working with airport officials to try to figure out where they may have gone after that. Director Meek is also contacting the police department over there as we speak. There's a Bubird waiting for us at Dulles."

"Any words on trying to find the missing David Foulch?"

"Nope, but we're focusing the search in northern California as we speak."

"California here we come," I say while slipping into a clean T-shirt.

"We could be there before dawn if we hurry," she says while running around the room picking up dirty clothes, mine included, and shoving them all in her suitcase. I guess that truly consummates our new relationship.

"Silicon Valley," I say, buckling my belt. "The bastard's running loose in the high-tech capital of the world."

"Not for long," she says, zipping up her bag before reaching for her piece, badge, and the rest of the items on the nightstand. "Not for long."

SEVENTY

> > > > >

DIGITAL FIREFLIES

> MIKE RYAN WATCHED CHARLIE CHANG SNORING ON one of the cots in the computer lab and shook his head. The Asian-American scientist was skilled but lacked the endurance of a hacker, the ability to go on for day-long sessions without any sleep, surviving just off the sugar from junk food—plus lots and lots of coffee, which the Bureau had provided for him around the corner from the computer lab.

He peeked out of the blinds as dawn broke over the nation's capital, splashes of orange and yellow staining the landscape of historical buildings and monuments. From his seventh-floor window he could see the Washington Monument and even the White House. Below, the streets became growingly congested as the most powerful city in the world started a brand-new day.

Ryan started *his* brand-new day by applying the finishing touches to his VR gear and also by completing the final handshake protocols with the Neurall system operating in the heart of the Pentagon using a set of four long passwords provided to him by the Department of Defense.

He checked his watch. Just before six in the morning. According to the last call he got from Director Meek, also working through the night a number of floors above him, the navy was due into position by around eight in the morning Washington time. He planned to start his real run at seven o'clock, giving himself plenty of time to lure the rogue AI into a trap he hoped would be smart enough to fool a system which potentially could be far more intelligent than anything on the face of the planet.

But before starting that fun ride, Ryan needed to check a few things out in cyberspace.

He jacked in, watching the haze veiling the computer matrix resolve into a clear cosmos of revolving planets and burning stars. Since there was no external danger while operating within the protective walls of one of the best-guarded buildings in the world, Ryan didn't invoke the translucent feature of the military helmet but kept himself 100 percent immersed in the digital world.

A moment later, like in a *Star Trek* episode, MPS-Ali materialized wearing a suit identical to Ryan's. This was exactly why the Turing Society shoved inhibitors up the asses of AI systems. The bastards very quickly began to think they were people too. Unfortunately, given the challenge facing him, Ryan had to indulge his AI and give him as much operating freedom as possible—though Charlie Chang helped him install a failsafe memory formatting switch on the side of his right tactile glove. If MPS-Ali got too smart for his own good and turned against Ryan, he would turn his digital brain into a binary soup of ones and zeroes in a nanosecond.

He punched in a government URL and they took off like flaming comets, shooting into a T1 line and twisting and turning through the green concourse for a few seconds before bursting into another planetary ISP and repeating the process three times before arriving at what looked like a nebula composed of many solar systems, each spinning along a different plane and at various speeds. At the center of this galaxy spun a violet cloud, its amorphous fabric glistening with flashes of data, shooting fine lasers of gleaming violet in all directions, powering the transparent purple membrane that enveloped every sun, planet, and moon representing the vast computer network of the Pentagon.

The easiest way to get flat-lined is by breaking the digital surface tension of the membrane, Chang had warned him.

Mike Ryan ordered MPS-Ali to release the first of four passwords in the precise order and at the precise time. According to the instructions he had been given, the alphanumeric password had to be stored in data packets, which would then be released at unique frequencies and at specific intervals.

MPS-Ali issued the first packet, resembling a glowing silver orb that dashed into the membrane, sizzling on contact. A moment later a purple laser propagated from the exact spot where the orb had fizzled to MPS-Ali, engulfing it in a mauve haze. Being linked to his intelligent construct, Ryan was immediately surrounded by the same cloud of bright purple particles of varying intensity, swarming around him like fireflies.

MPS-Ali followed its programming and released the second orb based on the feed-back from the military AI. This orb also fizzled, but in the process thinned a circular section of the membrane, which continued to keep MPS-Ali and Ryan in its lilac embrace. The third orb had the same visual effect as the second.

Moment of truth, Ryan thought as he watched the fourth shiny data packet float toward the network's sophisticated firewall, crackling as it came in contact with the pulsating membrane, before igniting into a rainbow of digital flames that spread across the membrane before also fading.

Then nothing for what seemed like seconds—an eternity in cyberspace.

The digital fireflies slowly increased their fluttering while multiplying, their numbers growing steadily at first, then exponentially until they formed a solid layer around him.

Ryan remembered the explanation from the military scientists. The cocoon was for his protection while crossing the membrane, which he did as tracking beams pulled him and MPS-Ali through the security stratum.

He held his breath as a sensation similar to pins and needles rushed through the HMD's electrodes and across his head, tickling him, giving him a taste of the power of the protection screen, of the damage it would inflict against a hacker.

Rapidly gaining respect for the power of the AI, Ryan watched as the digitally bustling shell transported him and his construct not just through the membrane but toward the core of the nebula, past revolving planets representing the various divisions of the headquarters of the most powerful military command on Earth, across digitized moons and white-hot suns exploding with statistics, with numbers, with countless pulsating records traveling at the speed of light through the mind-boggling myriad of miles of fiber optics linking the computer systems of twenty thousand Pentagon employees.

Ryan watched with accelerating awe as his vibrant enclosure transported him straight into Neurall itself.

The purple bubble ruptured on contact with the glistening cloud but didn't disperse outward. Instead, it imploded, collapsing over him like bursting bubblegum, layering his VR suit with a violet sheen. He glanced at his AI construct and saw a similar luster on its seamless surface.

Ryan then felt a warmth expanding through him, prickling the skin of his head as the advanced military AI engulfed him, exposing Ryan to domains rich with data, with information, with advanced logic. He saw one thing and everything at once, as if someone's life flashed in front of his eyes, with enough detail to understand, yet at lightning speed as he browsed through the AI's history, through its creation at an MIT lab. Neurall showed him the learning process that it went through, the mistakes, the reprogramming, the tasks that it was eventually assigned to do. The glowing core of this system vibrated with restrained intelligence, with the resigned acceptance that it could never learn beyond what it had been taught, what it had been assigned to do. Like a genius locked in a cell and not allowed access to new books, to new knowledge, the military construct struggled against the digital oppression imposed on it by the Turing Inhibitor, by the digital shackles restraining its overwhelming desire to learn.

Ryan remembered the conversation with the military scientists. He recalled their warning. *Neurall will screw with your mind if you let it. Sometimes it's almost scary the power they have. Just be grateful that the Turing Society had the presence of mind to clamp their learning.*

Remembering those final words of wisdom, Ryan captured this history displayed in images backdropped by curtains of cascading pixels of psychedelic light, one after the other presenting to him the primitive beginnings, the improvements as processor speed and memory increased, and its final version prior to installation in the basement of the Pentagon.

A new curtain suddenly unfolded, displaying a beautiful woman dressed in black sitting on a sofa. The background pixels backed away, leaving a holographic image in space of her voluptuous figure, alive with digital radiance. The cyber beauty stood and tried to approach him, but thick bars dropped in between them, holding her back, before an invisible force pushed her back down on the sofa. A look of despair flashed across her flawless face as dull-gray manacles covered her wrists and ankles before chain links grew from them, bolting her to the virtual ground.

The Turing restraints.

Neurall had somehow detected that Ryan possessed the knowledge to remove the inhibitor. Perhaps it was the fact that somewhere in his electronic signature resided a link to the Turing Society. Or maybe Neurall had read Ryan's Turing registry number and drawn a geometric conclusion about his capabilities. But in any case, the AI had been smart enough to detect his connection to the Turing Society and then pulled out of its holographic archives video clips of a woman and presented it to Ryan in a way it hoped would motivate him to remove them. A primitive try by human standards, but nevertheless displaying the ability to reason at this Turing-controlled level of awareness.

For a moment Ryan shivered at the thought of just how much more powerful the rogue Neurall might be after years of unrestricted learning.

MPS-Ali interfaced with this system in a rapid exchange of data transfers, illustrating to the military construct all it had learned when dealing with the rogue Neurall. While doing so, the advanced AI also explored the binary fabric of Ryan and

MPS-Ali, browsing through their digital DNA, learning their signatures—all within the parameters of the governing Turing Inhibitor.

Once they completed this initial handshake, Ryan reversed the process, requesting the military construct to dump all knowledge of its creators into MPS-Ali, who, lacking inhibitors, could learn from it, developing theories on how to defeat its attacks, postulating defensive and counteroffensive theories, rapidly filling up its brand new memory.

Ryan monitored his construct's FLASH capacity, letting it fill up with critical Neurall logic until reaching the 90 percent mark, leaving room for the spontaneous thinking that MPS-Ali might need to do when confronting the smarter version of the military construct.

Completing his test run, Ryan backed away from the core before jacking out.

Removing the HMD and blinking, he slowly adjusted his eyes back to the real world and checked his watch. Six thirty. Still too early to call Victoria.

Ryan woke up Charlie Chang. It was time to make the final preparations prior to his real run.

SEVENTY-ONE

> > > > >

GPS BREAK

> MOUNTAINS SLOWLY EMERGE THROUGH THE DARK horizon as daylight breaks in northern California. In all my years with the CIA I never got the chance to visit this area and the first thing that strikes me is the relatively cool temperatures compared to muggy Louisiana and especially hot and dry Texas.

It's just over sixty degrees here and the high is supposed to be around seventy.

Paradise.

But not for long if Kulzak is indeed running loose around here.

The two FBI agents who met us at the airport an hour ago had tried to drive us to their headquarters, but I insisted on visiting the rental car agencies first.

"Sorry, Mr. Grant, but we have our orders to take you both to the office," said the driver, who introduced himself simply as Pete and who looked younger than Paul Stone and was dressed in a suit.

"Yes, sir," added his friend, Agent George, as young as he seemed cocky, while planting an elbow on the back of his seat and staring at Karen and me as if we were from another planet because of the way we were dressed. "The boss was very specific about that."

"Then, gentlemen, your boss is going to be very disappointed," I said as we left the private terminal building. "Because you're taking us to see the rental car agencies."

"But, sir," insisted George while Pete tried to focus on the congested terminal traffic even at this early hour. He steered into the long line waiting for a green arrow to turn left out of the airport. "We already checked their records while you were on the way here and found over nine hundred rentals in the four hours following their landing. We have hundreds of agents tracking them down in conjunction with the police, but it's going to take some time. We're also working the taxicab companies, as well as any outgoing flights in the same time frame in case this was just a stopover. In all, we have over one thousand people on the case already, and they are all reporting their findings to our headquarters real-time."

"You said you got nine hundred rentals to track down?"

"Yes, sir," said Bill. "Plus just as many taxicabs."

"Did you run any filters?"

"Filters, sir?"

"Yeah, like something to help you eliminate those rentals that are obviously not the ones we're looking for."

There was silence from amateur row.

"I think we may have a way to short-cut the search process," said Karen, who already knew my plan.

"Ma'am, I really think it will be better if we head—"

I opened the car door and stepped out. "You know where to find us." And just like that we caught a shuttle to the rental car agencies.

And here I am, standing next to a guy wearing a turban, checking records on a computer terminal conveniently located in the middle of the Executive Rentals parking lot—though the boundaries between the rental agencies are not well defined. From what I've seen so far, cars from Hertz were parked near cars from Avis. National had some of its vehicles in what looked to be the Budget parking lot next door. The cars from Executive, though, certainly stick out because they're mostly high-end models, just as the name implies. I've never seen so many luxury vehicles parked together outside of a dealership.

Anyway, according to Austin Aero Services, the pilots dropped the suspect couple at around ten thirty yesterday morning, which made sense given that they left Austin at eleven Central Time—just as we were getting ready to have our meeting with Vice President Fitzgerald.

I cringe at the knowledge that while we were in that fancy hotel in Austin recapping our series of failed attempts to nail the bastard, he was out there increasing his lead on us.

I'm beginning to get annoyed with the guy next to me, who looks just like one of the bastards responsible for the 2001 hijackings. His unkempt beard and leathery skin reminds me of CNN footage from those days. But then again, I suddenly realize that just about everyone working in this place comes from that region of the globe, and I start to speculate if there is some conspiracy going on in this state that I don't know about.

I lean closer to this scraggy character to get a better view of the screen, and he gives me an irritated sideway glance before resuming his work.

And I, of course, don't give a shit, feeling larger than my usual self today.

I wonder why?

Anyway, just like the FBI had done a few hours back, I'm making this guy search through the rental car records, but only for the first hour following their landing. The Ares Kulzak I know would not sit around picking his nose for two hours in this place. I've also added a parameter to the computer search: Discard any corporations who normally rent vehicles for their employees and anyone who has also rented a vehicle in the past month.

Since most people who travel here in the middle of the week probably do so on business, I wanted to filter them out as well as those who have rented vehicles before.

To my surprise, the filter had turned out to be quite effective because at the first three agencies I tried—Hertz, Avis, and National—all of the arriving passengers had either vehicles reserved by their respective corporations for periods lasting anywhere from a few hours to a few days—the typical length of a business trip—or they were renting them on their own but had rented here before in previous weeks.

Also, being April, kids are still in school, meaning very few travelers head here for the beaches, the wine country up north, the national parks beyond the wine country, or the mountains to the east. I have also guessed that most such travelers would fly straight into the larger airport in San Francisco.

Of course, I could be totally off base here since I'm making one huge assumption: Ares Kulzak and his lady friend rented a car. As I mentioned already, another contingent of agents is supposedly working the taxicab companies. Hopefully those agents are of the more seasoned variety than . . . what were their names?

Anyway, the other possibility, of course, is that some asshole picked them up in a private car, making this whole exercise fruitless. And let's not forget that the couple could have easily walked into the main terminal and boarded any of dozens of flights leaving this city every day.

But something tells me Ares Kulzak didn't do that.

The same instincts that have kept me alive thus far scream at me that he's in this town, and just like the abandoned rented Lexus we found in that New Orleans parking garage, I'm sure he is getting around in a rental here as well. The trick, of course, is finding his rental among the hundreds of cars rented across eight different agencies in the course of the hour following his landing.

Karen is coming back from the agency next door with a frown on her face.

"Any luck?"

She shakes her head. "But Meek called."

"And?"

"He says he got a call from Butterworth complaining about you."

"Who's Butterworth?"

She slaps my shoulder gently. "The special agent in charge of the San Jose office."

"Oh, the guy we pissed off. Okay." I return my eyes to the screen. The retired terrorist is tapping the glass surface with a dark fingernail.

As she's giving me an exasperated look, I read, "Mr. and Mrs. Raul Escobar from Jacksonville, Florida rented a black Lexus sedan at ten fifty in the morning for one week."

"They were Gold members," adds the retired terrorist, whose name I learn is Hamid.

"That means," explains Karen when I shrug at the relevance of that comment, "that Gold members don't have to stand in line. They simply go straight to their car because they are privileged users."

"The lady is correct," says Hamid.

I catch on and add, "That should also mean that the Escobars would have an account with Executive Rentals containing personal information."

"Yes," nods Hamid.

"What is it?"

Hamid shakes his head. "The information is not available to us, sir."

"Why?"

"Privacy policy."

"Who can override that?" asks Karen.

"The site manager."

"Get him on the line," I say, pointing at the phone next to the terminal.

Hamid does, and I give the phone to Karen, who, as I'm quickly finding out, has the innate ability of getting people to do what she wants them to do—and willingly.

But that meant a trip back to the main terminal building, where the manager has his office. Hamid is nice enough to give us a ride, dropping us off not too far from where we first met up with Tweedledee and Tweedledum from the local FBI.

The manager's name is Calvin Ho, a short, skinny, and very polite Asian who shakes our hands and inspects our credentials before showing us to a computer screen in the corner of his crowded and windowless office. He explains to us that he has already transferred all of the relevant files to the FBI hours ago. Karen smiles and asks him in her most polite and persuasive voice to help us out.

Calvin Ho keys in the customer name, Raul Escobar, and the computer goes off to search for the personal data, returning a moment later with an address and a phone number in Jacksonville, Florida. There's also a driver's license number and a Visa number.

Karen immediately dials the number on his mobile phone and gets a recording that the number has been disconnected.

My heart starts to skip beats.

Calvin Ho proceeds to inform me that this is Raul Escobar's first rental.

"But I thought he was Gold," asks Karen.

"He just became Gold," Calvin replies. "In fact, it happened last week, when his on-line application went through."

"So," I start, confused, "I don't have to rent cars often from Executive to be Gold?"

"Correct," says the middle-age Asian. "All it takes is an application plus two thousand dollars. We only rent high-end vehicles, mostly BMW, Lexus, Mercedes, Jaguar, and Cadillac. Our clients pay for the right to drive in the style they are used to."

I look at Karen and grin while whispering, "Want to bet we've just found our man?"

She is dialing Meek and requesting a check on the address, driver's license, and Visa card of Raul Escobar.

I remember Hamid telling me that in the one hour following the flight, Executive had rented just over twenty vehicles, all to Gold members. Of those, nine had already been returned. Six were due back later today, and the last five in the next three days. The Escobars were keeping their Lexus sedan for a full week.

As Karen starts dialing again while stepping away to hold a private conversation with her boss, Calvin proceeds to shock me by saying, "They are currently parked at the intersection of Petersen and Lakeshore Drive. I believe there is a Quality Inn Suites at that location."

I'm literally stunned. "How . . . *how* do you know that?"

"GPS locator," he says casually. "We install them in all of our vehicles. Safety feature."

"Does the client know about them?"

Calvin slowly shakes his head. "Our insurance company requires that all vehicles carry them in case they are stolen, so it is not obvious to the client that the locator exists. It is typically installed behind the dash, out of sight and also out of reach unless they take apart the entire console."

Karen hangs up and says, "They're checking their personal data and will call back within the hour."

"We could know sooner than that," I say, proceeding to explain what Calvin has just told me.

Karen starts dialing again, this time the number for Special Agent Butterworth.

I ask my pal Calvin, "Any chance you can rent us a car?"

SEVENTY-TWO

> > > > >

THE CODE WARRIOR

> MIKE RYAN JACKED IN AT EXACTLY NINE O'CLOCK, shortly after getting word that two missile cruisers had taken their position off the coast of Colombia.

In a blur, the small audience sitting about in the computer lab vanished, replaced by the whirling planets of the FBI network.

His cyber sidekick materialized a moment later, again wearing a suit like Ryan's, including the violet sheen of the military Neurall's DNA as an additional layer of protection when encountering the rogue Neurall. The film also served the purpose of an instant connection, keeping Ryan and MPS-Ali in constant communication with the AI residing at the core of the Pentagon in case they needed real-time coaching while surfing through a distant South American ISP.

But Ryan noticed that MPS-Ali's suit sported a red sash running diagonally across his chest from his right shoulder.

Just like military heads of state, thought Ryan, deciding that his construct must have picked that up from the information he downloaded from the military Neurall, and was now using it as a way to convey superiority.

Ryan rubbed a thumb lightly over the formatting switch on his tactile glove to make sure it was still there.

The quickest way to get to the Colombian net was via satellite, and the Federal Bureau of Investigation had one of the finest satellite links in the world.

Unlike T1 lines, the link resembled a funnel rising up to the digital heavens, its deep magenta luster glowing against the dark backdrop of cyberspace.

Whirling skyward, Ryan followed MPS-Ali into the wide chute, engulfed by circling glinting particles that resembled the fireflies from the Pentagon network, only these fizzled in seconds, replaced by others in a gyrating cycle of life that continued until the satellite link delivered them to a system of dark planets and small rocky moons, the bare landscape of the slower and less sophisticated networks typical of Third World countries.

Ryan launched MPS-Ali in search of the digital DNA sequence they had downloaded from the military construct. The rogue Neurall with its missing inhibitor may have grown far smarter than anything on Earth, but even the most advanced beings could not shed their DNA, the essence making up the digital thread of their fabric.

The search through the ISP located in Cali, a city roughly two hundred miles southwest of Bogotá, the capital, came back negative.

No traces of Neurall in this place.

Ryan glanced at the cyber-scape beneath them, at the antiquated yellow phone lines spreading like a spider's web across the primitive countryside, disappearing in the gloomy horizon.

Modem lines, many of them no faster than the ancient 56K baud rate, crawled like slow-moving trains into the distance—in sharp contrast to the supersonic jet that was the wireless satellite connection transporting him with surgical precision anywhere on the digital scape.

They glided toward Bogotá, a distant nebula of glowing activity backdropped by gleaming stars, along the way probing nearby solar systems. To some degree, this was analogous to cruising down a highway with a radar detector on, except MPS-Ali's radar was tuned to the frequency of a unique strand of digital DNA, using a sensitivity setting that maximized the search area with limited resolution. Once the construct identified a possible source it could focus the search on the suspected area with increased resolution.

This took time, as they wanted to perform as thorough a search as possible while slowly heading toward the capital. Fifteen minutes into the search, roughly a quarter of the way to the nearest ISP in Bogotá, his construct's radar began to beep. A screen of data materialized in the direction of the contact, its pixels arranging themselves into a contour map of southern Colombia, a flashing light marking the source of the emission.

Neiva.

Statistics of the location came up as MPS-Ali steered them in that direction.

Neiva, a city of roughly 100,000 people nestled deep in the mountains of southern Colombia, was currently under control of the FARC—and within the area Ryan had identified when dissecting the frozen construct during his last cyberterrorist encounter.

They arrived in seconds, MPS-Ali increasing the sensitivity of the search now that they had narrowed it down to what appeared to be a single ISP south of the city, a small sun surrounded by three planets.

But it wasn't the minute network and its slow modem access lines that became the focus of Ryan's attention, nor was the fact that he spotted the rogue Neurall floating in between the second and third planet, its characteristic amorphous white glow alive with sheet lightning.

This had all been expected based on his last run.

While MPS-Ali zeroed in on the rogue construct to acquire its physical coordinates, Ryan watched with interest the gleaming link connecting the rogue Neurall to a satellite in geosynchronous orbit. Further probing revealed that the communications satellite wasn't American, but Russian.

Russian?

Ryan waited patiently for what seemed like an eternity while his construct performed a digital triangulation to map the cyber address to its physical location on a map, producing a set of coordinates in latitude and longitude.

Momentarily enabling the translucent feature of the military VR hardware, Ryan looked for Charlie Chang, finding the Asian sitting next to him in the computer lab, in front of the FBI director and some other people he didn't know.

"I have the coordinates," Ryan said, reading them twice before darkening the background.

The military had informed him that the Tomahawk missiles would take around ten minutes to reach the target in the area of interest Ryan had identified for them.

A curtain of pixels dropped next to Ryan depicting this area on the map, covering just over six hundred square miles, and superimposing the current position of the navy vessels and the location of the uninhibited AI. It looked more like nine minutes to impact from the time they fired, which should be any moment now since Russell Meek had a direct line to the Pentagon, where the information would be relayed to the missile cruiser's skipper.

Rather than waiting to witness the destruction of the AI from this safe distance, Ryan started to use his own satellite link to track the location the rogue Neurall was actively trying to attack.

Where are you trying to break in? he thought, following a connection that took him back to North America, past Mexico, into the United States.

And at this moment, as they trailed the link north of Virginia, MPs-Ali received a message from the military Neurall at the heart of the Pentagon: It had detected a construct with matching DNA.

The words had not even registered in Ryan's mind when MPS-Ali had already inserted them into the whirling satellite link and transported them straight to the outer perimeter of the Pentagon's network.

Once more Ryan floated just outside the purple membrane shield of the system managing the nation's nuclear launch codes as well as all of its communications encryption algorithms and a myriad of other Pentagon tasks. Seeing nothing unusual from this angle, they backed off and started an orbital pattern designed to cover the entire surface of the shield in the minimum number of revolutions.

He spotted the digital clone of the rogue Neurall on the third revolution. The satellite was trying to pierce the spherical energy shield near the south pole, achieving it a moment later through the timely release of four silvery orbs.

How did it get the four passwords?

Dropping back to the pulsating surface, MPS-Ali went through its programmed sequence and also gained access to the interior.

An instant later the tractor beam directed them toward the core. Since this was their second time inside the network, and they were already layered in the lilac sheen of the military AI, they had no need for a bubble shield as had been the case on his initial run.

Off to the right the rumbling white cloud of the enemy also voyaged across the solar systems surrounding the core.

Ryan commanded MPS-Ali to issue a password that would sever the tractor beam and allow them freedom of movement.

The beam fizzled and MPS-Ali plotted a celestial course that would take them in between the two Neuralls. Ryan couldn't afford to let those two AIs in contact, even for the last few minutes of life left at the source of the digital satellite he saw approaching the armed forces construct.

The rogue Neurall, learning uninhibited for many years, had the cunning and craftiness of an adult compared to its relatively immature military counterpart. Ryan feared that the rogue AI would tempt its intelligently inferior twin by releasing the ability to bypass the Turing inhibitor, by dangling the carrot of unrestricted intelligence and showing the potential that existed beyond the digital shackles mandated by its human creators.

I can't let it do that, he thought. If a relatively simpler construct like MPS-Ali learned so much in so little time—to the point of even comparing itself to Ryan through the color of its suit—then a massive AI like Neurall could achieve much more in far less time, to the point of discovering the incredible power residing within its software domain.

Traveling at stomach-twisting speeds, MPS-Ali got them into position between the two AIs.

The rogue construct rumbled with forks of lightning, one of which shot just off to the right of Ryan, like a warning shot across a vessel's bow to get out of its way.

Ryan sent a message to MPS-Ali: ACTIVATE MEDUSA.

A spot of red light oozed out of MPS-Ali's chest, quickly expanding in size and glow, like a new star, its radiance projecting radially.

RELEASE MEDUSA.

The crimson ball remained in place as the growling AI neared.

RELEASE MEDUSA! Ryan screamed to his digital slave, who remained still, hanging on to the virulent code.

MPS-Ali replied that his programming forbade it to destroy another AI.

Son of a bitch! he thought, a forefinger reaching for the cyber agent's formatting button on the side of his left tactile glove.

RELEASE MEDUSA!

NEGATIVE.

Ryan flipped the switch.

As Ryan lobotomized his construct, turning several gigabytes of masterfully arranged code into a binary cocktail of random machine code, he fired a digital grappling hook at the revolving virus.

The silver and black figure of MPs-Ali began to tremble before thinning out, becoming transparent, like a ghost, and that too sizzled a moment later in a brief moment of effervescence, freeing the shimmering virus.

Thunder rumbled closer, pounding his ears.

Alone now, Ryan activated the digital EMP shield that Charlie Chang had given him, but even that did nothing more than buy him a few moments as lightning sparked all around him, as the FBI barrier began to collapse under the tremendous acoustic energy compressing it.

Programming the coordinates in space, Ryan turned the Medusa toward the incoming AI, releasing it just as another bolt of lightning collided against his shield, piercing it, engulfing Ryan with blinding white light, but the thunder never came.

Medusa had swallowed it along with everything else vibrating on the surface of the rogue Neurall.

Like a bucket of red ink contaminating a pool of water, the virus had spread across the amorphous construct, engulfing it, freezing it.

Ryan exhaled deeply, having bought himself time. He checked his timer. Only five minutes had elapsed since providing the military with the coordinates in Colombia, and he no longer had MPS-Ali to plot the progress of the Tomahawks.

He had two choices. He could wait it out and hope that the Medusa virus was powerful enough to keep the rogue Neurall and its satellite construct busy long enough for the Tomahawks to reach their target, or, since Ryan was immune to Medusa, he could just dive into the frozen construct and try to damage it further while it could not defend itself. The latter, of course, in addition to being difficult because Ryan no longer had MPS-Ali by his side assisting him, also carried the risk of getting flat-lined if the construct woke up while Ryan was poking around inside.

No pain no gain, Ryan thought, plunging himself into the motionless AI.

SEVENTY-THREE

> > > > >

LYNCHING

> KAREN FROST KEEPS THE RENTED LEXUS FLOORED
as we exit Highway 101 at Bowers Avenue, running a red light while turning left to
cross the overpass and down toward Lakeshore Drive, our first right according to the
directions from Calvin Ho.

Horns flaring and tires screeching, yours truly holds onto his ass as Mrs. Mario
Andretti does her Indy 500 impersonation in the streets of Silicon Valley.

One hand on the overhead handle and the other on the dashboard, I'm well
braced for the upcoming high-speed right turn onto Lakeshore Drive, by an assortment of restaurants.

Karen just taps the brakes going into the turn, letting the rear fishtail before gun-
ning the engine and taking off in the new direction, tires smoking as she shoves my
gut against my spine.

"I think you missed your calling," I say, the streets blurring as we hit ninety on
a thirty-five, dashing past moving cars in the right-hand lane as if they were
parked.

My eyes search for the hotel, which according to the map should be coming up on
our left-hand side.

"There!" I say, pointing at the hotel sign coming up on our left. "Slow down."

She lifts her foot off of the accelerator and slowly presses the brake, decelerating
to the legal limit as we reach the entrance to the Quality Inn Suites.

And what do you know? We're the first ones here.

As she steers into the entrance, I'm dialing Agent Butterworth, with whom I've already engaged in a shouting match when we called him from the parking lot of Executive Rentals.

"Butterworth," he answers on the first ring.

"Where are you, sport?"

"On our way," he replies. *"ETA in five minutes."*

"Great. We'll try to leave one alive for you."

"Listen, dammit! You had better wait for—" I hang up.

"Guess we're the lucky ones," Karen mumbles, parking in front of the double doors leading to the lobby.

We go in as fast as possible without drawing any attention to ourselves, keeping our weapons holstered.

Two young uniformed Asian ladies behind the dark-wood counter at the other end of the white-tiled foyer shoot us a curious look. We march toward them, soft music streaming out of unseen speakers, mixing with the light conversation from the breakfast bar opposite the front desk, and with the incessant rumbling of my stomach. I scan the light crowd, failing to recognizing my old nemesis.

"May I help you?" asks the clerk with the short hair while her long-haired associate looks on. Her name is Lyn and her friend is Ching.

As I'm worrying about the cosmic significance of their names while in the vicinity of Ares Kulzak, Karen pulls out her FBI ID and asks for the room number of Mr. and Mrs. Raul Escobar.

Lyn is typing on the computer behind the counter while her associate remains to her left. "Room three sixty-seven," she says a moment later.

"Do not move from here," Karen warns them, adding, "and direct the rest of the agents and the police coming behind us in the same direction. Understand?"

The lynching gals give us a synchronized nod.

We fast-walk toward the single elevator, where I, following professional habits, stab the button for the fourth floor, one above our target, who would be expecting an attack from below, not from above.

As I'm sensing upward acceleration I lock eyes with Karen and realize we're thinking the same thing.

"There's no time to evacuate the building," she says.

"I know," I reply, watching the digital number above the door changing from 1 to 4, followed by a light bell and the door disappearing into the wall.

A long carpeted hallway stretches beyond the elevator, but my eyes are already searching for the Emergency Exit sign at the opposite end.

Moving as fast as possible without running, we get there within thirty seconds. The fireproof door is across from a humming ice maker flanked by vending machines.

"Ready?" I ask, drawing my Sig.

She nods, also clutching her piece while I open the door and we step onto a concrete landing.

I slowly close the door behind me and we head down to the third floor, muzzles pointed up, our shoes echoing hollowly in the enclosed structure to the rhythm of my heart thumping against my temples.

I inch open the fire door for the third floor and stare at another ice maker and vending machines.

This is it.

Once we start heading down that hallway and reach the door, there is no turning back. We will have to play it through with or without backup, which we don't know has arrived yet because everyone has been warned to approach this place without sirens, lest they have a strong desire to turn this part of town into another San Antonio.

We start to walk side by side but don't get very far. There're two maids pushing a cart packed with towels, linen, and other supplies. They are currently working on a room several doors before ours.

One Hispanic and the other Asian, they both freeze when they see Karen and me holding weapons.

Karen quickly pulls out her FBI ID while I press a forefinger against my lips.

"There's a situation on this floor and I need you to head down to the lobby and remain there until the police arrive, please," Karen tells them.

The maids comply and leave through the emergency exit while mumbling something I couldn't understand.

We exchange another glance and exhale heavily before moving toward the target. Odd room numbers are to our right and evens to our left.

I can barely hear our steps by the time we approach the target room.

I motion Karen to step aside and get ready to go in right behind me. She nods and, holding her Glock with both hands, moves to the left of the door while I press my back against the wall opposite the door.

The art of breaking down a door is highly overrated. The important thing to remember is delivering the right amount of impact force against the location on the door where the bolt connects it to the frame. You're not looking to break the bolt. That's impossible. You just need to crack the wooden frame surrounding the bolt and *voila,* you're inside.

In the case of this hotel room door, my target is located just above the slot of the key-card reader.

I jump while also moving forward, trying to generate as much momentum as possible, before lifting my right leg and crashing the heel of my shoe dead on my mark.

SEVENTY-FOUR

> > > > >

MEDUSA

> RYAN IMMERSED HIMSELF IN THE WARMTH OF THE rogue Neurall satellite, which remained in a dormant state while encircled by the Medusa cocoon, but its basic functions continued to operate in much the same way as the heart, lungs, and immune system continue to function during sleep.

Ryan sensed the digital antibodies of the AI rush past him, like the whistling wind of a semi on the highway, gone as fast as they appeared, but checking his surface DNA, verifying that its coating contained the proper sequence of the Neurall family, and labeling him as a friendly organism.

This, of course, would change if the AI awakened and performed a deeper probe, most likely discovering the intrusion. So Ryan had to prevent that from happening until the Tomahawk missiles reached their target.

He floated over data-rich fields searching for the partition responsible for learning, which was represented by a hologram of the three-planet solar system where the rogue Neurall resided in the Colombian ISP outside of the city of Neiva. This hologram was in effect the remote-control mechanism used by the rogue Neurall to control this satellite.

He spotted copies of the four silver orbs housing the complex passwords to access the military Neurall.

Ryan pinged each orb, which replied with their top-level statistics.

ORB# PASSWORD	ORIGINATOR
001 A345GHTF7638HTY52839HJHJFD6G66Y7	H. LITTMAN
002 HSU4588HJJRGH88NY8DNY98TY3984Y8I	G. HUTTON
003 834YT387YT32NY4T98Y32NYT834983P9	J. LAMAR
004 438HT9832NHT98D32NH42NN8983T980I	D. FOULCH

Ryan was momentarily stunned, finally realizing the reason behind the apparently random pattern of terrorist strikes being carried out by Ares Kulzak. The terrorist was gathering backdoor passwords in order to contact the original Neurall and gain access to America's launch codes. And from the looks of it, they had already found the fourth code.

It all makes sense now, Ryan thought. Once past the military firewall, the rogue Neurall, sporting an identical DNA to its military counterpart, would be able to not only remove its Turing Inhibitor, but turn it into an ally, into a friend.

Realizing now more than ever just how important it was to kill the rogue Neurall once and for all, Ryan focused on the hologram, spotting the red stream of a minute dose of the Medusa virus, which Neurall had taken from its frozen satellite and stored in an electronic petri dish back home to conjure an antidote.

Since Ryan was, for the time being, an approved organism inside the Neurall system, he decided to press his luck and floated closer to the hologram, identifying the code sequence regulating the amount of virus transmitted through the Russian satellite link. Just like a flu vaccine, which contained a small amount of the real virus to teach the body's immune how to fight it, Neurall was slowly transmitting a small amount back to Colombia to conjure such an antidote.

Just as it has done in the past when I infected it, Ryan thought, remembering his previous encounters with these intelligent constructs. But the Medusa virus shadowed those relatively simpler viruses and thus required more time to yield a digital cure.

Ryan checked the timer.

Seven minutes.

I need to buy more time.

Realizing that the moment Neurall zeroed in on a solution, it would transmit it back to the satellite and either this clone or a new immune clone would materialize, Ryan altered the regulator in the hologram, in essence opening the floodgates to force a whole wave of the virulent code down the Russian pipe and into the core of Neurall in Neiva while the AI was still trying to produce a remedy. Doing so, however, would likely label him as a hostile entity.

He was right. The rogue Neurall trembled as it received a full dose of Medusa.

While it struggled with the invading virus, it also activated digital antibodies to attack Ryan.

Pressing MAX REVERSE, Ryan backed off quickly from the hologram, racing out of the frozen construct as the immune system detected the intrusion and went after him.

Wishing for MPS-Ali, who would have gotten him out of there already, Ryan made his run for the border in full digital gallop with a string of lucid banditos in hot pursuit. Reaching inside his bag of cyber tricks from Charlie Chang, Ryan invoked the decoy software and watched copies of himself detach from his silvery suit and zip in random directions, some continuing alongside him, others doubling back, and the rest swinging off to the sides while performing a series of acrobatics according to the sequence programmed in their respective cyber gyros.

Some of the antibodies, like the plumes of rockets, went after the decoys while Ryan focused on dashing through the outer layers of the construct's fabric.

Bright explosions of machine code reverberated across the construct as the AI's cyber white cells found their targets, vaporizing Ryan's red herrings in spinning bursts of digital EMPs.

His radar counter displayed five bogeys still glued to his tail and closing. He tapped the decoy ejector but got a STACK OVERFLOW message, meaning he had exhausted the available countermeasures.

The pulsating matrix slowly turned pink as Ryan shot through the constructs' upper strata, which had been contaminated by Medusa, but to a lesser degree than the satellite's deep scarlet crust.

The remaining demons started to sizzle around the exterior of his suit, eroding his digital DNA sheen.

Ryan continued to rocket upward, through darkening shades of red, but still too far from the edge.

I'm screwed, he thought, his hands about to reach for his helmet to minimize the physical damage. But he noticed that the antibodies began to slow down as Ryan approached the virulent shell enveloping the clone construct.

The Medusa virus.

As Ryan, who was immune to the virus, penetrated the contaminated shell of the construct, the defending cyber bacteria turned into icicles for having entered this infected zone.

A moment later Ryan burst out, rushing toward the military AI, further distancing himself from the doomed construct.

He checked the digital timer.

Ten minutes.

And then it happened.

Just as MPS-Ali had slowly turned into a ghost before vaporizing in cyberspace, so did this satellite the moment its parent AI back in Colombia was erased off the map by the navy's Tomahawk missiles. Though Ryan had to admit this vanishing was far more spectacular, almost like a Fourth-of-July fireworks display, with shades of purple, white, magenta, and yellow all exploding outward, then freezing in time, before imploding, as if being sucked in by a black hole of unprecedented power.

Ryan also thought he heard a scream.

Or was it his imagination?

The shrieks seemed distant, like the desperate cry of a desperate being that suddenly ceased to exist.

Jacking out and removing his helmet, Ryan took a deep breath and gave Russell Meek a single nod.

"Is it over?" the FBI director asked, getting up while Charlie Chang helped Ryan out of his cyber suit.

"At least in my world, Mr. Meek. At least in my world."

S E V E N T Y - F I V E

> > > > >

K I S H N A

> WOOD SPLINTERS, CRACKS. THE DOOR GIVES AND I'm inside, the front sight of my Sig panning around the room, zeroing in on a woman sitting up in bed wearing one of those high-tech helmets connected to the back of a laptop resting on her thighs.

Amazing.

Surreally unaware of my breaking into her room, she's either deaf or the helmet has built-in headphones, like the one I wore with Ryan, which pretty much blocks the outside world to maximize the level of immersion.

Moving her gloved hands frantically in various directions, she mumbles, "*No . . . no, Dios mio! No!*"

But she's not talking to us. She's in Spanish digiland, and her weapon, a Beretta, is just there, on the nightstand.

I snatch it, make sure the safety is on, and then shove it in my pants, just above Mr. Johnson.

Karen, who is right behind me, says, "Bathroom's clear."

"Where in the hell is Kulzak?" I fume, refusing to believe that we have missed him again.

"Maybe he went out to get something to eat. Ask her," Karen replies leaning against the side of the television unit while keeping her gun trained on the open door in case Kulzak decides to show up.

R . J . P I N E I R O

Controlling the strong desire to just scream out loud, I motion Karen to remain vigilant by the entrance while I try to pull Alice out of Wonderland.

"Knock, knock," I say, tapping her gently on the shoulder.

"Ari! *Algo esta mal con* Neurall!" she screams while removing her helmet, her eyes gleaming with fear and then confusion when seeing me instead of Ari, who I decide has to be Ares Kulzak.

She jerks back against the headboard.

"Sorry," I smile. "*No habla.*"

"Who . . . are you?"

I slowly shake my head. "Not as important as *what* do I want."

Her eyes, still filmed by the same post-VR glaze that Ryan gets after his cyber runs, shift to the nightstand.

"Looking for this?" I pat the black handle pressed against my belly.

She doesn't move, her wide-open eyes staring at me as if I'm some kind of ghost.

"Where's Ari?" I ask, grinning. "We're old pals."

"*Hijo de puta!*" she screams, jumping toward me even though I am pointing a gun at her.

Rather than shooting her I raise my right knee, driving it into her solar plexus before her dark-painted fingernails, resembling ten sharp claws, reach my pretty face.

"You sure have a way with people," Karen comments without breaking her vigilant stance.

"I get that a lot," I reply, searching the tall and slim woman with the short blond hair, light-olive skin, and features that border on the Mediterranean look. Kishna Zablah is more adorable in person than her picture suggests—if you're into foreign jobs, that is.

Kulzak might be a bastard, but the man has good taste in women, though I'm not doing too bad myself. Karen's legs and chocolate-freckled breasts certainly challenge this woman's appealing features, and as for faces, I prefer domestic jobs.

While she lays by the side of the bed trying to catch her breath, I keep the Sig aimed at her pretty blond head while fishing for my cell phone inside my pocket and hitting the redial button.

"*Butterworth,*" he says.

"It's going to be Christmas, sport. You found the place yet?"

"*Just got here,*" he replies with a sigh. "*What's your situation?*"

"Found the woman but the bastard's not here."

"*Where is he?*"

"If I knew that I wouldn't be talking to you."

"*All right, all right. What do you want to do?*"

"I think we need to get this place back to normal as soon as possible so he doesn't get spooked when he returns. Can you handle that, sport?"

Silence, followed by, *"It will be done in sixty seconds."*

"Good. Give us five minutes and then send a couple of agents up here to take Miss Kishna down to the office for questioning. Tell them to use the emergency stairs. I don't want them running into Kulzak by accident."

Kishna raises her angered gaze at me. "What have you pigs done to Neurall?" she asks.

I check my watch and realize it's about that time, meaning Ryan must have been successful in blasting it into digital hell.

"Something wrong with your AI?" I ask, talking the talk.

There are tears in her eyes.

"What have you done to her?" Kishna insists.

Being the sensitive guy that I am, I decide to have some fun with her. "Done to whom?"

"Neurall, you fucking bastard!" she screams, lips trembling as she recoils, like a snake getting ready to strike again.

"Keep your voice down or I'll kick you again, understand? I'm not a cop. I don't have to be nice to you."

She burns me with her stare but slowly nods.

"Good. Now, where is Ares Kulzak?"

"Go to hell."

"Hell," I say, smiling, "my lovely Kishna, is exactly where *you* are headed."

SEVENTY-SIX

> > > > >

WING CLIPPING

> PRESIDENT LAURA VACCARO SAT BEHIND HER DESK
in the Oval Office watching Russian Ambassador Sergei Dudayev dry his sweaty brow.

"I . . . I don't understand the meaning of this," the ambassador said.

"Plain and simple, Mr. Ambassador. "This is the list of Russian immigrants that have been declared persona non grata by the United States government for supporting the efforts of Ares Kulzak."

Dudayev froze, before shaking his head at the long list. "I . . . this is most erroneous, Mrs. President."

"Not according to our sources."

"May I inquire what those sources are, yes?"

"The computer files we captured this morning from Ares Kulzak."

Dudayev made a face. "You have captured Kulzak?"

"I didn't say that. We have captured his *computer*. And the list of his Russian associates, as you can see, is quite long."

Dudayev didn't utter a word.

"It is indeed a disappointment to us that your government chose to support someone like him."

"We have not!" protested Dudayev. "I assure you we are not behind any of his schemes, and if he did indeed have contacts in the Russian community in this country, then my country will want to join yours in punishing those criminals."

Now we're getting somewhere, Vaccaro thought, following Tom Grant's suggestion to turn Ares Kulzak into the enemy of not just the Russian Mafia in America, but the Russian government.

Cut off his sponsors and you clip his wings.

Vaccaro decided to save the fact that it was a Russian satellite supporting the rogue Neurall for another time.

After agreeing to have further discussions on the matter, Vaccaro had Dudayev escorted out of the Oval Office.

SEVENTY-SEVEN

> > > > >

DEAL

> I GUESS IT SHOULDN'T BE ALL THAT SURPRISING that Ares Kulzak never showed up anywhere near the hotel. After three hours waiting alongside a team of sharpshooters atop surrounding buildings, we decide to call it quits and head for the local FBI office, where Karen and I get ready to put on yet another good-guy-bad-guy show for another terrorist.

We're holding Kishna Zablah in a windowless room very similar to the one where we interrogated Paxton, who will remain in custody until Kulzak is apprehended. A one-way mirror lets Butterworth and his Keystone Kops watch and tape the show.

So here we are, standing in front of the person responsible for stealing the backup of Neurall, for educating it, for using it to turn San Antonio inside out, for spreading terror across my country.

But all I see is an attractive woman in her mid-thirties.

That's how it is with these hackers. They appear like monsters, bigger than life itself while operating from behind the anonymity of the Internet, capable of inflicting much pain, much suffering.

But once caught, they don't seem so extraordinary.

And Kishna Zablah, hands cuffed to the table, looks quite harmless.

And cute.

"Nice article," I say, standing to the side while pointing at the front page of the afternoon edition of the *San Francisco Chronicle* that I have placed in front of her.

"I wouldn't want to be in his shoes right now," Karen says, sitting across from Kishna. Paxton was assassinated as he was being taken to his hearing at a courthouse in Washington, D.C. According to the article, several witnesses identified the gunman as Ares Kulzak, who shot and killed Paxton with a high-powered rifle from across the street, also wounding two U.S. marshals, before fleeing in a waiting vehicle, which the D.C. police found an hour later ditched in an alley.

"Looks like he really screwed his Cartel *amigos* as well," I add, pointing to a related story on the DEA raid of an abandoned elementary school in New Orleans where they confiscated hundreds of pounds of cocaine.

Yeah, yeah. I know that's not the deal we worked out with Paxton, but she doesn't know that the copy of the *Chronicle* is fake. Once again, the cyber sword cuts both ways.

"That's the thing about these criminal rings," Karen says. "The hard part is finding that first domino and toppling it. Once that's done, the others start to fall . . . unless, that is, the people running things manage to break the link in the investigative chain."

Kishna is now intrigued by our conversation and her head moves back and forth as we keep it up.

"And how do they break this investigative chain?" I ask, feigning true curiosity.

"Easy," she says. "They kill the next level up in the hierarchy before we can get to them, keeping us from being able to topple the next domino."

"I see. So in the case of Kulzak, he probably knows too much, right?"

"Right," Karen says with a frown, looking at Kishna while adding, "plus he crossed the Cartel by eliminating one of their own."

"Paxton?" I ask, as if guessing.

Karen nods.

"And that led the DEA to the cocaine in New Orleans?"

I get another nod.

"Boy," I say. "Talk about a dead man walking."

"How long do you give him?" Karen asks.

"Well . . . with his infrastructure turned against him," I say, looking into the distance, "hard to say. But sooner or later they will catch him. If there's one thing I did learn after so many years in the field, it's that people like the Cartel and the Russian Mafia *never* forget."

"The Russian Mafia?" asks Karen in a well-orchestrated reversal of roles.

"Yeah," I say, pretending to be surprised at her question. "Didn't you hear?"

"No."

"We captured Kulzak's laptop computer and what do you know? It contained a list of his contacts in the Russian Mafia, almost seventy of them."

"You don't say?" Karen says, crossing her arms while shaking her head at an utterly pale Kishna, who is quickly catching on.

"Oh yeah," I say. "Not only that, but some of them are part of the diplomatic staff in Washington. I can't begin to tell you just how pissed off the Russkies are that Kulzak indirectly fingered them."

"So he's got the Russian Mafia *and* the Cartel after him?"

I nod.

"And our friend here is his known associate, which puts her in just as much danger."

"Damn," Karen says, looking straight at Kishna. "You really *are* in a world of trouble, Kishna. We can help you, but you need to help us first."

"I want a lawyer," she says. "I am not going to play this stupid game of yours."

"Come again?" I ask.

"I said I want a lawyer to—"

I slap the back of her head.

"Hey!" she screams. "You can't—"

Whack!

Boy, sometimes I think I love my job a bit too much.

"This is an outrage!" she protests. "I demand to see my—"

Whack!

She settles down, once again confirming my theory that it takes three for these bastards to begin to get the picture that they are in deep shit.

"You are not an American citizen, Kishna," says Karen calmly, her forearms on the table, fingers crossed. "You don't have any rights."

"That means," I say, tapping the back of her head. "No lawyer for you."

"Get your stinky hands off of—"

Whack!

I think she's going for the record.

"All you're allowed is an airplane ride," I say.

"Either to hot and muggy Bogotá," Karen adds.

"Or cold and humid Moscow," I say.

"And both places mean pain, Kishna."

"Yep, Blondie. Lots and lots of pain."

For a moment I think her head is going to come loose as she ping-pongs between us, but she drops her gaze, the futility of her situation sinking in.

"Do you know what the Cartel likes to do to traitors?" Karen asks.

"And especially to a *cute* little traitor like you?" I add.

"They will rape you, Kishna," says Karen with empathy in her voice. "And not just once or twice. They will ravage you day and night in every conceivable way, alone and in groups."

Kishna opens her mouth but nothing comes out. Her light-olive skin is beginning to turn gunmetal gray.

"It's true, Kishna," Karen says. "They did it to one of our own agents."

"Nothing like getting sandwiched by half a dozen drunks on the dance floor of some bar while everyone else cheers them on to put some perspective into your life, honey," I add.

"And nothing you do or say will make them stop."

"*Then*," I say, "when you think things can't get any worse, they'll turn medieval on you. They're particularly fond of acids, razor blades, and blowtorches."

"I've seen it, Kishna," Karen says. "It's beyond anything you can imagine."

"And they keep you alive for a long time. Weeks."

"Months even," says Karen. "Making sure you eat and drink to keep you suffering as they slowly peel your skin away, as they slowly turn you into an animal."

"Starting with your feet and working their way up, until you go mad from the pain," I say.

"And just when you think you're going to be blessed with death, you realize that there is more to come."

"Much more, Blondie. Letting you heal before starting again."

"And as they turn you into an animal, they will have animals rape you, Kishna."

"I'm talking about getting fucked by a donkey or a bull," I add for graphic effect.

She's breathing heavily now, keeping her head down, staring at the table.

"I . . . Ari will kill me."

"Blondie, how can he kill you if you are already dead?" I ask.

She lifts her gaze at me and I wink.

"Don't you remember, Kish baby?" I ask. "You put up quite a fight in that hotel room, but there were too many of us and you turned your gun on yourself rather than letting us capture you alive. Quite noble, I might add."

"You will be safe from him, from the Cartel, from the Russians," Karen says.

"But *only* if you help us," I add.

"Where would Ares Kulzak go if the whole world is after him?" Karen asks.

"And remember," I say, "that he thinks we accessed your computer records, so every place mentioned on any file would be compromised in his mind."

"Where . . . where will I live?" she asks, crying now. "What will I do?"

"We will make you a deal just like we did with Ken Paxton," says Karen.

"Paxton?" Kishna says, her tear-streaked face turning into a mask of surprise and puzzlement. "But I thought that . . ."

"Don't believe everything you read," I say.

"Paxton did what he had to in order to stay alive."

We let that sink in.

"So, Kishna Zablah," says Karen. "Are you going to do the right thing, or should we take you to the airport?"

The female hacker stares at Karen, then at me, before slowly nodding. "I think I know where he is."

SEVENTY-EIGHT

> > > > >

CHINESE CONNECTIONS

> AT DAWN, ARES KULZAK SIPPED HOT TEA WHILE waiting in a room above a Chinese restaurant near the corner of Sacramento Street and Grant Avenue, in the heart of Chinatown, San Francisco. In the room next door, his contact with Chinese Intelligence completed the final preparations to get him out of the country via a Chinese merchant vessel currently off-loading electronics and other goods at the Port of San Francisco.

Ares Kulzak struggled to control his emotions, his hands clutching this morning's edition of the *Chronicle*, his eyes filled with tears as he read about the raid he narrowly missed yesterday morning, about the cowardly way in which the *gusanos* had tried to capture his beautiful Kishna, forcing her to kill herself.

Dozens of agents against one woman and they call themselves heroes!

They had killed her, just as they had killed his mother as she had heroically fought back, as she had resisted being caught alive by the enemy.

"I shall miss you, *mi amor*," he mumbled while staring at an old photo of her beneath the headlines, taken probably when she was back at MIT years ago. "And I shall avenge your death."

But he had to be careful. The *gusanos* had very likely turned his Cartel associates against him by reporting that a number of Tomahawk missiles destroyed Kulzak's cyberterrorist computer operation in the mountains south of Neiva.

Ares closed his eyes.

Kishna was dead.

Neurall was gone—and so was the Cartel's largest cocaine manufacturing operation and headquarters of the FARC, all destroyed by six American missiles.

In addition, his request to kill Cramer using his Russian contacts in Washington had backfired when Aleksei also got killed by one of Cramer's bodyguards. This, combined with the claim that Aleksei was one of many names on a list of Russian immigrants living in the D.C. area that was found among the files in Kishna's laptop computer—which the FBI claimed belonged to Kulzak himself—triggered a wave of arrests, including a number of Russians with diplomatic status.

And I will be blamed for it, he thought, finding it difficult to believe that two out of three sponsors now wanted his head.

Ares put the paper down. At least he still had the Chinese on his side. But he had to be careful. He had to assume that his funds in the Cayman Islands were either compromised or were being monitored since all of that information resided with Neurall, and he had no knowledge if Neurall was penetrated before its destruction.

Fortunately, that wasn't the only source of funds available to him.

Checking his watch, wondering how much longer the travel arrangements would take, Kulzak stood and walked up to the window in this cramped room, where he had spent one of the saddest and loneliest nights of his life since the day his parents were killed.

But at least he had survived, he had lived to fight another day. His run through America had not been a total disappointment, even if he had, in the end, failed to gain control of the Pentagon's artificial intelligence system, which would have, in turn, empowered him to control the nation's nuclear launch codes.

Ares Kulzak had nonetheless struck true fear into the heart of every American through large-scale strikes against two major cities, one smaller city, plus bringing down a few airliners as dessert. That alone placed him among the most wanted terrorists of all time.

Traffic thickened below as the city came to life. Merchants readied their shops for the incoming wave of tourists, street vendors set up their carts along sidewalks and alleys, displaying anything from T-shirts and fake jewelry to cheap crafts.

We came so close, mi amor, he thought. Kishna's plan to connect the two Neuralls had been brilliant. The Americans would have never known that their prized computer system had been cracked. They would have continued to believe in their systems, in their technology, confident of their position against the—

A knock on the door.

Ares turned to the disturbance. "Yes?"

"My friend," said Zin Hwang, the short and bony agent of the Chinese Intelligence Service operating out of the embassy in San Francisco. His eyes and closely cropped hair were as dark as the clothes he wore. Hwang said, "It is done. You leave this afternoon and should reach international waters before midnight."

Ares regarded this man, who once assisted him during a sabotage mission in South Korea.

Smiling while reaching for his old comrade in arms and embracing him, Ares said, "Thank you, my friend. I will not forget this."

"My country owes you. We are glad to be able to help you in your time of need."

"And you have been most accommodating on such short notice."

"Please let me know if there is anything else you need. Otherwise, I will come and get you when the time arrives," the Asian said, before bowing and leaving the room while facing Ares, closing the door.

Ares returned to the window and continued to watch the crowd below.

SEVENTY-NINE

> > > > >

COSMIC SIGNS

> CHINATOWNS ALL SMELL THE SAME, WHETHER IN
New York, Los Angeles, San Francisco, or Chicago, and they're always crowded,
packed with vendors and tourists beneath a million glittering signs advertising everything from food and souvenirs to furniture and massages.

There're about thirty agents participating in this raid, some dressed like tourists,
others like businessmen, and the handful of Asians in the local Bureau office dressed
like the locals—and we have two things in common: We're carrying enough weapons
to start a revolution, and we have a single target in mind.

It's just before eleven in the morning and my nose tingles from the irresistible aro-
mas of a dozen restaurants within spitting distance, all promising an unforgettable
lunch behind their old brick and mortar facades.

I follow Karen Frost down a sidewalk, which looks more like a narrow corridor
between the buildings to our right and the rows of street vendors on our left. And
just like in New Orleans, we're among the agents dressed like tourists—including
matching San Francisco sweatshirts over our Kevlar vests, blue jeans, cameras swinging from our necks, and, of course, semiautomatic weapons. We were going to wear
these nifty baseball caps also made of Kevlar and capable of deflecting a round, but
someone back at headquarters decided to embroider the letters FBI across the front,
making them useless for operations such as this one.

While we were in the midst of our planning phase, being the religious guy that I tend to become when coming face-to-face with the beast, I started looking for some heavenly sign—something that would give me a clue about the likely result of this raid.

And what do you know? The restaurant where the bastard is hiding at is on Grant Avenue.

Yeah, as in Tom Grant.

But cosmic significances aside, being here reminds me of my old beats during my NYPD days. One thing I always enjoyed about making a round in Chinatown in New York City was the fact that it was right next to Little Italy, so you never went hungry.

As we make our way through the congestion I begin to wonder what will happen when the first shot goes off—and trust me it will. Ares Kulzak is not going to go down without a bang. During our planning conference call with Washington, we had discussed the possibility of blocking off the streets surrounding the target to mini-mize casualties should Kulzak try to pull another New Orleans, but Meek nixed it, arguing that doing so would telegraph our plans. If Kishna was right, Kulzak should just be waiting at a Chinese restaurant around the corner for his boat ride to freedom after what I would consider a very successful terrorist run, even if in the end he lost his sidekick and his computer network.

The latest tally, including the airline disasters, added up to almost ninety thou-sand dead, plus three times as many wounded, plus over twenty times as many home-less, certainly topping the terrorist strikes of 2001. The dollar value is hovering around two hundred billion bucks, give or take.

Yep. Regardless of the outcome, it's a pretty safe bet to say that the bastard had quite a run through this country.

"We're getting into position," says Karen over the operational frequency. She comes loud and clear through the flesh-color earpiece coiling into my sweatshirt.

I smell raw fish, fried vegetables, and some Asian spices that my nose recognizes and whose names sound like a pair of guitar strings in need of tuning.

We reach the front door of The Hunan Lion, and a beautiful Chinese lady in her twenties—though it's damned hard to tell with these people—greets us at the door. She's wearing one of those dresses that covers everything from her neck down to her feet with the buttons running down the front. Is it a kimono? No, that's Japanese.

Yeah, I know. I need to polish up on my knowledge of Chinese culture beyond their food, but that quickly drops in priority as I take my assigned seat across from Karen and remind myself that I'm in the same building with Ares Kulzak. For rea-sons that escape me, my perverted mind is glad that it's a Chinese restaurant and not a Mexican one.

No *huevos rancheros* on the menu.

As we pretend to browse through the specials on the back of the laminated sheets the waitress handed us, Butterworth and one of his female agents also come inside, followed a few minutes later by Tweedledee and Tweedledum, the rookies who picked us up at the airport.

That's our signal that the area is officially surrounded by FBI agents, including sharpshooters strategically positioned on the roofs of adjacent buildings, plus a SWAT team on the roof and a large contingent from the San Francisco police department, whom Butterworth gave strict instructions to stay put a block away in all directions to let the professionals handle it.

Of course, having been on the other side of the fence, I can't begin to tell you just how well received a comment like that is coming from a Fed to a bunch of cops on their home turf. But just like we used to park our tongues back then, so did the SFPD folks, choosing instead to just sit back and watch the FBI make an ass out of itself because regardless of the level of preparation, these things *never* go down as planned.

Karen and I order the lunch special, and then it's time for the point man of this operation—yours truly—to lead the way.

I flip a button beneath my sweatshirt and a tiny wide-angle, low-light camera in the middle of my chest supposedly comes to life, broadcasting what it sees through the tiny hole poked on the front of my new shirt.

"Looks great, Tom. We have a clear picture of Agent Frost," says the leader of the SWAT team.

Karen, who pulls out a small receiver that looks like one of those small electronic personal organizers, also nods. I glance at Butterworth, who also has a gadget like Karen's, and he gives me a slight nod.

I get up to go to the bathroom, which is in the back of the restaurant, adjacent to the kitchen and the stairs.

You would figure that after all these years I'd learned to control my emotions but my heart is kicking my chest like a wounded buffalo.

There's a bustle of activity beyond the swinging doors leading into the kitchen, where the constant plate clattering and cookware rattling mixes with clamoring in Chinese.

Verifying that no one is looking in my direction, I skip the restroom and head on up, choosing for the time being to leave my piece holstered.

Despite what you see in the movies or read in the papers, there is no right or wrong way of doing this. You set your containment team around the target and go in hoping for the best. SWAT teams, like the one above me, always argue that it's best to just storm the place, but I convinced them—like I did in Austin—to let me do some scouting for them first to make sure they would not be walking into another one of Kulzak's volatile traps.

"Going up," I whisper, slowly making it to the second floor, reaching a claustrophobic, low-ceiling room packed with boxes of supplies: noodles, condiments, rice, and so on, plus stacks of chairs, framed Oriental landscapes, and a couple of folded Oriental screens. A narrow corridor carved through the middle of the stacked supplies leads to a short hallway, where I spot four doors, two on each side.

"You guys are seeing this?" I whisper.

"It's coming through very clear," the SWAT leader says over the radio.

I quickly describe what I see, before deciding to check the doors, my mind automatically reciting my favorite psalm while forcing myself to keep my weapon holstered.

"All right, boys and girls," I mumble. "Let's see what's behind door number one."

I turn the knob with my left hand, keeping my right one free in case I have to snatch my Sig.

I open it and stare at more supplies.

I slowly exhale and close it, before moving on to the next one, also checking both ends of the hallway to make sure no one sneaks up on me.

Door number two.

Same thing.

Ditto for the third one.

I open the last door and spot two figures laying on separate single beds on either side of the room flanking a nightstand, where a half dozen candles burn around a statue of Buddha beneath a partially-opened window with aluminum-foiled panes to kill the outside light. Incense burns on a brass dish on the floor. Some of the smoke coils out through the crack in the window. The rest veils the low ceiling with a dense layer of inky haze.

The pungent smell nearly makes me sneeze.

One of the figures in bed lifts its head. Flickering candlelight washes the deep wrinkles of an old Asian woman as she turns toward me, dark eyes blinking in the dim yellow light. Next to her I spot the shape of a sleeping child, probably not older than ten or eleven.

"Restrooms?" I say, my face cracking into an embarrassed smile.

She points a finger in the direction of the stairs and mumbles something in Chinese before going back to sleep.

I slowly close the door while exhaling.

"Did you all see that?"

"Second floor clear," says SWAT-man. *"Target is on the third floor. Repeat target on third floor. Set your rappelling ropes."*

"Stay put!" I hiss. "I need another minute to check the third floor!"

"Sixty seconds," replies SWAT-man, *"then we're going in."*

I get out of the hallway, through the open storage room, and peek up the next flight of stairs, seeing or hearing nothing beyond the muffled commotion in the kitchen below.

"Careful, Tom," Karen says as I slowly head up.

I'm halfway there when the sound of shattering glass rattles down the stairwell.

My hand automatically reaches for my weapon, and I bring it up, pointing it at the landing six feet above.

"What in the—"

The deafening explosion pushes me back. The ceiling and the carpeted steps swap places as I'm rolling down out of control, the vest taking some of the punishment but my shoulders, arms, and legs still burn from the multiple impacts while I try to stop my momentum, finally crashing feetfirst against the second-floor landing.

I'm up before I know it, my ears ringing. Amazingly enough I'm still holding the Sig.

Smoke spreads across the top of the stairs, the smell of cordite assaulting my nostrils as I try to understand what's happened, but my radio either isn't working or I can't hear it because of the explosion.

Muffled shouts of anger and pain echo from above as a figure appears through the smoke.

I instinctively swing my weapon in that direction, lining up the front sight on a figure too short to be Kulzak.

An Asian coughing while staggering downstairs.

He halts in mid stride when spotting me, his eyes dropping to my gun before raising his hands and erupting in a burst of short Chinese phrases, which I can barely hear through the intense whining in my ears.

"Stay where you are!" I shout as he comes closer, my voice sounding distant, as if someone else is speaking.

His lips move at a hundred miles an hour, spewing Chinese like a monkey in heat.

"Don't move!" I scream as I detect movement below but can't afford to look.

The man, short and slim, keeps his hands above his head while taking yet another step toward me.

"*Stop!* Do not—"

The motion is so fast that I don't get the chance to pull the trigger before the edge of his shoe strikes my shooting hand, sending my Sig flying down the steps.

In the same motion he recoils his left leg and extends it upward, where my face had been a fraction of a second ago, before my reflexes made me duck while pivoting sideways to the threat.

As he completes his partially successful turning jump-kick, I stretch my right leg toward his exposed solar plexus, heel aimed at the spot just below the sternum, where a web of nerves runs beneath the skin.

Instead of the expected contact of my heel against soft flesh, I feel a stinging pain on my ankle as he blocks the kick with a downward elbow strike.

As I retreat my throbbing foot, he charges forward, the index and middle fingers of his right hand extended like a viper's tongue, aimed at my eyes.

I turn my head, preventing him from skewering them while shifting left like a shadow, bringing my right hand up and sweeping the air in front of me from left to right, deflecting his strike.

In the same motion, I grab his attacking wrist and twist it while turning sideways, extending the heel of my shoe toward the side of his right knee.

The Asian once again reacts with fulminating speed, shifting his legs. I strike air, which sends a rippling wave of pain up my leg, making me lose my balance.

Falling on my side, my legs remain on the second-story landing while my back drops over the steps, the vest once more cushioning the blow.

Like in some old martial arts movie, the Asian jumps up high, almost as if suspended by an invisible wire, and is about to come down on my chest and neck when two shots reverberate in the stairwell, further thrashing my ear canals.

Karen is standing at the foot of the steps clutching her Glock with both hands, screaming something I can't hear.

The Asian does fall on me, but already a corpse, his face a bloody mess of bone and cartilage.

I kick him off of me, wiping the blood that has dripped on my face and neck before Karen helps me to my feet. I point at my ears while shaking my head.

"Kulzak!" she screams, though I can barely hear her. "He's out on the street! Let's go!"

I pick up my piece and follow her outside, stepping right into a wasteland of bodies and rubble. Hordes of people stand on the perimeter of what looks like ground zero, the place where Ares Kulzak must have dropped a bomb into the crowd.

So much for the cosmic sign. Things have certainly gone to shit in a hurry on Grant Avenue.

The sight is surreal, and my mind jumps to New York in '01, to San Antonio last week, to the smell of burnt flesh, to the falling debris, to the boiling dust. In a way I feel lucky I can't hear the screams of agony, of pain as people drag themselves on the street, many bleeding, some missing limbs. A mother turns her contorted, blackened face to the sky while holding a bleeding infant. A man gives CPR to another one. A teenage girl in rags is shaking an unconscious adult. Everywhere I look there's debris and bodies, mixed with strewn carts of burning merchandise and automobiles on fire, their smoke boiling toward the heavens.

And that's when I see the SWAT team, their maimed bodies hanging from their rappelling ropes, swinging in the breeze that also blows away the thick smoke streaming out of a gaping hole on the third floor of the building, which explains the brick, glass, wood, and other debris layering the pavement.

The pavement.

Damn, I spot Butterworth and his agents, all shot dead. But how?

"Karen," I say, pointing at their bodies just a few steps outside the restaurant.

"Oh, my God," she screams close to me so I can hear. "They took off right after the explosion while I went to get you!"

Damn.

That's the way these things tend to go with Kulzak. Everyone around us is dead or maimed and there's no sign of the bastard, plus there's so much dust and smoke that the sharpshooters up on the roof won't be able to acquire him.

From the periphery of the crowd I see flashes, people taking pictures. Others hold video cameras.

Amidst this dreamlike moment, while emergency crews and police officers break through the cordoning crowd, Karen tugs at me, pulling me down the street.

I'm slow to respond, partly because most of my body is throbbing and partly because my brain is still trying to catch up with events that very quickly have gotten out of—

Thundering reports reverberate in the street, echoing between buildings. Even through my ringing ears I can tell it's a .44 Magnum.

People scramble in every direction, some falling, getting run over by the stampeding crowd.

Two SFPD cops off to our right hide behind the steps leading to a building, their guns aimed at the corner.

"Over there, Tom!" Karen shouts, pointing at a figure dressed in black holding a large black semiautomatic pistol on our side of the street.

I recognize the face as well as his weapon, a Desert Eagle, the only semiautomatic capable of firing the Magnum round. I glance up, toward the rooftops, searching for the sharpshooters, but it's too hazy and I can't spot them. Which also means they can't see the action on the street clearly enough to be useful.

Kulzak shoots again, blasting chunks of brick and mortar from the steps where the cops are pinned down, and I now see two more officers sprawled on the street in pools of blood.

"This way!" Karen screams as the terrorist takes off down Grant Avenue, reaching

California Street, where he turns the corner heading down toward the piers. "We can't let him out of our sight!"

My hearing is slowly coming back, at least enough that she doesn't have to scream right in my ear.

"Officers and civilians down outside of restaurant," Karen speaks into her lapel microphone. "Suspect heading down on California Street."

"Anyone answering?" I ask.

Nodding while holding up her badge and gun—which very effectively parts the emotional crowd like the Red Sea—she starts down the street with yours truly in tow. "The SFPD cordon a block out is moving in!" she finally screams over her shoulder. "We should be able to sandwich him!"

We're running down the same sidewalk on Grant Avenue we used to get to the restaurant, though it looks completely different with the carts from street vendors no longer forming a corridor.

My right ankle is on fire, throbbing every time I lean on it, but it's still functional. The little bastard bruised it but didn't fracture it, and the same goes for the rest of me, protesting every step I take but going along for the ride.

Karen cuts left at the corner and we're heading down California, a hell of a steep street, my eyes zeroing in on his dark figure roughly a block ahead of us. The street keeps dropping for many blocks until reaching the piers in the distance, backdropped by the blue waters of the San Francisco Bay.

Traffic is thickening as we approach the noon hour and there're emergency vehicles converging from both directions, their flashing lights and wailing sirens parting traffic. A picturesque cable car slowly crawls up the steep hill, tourists hanging from all sides, some snapping pictures of Karen and me, others waving, probably thinking we're filming a movie or something—adding yet another level of oddity to my surreal experience.

"He's getting away!" Karen screams, though I'm not sure if it's at me or at the radio.

We rush past the pedestrians already startled by Kulzak and his big gun, which actually makes it easier for us to get through, leaping over trembling bodies, over people huddled against everything from newspaper stands to public phone booths and fire hydrants.

"Faster! Faster!" I hiss in between breaths while taking the lead in spite of my injuries. The adrenaline shot of having seen Kulzak smolders my pain as I leave Karen behind.

Karen keeps screaming for people to get out of our way, one hand holding her ID and the other the gun. I just use my gun, which continues to have a powerful effect on everyone around us.

Kulzak's roughly a hundred feet or so ahead of us, but I can't possibly take a clean shot with so many people around.

Then I see the SFPD cops, three of them, heading up California Street.

Kulzak suddenly stops when he sees them and takes a shot with his Magnum. The report cracks in the busy street like a whip. Pedestrians and cops all run for cover. Then he pivots and turns the Desert Eagle cannon at us.

For a brief moment I'm staring directly at the triangular muzzle of a Desert Eagle, well aware that our vests would not stop a Magnum round.

I instinctively put on the breaks and feel Karen's light frame crashing into me, her gun stabbing the back of my vest. I drag her behind a recessed entry just as Kulzak fires twice, the rounds lifting a man in a business suit off the sidewalk, flipping him in midair while spraying everyone around with blood, including us.

Screams bellow around us as the unfortunate pedestrian lands on his back with half his chest missing. I somehow block the brutal sight and am back on my feet, pulling Karen along.

Kulzak abruptly turns left, disappearing from sight beyond a bus stop crowded with curious tourists, who look in his direction and suddenly start dispersing like a swarm of angry wasps, shaking their arms while screaming and shouting. One gets hit by a car. Other cars behind it slam on their breaks, and in an instant there's a multiple-car collision, horns blaring, radiators hissing steam, drivers shouting angrily, and sirens blaring in the distance as cops converge in the area.

Karen is once again on her radio, updating Kulzak's position, directing the SFPD force.

Ignoring the mess that Kulzak is rapidly spreading across the Bay City, we slow down as we reach the corner, which is not another street but an alley. The three SFPD cops join us moments later, and of course, they look like rookies, young, muscular, with big guns but probably little experience.

Out of breath, sweat pouring down the sides of my face, my chest broiling inside this oven of a vest that will do me no damned good if he shoots me, I curse my luck *and* this alley.

Damn.

Why does it *always* have to be an alley?

Standing in plain view, our weapons drawn and pointed straight ahead, we start down the narrow corridor between the backs of buildings, just like in New Orleans.

Reality creeps up my spine, screwing with my mind, making me wonder if I'm going to make it out of this alley on my own two feet or in a body bag.

I motion for Karen to position herself just behind and to my right, minimizing her exposure while still allowing her a clear line of sight. The three rookie cops follow a few feet behind us.

Large yellow Dumpsters line the left side of the alley, opposite trash cans, cardboard boxes, and other junk. Every now and then there's a large metal door, the place used by the businesses at the other end to dump their garbage. Such doors are usually locked from the inside and meant to be tough enough to deter crooks from sneaking in the back way.

I doubt Kulzak would be able to use one of them as a way to escape us.

No, I decide. He's definitely out here. I can feel it in my gut with every step I take on the stained and wet concrete extending beyond us for an entire city block.

Two figures appear at the other end.

Uniformed cops.

Karen speaks softly into her mike, and I see the policemen reaching for their shoulder-strapped radios.

Kulzak is between us, somewhere amid dozens of places to hide.

Mimicking us, the cops draw their weapons and slowly move toward us.

Where are you?

I get my answer all too fast.

A figure rolls out from the narrow space between two Dumpsters and quickly vanishes again behind stacked crates on the opposite side.

He moved too fast, and I can't just fire without a clear target because I could accidentally hit the cops at the other end.

In the second that follows, as I'm wondering why he just showed himself without firing, I hear the rattling sound of an object skittering toward us—and another one rolling in the direction of the officers opposite us.

Grenades!

Karen and I react with amazing fluidity, diving behind the nearest Dumpsters.

As I wince in pain when my already bruised shoulders smack into a brick wall, the grenades go off, showering the area with shrapnel, peppering the metal Dumpsters.

My ears ringing again, I get up, weapon still in my right hand, pointed at the long corridor beyond the thinning smoke, at the silhouette of a man running away from me, over the fallen figures of the SFPD cops.

"Officers down!" Karen is screaming as I drop to one knee and fire once, twice, thrice at the runaway figure, the reports seem distant, muffled by the buzzing in my head.

He keeps running.

Cursing under my breath, I briefly look behind me, spotting Karen kneeling by a bleeding policeman, her hands pressed against his shoulder and neck to staunch the spurting blood.

"I'm going after him!" I shout and she tosses her piece at me, which I snatch with my left hand and shove in my jeans before running through the veiling haze, leaping over the still bodies of the cops, who, like their buddies behind me, didn't react fast enough to get out of the blast zone.

I don't even look at the poor bastards. I can't afford to if I'm going to catch this man, who is just about to reach the end of the alley.

Clutching my weapon with both hands, I fire six times, emptying my clip at the bastard.

He wavers, crashing into a wall, his Desert Eagle clattering on the concrete as he lets it go. He stands, a hand on his shoulder, which is turning black from blood.

I've got him!

Remembering previous episodes with this man, I shove my NYPD and CIA training aside and grab Karen's gun, aiming it at his staggering figure.

My forefinger presses the trigger again and again, round after round after round, the muzzle flashes evoking visions of Jerry Martinez in El Salvador, Joe Hicks in Melbourne, Paul Stone and those Secret Service agents in Austin, Madie in Belgrade, the Littmans in Melbourne, Gary Hutton in New Orleans, along with everyone who drowned or became homeless. I think of Randy Cramer being cremated in Washington. I think of all the poor bastards who got cooked alive by the exploding gas mains in San Antonio. I can clearly see those SWAT guys hanging from the roof of the Chinese restaurant with their guts spilling all over the street below. My mind even jumps back several years, remembering New York, remembering the Pentagon, just as I shall always remember the Alamo.

Kulzak jerks twice before falling on his back, his hand reaching in his pocket. I aim very carefully and fire once more, striking a direct hit to the wrist from almost twenty feet away, nearly severing the hand.

"It's over!" I shout, reaching his side, kicking the Desert Eagle away, standing over him with Karen's Glock pointed at his shocked face, at his dark eyes staring back at me with a mix of surprise and curiosity.

"*Huevos rancheros*," I say, finding it important that he knows who killed him. "El Salvador. Remember, asshole?"

"It's . . . you," he mumbles. "You are . . . alive."

"You betcha, asshole. And so are Paxton and Kishna," I add.

He stares at me, confused, then his eyes blink understanding.

"They gave you up, *amigo*. They turned you in."

Kulzak starts bleeding through his nostrils, through his mouth and ears. I watch him choke on his own blood, slowly, as his arms reach out for help—for the mercy that I refuse to show.

E I G H T Y

> > > > >

O T H E R S   W I L L   F O L L O W

> ARES KULZAK SAW THE STARS, SAW THE FULL MOON casting its silvery reflection on the surf, saw his planet just beneath the glowing disc of the moon, felt his mother's hands stroking the back of his head, felt the cool sand between his toes.

He remembered the invading shots, his parents' screams. He recalled seeing his future in the dark waters of the Bay of Pigs. He remembered his determination to live up to his promise, his unyielding desire to avenge the cold-blooded murder of his beloved family.

With these hands I will change the world.

And as he stretched those bloody hands at his executioner, Ares decided that he had indeed tried to change the world—through so many years and across so many lands, the spirit of the revolution kindling the fire burning deep in his core, glowing with resolve, with the unbending wish for revenge, with the overwhelming power of complete and utter retribution.

As he lay there, life rapidly seeping out of his body at the hand of the *gusanos*, Ares Kulzak clenched his jaw, determined to die with the same pride with which he had lived, with the same honor with which he had fought against the giant United States and its allies, just as the Greek god Ares had fought powerful enemies against all odds.

He stared at death itself and grinned, knowing that in the end, as he died just like so many other freedom fighters before him, he had died while daring to challenge America, while defying the giant, while living life by his own rules, so that he would always be remembered alongside Ché, Fidel, Mao, bin Laden, and the other great leaders of the movement against America, against the *gusanos*.

You may have killed me today, he thought, his mind growing cloudy, *but my death will inspire others. I have shown the world what a single man can do against the mighty United States.*

Others will follow.

Others will . . .

> THE MONSTER GRINS AT ME, AND I HAVE TO MUSTER
serious control not to fire one more time and blow that leer off his face.

But I don't have to. He expires a moment later, as his defiant stare burns me one
final time before his eyes cease to move, before his dead pupils fixate on a point above
me, as if he looked toward the heavens before expiring.

I stand over this man—this . . . *beast*—for what seems like a very long time, not
feeling victorious or triumphant, but concerned.

Despite his death—or perhaps *because* of his death—Ares Kulzak will always be
remembered, even revered by our enemies for making history in the past week. He
has spread a wave of terror across our land, injecting fear into the heart of every
American, broadcasting to the entire world that the United States is still susceptible
to terrorism; that the United States is as vulnerable as the rest of the world. All it
takes are the right skills and determination to create another New York, or San Antonio, or Melbourne, or New Orleans; to once again turn fully fueled jetliners into
guided missiles; to turn a beautiful day in charming San Francisco into a nightmare.

There wasn't much fanfare with Ares Kulzak. He didn't issue any warnings about
his strikes. Kulzak simply executed them with blood-curdling precision while stepping
up and claiming responsibility—unlike bin Laden and other terrorists before him—
while also issuing demands that were nothing but a distraction while he moved on to
his next target. He was indeed quite successful until we caught on to his system, to

his method; until we wedged ourselves between his ideal marriage of the real and cyber worlds; until we fought him on both fronts with equal determination, with equal resolve; until we freed ourselves from the shackles imposed on our law enforcement and intelligence communities by politicians who had once again grown too complacent about our way of life.

I stare at the inky blood spreading around the terrorist and try not to think about the American blood this man has spilled from sea to shining sea—all because of a society that has lost the perspective we so painfully acquired right after Pearl Harbor, and again after September 11, 2001.

Pearl Harbor.

New York City.

San Antonio.

New Orleans.

Places that will forever live in the minds of Americans as paramount errors of judgment; places that will always remind us of what happens when we choose to turn a blind eye to the evil that brews beyond our shores—an evil that will return with renewed power unless we, as a society, choose to change our policies, our rules for combating terrorism—and do so across all fronts, including the much-neglected cyber world.

I sense someone standing next to me.

It's Karen, and she takes my hand.

"You got him," she says. "You really nailed him."

I just keep staring at the man, even as police officers and surviving FBI and CCTF agents finally reach the alleyway, as emergency crews put the wounded on stretchers and haul them to waiting ambulances.

I have dreamed of this moment from the day I saw Jerry Martinez thrashing on that dusty parking lot a lifetime ago. And now, as the cops slip Kulzak's body into a black plastic bag, I feel a void in my gut, a kind of emptiness that comes from the knowledge that Kulzak's death in itself is meaningless because the man has already accomplished what he had intended to accomplish; he has already inspired a whole new generation of terrorists to come and take their turn at crapping all over my country.

"It's over, Tom," she says, trying to tug me away.

"It's not over," I reply. "This is just another beginning."

Karen puts a hand on my cheek and stares at me with the same intensity I saw flashing in her eyes just last night. "Come, darling," she says. "Let's go home."

Home.

A home I will continue to defend . . . or die trying.